UNCOUNTED

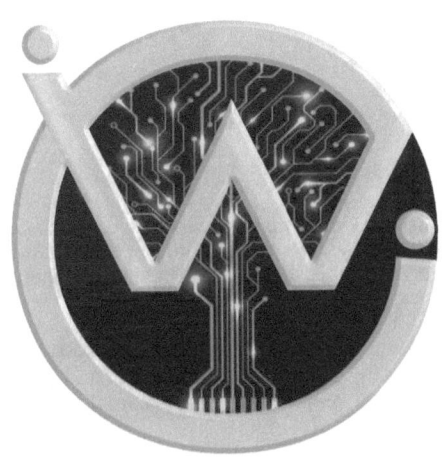

THE WORLD COLLECTIVE BOOK 3

SUSAN CULLEN

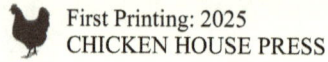 First Printing: 2025
CHICKEN HOUSE PRESS

Library and Archives Canada Cataloguing in Publication
CIP data on file with the National Library and Archives

ISBN hardcover edition: 978-1-990336-88-1
ISBN trade paperback edition: 978-1-990336-87-4

Chicken House Press
282906 Normanby/Bentinck Townline
Durham, Ontario, Canada, N0G 1R0

www.chickenhousepress.ca

To the reader,

May you know you are loved, that your life has a purpose, and a better tomorrow is possible.

When the storms rage,
when the floods come,
I will hold fast to you.
When the wind howls
and the sun scorches,
I will hide in your arms.

UNCOUNTED

Susan Cullen

CHICKEN HOUSE PRESS

CHAPTER ONE

"**T**ELL ME THIS IS GOING TO WORK," TALI PLEADS.

"It's going to work."

The promise is easy to make because it's the only option. It doesn't matter that we're fugitives from the World Collective, fleeing Unity after escaping with Tazib with nothing but two commandeered pods. It doesn't matter that we can't meet the United People's demands and have no patch to stop an early Thanatos death.

"It's going to work," I repeat, reaching for Tali's cold hands and holding them in mine. "We are going to save Ky."

Tali and I crouch behind the remains of a crumbling brick wall as we wait for Tazib's signal. From our hidden vantage point we are able to study the jumbled assortment of dilapidated buildings and random junk that forms the United People's secret compound. Beyond the unsuspecting structure and across the river, the tall metal and stone towers of Fordtown rise into the midmorning sky, their peaks disappearing in the low grey clouds.

"But the deadline, it's any minute now. What if the United People have already…" Tali's wide blue eyes glaze with fresh tears and her voice drops to a near whisper. "What if he's already dead?"

"He's not."

"But—"

"Ky's alive." I squeeze Tali's hands. "I'm positive. And who knows? Maybe Merari gave in to their demands and uploaded the patch to everyone's system. Maybe the United People are about to release Ky. It's possible. We're disconnected—we don't know what's happened since we fled Unity."

Tali's eyes drop to our hands as a shiver shakes her thin frame. Despite my conviction that Ky's alive, we both know Merari would never cave to a group she considers terrorists, no matter what feelings she may have for her offspring.

Heat burns in my chest, warming me despite the fact I'm wearing only pyjamas. The Collective was supposed to protect us. The creation of The Code, our reliance to follow its direction in our vital roles and our deaths, was all to ensure a world where everyone could experience a full life with order, peace, and wellness. But all along, the WC has been hiding and manipulating the truth to suit their purposes. They lied about the accident that took my foot and killed my classmates, and about the virus that runs on Thanatos, to name a few. It is clear the only value they truly uphold is control.

And the United People are no better.

They already have the patch. I gave it to them by handing it over to Libni. At the time, I thought it was the right thing to do; and even when they first made their threats, I clung to the hope it was all an elaborate ploy. A desperate bid to get the World Collective to admit the truth to their citizens—a way to force their hand, making sure everyone received protection from an early Thanatos death. But how wrong I was. When they threatened to disable all working patches, when they threatened to kill Kyven, an innocent kid whose only crime was being Merari's offspring... Well, that showed the United People are nothing but monsters in a different form.

"Tali, I'm telling you, this is going to work." I speak to Tali's bowed head, my body tense with anticipation. "We're going to get Ky out before anything happens to him."

"But Tazib's right," Tali sighs. "It isn't a very good plan."

Tazib. I fume silently, scowling at the low clouds where the pod carrying Tazib and Loren hovers out of sight. If he had his way we'd be miles from here, fleeing to whatever safe spot he's been hiding away in with the Uncounted. The only reason he relented to this rescue was because the freckled teen Eldon agreed we couldn't stand by and do nothing. But, while I find Tazib's utter disregard for whether Ky lives or dies unsettling, it's because we have Tazib I believe we can pull this off. What he managed to accomplish with the relatively simple interface of the commandeered WC pods is nothing short of astounding. Not only was he able to ensure we wouldn't be tracked, he somehow managed to access the larger network, proving there is no technical aspect of the Collective that the crazy-smart teen hacker cannot manipulate to his advantage. Five minutes. That's all it took for him to find Ky and confirm he was north of Fordtown. Five minutes—when DATA and all of the World Collective's smartest technical experts said Ky was offline and untraceable. And now that we know Ky is being kept in the secret compound just outside Fordtown—the very place that Tazib managed to kidnap my brother without anyone being the wiser—I know this plan is going to work.

The crunch of gravel draws our attention back to the jumble of buildings. I peer around the edge of the wall as Eldon runs from the the far corner, hunched at his middle like that will hide his long arms and gangly legs as he crosses the open space to our hiding spot.

"I found it," he puffs, his face red from the run. "There's a way in, right where Tazib said it would be. It will take two of us to pull the metal aside, but then we should be able to wiggle through. Come on."

Eldon jogs back the way he came and Tali and I hurry to follow him. Loren's shoes are much too small for me and snap loudly against my heels in the quiet. I'm thankful she insisted I take them as running barefoot in this desolate place would have been inviting disaster.

"Eldon, hold up."

Tazib's command is transmitted to our tragus implants and Eldon stops so suddenly Tali and I collide with his back. We pause at the corner, crouching behind an overgrown bush.

"You sure using our implants won't get us caught?" Loren's voice asks in my ear.

I have to smile at Loren's tenacity. Chances are she's standing at Tazib's elbow, drilling him with her death stare until he answers. Since fleeing Unity she's made no attempt to hide her distrust of him. It was her idea to stay with him in the pod, as she said, to make sure he didn't attempt anything funny or abandon us.

"No," Tazib sighs. "I've already told you. I'm not using the WC's network, just the local signal through the pods."

"Whatever," Loren huffs. "But I have to say, I do NOT enjoy having your voice inside my head."

"Yeah, it isn't a thing you get used to," I mutter. "What's the hold up, Tazib?"

"I'm just seeing if I can get into The Code from here. It might be possible to get rid of any…" He pauses. "Obstacles."

The skin at the back of my neck crawls.

"You don't mean…? No." I shake my head. "No. We are NOT activating anyone's Thanatos."

"Why not?" Tazib asks. "They will kill him—without a second thought. Why do you afford them any compassion?"

"Because I'm not them. And I'm not you."

"That's why you need me." Hearing Tazib this way, a bodiless voice full of self assurance and a complete lack of morality, is like jumping back in time. "You need me to make the hard calls, Ry, to do the necessary things."

"No," I repeat. "We rescue Ky without killing anyone."

"I'm with Ry on this." Loren's voice quivers with barely contained rage. I would not want to be standing next to her right now. "Use all your fancy tech smarts to help in some other way, but we don't do that. Got it?"

"Fine," Tazib huffs. "Don't take advantage of my skills."

"Don't worry, Ry," Loren reassures. "I'll keep an eye on him."

"Thanks, Loren." I nudge Eldon's back. "So where's this opening?"

"See that corrugated tin?" Eldon points to what looks like nothing more than a tower of boxes and scrap metal. "The door's behind that."

The United People deserve credit for their ingenuity. According to Aliah, they've been at work for years, quietly moving in the sidelines to bring down the system that's monitored our lives, hiding in plain sight by taking advantage of their vital roles and making use of places like this, the abandoned and forgotten parts of our past.

"Let's go." Tali's voice is high and pinched with anxiety. "We need to hurry."

We sprint the short distance to the tin and pull it aside together, cringing when it scrapes against the pavement. Behind it lays a simple door; no scanner or lock, but a straightforward latch. I fumble to slide it back, my hands stiff with cold, but it gives way and I push it open before slipping through the gap.

Inside, I'm met with a suffocating staleness; a musty, rotting smell. Eldon and Tali squeeze in behind me and we silently move down the hall. The United People's compound is a mess of crumbling buildings tied together with hobbled hallways like this one, linking a variety of structures all disguised from the outside to hide the truth of what lies beneath. Water marks stain the ceiling and the flooring is uneven and patchy as the surfaces repeatedly change. We pause when we reach the first turn, peering cautiously around the corner.

"This looks familiar," I whisper, knowing the others will be able to hear me clearly through their implants. "I think we're heading to the rooms where they kept us for questioning when we were here before."

Tali's face scrunches. "It's so strange I have no memory of that. It makes me feel so... off."

I can understand how Tali feels. Her memories of this place aren't the only ones to have been erased. Tazib was in my dorm group, but I have no memory of our time together. The WC erased every trace of him from my childhood and every time Tazib brings up something from our shared past it's like I'm trying to swim through thick fog as I struggle to remember.

We continue to move cautiously through the dilapidated corridors until we reach a short hall with a series of doors.

"Little help, Tazib?" Eldon asks in a hushed voice. "Can you tell which room has Ky?"

"Sure. Just keep walking… keep walking…" Tazib says as we creep down the hall. "There. Stop," he instructs. "His signal is directly opposite you."

We examine the solid wooden door and surrounding wall for a scanner or panel, but both are frustratingly empty.

"How do we get in?" I ask. "There's nothing to access the lock."

"You're on your own. I've got nothing from up here."

Eldon reaches for the doorknob, giving it a twist. "This is old, really old and really solid." He kneels, peering at the handle. "Looks like we need a physical key."

"A key?" I reach for the knob, twisting it with both hands in a futile attempt to pop the lock.

"Yeah, you know, those metal things you stick in the hole." Eldon points to a slot in the handle. "But we don't have one."

"And it's not something we can hack." I groan. Frustrated, I slap the door, leaning my forehead against its immovable presence.

"Hello? Is someone there?" a faint voice calls.

"Ky? Can you hear me?" I press my ear against the door.

"I hear you." Ky's voice is clearer, like he too is pressed against the other side. "Who are you?"

"It's me, Rygita. I'm going to get you out."

"Thank The Code." Ky laughs. "I mean, these guys have been great hosts, decent food and all that. But locking me in this dump is not cool. Not cool at all."

"Is there any way you can open the door from your side?" I ask.

"Ah, no." Ky's voice drips with sarcasm. "If there was, do you think I'd be hanging out in here?"

"What do we do?" Eldon asks. "We can't just stand here. Someone might come."

"What if we climbed up there?" Tali points to a dark hole in the ceiling where a tile has fallen, revealing the space between the ceiling and roof. "I bet there's empty space above Ky's room too. I could climb over and pull him up."

Eldon joins Tali under the hole, jumping lightly on his feet as he attempts to peer into the dim space. "I bet you're right." He grins at Tali. "Great thinking. Here, I'll give you a boost." He links his hands together, offering her a step.

"No, wait." I grab Tali's elbow. "I'll go."

"But I'm smaller," Tali protests. "Less risk of me falling through."

"Yeah, but will you be able to pull Ky up?"

"Ry—"

I step onto Eldon's hands, grabbing at the edge of the hole when he boosts me. Shimmying onto my belly, I pull myself into the gloomy interior.

"Let Ky know what I'm doing," I tell the others as I peer in the direction of his room. There isn't much space above my head and I have to be careful to stick to the joists to avoid falling through the ceiling as I wiggle along, the thick layer of dust and cobwebs tickling my nose. The small space is disorienting, so when I reach a barrier, I hesitate, surprised I'm already at the outer wall.

"Why are you stopping?" Tali whispers. "You haven't gone far enough. You're still outside his room."

"I am?" I look again at the barrier in front of me. It is a collection of boards, maybe two inches thick, spread evenly across the space. "There's something in the way."

"Maybe the wall goes to the roof?" Eldon suggests, and I realize he must be right. In the dim light, I can just make out the open space continuing beyond.

"Okay, give me a minute. I'll get through."

I wiggle my shoulders through the beams, cringing when my hand flattens a pile of animal droppings. The tightness of the space sets my heart racing, but I close my eyes against the panic. I don't have to be afraid, not when I know how to listen for the music. Though the dust dries my throat, I force a hum over my lips.

"Ry? Are you humming?" It's Loren's voice that breaks into my thoughts. "What's wrong?"

"I think I'm stuck."

It's true. I'm stuck. My hips refuse to squeeze between the beams. The space is too narrow.

"This isn't going to work. I'm too big."

"Ry? I can hear you," Ky calls. "Give me a second. I've got an idea."

Below me, a grunt is followed by the sound of something heavy being pushed across the floor. A moment later, the ceiling tile directly in front of me is pushed aside, flooding the space with light that temporarily darkens my vision.

"Ry? You there?" Ky's dark hair pops into view, just the top of his head as he teeters on whatever he's stacked to reach the ceiling. "I can't quite make it. Give me a hand."

I reach for Ky's outstretched hand, groaning as I attempt to pull him towards me.

"I can't… I don't have a good grip. I need to be closer," I grunt.

"Okay, let me try again."

Ky's head drops from view and I hear him strain to move everything closer to the wall.

"Someone's coming." The urgency in Eldon's voice is as good as a blaring alarm. "Tali, quick. We have to hide!"

"Ry, cover the hole," Ky frantically instructs as he hurries to dismantle his pile.

I shove the ceiling tile back into place, my heart hammering as I listen to the sounds below me. Heavy footsteps. A pause. A metallic click. The groan of a door.

"Hey guys, back at last?" Ky's voice is loud and clear, his usual cocky tone masking his breathlessness. "I got a little bored so I thought I'd do some redecorating. What d'you think?"

"Time's up," a deep baritone answers.

"Time's up?" Ky's voice cracks. "You don't mean… Merari…. She didn't give you what you want?" His laugh is tight and painfully high. "I guess I should have told you. She's a rule follower, got to do everything by The Code, you know?"

"Will you come willingly?" The deep voice is familiar, one I've heard before in this very compound. Kohath, the leader of the United People.

"Are you going to carry out your threat? 'Cause if so, no. No, I do not come willingly!" There is a scuffle of feet as Ky's shouts grow louder. "Stop it! Let me go! You can't do this! Don't do this! Please!"

"Ry, what's happening?" I barely hear Tazib over Ky's panicked cries as he is pulled from the room. "Do you have Ky? I can see his signal moving but yours isn't."

"No," I whisper, frantically wiggling to free myself from the beams. "They're taking him away. What do we do?"

"We still have one option."

"No," I snap as the commotion below me grows louder. There is a surprised grunt and a heavy thud as Tali's thin voice cries out.

"Ky!"

I scramble back towards the open tile, abandoning caution as the shouts increase.

"Freeze! Don't move!"

"Let him go," Tali pleads. "Please don't hurt him."

I've reached the opening and I twist to peer down at the scene below me. Kohath is at the far end of the hall, his once warm smile gone as he stares down at a quivering Tali. Beside him, a guard holds a bound Ky, a device of some kind jabbed into his ribs. Ky's face is pale with terror, his pupils dilated to points of darkness. Meanwhile, Eldon struggles with a second guard, the two wrestling to stand, though it's clear Eldon is taking the worst of the beating.

"Our demands were clear." Kohath nods at the guard holding Ky who proceeds to shove him around the corner and out of sight. "The WC has toyed with the lives of its citizens for long enough. Change can be painful but it is necessary if we hope to have a future."

The second guard has managed to gain the upper hand and he

shoves Eldon to the floor, knocking his head against the hard tile with a hollow thump. Eldon moans, his eyes rolling back in his head as his body sags.

"What a pitiful rescue attempt," Kohath scoffs. "I'd expected Merari to send someone, but children?" He shakes his head. "It just demonstrates how badly the world needs us. Get the boy restrained," he says to the guard.

"No!" Tali cries, throwing herself at the guard and clawing at his back.

Kohath laughs. "There's no point resisting. More guards are on their way. Won't this be a statement? The public execution of Merari's offspring and a member of DATA."

I don't wait to hear more. I drop down from the ceiling with a shout, landing on top of the guard as Tali jumps back just in time. Scrambling to my feet, I grab Eldon.

"Tali, grab his other arm." I struggle to support Eldon's stumbling frame as I rush away from Kohath.

"What about Ky?" Tali cries as she hurries to help me.

I don't answer.

We race back through the halls, squeezing through the hidden door, and dashing across the open space to where we'd hidden our pod in the remains of a roofless structure.

"You guys need to move," Tazib announces as we stumble inside. "There are a lot of angry dots heading your way."

"I got it," Eldon moans, setting his palm on the metal scanner and raising the pod into the sky. He touches the side of his head gingerly, wincing at the growing bump.

Tali crumples into one of the two chairs, silent sobs shaking her thin shoulders as the twisted structures of the United People's compound are swallowed by the clouds. I remain standing, watching the swirling mist glide over the round surface of the pod, equally flooded with relief and regret.

We've escaped capture.

But we've left Ky behind.

CHAPTER TWO

FOR HOURS, WE FLY OVER A LAND OF COLOUR AND LAKES, the landscape void of everything familiar. Other than the occasional glimpse of a crumbling ancient city or a ribbon of broken pavement, there is little to indicate people have ever lived in these wild places.

Eldon and Tazib have taken a number of precautions to keep us hidden from both the Collective and the United People. Besides disabling our personal tech before leaving Unity, they keep us off the system by flying the pods manually, a mind-blowing feat I didn't even know was possible. Eldon flies the joined pods now as Tazib rests, something I should try to do. But as exhausted as I am, I've spent the majority of the trip watching the flame-coloured forest blur below me as I'm carried far from the ordered world of the Collective.

I'm doing this. I'm leaving everything I know behind and heading into the wilderness. With Tazib.

Turning from the window, I balance myself on the low shelf that runs around the pod. Only a foot away lies Tazib, asleep on one of the chairs. It's hard not to stare. In sleep, Tazib is so peaceful, so relaxed, it's easy to see how young he is. He's only 14, maybe close to 15, but still, he's my age. For all the time I've spent across the table from him in the holding facility there is still so much I don't know, so many parts to his story that remain untold. Like how long did it take him to recover from the burns that cover the majority of his body? Was he in the same healing centre as I was? Did the same people who cared for me care for him? And when did he leave the WC? He would have been so young. Did he go alone or did someone lead him to the wilderness like he's doing for me now?

Tazib's dark lashes flutter as he mutters in his sleep, his brow furrowing. Perhaps he's having a nightmare, reliving that terrible day the chain of pods carrying our dorm crashed to the ground in a blaze of fire and twisted metal. It used to be a near-nightly occurrence for me, reliving the terror while trapped in a coffin-sized box, but I haven't had those nightmares for weeks now. Not since before my coma. Not since I learned to listen for the Composer, the one who creates the perfect music of the woods.

I close my eyes and listen for it now, the melody that tells me I am loved and that there's a plan. It helps ease the tightness in my chest, though it doesn't take away the pain. There's been too much death to be free of that completely. Far too many deaths and more to come unless we can find a way to fix Thanatos.

The soft whoosh of the doors signals someone has entered and I open my eyes to find Loren gawking at Tazib.

"I can't believe I'm saying this, but looking at him now…" She shakes her head. "It's hard to believe he's responsible for so many deaths. He's just like us."

"I know." It's reassuring to know Loren feels as conflicted about Tazib as I do. I'll never be able to forgive him for killing Jep; but unlike most people, I know he isn't responsible for everything that's happened. Heat flares in my chest. "He's done terrible, horrible things, but he isn't as evil as the World Collective." My quiet voice trembles. "They're the ones who created Thanatos and then covered up that it had a fault. So many are dead because they care more about their perfect control than the lives of their people."

"The United People aren't turning out to be much better." Loren sighs as she moves to my side. "I knew our plan sucked, but still... I hate that we left Ky behind."

My hands instinctively reach for Mom's necklace, but it isn't in its spot around my neck. Without its reassuring weight I feel off-balance. "Maybe it was a hollow threat. Maybe they've released Ky and he's fine."

Loren doesn't answer and I press a hand against the ache in my chest. We both know the truth. As the hours have crawled by, all hope that maybe, just maybe, the United People won't harm Ky has shrunk bit by bit until nothing remains.

Another failure to add to my long list.

"So, what happens now?" Loren asks, turning to look out at the untouched landscape.

"I'm not sure." I know that isn't what Loren wants to hear, but it's the truth. I have no idea what's next. No idea where we're going or what we'll find when we reach whatever secret location Tazib's been hiding in. I have no idea what the World Collective or the

United People will do next. No idea how to fix Thanatos. The number of unknowns would be crippling if not for the music. "What I do know is that we can't go back, not after freeing Tazib. Are you sure you made the right decision? To come with me? You could have started over."

Loren shakes her head, her straight dark hair swinging over her shoulders. "There was no life for me there. I killed Mart."

"It was an accident."

"One I didn't prevent, same thing. I had to get away, Ry. Walking around Unity, every pond, every group of dorm kids, it was only going to remind me. No matter how the WC tried to cover up his death *I* would know, and how could I live with that? No." She shakes her head vehemently. "I couldn't stay." Loren clamps her teeth together, her nostrils flaring as her eyes glisten.

I bump my shoulder against hers, offering a sad smile. There's a part of me that could be mad at Loren—little Mart would be alive if she'd been doing her role—but I'm not. Instead, there is only deep sorrow for her. She should never have been placed as dorm leader. With her hot temper and short fuse, asking her to have unlimited patience for a half dozen 3-year-olds was insane. It is just another example of how broken things have become within the World Collective.

"Do you think it will ever stop hurting?" Loren asks as a single tear escapes, leaving a shimmering trail down her cheek.

"I don't know if it will ever not hurt, but I think it will get easier, with time." I lean my head against hers, closing my eyes as I listen for the melody, desperate to stop the whisper of fear. If we have time...

"No need to sleep standing."

My eyes snap open to find Tazib studying Loren and I.

"There are two reclining chairs," he says. "Or do you still not trust me?"

Loren stiffens and pulls away from my side. "Were you awake the whole time?"

"Maybe." Tazib shrugs noncommittally as he raises the chair from the reclined position. He laughs at Loren's fierce scowl. "Look, you're not going to get any judgement from me. We've all made poor decisions, some bigger than others." He stretches, wincing as he straightens his arms. "I'm so stiff," he complains as he massages his biceps. "Stiff and itchy. For all their 'perfection' that bed in Unity sucked and they refused to let me use lotion more than once a day." He shakes his head. "You'd think they'd know burn victims need to be careful not to let their skin dry out."

"You were locked up in a holding centre, guilty of murder." I cross my arms. "Your comfort wasn't a priority."

"Fair enough." Tazib grins. "Going to make it that much better to get home."

Home. I'm not sure I know what that means anymore. Ol'Syd had been home, but with all the people I care about no longer there, would it still feel like it? Unity was supposed to become my home, the place I would put down roots, grow friendships, find love, serve my purpose, and one day die and regrow with a tree of my own in New Growth Grove. But I wasn't there long enough for any of that to happen, and with the world as uncertain as it is, is any of that possible now?

Tazib moves to the window and looks north to where mountains rise into the sky, their snowy peaks hidden in clouds. "I can't wait for you to see Sota," he says. "I think you're going to like it. It's like nothing you've ever seen before, completely stunning." He turns towards me, his expression softening. "And the people, well, I think they're your type of people, Ry."

I shift away from Tazib, wishing the pod was bigger and I could put more space between us. Yes, we were close back in the interrogation room in Unity, but there he was restrained. Here, miles above the ground in a glass pod with nowhere to escape... "My kind of people, huh? If they're anything like you, I doubt we'll get along."

"Whatever do you mean?" Tazib feigns hurt. "I'm clearly not the only one in your life with death on their hands."

Loren sucks in a sharp breath, her hands balling into fists at her sides.

"Hold on now." Tazib shields himself with open palms. "I've heard about your temper. Don't go getting yourself all twisted in knots. I know we aren't the same. I'm just saying" —he waves between himself and Loren— "Maybe you should stop looking at the differences and start looking for the similarities."

Loren huffs but unclasps her hands. "How much longer until we get to this wonderful place of yours?"

"Not far now, see that peak?" Tazib points to a barren grey ridge. "Sota is on the other side."

The landscape below has transformed from rolling hills and flat plains to a marvel that takes my breath away. Tazib is right, this is like nothing I've seen before. The land is marred with rocky ridges and deep furrows where rivers crash with white foam. Before us, mountains grow larger, natural structures that put the tallest buildings in Unity to shame. The lower parts of the mountains are covered in pines, firs, and maples, their fall foliage brilliant in the late afternoon light. Higher up, the rock is laid bare with only a few straggly trees clinging to the cliff faces, their forms bent at strange angles from years of being battered by the elements.

Tazib waves through the glass, signalling that he will take over flying. As soon as Tazib has control, Eldon joins us.

"We are so close!" Eldon cheers, placing a long arm over Tazib's shoulder. "You ready to be home?"

"It's been too long," Tazib answers. "Did you let them know we're coming? And that we have company?"

Eldon nods, his freckled face breaking into a grin. "Yep. Momma Aimee's super excited. Sounds like she's prepared a feast."

The smile that forms on Tazib's face is transforming, a lightness I haven't seen before. He rubs his stomach and moans with pleasure. "Yes. WC food was so bland. I'm more than ready for a Momma Aimee meal."

The mention of food sets my own stomach grumbling. My last meal was a long time ago; and unfortunately, the pods Eldon commandeered from Unity have no snacks on board. It's been a long, hungry day.

The pod door opens again and a red-eyed Tali enters. Her dark hair falls across a shallow and pale face.

"Tali." I cross the small space and pull her bony frame into my arms. "Tali, I'm so sorry we couldn't save Ky."

She turns her face into my shoulder, her whole body trembling. "We should have moved faster. Gotten there sooner. Fought harder. We should have done more."

"You should've let me do my thing," Tazib asserts. "But it doesn't matter. Stop blaming yourselves. You didn't cause this. Blame the World Collective or the United People, The Code and Thanatos, any of it, or all of it. All their planning and plotting..." He shakes his head, his laugh cold. "If I've learned anything over the years it's that you can never predict what is going to happen next. Chaos wins. Always."

My chest tingles. "There is more than chaos, Tazib. Just look at the world around you." I wave to the windows. "These mountains, the forest. They are stunning and beautiful and awe-inspiring without the WC's order and reason, or the United People's plotting. Even without perfection it isn't chaos because each rock and tree and mountain are where they're supposed to be. They have a purpose, Tazib, because there is a plan. I believe that in the deepest part of me."

"And I believe people shouldn't be a number in a program. That we should all have faces and a voice. But that isn't the world we live in," Tazib snaps.

For a moment, the pod falls into stunned silence. Tazib's never been so blunt before, and it is more than a bit startling to hear his thoughts laid out so succinctly, especially since they mirror my own.

"Look." Eldon bounces on his toes. "We're almost there. Watch, this is the best part."

As our pods crest the peak of the mountain, a stunning vista opens below us. A long, clear blue lake shimmers in the setting sun, so pristine and framed by such beauty it doesn't seem real. We follow the lake north, the mountains rising on either side, one side cast in light and the other in darkening shadows as the sun sinks below the peaks.

"Where's the city? If we're close, shouldn't we see something?" Loren asks, her tiny nose wrinkling as she leans closer to the glass. "There's nothing here."

"Just the way we want it," Tazib drawls.

"There's a shield," Eldon grins as he points to a spot where the lake narrows. "This is my favourite part. Keep watching."

The pods are sinking towards the lake with alarming speed and I fight the fear that accompanies every descent. Shouldn't we be sitting down, each in our own pod? It can't be safe to land with all five of us standing here together. I lower myself into a seat.

"Don't want to watch?" Tazib asks.

"I can see from here." It isn't totally true. With Tali, Loren, and Eldon in the way, there is little I can see of the growing mountainside, and that's okay with me.

"Oh!" Loren gasps. "Did you see that? It appeared out of thin air! How'd you do that?"

Between their bodies I can just make out buildings set into the side of the mountain. They are small, only one or two stories tall, with roofs shingled in a grey material that matches the rocky area.

Eldon bounces lightly on his toes, grinning at Loren's astonishment. "It was Tazib's idea. Everything already sorta blends into the forest, he just amplified it with a few projections. If you sit on the other side of the lake and really look, you can tell the trees and rocks repeat in this section, but you'd only realize if you knew where to look." He scrunches his nose, glancing quickly at Tali. "I could show you sometime, if you want…"

Tali stares ahead vacantly, not seeing Eldon's look of hope. "Seeing what you use for projectors would be kind of interesting," she says without her typical enthusiasm.

Eldon's face falls. "Yeah, for sure. I can show you that, if you want."

"What are those?" Loren points to something lower that I can't see from my seat.

Eldon casts a quick glance at Tazib. "Ah, those are just a safety precaution. Oh look, there's Momma Aimee." He waves eagerly, nearly knocking Loren in the head with his elbow. "Oops, sorry, bit crowded in here. Guess some of us should move to the other pod for the final descent."

He, Tali, and Loren leave, though I wonder if there's any point. We must be almost on the ground. But once they go, I have a better view, and I realize we are still high up in the air. As Tazib lowers the pod, the buildings and the mountain rise above us.

"Nervous?"

Tazib's question catches me off guard and I tear my eyes away from the strange jumble of a town to find him watching me.

"A little."

"Everyone's going to love you." Tazib's smile does little to calm my nerves. "People always do. The World Collective hedged their bets right when they picked you to be the mascot of hope."

I look away, uncomfortable at the truth in his words. "It's not that," I say. "I grew up believing no one could live outside the WC. It felt natural to trust The Code to determine my purpose, to count my days. Now I have to learn to live outside all of it. It's... It's a big adjustment."

"Guess I wasn't there long enough to be so indoctrinated. But don't worry. We'll get you sorted out."

"I'm not here to join your group, Tazib." The pods have nearly finished landing in a clearing by the water's edge. "I'm here because you said you know how to fix Thanatos. I'm not running away from the WC. I will work with you until we get this figured out, and then I'm taking it back to them."

The pod has settled but Tazib doesn't immediately open the door. "Do you think you can do that? Actually work with *me* to end this?"

I meet his gold-flecked eyes, understanding the question he doesn't voice aloud. Am I willing to work with the terrorist hacker who killed my best friend and nearly killed my brother?

"I'm here, aren't I?" I ignore his outstretched hand and stand on my own.

Tazib has done terrible things, there is no denying that, but he's also been able to accomplish more than all my mad fumblings have managed. That's why I'm here. But trust him?

No. I'm not ready to do that.

CHAPTER THREE

THE POD DOOR OPENS WITH A BLAST OF FRIGID AIR, A reminder of both how far north we've travelled and my poor attire. Not relishing the idea of meeting Tazib's people while barefoot and in my pyjamas, I hesitate, wrapping my arms around my middle as Tazib hops out of the pod.

"Momma Aimee!"

Tazib dashes across the clearing, racing into the open arms of a heavily bundled form. A throaty musical laugh is blown back to me on the wind as the two embrace, the hood slipping back to reveal the jovial face of a woman bowed with age. I'm thankful the whistling wind disguises my gasp of surprise. The woman is old, older than anyone I've ever seen before. I'm unable to pull my eyes away from the pair as Tazib's youth accentuates her many wrinkles, the folds of skin under her chin, and her sagging cheeks. White hair crowns her head, a wavy mess that frames the joy on her face as she clasps Tazib, looking at him with such pride. She only releases him when

Eldon bounds forwards, ready to receive a hug of his own. Then she turns to Loren and Tali, greeting each of them with warmth before directing them to one of the nearby wood buildings. All of this I watch from the door of the pod, shivering in my polka-dot pants and ragged T-shirt until the woman looks my way.

"You poor thing!" she cries, hurrying to me with small shuffling steps. "You must be a block of ice. Tazib, you fool. Don't just stand there. Run and get the girl something warm to wear."

"Of course, right away, Momma Aimee." Tazib tucks his head and runs along one of the many paths leading up the mountain.

"That boy," the woman says, shaking her head. "For all his smarts he can be utterly clueless. Here, take my coat." She begins to shrug her shoulders free of the heavy jacket.

"No, I can't," I protest. The temperature is dropping fast with the sinking sun, and though I eye the thick lining with longing, I'm mortified at the idea of depriving such an elderly individual of their coat. "I'll be fine once I get inside," I reassure her.

"At least take my gloves," she insists, pulling them off to pass to me as I step out of the pod. Her eyes drop to my prosthetic but she is quick to raise her gaze to my face with a smile. "Come on, let's get you indoors. I'm Aimee, but everyone calls me Momma Aimee, and this is Sota." She waves to the buildings that cover the mountainside. "We're glad you're here, Rygita."

Aimee's voice is deep and raspy, but strong and commanding, with no sign of frailty. She leads me towards the nearest building where Eldon, Tali, and Loren wait at the door. Though her shoulders are stooped she is surprisingly tall, and her frame blocks the worst of the wind as I gratefully tug the gloves over my frozen fingers.

Matching my steps to Aimee's slow pace, I examine the squat, tiny buildings. Made with materials from the surrounding landscape, they blend easily into the mountainside. Huge logs still covered in bark form the frames, while stripped logs chinked with green moss form the walls. Windows look out towards the lake, their glass framed by cheerful curtains and window boxes of what once would have been colourful flowers that have now browned in the cold weather.

"Get indoors now, all of you." She motions for Eldon to enter the quaint lodging. "Eldon, dear, did you eat anything while you were away? You're much too skinny." Her eyes roam over Tali's frame. "You too, dear, all elbows and knees, the pair of you. Doesn't the World Collective know teenagers need the good stuff? Put some meat on those bones, I will. I have just the thing."

Following her inside, I nearly duck, surprised the ceiling is so close to my head. The small space is dominated by a large fireplace with a blazing fire and a worn couch is tucked under the window and framed by a collection of armchairs. Across the room, a long table is lined with mismatched chairs, leaving hardly enough space for a long, low cupboard. The space is cluttered with personal touches, instantly giving an impression of comfort and home.

Home. That's what this place is. It isn't a complex; no giant lobby full of ponds and fountains, no elevators, no dining hall. Just a simple home.

Aimee hangs her coat on a hook by the door and tugs off her boots before bustling through a swinging door by the table. As the door swings closed, the most delicious smell wafts back to us. "Have a seat at the table and make yourselves comfortable," she calls. "I'll be right back with the good stuff."

"It's all so tiny," Tali whispers, running a finger over the rough timber walls.

"Tiny?" Eldon pulls out a chair and sits at the table. "Momma Aimee has the biggest place in Sota. She's our welcome committee and meeting leader. You guys are all skewed weird because you grew up in the WC where everything is super oversized."

"You didn't grow up in the Collective?" Loren doesn't hide her bewilderment.

"Nope, I grew up tech free. Only got this a couple of months ago, when Tazib needed me to… When he needed me in Unity." He holds up his wrist, showing a scar that's a little bigger than typical of an implant.

"Wait." Loren's eyes narrow. "This is all working out too conveniently. Were you in Unity to spy on us? You *were* awfully friendly to me when we first met."

Eldon flushes as he rubs his hand along the back of his neck. "I wasn't spying, not really, just waiting. And it's good I was there," he rushes. "If I wasn't, we wouldn't have gotten Tazib out."

"Speaking of which, where is that boy?" Momma Aimee backs out of the kitchen carrying an armload of bowls. Eldon jumps to his feet, taking the bowls from her, and setting them along the table. "What's taking him so long? Is he bringing back a whole wardrobe?" She opens a drawer in the long cupboard, grabbing a handful of spoons. "Here, dear," she says to Tali. "Would you set out the cutlery? And you—" She crooks a finger at Loren. "Come give me a hand in the kitchen. You, Ry, get over to the fire. You are much too pale, and don't think these old eyes can't see you're still shivering."

Though we've only just met her, there is something about the old woman that drives one to please her. I watch from my spot by the fire as the others hurry to obey Aimee's bidding.

When Tazib returns with a gust of cold air, he kicks off his shoes in the doorway. "I'm back, Momma Aimee!"

"Took you long enough," she calls from the kitchen.

"Here." Tazib dumps a pile of mismatched clothes on the couch. "I raided Maisie's closet. Couldn't find her so here's hoping she doesn't throttle me. Should be close to your size. You can change in the bathroom in the back." He points the way down a small hall. "And Momma Aimee has a box of old shoes in the hall closet. Hopefully you can find something that fits."

I rummage through the pile and pull out a pair of pants, plain tank top, heavy sweater, and a pair of thick socks before heading to the bathroom. The clothes are worn, the knees nearly threadbare, and the style is more what I remember Jezza wearing when I was 6. Everything fits pretty well expect for the pants which rise above my ankles. Still, a hundred times better than pyjamas.

When I return, the long table is covered with steaming bowls of mashed potatoes and baskets of fresh bread. At the centre sits a giant pot, the source of the amazing smell. Aimee stands over it, a large ladle in hand as she carefully fills the bowls as they are passed to her.

"Come child, take a seat and hand me your bowl," Aimee instructs with an outstretched hand. "You can't eat what you don't have."

I slip onto an empty chair next to Loren and hurry to pass my bowl to be filled with the rich, dark stew.

"You can dip the bread or add mashed potatoes," Aimee directs. "Whatever suits your fancy."

"I'm a potato fan myself," Tazib says. A glance at his bowl shows he isn't kidding. A mountain of mashed potatoes rises from the stew and he eats with an enthusiasm that reminds me of Rube.

Rube. I quickly look away from Tazib, my chest squeezing uncomfortably. I haven't spoken to my brother since Dad was arrested. The fact that I played a part in Dad's arrest is something I doubt Rube will ever forgive. I've never felt so disconnected from my brother; and now that I'm a fugitive from the Collective, there will be no opportunity to fix things between us.

"This is sooooo goood," Loren moans. "Why aren't you eating?" She elbows me, shaking me from my self-pity.

Blowing on my spoon, I try a mouthful of the stew. It is divine. The perfect thing after going so long without eating. I eat half the bowl before adding mashed potatoes which creates a whole new element of pleasure.

The door of the cabin slams open, rattling the dishes on the table.

"Sorry we're late!"

Dominating the small doorway is a burly man with large shoulders, thick forearms, and a bushy red beard. Intricate tattoos of geometric shapes interwoven with landscapes of treed mountains creep up his neck and trail over his exposed arms. "I hope there's still some food left, what with Tazib and Eldon back," he grins and pulls off his boots. When he steps away from the door, he reveals a short teen girl who was hidden by his large frame.

"Maisie!"

Both Eldon and Tazib jump to their feet, rushing to sandwich the newcomer in a hug.

"What? No hugs for Al?" The big man laughs, clapping the two boys on the back.

"Come, come eat." Aimee fills more bowls.

Tazib and Eldon drag the girl back to the table. As she takes a seat across from me, she pulls off her hat, revealing shoulder length blonde hair, buzzcut on one side of her head, which allows a clear view of the trail of piercings lining her ear. Her ears aren't the only thing pierced. Her nose, eyebrow, and lip all flash with spikes and studs.

"Hold up." The burly man pauses at the end of the table, a dark scowl accentuating his thick eyebrows. "Who are they?" He motions to Tali and Loren.

"Al, this is Tali, Loren, and Rygita." Aimee points to each of us in turn.

"I know who Rygita is," Al grumbles. "But who are these other two and what are they doing here?"

"Ah, we're here because we risked our lives to free Tazib," Loren quips.

"And we're grateful to you," Aimee says. "Al, sit down. There will be more than enough time to discuss everything later."

"It's my job to keep this community safe," Al's deep voice rumbles. "A job I take very seriously. Which is why I want to know why we have unexpected guests."

"Al, you knew Tazib would be returning with Rygita. That was the plan."

"Fine. Yes. Rygita was a risk I understood was worth taking. But who are these other two?" Al huffs. "They shouldn't be here."

"And where can we go?" Loren demands. "I can't go back to the

WC. None of us can after what we did. You should be thanking us. Not kicking us out into the wilderness!"

"No one is kicking you out," Aimee soothes.

"Having them here is only going to bring death on all our heads!"Al's hands wave as his voice rises. "We should split them up, send them to one of the Uncounted's smaller sites, lower the risks. We know the WC is going to come looking. Not just because Tazib escaped, but because we've got their little darling."

"I made sure they're completely unconnected." Eldon's voice cracks as he glances from Al to the three of us. "And I had Tazib double check to make sure."

"They're fine, Al," Tazib says, returning to his meal, unfazed by the large man's anger. "I've taken care of things. They aren't going to be tracked and no one's going to find us."

Al huffs but drops into his chair. "Fine," he grumbles, his hands still fluttering wildly. "They stay. For now."

"We will need to find places for them," Aimee says. "I can take one and Priya has offered to host one as well. I did ask Jolan and Mikom but their hands are already full, what with their gaggle of children." She chuckles. "It would make a lot of sense for Rygita to stay at your place. You have room for one more, don't you, Al?" The old woman smiles sweetly with a confident twinkle.

Al sighs. "I'm sure I can squeeze another in."

Aimee nods. "Wonderful."

"Wait." Loren looks between Al and Aimee. "You're just dividing us up like portions? Don't we get a say? What if we want to stay together? We don't know you."

I've missed Loren's brashness. She's given voice to my own

thoughts. "Besides," I add. "You should know we aren't planning on staying long. As soon as we get what we need, we'll be on our way."

"Aren't you listening?" Al barks. "The Uncounted must remain secret, hidden."

"So what?" Loren bristles. "We have to stay here forever? 'Cause look, even though we can't go back to the WC right now, we have no interest in joining your group or whatever you are."

"Whatever we are?" Al rumbles. "What? Do you think we're some kind of terrorists?!"

"Al." Aimee gives him a pointed look.

"We are *not* terrorists," Al mutters.

"What Loren is trying to say..." I place a calming hand on Loren's arm though my own heart is racing at the sudden charge in the room. "...is that we didn't know our presence would cause so much trouble or danger for you. People getting hurt is the last thing we want, trust me. We didn't come to hide out from the Collective. We're here because Tazib said you had a way to fix Thanatos."

Maisie's head snaps to Tazib, her pierced brow arched and eyes questioning.

"You told her we had a way to fix it?!" Al thunders.

"I may have embellished a little," Tazib drawls as he licks his spoon clean.

The surprised expressions of the others raises a lump in the back of my throat.

"Tazib." My voice wavers. "Tell me you know how to fix Thanatos."

"I don't."

"But you said—"

"I said I had a lead on finding the cryptography key." Tazib looks up from his bowl, his eyes locking on mine. "You. You're the lead."

01010111 01100101 00100000 01100001 01110010 01100101 00100000 01110100 01101000 01100101 00100000

01010101 01101110 01100011 01101111 01110101 01101110 01110100 01100101 01100100 00101110

My body goes rigid, my neck and shoulders tightening so quickly a headache is already creeping up my skull. "What does that mean? How am *I* the lead?"

"Tazib, dear. Did you tell her nothing?" Aimee frowns at Tazib.

He shrugs. "I couldn't say much, not while I was in the holding cell. Couldn't risk anyone else hearing."

"What?" I gasp. "Why not? DATA's whole purpose was to stop what was going wrong. There was a whole team of people just waiting for information that could help!"

"A team lead by a United People member," Tazib answers. "And just look at how amazing they've turned out to be. I couldn't tell you. Not then."

"What about in the pods? After we escaped? Why didn't you tell me then? What does it even mean?" I repeat. "How can *I* be the lead? I didn't even know what a cryptography key was until we learned Thanatos needed one!"

"I think some explanations are in order," Aimee states. "Please, everyone eat. Let's not lose our tempers. Let's see, how can I summarize...?" Her lips purse, accentuating the fan of wrinkles. "The Uncounted have remained separate from the World Collective but not oblivious. Tazib saw what was happening with Thanatos and The Table decided to get involved. We began with research, and in that research we discovered some very old records that mention a tie between your genetic ancestors and the first Thanatos. Like many records, large parts of it were corrupted, even our best techs were unable to recover much. But what we could see is that something, a key of some kind, has been passed down. We assume this is the cryptography key needed to gain complete access to the Thanatos code."

"Are you sure this is wise?" Al asks. "Telling a bunch of kids everything?"

"They are the ones who put their lives on the line to free Tazib. They deserve to know what we know. And Rygita has a right to know her role in our plan."

"And what is that?" I ask, my voice breaking as I struggle to remain calm.

"We know that without a patch, the only way to save lives is to get to the root of the problem in the Thanatos coding itself. And to do that, we need the key."

"The key that may be hidden in me. How is that even possible?"

Aimee smiles. "The World Collective got very good at science, as I'm sure you know, and they love hiding things in the most complicated of places."

"What does that mean?"

"We believe the key could be in your genetic code."

"Seriously?" Loren blurts. "How in the world do you go about finding something like that?"

"Well, it's going to take time," Aimee admits. "But we aren't too bad at science ourselves. First thing tomorrow, Tazib will show you the lab. We will take blood and tissue samples, body and brain scans, and use any other tools that may help us find the key."

The way her voice wavers when she says "other tools" sends a quiver of unease down my spine.

"Wait, my genetic code isn't the only place the Collective could hide something. Knowing what they can do with MEMORY, could it be…?"

"Hidden in your memories?" Aimee finishes for me when my throat closes. "It is a possibility."

"Is that what you were looking for?" I ask Tazib. "When you had Kota—"

Tazib jumps to his feet. "I think we need more potatoes. More potatoes anyone?" Without waiting for an answer, he disappears through the swinging door to the kitchen.

"I react to MEMORY," I hiss through clenched teeth. "When I'm under, it's like my cells are being torn apart."

"We know." Aimee leans back in her chair, her expression serious. "And that's why we don't think we should use it on you."

"But Tazib—"

"Tazib doesn't make the decisions around here." Her throaty voice is both authoritative and soothing. "Subjecting you to MEMORY is something we will only do as a last resort. The Uncounted do not toy with lives, Rygita. You are safe here."

"Safe? How can I be safe?" I choke, my voice rising. "You want me to trust you after you allowed Tazib to murder my friend? After he tried to kill my brother?! After he almost killed me?!"

My whole body shakes with anger and exhaustion. Yes, I chose to free Tazib. And yes, I travelled here with him of my own free will. But it was only because I had no other choice.

A deep hush falls over the room. Al and Aimee cast a quick glance at each other before turning to Eldon. Sensing all eyes on him, Eldon flushes crimson.

"I guess I didn't tell you *everything* Tazib was doing," he mumbles.

"Tazib!" Al barks, his thunderous voice rattling my already frayed nerves. "Get out of that kitchen this instant! You have some explaining to do!"

Tazib emerges, his head bowed.

"Is this true?" Aimee questions, her face paling. "Tazib, did you kill innocent people?"

Tazib's head drops further. "I'm sorry, Momma Aimee, but I saw no other way."

Aimee sags back in her chair, closing her eyes with a grimace.

Al, on the other hand, shoots to his feet. "You self-centred, headstrong—"

"I get things done," Tazib says, raising his chin to meet the glares from the table. "It's never been a secret that I'm willing to do whatever it takes."

"But at what cost?" Al's nostrils flare. "You were captured."

Tazib opens his mouth, but Al cuts him off.

"And not just you. Kota too. And where is he now?"

Tazib's mouth slowly closes.

"Yeah, that's what I figured. You haven't given him a second thought, have you? You were all wrapped up in your little plan. Didn't think to rescue him, did you? And what do you think is going to happen to him? Where do you think he is now?"

A pit of dread opens in my stomach. There is no doubt the WC will convict Kota of terrorism. He's as good as dead if he isn't already. The image I had of him as a human jungle gym jumps to my mind. I wasn't a fan of what he did to me, but he was only following orders—Tazib's orders.

Tazib stands rigid, the muscles in his neck visible as he clenches his jaw. "Things didn't go as planned."

"No kidding," Loren mutters.

"Tazib." Aimee's strained voice seems to impact Tazib more than Al's anger. "Your actions cost us a valuable location, countless resources, and let's not forget the risk Eldon took to live in Unity. All was an acceptable cost when we considered the implications of leaving Thanatos unchecked, but taking lives…"

"Eldon always wanted to see Unity," Tazib interjects. "And it worked, we got Ry here, we can find the key now."

"That does not make it right."

"What do you want?" Tazib asks softly. "You want me to go break out Kota? 'Cause I will."

"We want you to set aside this strange vendetta of yours!" Al barks. "To actually think about how your actions impact those around you!"

"What is done is done." Aimee sighs, pinching the bridge of her nose. "We have given Tazib a great deal of power and resources. He is responsible for his choices, but we too have a responsibility." Her features sag. "Tazib, because of your actions, you will be banned from the lab."

"Banned?" Tazib's eyes widen. "But I know what we're looking for. They'll need me."

"The others know what we are looking for."

I can feel Aimee's authority in the way Tazib shrinks under her gaze.

"Tazib, I understand you feel strongly about Thanatos, about Rygita, but we have clearly allowed you freedoms and resources beyond your years. You are an exceptional child with exceptional abilities, but you are just that, a child." She runs a hand down her face. "We will need to discuss this with the others," she says to Al. "We all share a blame in Tazib's actions by failing to treat him as the child he is."

"I'm sorry, but seriously?" Loren coughs, scowling at Aimee. "Are you apologizing for what *he* did?"

"I'm taking ownership for my actions," Aimee says. "Isn't that what you wish the World Collective would do? Yes, Tazib carries blame, but it is important to recognize the underlying issues. If we want the world to change, we must change the systems that allowed or encouraged terrible events. If we don't, we will continue to repeat the same mistakes, over and over until the end of time."

"But shouldn't there be more?" I blurt. "He killed my best friend! Shouldn't his punishment be more than a simple lab banning?"

"What do you have in mind?" The old woman turns her full gaze on me. "A public execution? Do you demand a life for a life?"

"Yes. No. I don't know," I falter. I wiggle on my seat, unable to look at Tazib. I hate him for what he's done, but demanding his death? Wouldn't that make me just as terrible?

"It isn't so simple, is it?" Aimee states. "It never is."

For a moment the room is quiet. Tazib shifts uneasily on his feet while Aimee rubs a wrinkled hand over her eyes.

"I have a question." Tali sets her spoon beside her untouched stew, looking up at the table with red-rimmed eyes. "About Thanatos." She rubs at her wrist, at the slightly raised spot where the implant lies under her skin. "Are we safe from it? You said we're disconnected. Does that mean it won't happen to us? It won't activate?"

Al coughs and Maisie shifts in her seat.

"No," Tazib says softly. He looks from me to Tali and Loren. "You are disconnected from the system, but Thanatos continues to run on each of you individually. The moment it is uploaded at birth, there's no way to turn it off."

"Oh," Tali gasps, chewing her lip as her eyes drop to her arm. "So, it can still kill us? We're no safer than before?"

"No. Not until we find that key."

CHAPTER FOUR

THE TABLE DROPS INTO UNEASY SILENCE AS WE RETURN TO OUR meal. Al continues to scowl as he devours his stew, oblivious to the dribbles splattering into his beard. Tali pokes at her bowl, her shoulders slumped and head resting on her hand while Loren vibrates with barely contained rage. I bump her shoulder, trying to break the tension, knowing she finds it easier to be angry than to process all that's happened. I can't say I blame her. I keep my eyes on my food to avoid seeing Tazib across the table. While part of me is relieved the Uncounted were unaware of what he was doing, his punishment—being banned from the lab—feels like a slap on the wrist. Shouldn't there be more?

Eventually, the table returns to awkward chatter as Aimee steers the conversation to the happenings of the community while Eldon and Tazib were away. I find the whole experience strange, watching Tazib interact with these people like a regular teen, but I also find it weird how all the Uncounted members speak with their hands.

"Anyone want thirds?" Aimee asks. When everyone shakes their heads, she gathers the large pot, backing into the kitchen. "Al, could you ask Maisie if she'll need to borrow any bedding for Rygita?" she calls from the kitchen.

"Sure thing." Al turns so he is facing Maisie, his hands moving expressively. "Momma Aimee wants to know if we need more bedding."

Maisie doesn't answer, but moves her hands, and I notice that they aren't fluttering like mine do when I'm overwhelmed and trying to make my point. There is a pattern, an order to her movements.

"She says we got more than enough, but thanks," Al hollers.

Seeing my befuddled look, Maisie smirks, the pierced brow rising. She taps Al's arm before again moving her hands quickly before her.

"Maisie says if you haven't figured it out by now then you are a special kind of slow." There is no mistaking the laughter in Al's voice. "She is deaf. Has been from birth. She speaks with her hands and is pretty amazing at lip reading."

I try to keep my face neutral, but I'm sure I fail. Deaf? Deafness was one of the weaknesses the World Collective solved over a century ago. "If she can't hear, how does she—"

The scowl that appears on Maisie's face cuts me short. Her hands move rapidly.

"Don't you dare underestimate me," Al translates. "Just because I can't hear doesn't mean I don't understand what's happening."

Tazib nods. "I second that," he says, a grin spreading on his face. "Underestimating Maisie is not a mistake you want to make. If anything, you should be thanking her. Without her, you'd still be wearing pjs."

Colour heats my face. How many times have strangers met me and made assumptions about my abilities based on my prosthetic. It's one of my biggest pet peeves and here I go and do the same thing.

"Don't worry," Tazib says. "She forgives easily. A good thing considering you're staying with us." He points between him, Eldon, Al, and Maisie.

My stomach turns at Tazib's smile. I'm still trying to wrap my brain around the fact that I'm here, eating a meal with Tazib, and now I have to live with him? This is just great.

Darkness has fallen when Al declares it's time to leave. Loren will be staying with Aimee, and Tali will be staying with someone called Priya. I give each friend a hug, wishing I could trade places with them, though I doubt either of them wants to sleep in the same house as Tazib any more than I do.

After exiting the little house, Al leads us up a steep path with more stairs than flat areas. The night air is chilly and I pull my hands inside the sleeves of my sweater while tucking my chin into the collar. Eldon rubs his bare arms, and though he tries to hide it, Tazib is shivering too. Only Al and Maisie appear unaware of the cold night air. Al has the sleeves of his shirt shoved up his arms and Maisie is dressed in a T-shirt and pants that have more rips than material.

I try to look around as we climb upwards, but it is virtually impossible. The dark path is lit only occasionally with the little light that escapes a curtained window, and even though I train my eyes on the ground, I keep catching my prosthetic on the uneven surface.

"Your eyes will adjust," Tazib offers, catching my arm after a particularly bad stumble nearly sends me tumbling into a tree. "Bet you've never been anywhere so dark before."

I jerk my arm away from Tazib's touch.

"I missed the dark," Eldon quips. "And the quiet. Unity was cool to visit, but I don't think I could live there. It was so hard to fall asleep."

Now that he's mentioned it, I'm keenly aware of the silence. There are no pods whirring over our heads, no elevators zooming up the sides of buildings, no chatter from hundreds of bodies, no beeps from scanning devices. I shiver. The usual sounds are gone, but the more I listen, the less I'd say it's quiet. There are so many new sounds: hoots and cries from the woods around us, the wind moving in the tall pines, the branches groaning. Something snaps loudly in the bush just off the path and I jump.

"You'll get used to that too," Tazib chuckles.

By the time we reach Al's house, we are high up the mountainside. The climb has warmed me and I turn towards the view below as I catch my breath. From here, I can see the wispy trails of smoke from hidden chimneys, the shimmer of the lake far below, and the outline of the mountain on the other side against the dark grey sky. No doubt I will be met with a stunning view in the morning.

"Home sweet home," Al booms, sending some small creature skittering into the woods as he shoves open a heavy wooden door and leads us inside a long, low, timber-framed house. Hitting a switch, the front room is flooded with light, revealing a space even smaller than Aimee's. It is cold and damp with a strange smell of pine mixed with wet shoes.

"I'll make a fire, get the place warmed up." Al signs as he talks. "You'll want to open the door to your room." He nods to Tazib and Eldon. "It's been closed up a while so it'll be pretty chilly. Maisie, how about you find some extra blankets, make a bed for Rygita in your room."

Maisie and Eldon disappear down the hall.

"Can I do anything?" I ask.

"Sure. You and Tazib can bring in more wood." Al opens the grate to the fireplace and pokes the ash with a long metal rod. "The air has a bite tonight, going to be a cold one."

"On it," Tazib crows. He motions me to follow him back outside and around the side of the house to where a long pile of wood is stacked neatly next to the wall.

It's hard not to stare at Tazib as he collects an armload of logs, at how cheerfully he does what he was asked.

"Wood is the main source of heat in Sota," Tazib explains, mistaking my befuddled look. "There's no shortage of it, but it's a lot of work."

"It's not that." I keep my eyes down as I fumble to collect the rough logs into my arms. "It's you... You're so different here."

"Not sure what to tell you," Tazib says, adding one more log to his impossibly huge armload. "I'm just being me."

"You're so calm about getting in trouble," I say as I struggle to stand with my armload. "Not that I think your punishment is nearly enough."

A shadow crosses Tazib's face. "They knew how to hurt me—banning me from the lab—right when we finally have the person we've been searching for."

"Do you really think the key could be in my genetic code?"

"Maybe." Tazib leads the way back around the house. "Though I think there's a better chance of finding it in your memory."

"You were looking for it, when you had Kota use MEMORY on me, weren't you?"

He nods. "I was hoping you would remember me, but yeah, I had my suspicions."

"And did you find anything?"

"I don't know. I got arrested before I saw the footage."

"Well, it's not going to happen, not if I have any say."

"They won't force you, but you need to do it. I'm positive."

"MEMORY almost killed me," I growl. "I nearly died."

"But you didn't." Tazib leans towards me. "Think about it, Ry. Why do you react so poorly? My guess is it's *because* they've hidden the key in your memories."

"So," I counter. "What if going under kills me this time? What happens then?"

Tazib shrugs. "It's a necessary risk. It won't happen—" he rushes. "But if it did, we would at least have the data we need to stop Thanatos."

My mouth drops open. That's it? All that work to get me on his side and this is his plan? To hook me up to a machine that could possibly kill me with the hopes that maybe, just maybe, he'll find some way to stop Thanatos?

"You're insane," I mutter, pushing past him.

"And you're going to do it. You're going to do it because nothing else has worked. You'll do it because it's the only way to protect Rube, Tali, Loren, and even the dimpled Darr." Tazib's footsteps crunch behind me on the gravelled path. "Where is Darr, by the way? Not that I care…" he drawls. "But I thought he'd be a part of the breakout, that he'd be here."

I don't answer because what happened between Darr and me is none of Tazib's business. I struggle not to drop the logs in my arms as I think back to the last time I saw Darr. I still can't get over the fact that he turned me in. His face that morning when I wouldn't back down from my plan to free Tazib… I'm not sure there's a way to salvage what we had. I can't forget the hurt I saw in his eyes, his anxiousness and determination. Darr was sure he was protecting me, that he was doing the right thing. But can't he see that none of us are safe while the Thanatos virus exists? We have to fix it, and we have to be willing to do whatever it takes. It's why I broke Tazib out. It's why I'm here with him now.

Heading back into the house, we drop the wood next to the fireplace where Al is coaxing a small fire to light.

"Which of us didn't finish your sandwich?" Eldon calls as he returns from the back hall with an armload of dirty dishes. "'Cause this thing is positively green." He waves a plate covered in green-grey fuzz.

"That's what you get when you don't clean your room." Al's laugh is more like a bark, loud like the rest of him. "Doubt either of you have any clean clothes to wear either. You'll have to take a load to the wash tomorrow."

Maisie enters after Eldon, waving her hand in front of her nose. I watch as the three of them rapidly sign to one another. It's strange —their banter is silent, but it's clear there is a deep bond between them. They act like siblings, teasing each other in that loving way.

My heart aches as my mind jumps to Rube. I miss him so much. But even if I could call him, would he even answer? Dad's been sentenced to mine plastics for the rest of his life because of me. Rube will never see Dad again because of me. No, I doubt Rube is ever going to forgive me.

"Maisie will show you where you're sleeping," Eldon says, interrupting my gloomy thoughts and drawing my attention to where Maisie waits.

I follow her down the hall. She pushes open the first door on the left, showing me a simple bathroom with a tub and shower combo. The next door opposite stands open. Maisie plugs her nose before doing two slow motions.

"Tazib's and Eldon's?" I guess.

Maisie nods with a smirk. She continues down the hall, signing again before a closed door.

"Your dad's? Wait, he is your dad, right?"

Maisie nods her head, again doing a slow sign. There is a challenge in her eyes, a dare to prove I'm not as stupid as she thinks I am. She does the sign again, not moving as I shift on my feet.

"Are you signing *dad*?" I ask. I try to mimic her movements. Her scowl deepens as she repeats it again. "Like this?" I work to place my fingers the way she has hers, trying the sign again. "Dad," I say.

Satisfied, Maisie turns and opens the last door. Unlike the bathroom, which was set on the mountain side of the house and only had one small, high window, Maisie's room faces the lake, and the outer wall is dominated by a large window seat covered in mismatched pillows and a pile of blankets. Stepping into the room, it feels small. There is so much stuff. Maisie's bed is tucked in the corner, making space for a large desk covered in tools and the remains of some machine that has been pulled apart. The other corner has a large drum set, the bass drum scrawled with the words "Death to the WC" in angry red lettering. But what makes the room feel really small is the fact that nearly every wall is covered in shelves, each overflowing with odd pieces of metal, jars of bright coloured stones, feathers, and pinecones. And books. More books than I've ever seen in my life. They're everywhere. Piled by her bed, crammed on the shelves, covering her desk. I step closer to the nearest shelf and pick up a book, turning its dog-eared pages carefully. The cover is mostly missing, the spine is broken, and it has a strong smell of mildew, but it's real.

"I've never seen so many books." I turn the pages, reading a couple of lines. "Everything is digital within the Collective."

Maisie shrugs and flops onto her bed. She points to the window seat and mimes sleeping.

"Oh, thanks." I look around the small space and back to Maisie with fresh curiosity. "Have you read all these?"

Maisie grins with another nonchalant shrug. She leans over her bed and pulls open a drawer built into the base. Fishing out a clean pair of pjs, she tosses them to me.

I head to the bathroom to change, pausing at Tazib's and Eldon's door where the murmur of voices is punctuated by laughter. When I return, Maisie is already in bed, reading in the small pool of light from her bedside lamp. I rearrange the pillows to one end of the window seat and spread out the blankets. There is a chill coming off the glass, but I'm comfortable once I snuggle down into the covers. I look at Maisie across the room. I'd like to chat, to ask the million questions rattling around my brain, but she doesn't look up from her book.

I roll over and peer out into the dark night sky. The day has been impossibly long. And strange. It's like I've stepped back into another time and place, or an alternate universe. Unity feels light-years away, everything happening there so distant and separate from this place. But that's not true. No matter how many miles we travelled, the problems have followed. Thanatos still runs, threatening the lives of everyone I care about.

I pull my knees to my chest, curling into a ball. Tomorrow will be spent in the lab, searching for the crypto key. I know Dad said Mom's ancestors were involved in the creation of The Code, but it's hard to believe my family, my genetic history, may have the answer to stopping Thanatos. It seems impossible. But on the other hand, I believe an unseen Composer guides the world with music, so why not? Why not hope for the impossible? At this point, what do I have to lose?

It's a silent hike down the mountain the next morning. Though he's banned from the lab, Tazib's been tasked with showing me the way since there are no digital maps of Sota's many twisting paths. I watch his back as he carefully maneuvers the rocky path. I don't understand him. I've seen him angry, indifferent, calculating, and even broken. But here, watching him at breakfast with Al, Maisie, and Eldon, he is happy and carefree, and that image—the idea of Tazib happy—does strange things to my gut and heart.

In an attempt to distract myself, I turn my gaze away from Tazib to the stunning beauty of this place. Instead of tall buildings winking with lights, frost-covered trees glitter. Instead of pods, large birds circle on unseen winds. Wisps of fog rise from the lake, adding an otherworldliness to this untamed place.

"This way."

Tazib turns down a new path leading away from the main grouping of buildings. A thick bed of pine needles muffles our steps and between the tall trees I catch glimpses of a clear blue sky marred by a single column of smoke. When we break from the forest into a green clearing, we are rewarded with an unobscured view of the far mountain reflected in double on the smooth surface of the lake.

When I gasp, my feet halting, Tazib chuckles. "Guess it is pretty amazing, but wait until you see the lab. It's this way." He nods to the rocky base of the mountain where a pair of buildings sit tucked against the stone like they were carved from it. Between them is a large pool that billows white clouds of steam. "It's a natural hot spring," Tazib explains as we pass. "We use it to generate power for Sota, that and what we can get from solar panels. It's got lots of great minerals and stuff. Does wonders for sore muscles."

Tazib leads me inside the second of the two buildings. Camouflaged with the mountainside, the structure is unremarkable and looks no bigger than Al's cabin; but stepping inside, I see I've been misled. The space opens into a corridor that travels deep into the rock. Tazib leads me down its well-lit path and into a large lab where I can't help but let my jaw drop.

So far, everything I've seen in Sota has appeared rather primitive: wood fireplaces, few lights, simple bathrooms, kitchens with no fancy equipment. But the lab is another story. It isn't just a lab with all the microscopes, beakers, fridges, and Bunsen burners you'd expect to find. There are medical tables, electronic screens, and a complete, contained server room. All the tech is state-of-the-art, everything you'd expect to find in a lab in Unity, with a number of extra devices I don't recognize.

Tazib watches my reaction with an amused twinkle. "We may live outside the Collective, but that doesn't mean we're uneducated." He waves around the room. "The truth is, people here are hands down smarter than the average WC citizen. We have to be. No specializing in one role—we have to know how do to all the roles. Makes us better problem solvers and adaptors, things the WC is sorely lacking."

Tazib leads me across the large lab to a little office full of cozy chairs. Here, three adults sit talking over steaming mugs.

"Here she is," Tazib announces. "The Collective's little survivor and the key to solving everything. Ry, meet Mikom, Jolan, and Priya."

"Hello." A man with long dark hair reaches for my hand, giving me a funny look when I press my palm against his. "It's wonderful to meet you, Rygita. Like Tazib said, I'm Mikom. Sota's tech expert, well, one of them." His eyes meet Tazib's behind me. "Under normal circumstances, Tazib would be working with us, but…"

"But I'm banned. I know, I know." Tazib waves his hands in submission. "Don't worry, I'm going. Just had to say hi."

"We're glad you're back, Tazib." One of the two women stands, pushing herself off the couch with a groan. Her hands cup a *very* large belly. "Though we wish you had made different choices." She turns to me with an uncertain smile. "Hello, Rygita. I'm Priya, Sota's medical expert, though I'll be taking a bit of a break in the near future." Her eyes drop to her swollen stomach, her voice softening. "Three more weeks until I meet this little one."

"And I'm Jolan." The second woman's pale blue eyes crinkle when she smiles. She flicks one of her two long braids over her shoulder. "It's my job to keep things organized around here."

"Nice to meet you." I give each a smile, allowing my years of awkward interactions with strangers to guide me.

"Well," Tazib says. "I'll let you get to work finding that key." He waves a farewell as he leaves the lab.

"So, where do we start?" I ask, suddenly nervous.

"Let's start simple," Priya suggests. "How about bloodwork?" She leads the way out of the small office and I slow my pace to match her pregnant waddle.

"Bloodwork's fine," I say. "I happen to have a bit of experience with it."

"Oh, we know," Jolan says. "We know all about your past." At my sharp look she adds, "Don't worry, we understand WC press updates never tell the whole story, so we've looked a bit deeper." She nods to where Mikom sits at a computer that would rival the ones the DATA team used in Unity. "Plus, we've had Tazib's insights."

Priya motions for me to sit in a padded chair and I pull off my heavy sweater, readying my arm for her needle. It's hard to stop my frown. Reading my files doesn't mean they know me and I seriously doubt the accuracy of Tazib's "insights."

"That's quite the face," Priya says, as she ties a band around my upper arm. "Is something wrong?"

"No." I shake my head, forcing my face to relax. "I'm good. Let's find the key."

"No, something's bothering you. We won't rush you."

My chest squeezes. I want to rush. I want to find the key as quickly as possible so I can fix Thanatos and life can return to normal. At least, something closer to normal.

"It's just…" I take a deep breath. "It's just that I don't know you. I don't know anything about the Uncounted or this place or what you know and don't know. Hearing you say you know me… You can't. You don't. No matter what Tazib's told you."

It's hard to look at Priya, she already appears so worn and exhausted, so I drop my eyes to the floor. Mikom's chair squeaks as he pushes away from the desk.

"We're sorry, Rygita. You're right. You don't know us and we don't know you. Not yet anyway. Will you give us the chance? Can we go on this journey together?"

I pull my eyes from the cement floor to find Jolan's hand on Mikom's shoulder. He cups her hand and gives me an apologetic smile. Priya too has taken a step back and waits for me.

"I don't have much of a choice," I answer.

"Sure you do," Mikom says. "You know where to look for the key now. You could go back to Unity and do this on your own."

"I wish that was true." I bite my lip. "But after what I did, breaking out of the holding centre, it wouldn't be safe for me."

"Then let us help you." Priya crouches at my side, her knees cracking as she squats. "I know you may find it hard to believe, but we want to stop Thanatos just as much as you do."

"Really?" I look up at these people, at their unscarred arms and implant-free bodies. There is something reassuring about the trio of adults, something that gives the impression they'll look out for me.

"Really," Jolan and Mikom echo.

"Alright," I concede. "Let's do this."

Time in the lab is like stepping back to my days in the healing centre. All the things are familiar: bloodwork, scans, tissue samples. It isn't bad. Priya has a serious sweet tooth and believes every procedure should be rewarded with a cookie. She handles all the medical equipment while Mikom uses the tech, operating the equipment like it's an extension of himself. He and Jolan are a couple, one that is openly affectionate with each other. She is the one who keeps everything on track, checking lists and brainstorming new ideas, even though she is often called elsewhere and has to leave.

"I think that's a good start," Mikom announces after a couple of hours. "How about we break for lunch?"

"Sounds good," Priya says. "I'm famished."

"How?" Mikom laughs. "You must have had at least half a dozen cookies."

"So?" Priya pouts. "I'm growing another person, I think I've earned them."

"Fair enough." Mikom's laugh echoes in the cavernous lab. "If I've learned anything from watching Jolan birth four babies, it's that the pregnant woman is always right."

"Four?" I blink at Mikom. "You have *four* kids?"

"Yep," he says, practically radiating fatherly pride. "I heard you are good with kids. You'll have to come by sometime. Jolan and I are always looking for help. Speaking of which, I should get moving. She doesn't love managing the lunch meltdowns on her own."

"What time do you want me back in the lab?" I ask, as I grab my sweater and follow Mikom and Priya to the door.

Priya stops, her hands cupping her back as she shoots Mikom a glance. "How much did Momma Aimee explain about how our community works?" she asks.

"Not much," I answer, looking between them.

Mikom leans against the door. "Jolan would be better at explaining this," he sighs. "But I guess I'll have to do. The Uncounted have survived by remaining unconnected and distinct from the World Collective. Not just in terms of technology, but in the ways we do things."

"It's something we take very seriously," Priya interjects.

"It is," Mikom nods. "There's a lot I could say about how we do this, but only one really impacts you, and that's in how you are viewed among the Uncounted."

"Viewed?"

"Yes, as a child," Mikom continues. "I know in the WC, once you're activated for your vital role you're considered an adult, but here, well, we still see you as children. Children who have faced more than most adults could handle," he adds quickly. "But still children."

I pull the sleeves of my sweater over my knuckles as I frown. Sure, I haven't always felt grown up since being activated, but I'm also not liking where this conversation is going.

"Rygita, our expectations for you and your friends are vastly different from what was expected of you within the Collective. Yes, we expect you to contribute to the community, but only in tasks that are appropriate to your age."

"What are you saying?" I cross my arms over my middle, pinning my anxious fingers to my sides. "What does this have to do with coming back to the lab after lunch?"

"I'm making a mess of this, aren't I?" Mikom says to Priya.

"What Mikom's saying is that we don't expect you to spend your day in the lab," Priya says.

"What?" I stutter. "But I have the key. If I'm not in the lab, what am I doing?"

"Al will probably assign you some chores," Mikom says.

"And then you'll have some free time to do whatever you want," Priya adds. "Go to school, visit with your friends, draw, build, hike. Be a child."

"But we need to stop Thanatos." Heat flares in my chest. "People are dying!"

"We know," Priya says. "And we are taking it seriously. Mikom and I will be analyzing everything we collected today, and tomorrow morning you will return and we'll go at it again. We aren't shutting you out, Ry," she stresses. "We're protecting you."

"But you are shutting me out!" My voice trembles as I struggle to remain composed. "I could help with analyzing. Loren too. She aced science. Even Tali is amazing—the things she remembers. We should be here, helping."

"We know it means a lot to you—"

"It's our lives!"

"And it's a responsibility children should not have to bear." Mikom steps forward, his eyes kind. "The Uncounted handle things differently from the World Collective, but no less seriously. We have a thing here, we call it The Table. Instead of using a computer program to make our decisions, we gather qualified individuals who weigh the risks and benefits of every problem and situation. The choice to bring you here to Sota was one made at The Table. Searching for the key in your genetic past was another. By using The Table to make decisions, the responsibility rests not with one person, but many. This is our way. If things fail, it will crush all involved, but The Table will carry the blame. This isn't something for a child, do you see?"

I shake my head. Don't they understand I already carry this burden? Shutting me out of the lab isn't going to change that.

CHAPTER FIVE

AFTER LUNCH, I'M GIVEN A HANDFUL OF CHORES TO DO WHILE the "adults" analyze my samples. I'm still fuming at being shut out of the lab. Sure, my skills may not be top tier, but I'm not clueless either.

It doesn't help that Al's paired me with Tazib for the afternoon. It is so strange, to be wandering freely with Tazib, the most wanted terrorist in the World Collective. I can't get over how different he is here. His whole countenance has changed, he's so full of life and light. Even his posture is different. If I hadn't seen it with my own eyes, I would never believe this is the same guy who kidnapped my brother and watched with indifference as he suffered.

After canvasing other families in the community for some better-fitting clothing for me, we tackle the long list of chores we've been assigned. Tazib attacks each task with enthusiasm, chatting with everyone we meet, catching up on the things he missed while away, and showing genuine interest in their answers.

"They like to keep us occupied with busy work," Tazib says as we climb back up the mountain at the end of the day.

I don't answer. I've hardly said anything all afternoon, my mind too busy imploding as I try to make sense of this place and this version of Tazib. I keep my eyes on the back of his sneakers as he climbs the steps ahead of me.

"I know it bugs you as much as it bugs me," Tazib continues. "They block us out of big decisions because of our age, but they fail to recognize it's our lives they're playing with. They say this is how the Uncounted have survived." He laughs dryly. "But they were barely surviving when I arrived. Change can be a good thing, a needed thing."

Reaching Al's house, we are met with the smell of something burning and a deafening racket of drums.

Tazib groans. "Must be Eldon's turn to cook supper."

In the kitchen, we find Eldon waving smoke from the open oven.

"I don't know what I did wrong," he yells over the drums. "I followed all the steps!"

Tazib grabs a towel and pulls a black mass from the oven, dumping it into the sink. "Guess we're having toast and beans tonight."

"What is that noise?" I shout, my head already starting to ache.

"Maisie," both Eldon and Tazib answer.

They lead the way down the hall, throwing open Maisie's door to reveal Maisie covered in sweat, the muscles in her arms flexing, head nodding as she pounds out a beat I feel in my chest.

Seeing us in the doorway, she stops, a large grin on her face. Setting the sticks on the snare, she signs to Tazib.

"Yeah, it was a bit loud," Tazib answers aloud and with sign. "But it was rocking. The smell?" He elbows Eldon in the ribs. "Guess who was assigned supper?"

Maisie groans.

We would have gone to bed hungry, but our unsatisfied bellies were rescued by a knock on the door and the arrival of Tali and Loren along with three pies.

"Aimee sent us," Loren explains. "We're supposed to tell you there's a Table meeting at her house," she tells Al. "And not to worry. She has more pie."

"An impromptu meeting," Al mutters, grabbing his sweater from the peg by the door. "This can't be good."

We take the pies to the kitchen where Tazib grabs clean plates and cutlery as Maisie puts a kettle on to boil for tea.

"There's apple, pumpkin, and strawberry rhubarb," Loren explains. "That woman can cook."

"Pumpkin for me," says Tazib.

"I'll take one of each." At Maisie's scowl, Eldon shrugs. "What? I'm not going to apologize. I'm hungry and I missed pie. You'd think for being all 'perfect' and everything the WC would actually serve decent food."

"Maybe it's the people in the kitchen." Loren cuts herself a piece of strawberry rhubarb. "That's where they were going to send me."

Her laugh is sour. "They thought it was the safer option, but it's more likely I'd accidentally poison someone. That's what I keep telling Aimee, but she seems determined to get me cooking."

"Well, if you learn how to make pie, I wouldn't complain," I say, taking a bite of my slice of apple. "This is amazing."

Maisie collects the kettle and pours tea, passing a mug to Tali.

"Thank you." Tali smiles uncertainly, touching her fingertips to her lips before lowering them to her open palm.

Maisie's eyes widen in surprise and she nearly drops the kettle in her hurry to free her hands.

"I know some," Tali answers. "If you go slow."

Maisie slows her signs and Tali watches her hands carefully, often mimicking the actions.

"I used to waste a lot of time researching all sorts of random things," Tali says. "Especially anything from the past that we've stopped using. I don't know many signs, but I know some of the basics."

Maisie smiles, revealing two large front teeth as she signs.

Tali blushes. "Yeah, well, I kind of have a thing for remembering useless facts. But I guess this time it's turned out to not be so useless. I don't trust myself to sign much back though. I'd probably say something stupid."

"I do that all the time," Eldon laughs.

Loren selects a flowered mug and pours herself a cup of tea. "You three seem pretty comfortable with each other," she nods to Tazib, Eldon, and Maisie. "How long have you known each other?"

Maisie frowns and signs to Tazib.

"Maisie would appreciate if you'd keep your face towards her when you talk," Tazib explains. "But to answer your question, I've known Maisie since I got here."

"When was that?"

Tazib licks his fork clean, setting it on the edge of his plate. "Six years ago."

Six years. Tazib would have been 8, two years after the accident. Was that how long he was in the hospital? How did he get from there to here at only 8?

"And I arrived five years ago," Eldon answers after being careful to swallow his mouthful. "After Tazib found me. Rescued me really."

"Tazib rescued you?" Loren asks, scepticism dripping.

Eldon's head wags. "He did. I was basically starving, I wouldn't have made it though another winter."

"Wait. What do you mean?" Tali pauses with the fork part way to her mouth. "Why were you starving? Where were you?"

"The middle of nowhere."

"But why?"

Eldon sighs. "Honestly, I don't really know. We had this little house my dad built. He called it our homestead. I was born there. Me and my sisters. Life was hard. Really hard. My older sister, Lacey, died when I was 4. She was chopping wood and the axe slipped. Mom and dad couldn't stop the bleeding." He shudders, his face growing pale as he relives the memory. "That was the first time I heard my parents arguing. Mom wanted to take Lacey somewhere to get help. But Dad said they couldn't. After that, I started asking questions. They never told me the whole story, but from what they did tell me, I think it had something to do with the role Dad was assigned. He wasn't comfortable with it, tried to push back. He would complain that the WC wanted robots not humans, and there was no way he was going to let them get their hands on us."

Eldon fiddles with the cuffs of his sleeves, pulling them down over his long fingers. "Whatever reason they had for wanting to be out there, far from help, must have been pretty good, because they paid for it with their lives. One by one, our family kept getting smaller, and the number of graves at the edge of the woods kept growing until at last, it was only me. I had pretty much given up, even considered digging my own grave, but I didn't have the energy."

"How old were you?" Tali asks.

"Not quite 9. I had never seen a pod before that day." Eldon grins at Tazib. "When I saw that metal and glass thing hovering over the house, I thought my heart was going to pound right out of my chest. I couldn't decide if I should hide or fight, but I was too weak to do either, so I simply watched as this *thing* flattened the few plants left in the garden. When a *boy* stepped out, well, I figured I'd died and this was some being come to take me to the other side."

Maisie laughs loudly, her hands flying, and soon Eldon and Tazib are snickering too, their laughter growing more unrestrained with whatever Maisie is signing.

"What's so funny?" I ask.

Tazib gasps as he tries to get his breath. "She's just pointing out what an unlikely angel I am."

"Angel?" Loren frowns. "What's that?"

"Oh, yeah, WC clones." Tazib shares a knowing look with Maisie and Eldon. "It's just something from before the World

Collective. All you need to know is that I am NOT an angel."

This sets Maisie and Eldon off again, Eldon laughing so hard he nearly chokes.

A knock on the door pulls Tazib away, still wiping tears from his eyes. When he returns, Mikom is with him, and as soon as we see Mikom's face, all laughter fades.

"Did you find something in the samples?" I ask, hoping Mikom's solemn face is a strange version of a good news face.

"Not yet," he shakes his head. "But it was only the first day. No, I'm here because I intercepted a message from the United People."

"Ky?" Tali's voice quivers. "Did you see Ky?"

"The United People are claiming they've released a virus to disable all existing patches. But I haven't been able to verify that."

"What about Ky?"

"The young man, Kyven, was present for the message," Mikom says slowly.

"Is he okay? Did they hurt him?" My voice is nothing more than a squeak as my lungs contract.

"After much discussion, The Table decided it would be best to show you. Tazib, Maisie, I'm guessing you have some equipment we can use?"

"Of course." Tazib jumps from the table, hurrying to his room and returning with an armload of portable tech. "Just give me a sec."

He hurries to connect everything, and when he's finished, Mikom projects a still image on the wall. Tali gasps, clapping a hand over her mouth.

The paused video shows a plain room, bare except for a single chair and a vitals monitor. In the chair is Ky, his hands bound in his lap and legs bound to the floor. He is pale except for his flushed cheeks and a rim of red around his wrists where he has pulled against the restraints.

"This may be difficult for you to watch," Mikom says gently as he presses play.

"Guys, please don't do this." Ky struggles in the chair, wrenching his arms as he tries to free his hands. Hearing him plead, his fear so visceral, sets my full stomach rolling.

"It is time." Kohath's deep voice says off screen. "Leaders of the World Collective, you have failed to save your people. Death is on your hands. The deaths of all who have had their Thanatos too early and the deaths of many more with your failure to stop your creation."

As he speaks, Ky continues to struggle, sweat beading on his forehead.

"People of the Collective," Kohath continues. "I know what your leaders are telling you. They claim you are all in the same position, all facing the same risks. They tell you that this problem with Thanatos was caused by an outside source. But it is lies. All of it. The virus destroying Thanatos has existed since the beginning.

"It takes only a microbe to cause an infection. A sliver of harmful material can lead to the loss of a limb or worse if left untreated. This is the World Collective. Thanatos was created with a flaw, one that could have been treated if the WC cared more about its citizens than maintaining order and control. Now, what began as a sliver has grown into a cancerous beast that will devour us all.

"But wait, that is not the truth. Your leaders have a secret. One they are so desperate to keep that they throw away the very values this world was created upon.

"They have a patch. One that protects them from dying before their time.

"Do you not see? Look to your leaders. Do they not age and grow old while all others celebrate their Thanatos?"

"Please," Ky whimpers.

"Time's up." Kohath's voice thunders through my skull. "The World Collective brings only death. It is time to set aside the old. Time to turn to the new. Join us, the United People, or remain with the Collective and face your deaths. The choice is yours."

Tears stream down Ky's cheeks as he continues to thrash against his bindings, but his movements have changed. The shaking comes from his core and is more a spasm of pain than the struggle of someone trying to break free.

"His wrist," Loren says softly.

The restraints on his arms have shifted, revealing a green light shining through his skin. On the monitor behind him, the line indicating his heart rate spikes erratically.

"What's happening?" Tali cries.

"Thanatos," I breathe, noting the sweat stains on his shirt, the way his cheeks cave, the hollowness to his glazed eyes. "It's killing him."

"How?" Tali shouts. "We just saw him! He was fine. Thanatos isn't supposed to look like this!"

"Merari, you may think you are untouchable, but that is not the truth." Kohath's voice is calm despite Ky's moans of pain. "We have released a virus, one to render your precious patch obsolete. Death is coming for you. See, it is here now."

Ky cries out, his eyes rolling back in his head before he falls limp. The erratic lines on the monitor smooth into a straight line as the feed ends.

01010111 01100101 00100000 01100001 01110010 01100101 00100000 01110100 01101000 01100101 00100000

01010101 01101110 01100011 01101111 01110101 01101110 01110100 01100101 01100100 00101110

The room is silent. Each of us sit unmoving, hardly daring to breathe as the final image sinks into our minds, leaving spots of darkness like a too bright flash. My hands reach for my chest, for my missing necklace, as my mind reels. I can't believe they did it. They killed an innocent kid.

"I... " Tali gasps as she struggles to speak. "I don't understand... He's dead?"

"I'm very sorry for your loss." Mikom's voice is gruff and his eyes shimmer.

"No," Tali shakes her head, her eyes brimming with tears. "I... He can't be..." She jumps to her feet. "I need the bathroom."

Eldon points the way and Tali dashes from the kitchen.

Mikom sighs. "Again, I'm sorry." He unhooks the equipment, stacking it neatly in a pile. "I know his death hurts you deeply. But take heart. We want to help you. We want to put an end to this as much as you do."

His words ring empty, promises made because those are the things to say.

"I should check on Tali."

For a second, I stand at the closed bathroom door, listening to Tali's muffled sobs. Silent tears run down my cheeks as I close my eyes, desperately searching for the Composer's melody.

"Tali?" I knock. "It's me, Ry. Want some company?" Trying the handle, I open the door a crack, catching sight of Tali leaning over the sink, her shoulders bent and hair obscuring her face. "I'm coming in," I declare, slipping in and closing the door behind me. "Tali?"

"They killed him," she hiccups, falling into my open arms. "Just to prove a point. Because we couldn't give them what they wanted." I rub her back as she struggles to catch her breath. "They said they were for a future for all. But what about Ky? What about his future?"

"Oh, Tali, I'm so sorry."

"Everything's all wrong. This wasn't supposed to happen. When I was activated..." She pulls away and grabs a wad of toilet paper to wipe her face, her cheeks blotching as she takes a shuddering breath. "I thought I knew who the bad guys were: Tazib and terrorists. They were the ones hurting people. They were the ones we needed to stop. But now…"

"I know. The United People are evil."

"And Libni works for them!" Tali's red-rimmed eyes blaze. "We worked for her! What if we helped?!"

I bite my lip. I did help Libni. Guilt threatens to crush me, but I shove it aside.

"Tali, I won't give up. We're going to find that key and fix this."

"Who cares!" Tali's voice catches. "Ky is dead! Fixing Thanatos isn't going to bring him back. Nothing will!"

"Oh, Tali. Come here." I open my arms again, but Tali shakes her head, her stringy hair catching on her wet cheeks.

"No. Don't you get it? He's dead because we didn't save him."

"We tried our best—"

"It wasn't enough!" Her chest heaves. "If you had let me go... I would've fit! I could have gotten him out!"

I drop my arms, a cold chill raising the hair on the back of my neck. "We don't know that," I whisper.

"No, we don't," Tali snaps. "And we never will." She sags to the floor, burying her head against her knees, all her energy evaporated in an instant. "I can't believe he's gone."

I lower myself to her side, our legs cramped in the small square of floor space. Knowing there are no words that can ease her pain, I simply hold her, letting her cry herself dry.

CHAPTER SIX

MY DREAMS CARRY ME TO A FAMILIAR PLACE WHERE TREES tower above me, their rough bark nearly hidden with lush moss and trailing vines. The undergrowth is thick but easy to pass through, the large ferns brushing my arms like feathers. These dense woods should be intimidating, but I never feel lost or afraid. Here I've learned to listen, to hear the words in the melody of the perfect music; music that tells me who I am, that I'm not alone, and there is a plan. In these woods, I've learned to use my voice, to sing when doubts and fears overwhelm me.

If I could, I would dream forever. I would endlessly wander these overgrown paths instead of waking to face the stress and worries of another day. But night is all I get, and each night I treasure the time I have to soak in the melody, always moving forward, always searching for the Composer.

Ahead of me, light filters between the trees, long fingers of sunbeams dancing among the trunks. I push through a number of young saplings and find the forest thinning. Before me, stone structures rise between the trees, and there is a new hum of energy to the music, a bustling busyness.

Tripping over a stone, my eyes are pulled to my feet. The soft bedding of pine needles has been replaced with a solid path, one made up of smooth stones. Picking up the offending rock, I cup it in my hand, surprised such a small thing can be so heavy, before moving down this new path that leads into the city.

At least, I think it's a city. It's nothing like any place I've seen before. It has elements of Ol'Syd and some of the brick buildings remind me of Fordtown, but it is too different to be either. Rather, it resembles an ancient city, a mismatch of images I've seen from before the fall. The streets are lined with uneven cobblestones and the limestone of the larger buildings is worn smooth from years of weather.

Barefoot, I meander down the streets, the stones warm from the sun and the grit grounding me to this place. The road leads up the hill the city is built upon, and as I follow it, I watch the people going about their lives: hanging clothes on lines to dry, trading baskets of apples for a loaf of bread, repairing a broken window. No one pays me any attention so I'm free to eavesdrop on the old men gossiping in the shade of a tree, the happy banter of a group of children playing with colourful stones, a lovestruck couple walking arm in arm.

It is a steep climb and my legs are burning and my chest is heaving when I finally crest the hill. On all sides, the city fans out below me, fading into the endless forest like the two have been here since the start of time. But here, at the top of the hill, is the heart of the city. A garden more than a city square, it is framed by a low wall covered in fragrant blooming vines and flowering trees. A large pond bubbles in the centre where tall reeds sway at its edge, birds bending their stalks as they trill in song. Even from a distance I can see the small fish swirling beneath the waters and the ripple of rings as a vibrant green frog dives from sight.

My heart leaps. Some part of me knows this is where I'm meant to be and I race forward, my dress whipping against my legs. I revel in the feeling of the stone road giving way to lush grass as I start to laugh, quiet at first, but quickly growing loud and rambunctious. But I don't stop there. This space demands sound. Not just any sound, but the perfect symphony. And since I can't hear it, that means I must sing it.

I fling my arms wide, spinning as the notes spill from me, a thrill of melody with no words. *This*—this is what I'm meant to do. To dance and sing at the top of my lungs. My feet in the grass, arms flung wide, hair in my face, skirt twirling. Singing is the only way to release the joy that bursts from my soul.

But as much as I'm driven to sing and dance, my feet slow far too soon, and a heaviness crushes the breath from my lungs.

That's when I notice I'm not alone.

Around me, the low walls are lined with spectators. The people of the city have followed me and they regard me with unreadable expressions. I blush, suddenly self conscious of how foolish I must look.

"What are you doing?" a stern voice demands.

Uncertainty swallows me like a tidal wave. I scan the faces of the crowd. Some are obviously mystified at my strange performance, but many scowl. Worse, cameras have appeared and they hover around me, buzzing like flies, revealing my foolishness to the world.

I duck my head, ready to run back down the streets, back to the safety of the forest, but I pause when a small hand slips into mine. Looking down, I find a young child grinning up at me, joy radiating so clearly on their face they're almost glowing.

My breath catches.

The Composer.

"Don't be afraid." The voice of the Composer is one I'd recognize no matter what form they took. "They're only waiting."

"Waiting?" I look out at the crowd. "Waiting for what?"

"For you." The child Composer grins. "For you to see them as they really are. But first you have to let go."

01010111 01100101 00100000 01100001 01110010 01100101 00100000 01110100 01101000 01100101 00100000

01010101 01101110 01100011 01101111 01101101 01101110 01101110 01101101 01100101 01100100 00101110

Like every morning for the past week, I'm startled awake by the loud bang of the bedroom door. No matter how many times I ask Maisie to be careful, she somehow succeeds in slamming the door every morning, and I'm starting to wonder if she's doing it on purpose.

Pulling the covers from my head, I emerge from my cocoon to find the glass covered with frost, fracturing the view of the lake and mountains. Each morning has been colder than the last so I dress as quickly as possible, the room downright chilly and the floor a block of ice. After a quick trip to the bathroom, I hurry down the hall to the much warmer kitchen where I find Eldon and Al at the table finishing their breakfasts.

"Morning," Al nods. "It was Eldon's turn. He made porridge. It's on the back of the stove keeping warm."

I grimace as I take the pot and scoop the lumpy, grey substance into a bowl. Al keeps the house running with a strict rotation of chores. Cooking, cleaning, stacking wood, laundry, the tasks are never ending, and for me, a WC citizen who never had to do any of them before, they all involve a learning curve.

"I know." Eldon's face flushes. "It's terrible. But here. Try this." He pushes a small jug towards me. "It will help. Promise."

"Don't feel bad," I tell Eldon as I pour the dark, thick liquid into my bowl. "At least you know the basics."

"Barely," Al laughs. "Whoa, easy there." He nods at my bowl. "Save some for the rest of us."

Setting the jug back down, I catch a drip with my finger, popping it in my mouth. "Oh," I gasp. "You didn't say it was sweet!"

Eldon shrugs with a grin. "It's maple syrup, of course it's sweet."

"I didn't know. I thought it was like milk or something." I poke at the brown mess in my bowl, eyeing the near-empty pot.

"There's no more," Al shakes his head. "You eat what you got." He pushes his chair back with a groan. "I'm heading out. Good luck in the lab, Ry. Here's hoping today's the day you find something."

Al grabs his jacket and heads out as I take a bite of my super sugary breakfast. There have been a lot of things I've struggled to adapt to, living here among the Uncounted, but the freedom to choose my own portions along with regular access to sweets has not been one of them.

"Morning," Tazib crows cheerfully as he crosses the kitchen to the sink, filling it with hot soapy water. "You walking Tali to school again, Eldon?"

"Yeah," Eldon says with a sheepish grin as he hands Tazib his empty bowl.

"How is she liking our little school?" Tazib asks. "Bet she finds it a lot different from what they have back in the Collective."

"She's loving it," Eldon answers. "She really likes the group projects and getting to do presentations. She doesn't get all flustered like I do," he adds, his cheeks flushing.

I'm glad Tali has the opportunity to simply be a kid here in Sota. She's been given no responsibilities beyond our new chores—and even school was optional. The adults at The Table decided they had no expectations for Tali, wanting to give her time to heal from her grief. Without a role to perform, Tali has spent her time going to school in the morning and exploring the mountainside with Eldon and other Uncounted youth in the afternoon. The unstructured time has helped, but I often catch her staring into space, her once doll-like eyes now clouded with sorrow.

"Tali said you have a big test coming up?" I ask.

"Yeah, counts for ten percent of our grade. Tali's going to ace it. She's super smart." Eldon's grin is endearingly sweet.

"Why don't you ask her to help you study? I know she already has plans to come over tonight to work on learning new signs with Maisie."

"I noticed she's getting pretty good at signing," Tazib says as he begins washing. "You been tutoring?"

"Nah," Eldon shakes his head. "That's all Maisie. But yeah, Tali is catching on fast."

"That's Tali." I give up on my drowned porridge, scraping the remains into the compost, and passing my bowl to Tazib. "She's a quick learner with an impeccable memory."

My attempts at learning sign haven't been so stellar. The way Tali is absorbing it makes me wonder if we should trade hosts. Tali would be comfortable here at Al's, reading Maisie's books and learning more sign. And I wouldn't mind putting some space between me and Tazib.

"Is Loren coming over too?" Eldon asks. "Because that might make it hard to concentrate."

"You have a point," I concede. Loren is determined to learn how to play the drums. I don't know how Al stands the racket. When Loren plays, it is an instant headache, but when Maisie plays, the whole house shakes, each thud of the bass vibrating through our chests, the snare rattling our teeth.

"Well, I should head out. See you guys tonight." Eldon tugs on his shoes, dashing out the door with his sweater tucked under his arm.

"I think you're on for drying," Tazib says, nodding to where a towel hangs on a hook. "I'm running out of space."

Living with Tazib has been confusing. Watching him here, where he is treated no differently from Eldon or Maisie or even myself, has been mind-boggling. Each time he laughs and jokes with Eldon, each time he clears the table without being asked, the way he serves throughout the community, it all brings such a tangled mess of feelings. He's a kid, like me, I get that. I saw his vulnerability back in the interrogation room in Unity. But I can't reconcile this version of Tazib with the other sides I've seen of him. I can't forget the way he toyed with me, manipulating me to do his dirty work. The times he showed his utter disregard for the value of a person's life. The fact that he murdered Jep and nearly killed Rube.

"It snowed a little last night," Tazib says as I begin drying the dishes. "Paths will be slick. Want me to walk you to the lab?"

"I'll be fine." I focus on the bowl in my hands, finding it easier to not look at Tazib, to not notice the way his hair ruffles when he pulls a sweater over his head, or the fact that his movements are slow and stiff first thing in the morning. If I can't distance myself from him in real life, I'm determined to at least create a space in my head.

"Think they'll let me back in the lab yet?" he asks as he takes the cloth to the table, wiping the surface clean of sticky drips of syrup. "It's been over a week with no results."

I don't answer though I feel Tazib watching me as I stack the dried dishes, his observation opening the acidic pit in my gut. I'm more than aware of the passing of time, of each failed attempt to find the key in my genetic code. Every minute without the key costs another WC citizen their life.

Tazib returns to the sink and pulls the plug. "They aren't going to find it," he says, watching the water swirl down the drain. "The key isn't in your genetic code, it's in your memory."

This isn't the first time Tazib's made this comment. Throughout the week, any chance he gets he comes back to this—the need for me to submit to another MEMORY experience. Sometimes I wonder if he thinks it will change how I see him. He's constantly dropping details from our shared time in the dorms, little moments he expects me to remember, like telling me will somehow unlock that part of my brain and magically restore us to the friendship we had as children. But can't he tell I'm not the kid I was before the accident? He isn't either. And remembering child Tazib isn't going to make us best friends today. It won't erase what he's done.

I set the last dish in the cupboard and hang the towel to dry. "I should get to the lab."

"Ry." Tazib reaches for my arm, hesitating just before touching me. "Look, I know I've hurt you. You have valid reasons for not trusting me." I keep my eyes on Tazib's feet, on the tiny hole in his sock over his big toe. "But we want the same things. We want the world to change. I can help you achieve that, but you have to work with me, not against me."

Heat flares in my chest and my eyes snap to his face. "I've given up everything for you. Don't you see that? I can't go back to the Collective, not until this is fixed. I can't see Rube—I can't even talk with him!" My eyes burn but I blink the tears away, fanning the flame of anger. "And it's all because I believed you had a way to stop this. But you don't!" My hands tremble at my sides. "*You* have nothing to offer. If there is a key, it's with *me*, not you!"

"It's not if," Tazib says. "You do have the key. And you do need me."

"I don't need you," I growl.

"The others aren't willing to push boundaries. They're more concerned with keeping everyone safe, even you. *I'm* willing to do whatever it takes, and I know you are too. You have to ask them to use MEMORY. And when they find the key in your memories you'll need me to actually do something with it. The Uncounted say they want to help, but think about it, Ry, Thanatos doesn't threaten them. If they think the risk is too great, they'll hold back."

My jaw aches as I clench my teeth. "I'm going to be late," I snap, grabbing my heavy sweater from the chair.

I let the door slam shut behind me.

Stripes of sun and shadow flicker in my peripheral as I stomp down the mountain. Everything about Tazib rubs me the wrong way

—even ten minutes with him leaves me in a rage.

It's been over a week of scans and samples, and though no one will say it, it's clear every attempt to find the key in my genetic code has come up empty. It's also clear that neither Mikom, Jolan, or Priya will suggest using MEMORY. A hundred times a day, my eyes dart across the lab to the panel labelled MEMORS. Little of the device resembles the one Libni used on me back in Unity—instead of a sterile, reclined chair, the one here is more like a modified couch—but no amount of colourful pillows and mismatched, patchwork blankets will disguise the restraints or the two metal panels.

Reaching the lab, I weave through the equipment to the little office in the back. Here, the walls are painted black, the expanse covered in equations, lines of code, names, places, and details written in white. My eyes are drawn to a section where my name is circled. Radiating out from it are facts from my life, my parents, Rube, details of the accident, Loren, Jep, DATA, Unity. Lines crisscross to other areas on the wall, but it is hard to tear my eyes away from those names that have been crossed out, a simple x, marking the fact that they no longer have a part to play.

"It's too easy to forget they were more than a name." Priya joins me, supporting her lower back with her hands as she looks up at the wall. "I'm sorry for all you have lost."

I reach out and touch Dad's name, my fingers leaving a smear in the chalky substance. "It's why I'm here. I can't lose anyone else." I look at my life, laid out in black and white before me. As much as I hate it, Tazib's right. We're out of options and we are running out of time. "Priya, we need to talk."

"Of course." Priya moves to the kettle, pouring herself a cup of tea. This has become our routine, hot mugs cupped between our hands after the cold walk to the lab, starting each morning with a debriefing of the day before, going over lab results and discussing where else we can look in my genetic make-up.

Readying my own cup, I join Priya on the long couch, hardly believing I'm about to do this willingly. "It's time we consider using MEMORY."

"Oh," Priya gasps, clearly not expecting my request. "Are you sure? We're still waiting for the results of yesterday's samples."

"We both know we won't find anything. We've already checked everything twice." I watch the bubbles pop in my tea. "It makes sense; we know the World Collective has buried information before, erasing memories to suit their fancy. So yeah, I think we should try MEMORY."

"Sorry we're late," Jolan huffs as she and Mikom hurry into the lab. "Our gaggle of children didn't feel like going to nursery today. Thankfully, Tali came by and helped us get them out the door." She pauses when she sees my face. "What'd we miss?"

"She's decided to use MEMORY," Priya explains.

"Really? I thought it was the last thing you wanted," Jolan says, pouring herself a coffee. "Because of the way you react."

"It is. But we're running out of options and time."

Mikom sighs. "I hate to say it, but I agree. I'm sorry, Ry. If it was in my power for you to avoid this, I'd do it."

"He means it," Jolan snorts. "He broke his own rule about keeping distance from the WC and hacked into what they had from your MEMORY experience in Unity."

"And?" I ask eagerly. "Did you find anything?"

"Sadly, not what we are looking for," Mikom admits. "But it's clear you're a special case. Most subjects only jump back to what the controller wants to see, usually not more than a week, maybe a month. But you, you just flew back in time."

"Is that a good thing or bad thing?" I ask.

"Depends," Mikom answers. "It isn't typical and it clearly poses a greater risk to your health, jumping so far back so quickly, but it could be a good thing for us. If the cryptography key is hidden in your memories, it's likely to be when you were very young, and the ability to go that far back will be an advantage."

"And what if it isn't there?" I ask, running my finger along the rim of my mug, unable to watch their faces as I voice this fear that has grown over the past week. All this effort, this idea that I hold the key, what if we're wrong? What if we've been doing nothing but wasting time as more people die an early death? "What if you and Tazib are wrong and there is nothing to connect me to the cryptography key? Worse, what if there is no key at all? It's been so long. Maybe it's lost, I mean really, truly lost, and there's no way to recover it."

"No, there's a key, I'm sure of it," Jolan says. "The makers of The Code thought of everything. They knew what they were doing and they did everything in their power to protect The Code. They made a key, but they wanted—they *needed*—to keep it secure. Using people as an unknowing 'safe'"—she air quotes—"makes sense. And everything we've found in our research points to you and your family."

"But we understand examining our pasts can be a scary thing," Mikom says. He meets my gaze, his eyes full of compassion. "So this is your choice. No one here will force you."

I drop my eyes back to my cup. The tea has gone cold and I watch it slosh up the side as my hands quiver. I don't want to be put under MEMORY again, but what if there is something in my past that could lead us to a way to fix this? If I don't try, more and more people are going to die. It's only a matter of time until I lose everyone I care about and that's not something I can live with.

The choice is mine and I know my choice. If there is even the smallest chance that risking my life could save my friends then I have to do it.

"Okay," I say softly, setting the mug aside. "Let's do it."

"You sure?" Priya asks.

I take a deep breath. "Yes. But we've got to do it now, before I have too much time to think about it."

"Alright."

Mikom jumps to his feet, heading across the room to ready the equipment.

"I'll get Maisie," Jolan says, quickly leaving the lab.

Priya winces as she struggles to push herself off the couch so I offer her my arm. "Thanks," she pants with a laugh. "This belly is just so big. Come." She opens a cupboard and fishes out a folded healing centre gown, passing it to me. "Take this to the restroom and change while we finish setting things up."

I reach for the clothing, my hands trembling as I hug them to my body. This may be my choice, but that doesn't mean I'm not terrified.

"It's okay to be scared." Priya's hand drops to her protruding belly. "Things can be both good and frightening at the same time."

"Is this your first?" I ask.

"It is." Priya sighs, her generally cheerful face paling as her eyes mist with tears. "I'm sorry. It's just, I never expected to be doing this on my own." Her gaze shifts past me, unseeing. "I lost my husband right before I learned I was expecting. It's so unfair he'll never get to meet this little one. So unfair."

"May I ask what happened to him?" I ask gently. "I mean, you don't have to tell me if you don't want to. It's none of my business," I rush to add.

"Nonsense," Priya says, reaching for my hand. "You should know. It may help you understand why I'm committed to finding a solution to Thanatos. My husband joined the Uncounted when he was a teen. He fled the World Collective when he was activated—he didn't want to be sent halfway around the planet—and he had already met someone from the Uncounted, so he had a way out. It doesn't happen very often, people fleeing the WC reaching an Uncounted community, but it happens more than you think."

Priya closes her eyes with a grimace. "You can escape the World Collective, but you are never truly free from it, not with that terrible tech under your skin." Her eyes drop to my wrist, her face darkening. "When we woke to that green glow…" She squeezes my hand tightly, her voice quivering. "I'm committed, Ry. I'm committed to finishing this. They can't have anyone else."

Unsure what to say, I squeeze her hand in return before turning for the washroom on the other side of the lab. I'm just about to undress when a loud alarm startles me. Setting the hospital gown aside, I peek outside to find Mikom hurrying from screen to screen, typing in commands with a worried frown. There is no sign of Priya.

Abandoning changing, I cross the lab to Mikom. "What's

happening?" I ask over the incessant wailing of the alarm.

Either Mikom is too busy to answer or he doesn't hear me. Jolan dashes into the room, pushing me aside to reach her computer.

"I'm activating the Ark procedures," she says, still breathless from her race back to the lab.

"Did you find Maisie?" Mikom asks.

"I hadn't gotten that far before I heard the alarm."

"What the blazes is going on?!" Al barrels into the room, startling me with his thunderous voice and surprising speed. Eldon and Tazib follow him, jogging to keep pace with his monstrous strides.

"An unidentified pod has been detected," Mikom says, showing a map of the area on one of the screens. "Here."

Al leans towards the blinking dot. "And it's moving this way?"

"It's heading straight for us," Mikom states, his forehead puckering with worry lines. "At its current rate of speed it will be here in ten minutes."

Al swears.

"I've activated project Ark," Jolan says. "I'm already getting notifications of people responding. Everyone except Momma Aimee."

"Of course she's taking her time," Al grumbles. "Probably waiting for something in the oven. Eldon, use those long legs of yours. Go, quickly."

Eldon sprints from the room.

"Now might be a good time to use the self defence system I created," Tazib suggests. The flecks of gold in his eyes glow with eager hope.

"What?" Al growls. "You want to send them crashing into the side of the mountain? Think, boy. What better way to alert the World

Collective to our location. I don't think so."

I peer at the approaching dot on Mikom's screen. "I don't get it. Why are you so worried? You have those projection things. I couldn't see Sota until we were right on top of it. Won't they keep you hidden? Shouldn't the pod just fly over?"

Mikom shakes his head. "Pods don't travel this way. Ever. If it's here it's for a reason, and Sota is the only location of note in this region."

"Ry does have a point," Jolan says. "If the pod passes by without finding us, they may move on. Tazib, is there any way you can redirect it? Send it off course just enough that it misses us, but not so much they notice the change?"

"I'm more than happy to try." Tazib cracks his knuckles with an eager grin. "Does this mean I'm forgiven?"

"We'll see about that," Jolan answers noncommittally.

Tazib drops into a chair, spinning with a flourish to the screen. The alarms continue to blare as we watch him flick through screens and code with impressive speed.

"Well, this is interesting…" Tazib's nose wrinkles as he stares at the data. "I've hacked the pod's interface, no issues there, but it's not showing any occupants."

"No occupants?" Jolan echoes. "Why would an empty pod be in the middle of nowhere?"

"Oh, I highly doubt it's empty," Tazib says as he continues typing. "Give me a minute, I'm sure I can figure out who is flying this pesky bug."

"Flying it?" I glance back at Mikom's computer, the dot growing closer and closer to our location. "You mean it's being controlled manually?"

"Sure looks that way."

"Would that mean it is one of yours?" I ask.

"Uncounted aren't the only ones who know how to manually fly a pod," Mikom says. "While it isn't common knowledge, there would be individuals who know how among the WC and the United People."

"Whoever this is, they're good at what they do." Tazib's smile continues to grow as he works. "This is actually a challenge."

"One we do not have time for." Al paces. "Where is Eldon? He should be back by now."

A terrible screeching, grating sound cuts Al short and has me clapping my hands over my ears. Turning to the awful noise, I'm shocked to find that the back wall of the lab has split open to reveal a long, dimly lit corridor and a breathless Eldon.

"Momma Aimee is in the Ark and it looks like everyone else is making their way there too," he gasps, gripping his knees as he catches his breath.

"Good." Al moves to the opening in the wall, motioning for us to follow. "Let's get moving. The Ark is where we should be too."

Eldon straightens, wagging his head in affirmation and trotting back the way he came.

"The pod is less than five minutes out," Mikom states, closing his screen and reaching for Jolan's hand. "We'll meet you at the command centre after we've found our kids." Together, he and Jolan proceed into the hidden corridor.

"Sounds good," Al nods.

I move to the opening in the wall but Tazib remains at his screen, typing furiously.

"Just one more minute…"

"Now, Tazib," Al barks.

Tazib flinches but doesn't move. "I was asked to do a job and I'm going to do it."

"Go," Al waves for me to follow the others as he crosses the room to Tazib. I watch with amusement as he hoists Tazib over his shoulder like a sack of dirty laundry or an unruly toddler, ignoring his strangled cry of protest. "Didn't I tell you to go?" Al's blue eyes flash as he stomps into the tunnel, slapping a button on the wall.

"Yes, sir." I smile, enjoying the sight of Tazib flailing on Al's shoulder a little too much. But as I watch his fruitless wiggling to free himself, the glow of his abandoned screen catches my eye. "Wait!" I shout over the deafening screech of the wall returning to its place. "I know who it is! I know who's in the pod!"

"You saw the screen?" Tazib asks, twisting in an attempt to see for himself.

"I did, quick, open the door!"

"Not a chance," Al mutters. "Let me guess, it's some World Collective special agent come to take you back."

"No, it's not a special agent." I shake my head, my curls bouncing around my face. "It's Ora!"

CHAPTER SEVEN

"**O**RA, MERARI, THE KING OF TIMBUKTU, I DON'T CARE.** I'm not opening that door." Al sets Tazib on his feet, giving him a shove down the corridor. "Move it. We're not safe until we're in the Ark."

Tazib smooths his ruffled hair, shooting Al a look of contempt that could curdle blood. "Ora?" Tazib says to me. "The medical officer who gave you your prosthetic?"

I nod as Al herds us down the corridor which is nothing more than a roughly cut tunnel dimly lit with bare bulbs.

"Do I have to carry the pair of you?" Al threatens. "Because I will."

"But—"

"No buts," Al shoos us forward. "Safety first. You can talk all you want when we reach the others."

We pass through two more sets of heavy doors before reaching a large room deep in the heart of the mountain. Stepping inside, I quickly lose sight of Al and Tazib, momentarily distracted by the enormous space crowded with people and stuff. So much stuff. There are tents, a huge kitchen area, tables and chairs, and rows and rows of shelves lined with food, medical supplies, and equipment. But the large cavern isn't just equipped with the necessary materials of an emergency shelter. There's a swing set and slide, a fenced off area with a soft carpet littered with baby toys, and many other forms of entertainment. And over the commotion of voices, I'm pretty sure I hear the musical clucking of chickens.

"Ry!" Loren sprints across the large space, pulling me further into the hall. "Do you know what's happening? One minute Momma Aimee is showing me how to knead dough and the next Eldon is shoving us in the closet." She laughs. "I mean, that's what it looked like. It looked like a regular closet, but Eldon tugged on this old shoe on the shelf and the whole back wall swung away to reveal a tunnel that led us here. This place is insane!"

"There was an alarm," I answer. "They detected a pod heading this way."

Loren's flushed face pales. "Do you think?... Ry, the WC can't find us. We broke out Tazib. We're terrorists now."

"Loren." I grab her hands. "It's not the WC, at least I don't think so. It's Ora."

"Ora?"

Loren follows me through the crowd as I head over to what must be the command centre: a large, raised platform in the middle of the cavern that is covered with a variety of equipment and computers. Jolan, Mikom, and Tazib wade through screens of information as a pacing Al watches. At the base of this platform are couches and chairs and here we find Momma Aimee and a vibrating Eldon.

"Rygita." Aimee moves a half-finished blanket of blue and yellow yarn off her lap and pushes herself to her feet. "Come. Tazib says you know the occupant of the pod?" Taking my arm she escorts me onto the platform.

"I don't care who's in the pod," Al grumbles. "The fact that they've disguised it as empty is proof they're up to no good. A sneaky saboteur no doubt."

"It's not a saboteur," I assure, drawing the attention of the others. "It's Ora. I saw her info on Tazib's screen. She's a medical officer, one I've known since the accident. She's a good person. You don't have to do all this." I wave at the mountain cavern. "You can trust Ora."

Al huffs while the others eye me with scepticism.

"Mikom, can you confirm she's a medical officer?" Jolan asks as she scoops up their toddler to balance on her hip.

"Give me a sec." Three of Jolan and Mikom's children climb over Mikom as he works at a computer. He taps a file and Ora's face fills the screen. "Checks out."

"I don't care who she is," Al's low voice rumbles. "The question is, why is she here? And how? How did she find us?"

"The pod has landed," Tazib announces, pointing to a screen with an overhead shot of the grassy landing area. I move to his side to watch as Ora steps cautiously from the pod.

"This isn't good." There is no mistaking the certainty in Al's voice. "She landed. She's seeing Sota." He turns to the group. "This location has been compromised."

On the screen, Ora wraps her arms around her middle, shivering as she looks at the wood-framed houses.

"We aren't discovered yet," Mikom states. "If she doesn't find anyone there's a chance she'll leave."

"Doesn't matter," Al rumbles. "She knows our location. We have to apprehend her."

"Apprehend her?" I gasp. "Why? She's not hurting anyone by looking around. And besides, we should go to her, see why she's here."

Momma Aimee takes my arm. "Look around, Ry. My people, the Uncounted, need to be protected. Ora or not, keeping this location secret is the most important thing. Think of the state of the world. The Uncounted have survived this long by staying separate and hidden from the world. We must remain cautious."

I look past Momma Aimee at the large cavern bustling with people. So many people. Couples with toddlers, seniors being assisted by teenagers, kids racing around the room. Chatter, the cry of a baby, and glee-filled shrieks of children fill the large space with vibrancy and life. A lump grows in my throat. Sota is so alive, so full of community. Seeing tiny children holding the fingers of someone four times their age, watching a grey head bend to listen... How did the World Collective abandon this? These relationships, the care these people have for one another, the bonds that unite ages and people together... For all its "perfection" the WC missed the most important bits.

"Hold on, what's that?" Al barks, drawing our attention back to Tazib's screen where a second figure steps out of the pod. A figure with perfect long hair and a signature pout.

"Is that *Aliah*?" Loren's voice drips with disdain. Her eyes narrow as she studies the screen from her lower vantage point.

"What is *she* doing here?"

"Aliah?" Momma Aimee echoes, turning to me while Mikom swings to his computer to search for her details. "Is this another friend?"

"Not exactly." I watch as Ora moves to knock on a cabin door. Aliah stays near the pod. Even with the poor quality of the feed I can tell she is scowling as she examines the mountainside community. "Aliah is a bit more complicated than Ora. I'm not—" I stop short when both Aliah and Ora suddenly swing towards one of the many paths that wind through Sota.

"No, no, no," Jolan groans. "What are they looking at?"

The security feed offers no audio, but it's clear something has caught Ora and Aliah's attention. Both look to the path that leads up the mountain. When Aliah jogs out of the frame Tazib hits a couple keys to change the camera angle.

"It's Tali."

There is no mistaking Tali's thin frame and dark hair streaked with fading purple. She sprints down the path towards Ora and Aliah, waving her arms and clearly shouting to get their attention.

"What is going on?" Al thunders as he leans over Tazib, as if getting closer to the screen will allow him to hear what is being said.

Tali grabs Ora's arm, pulling her back the way she came and talking so quickly I doubt even Maisie could read her lips.

"Don't you have more angles?" Al bellows. "Get us closer!"

Tazib enters more commands and flicks through screens showing different sections of Sota and allowing us to follow Tali, Aliah, and Ora as they hurry up the path.

"Wait, what's that?" Jolan points to a different section.

Just outside the doors of a cabin, Priya is crumpled on the ground, her legs bent beneath her, and her face contorted. Maisie is at her side, attempting to pull her to her feet, her own face pinched with alarm.

"Eldon, I told you to alert everyone," Al splutters. "Why are all these people outside?"

I peer at Priya. She had been with me moments before the alarm. Why did she leave the lab?

On the screen, Tali continues to lead Ora and Aliah up the path towards the cabin. Al's string of swearing grows louder.

"She's leading them right to them! Maisie, move!" He roars at the screen. "Get Priya out of there before they see you!"

"This is the worst thing that could happen." Jolan cups her toddler's head to her shoulder as she shakes her own. "All our work building this community. Gone."

"I hate to say it, but I guess we should start evacuating." Mikom stands, setting his children on the ground as he looks over the large hall. "It's not safe to stay here any longer."

"Wait." I wave at the screen where Tali continues to tug Ora up the path. "Look at Tali, she's so pale and talking so fast. I bet Priya left the lab to go find her. Tali wouldn't have known what to do when the alarm went off. But something went wrong. Just look. Priya's in pain."

Tazib zooms in as close as the camera is able, and though the feed is grainy, it is clear Priya's chest heaves and her face is scrunched in concentration.

"She's in labour," Momma Aimee declares.

"But she's not due for two more weeks," Jolan counters.

"She's in labour all the same."

"And Tali is taking Ora to her." I point as they emerge from the trees.

As soon as Ora sees Priya she races forward, dropping to her knees, and reaching for Priya's wrist.

"What's she doing?" Al roars.

"She's helping," I snap. "It's what she does. If something is wrong with Priya or her baby, Ora will know what to do. We should go to them, help them instead of watching from here."

Momma Aimee closes her eyes, folding her hands and resting them on her lips. She bobs her head, making quiet thinking sounds while the others watch her, waiting until she opens her eyes with a nod. "Send our medical team and bring all of them inside."

"All of them?" Jolan questions.

"I think we should evacuate," Al repeats.

"First we take care of Priya and speak with these visitors. Learn their intentions."

"If they're from the Collective we don't have time."

"We'll continue to monitor for any other pods. If we see anything suspicious, we go."

"Fine." Al spins on his heel, his large strides quickly taking him across the room. Eldon trots after him, and even though they are on the other side of the room, there is no mistaking Al's grumbles as he sends Eldon back.

"Tell us about these friends of yours," Momma Aimee says, moving to stand by my elbow as we watch the silent tableau on Tazib's screen.

"Ora was the one who saved my life after the accident, the one

Tazib and I survived." I watch as Ora gently prods Priya's extended belly. "She is the gentlest person you could ever meet. Taking care of people, her medical genius, it comes naturally to her."

"And Aliah?"

Aliah stands off to the side, barely visible at this camera angle. I bite my lip, aware Momma Aimee is watching me instead of the screen.

"Aliah is a stuck up, suck up," Loren spits from her spot on the couch. "Polar opposite of Ora. She only thinks of herself and how she can twist a situation to her gain."

"Is this true?"

"It is," I admit. "I don't trust Aliah. She works for Libni and the United People."

"The United People?" Jolan swears and one of the children climbing over Mikom is quick to repeat the word. Mikom clamps a hand on the child's mouth, shooting Jolan a pointed look. "Sorry." Jolan shifts the toddler on her hip. "But this is bad. Really bad. The United People are no better than the World Collective. We don't need either group learning our location."

On the video feed, Aliah turns suddenly, and we don't have to wait long to see why. Al storms into the frame, leading a group of six individuals, two of which aim small metal devices at Ora and Aliah. You can almost hear Al barking orders as he barrels straight for Aliah, who backs away with hands raised. Ora too raises her hands and getting to her feet, steps away from Priya, but she doesn't take her eyes off the prone woman. While one of the armed men restrains Aliah, Al pulls Ora further from Priya, securing her hands together while the others move Priya to a stretcher. Al then moves to grab Tali's arm, shaking her and shouting in her face. Poor Tali, even from this poor camera feed we can see her eyes grow wide with fear. Maisie jumps between Tali and Al, rapidly signing to her dad. I turn to Jolan, aware that those who understand sign will know what is being said, but she doesn't look my way, and when I look back at Tazib's screen, the group has disappeared.

I watch the far door anxiously, racing across the room the moment it opens.

"Ora!"

Ora's bowed head snaps up at her name. "Rygita, you're here. We found you."

Ora's eyes are rimmed in red, her cheeks sunken, and her lips cracked. Al shoves her towards the command centre. For such a large space, the room has become impossibly quiet as children and adults alike still to watch the cuffed forms of Ora and Aliah pass.

"Ry!" Tali races into my arms, her voice high and breathless. "It was so scary. All these alarms sounded and I had no idea what to do. I went looking for Priya and I found her on the ground. I think she slipped and fell. Maisie found us and we tried to move her, but she's gone into labour. Then I heard the pod. I was just trying to find help, but Al says I've put everyone at risk. I didn't mean to!"

Behind Tali, the others arrive carrying Priya on the stretcher, Maisie still holding her hand. Priya pants loudly, her forehead slick with sweat, as they hurry to move her to a tent.

"Tali, here, now!" Al thunders from the command centre.

Tali grabs my hand, squeezing it tightly as we make our way back to the platform.

"Why did you approach the pod?" A vein on Al's forehead

throbs as he rails at Tali. "Did you send a message? How many more should we expect?"

"I didn't send for it," Tali stutters. "I was looking for help, for Priya. I had no idea who was in the pod. Honest."

"You." Al swings to Ora and Aliah. "Who are you? Why are you here?"

Ora sways on her feet. "My name is Ora," she says in her typical soft voice and after Al's thundering it seems even quieter. "No one sent for us. Please, we didn't mean to cause alarm. It is not our intention to harm your community."

Al huffs. "No doubt the Trojan Horse thought the same thing."

"No one is going to follow us." Aliah frowns at Al, matching his scowl with one of her own. "I'm no amateur. I made sure our pod was untraceable. And not just our pod" —she cuts off Jolan's humph of disgust— "but our personal tech too. Here." She thrusts out her cuffed wrists. "You can check. No one is going to track us."

Mikom takes Aliah's wrist and scans it with a small device before turning to a screen to confirm her claim.

"Please," Ora says. "We are not here to threaten your community. We are here because I need to speak with Rygita."

Her eyes find mine and my heart jumps. Something is wrong. Really wrong.

"I'm here." I step forward. "What's happened?"

"Hold up," Al thunders. "I'm the one asking questions!"

Ora groans, her body folding in on itself as she crumples to the floor.

"Ora!"

Al tries to block me but I slip past, wrapping my arm around

Ora's shoulders. When did she get so thin?

"Alright, now." Momma Aimee directs. "Let's get those cuffs off and find a chair and a glass of water."

"She's a threat—" Al begins, but Momma Aimee waves him off.

"Tazib and Mikom, is there any sign of other pods? Any signals leaving the community?"

Mikom and Tazib shake their heads.

"Good, so for the moment we can assume we are safe. We'll get to the bottom of this, but let's treat our visitors with human decency." Momma Aimee watches as Al removes Ora's cuffs and then offers Ora her arm to assist her onto a chair. As Ora settles she rubs her wrists.

My stomach drops.

"Ora." I can't bring myself to say more. My eyes remain locked on the green light shining under her skin. Ora's Thanatos has been activated. She is going to die. I kneel before Ora, taking her hands in mine, my thumb tracing the tech under her skin.

Ora releases a long sigh. "I've witnessed hundreds of Thanatos'. I understand how it works. But experiencing it..." She shudders. "I wish I understood sooner."

Someone has brought Ora a glass of water and she takes a long sip. Straightening, she looks towards the tent Priya was taken to.

"I did a scan," Ora says. "It's a uterine rupture and the infant is experiencing perinatal asphyxia. Will you be able to handle that?"

I have no idea what any of those terms mean, but from the way Jolan and Momma Aimee draw in a breath I know it isn't good.

"I can help," Ora continues. "If we act fast we should be able to save her and the baby."

"You're sure you weren't followed?" Al asks, his voice more

restrained as his anger cools.

"Have Tazib check the pod," Ora answers. "He will be able to confirm if Aliah was successful in disguising our movements or not."

"Oh, Aliah did a good job," Tazib nods, shooting Aliah a look of appreciation.

Aliah doesn't acknowledge Tazib's admiration. Instead her eyes roam over the large hall with an interest that makes my skin crawl.

"Alright," Momma Aimee states, clapping her hands together. "Let's get this healer to the medic tent. Is there anything we can do for you? Something to help with..." She points to the green light.

Ora shakes her head. "I'm afraid there isn't much you can do. Painkillers help."

"We have those."

Ora stands, shaking out her hands.

"Wait, why did you have to find me?" I ask.

Ora turns and it takes a moment for her eyes to focus on me. "I have news and a favour to ask. But now isn't the time. Later." She follows Momma Aimee into the tent.

"And what are we supposed to do with this one," Al mutters, nodding towards Aliah. "You've been awfully quiet. Do you have medical experience?"

"No." Aliah's long hair swings across her back as she shakes her head.

"Why are *you* here?" It's hard not to glare at Aliah. The last time I saw her she was escorting me to the holding centre, locking me up as a terrorist because I plotted to break Tazib out. I very much doubt she had a sudden change of heart and came to apologize.

"Ora sought me out. She needed to find you and didn't want anyone to follow. I helped with the technical aspect."

"That's it? You're just helping Ora?" I snort. "As if. Why are you really here? Are you spying for Libni? Helping the United People plan how to take down another group of people after you've finished decimating the World Collective?"

Aliah juts her chin out as she meets my stare. "No. I'm not helping Libni. Not anymore."

"I don't buy it." I spin to the others. "Don't trust her. She may look sweet and little, but it's all an act."

"She did a good job covering her tracks," Tazib pipes up from his computer. "A really good job. I might have to use this coding myself." Tazib grins at Aliah, giving her a thumbs up.

"What do we do with her?" Al asks again.

"Lock her up," I mutter.

Jolan nods. "I think that's wise. At least until we can make sure it is truly safe. We can discuss this further later, after..." She glances at the medic tent. Despite the bustle of bodies and voices there is no mistaking the low moans of agony.

"I don't like this." Al takes Aliah's arm, leading her away. "I don't like it one bit."

CHAPTER EIGHT

"**W**E HAVE A NEW BABY GIRL,"** MOMMA AIMEE announces hours later. She lowers herself wearily into an armchair.

"How is Priya?" Jolan asks, reaching for Mikom's hand.

"She lost a lot of blood." Momma Aimee rubs the back of her neck. "But thanks to Ora, she'll make a full recovery." She looks over as Ora emerges from the tent. She appears tired and pale, and there is blood on her sleeves, but she has that look of satisfaction, of knowing she did her job well. "If it wasn't for her, we would have lost them both. We owe you our thanks," she says as Ora drops onto a worn couch.

Ora brushes her bangs from her eyes. "It's my purpose," she says with a tired smile.

"I'd offer you some food, but I'm too tired," Momma Aimee chuckles. "But I think it best we get your story. I know you are exhausted, but we need to know how you found us and why are you here."

I crowd in closer, sitting on the floor since there is no more room on the couch with Tali, Loren, Eldon, and Maisie.

Ora takes a deep breath. "I found you by using Rygita's prosthetic."

All eyes swing to me as my own drop to my foot. Al swears.

"I thought Aliah's tracker was disabled," I stammer.

"There was a tracker on you?" Al thunders. "And you didn't think to tell me?"

"It was disabled," Ora tries to calm Al. "That's not how I found you. No, I created Rygita's foot. I built the programs that run on it and I've kept a pathway open, even after you left Ol'Syd." Ora finds my eyes. "It was in case you ever needed my expertise," she explains.

"Mikom, explain what she's talking about," Al barks.

Mikom shrugs. "It's possible. We don't have much information on how the WC creates prosthetics so I don't really have anything to go on. But I suppose it makes sense. It would allow her to have access to data."

"But you always have me scan for data."

Ora nods. "Yes, I respect your privacy, your right to decide what information to share. I only used the access at the very beginning, when we were making minute changes daily, sometimes hourly."

I believe her when she says she didn't keep using it. Ora's always had such respect for orders and procedures.

"So, why?" I ask. "Why did you want to find me now?"

Ora licks her lips, rubbing the light under her skin. "I don't know how much you know. So much has happened so fast." We wait as she straightens, looking from face to face before settling on me. "Do you know about Kyven? Did you see that message?"

I'm silent as I nod my affirmation. More than a week later and I'm still reeling at the fact the United People would go so far as to murder an innocent kid.

"So you heard the United People's claim, that they disabled all patches. I thought—I think everyone thought—it would take time before we saw any proof." She shakes her head. "But it was only days…" Her soft voice drops to a whisper and she stares blankly into space before blinking and refocusing on my face. "It will be easiest to show you."

Ora spreads her fingers into a frame before her, pulling her hands apart to grow the screen. In the paused recording, Nela stands in front of the Chrysalis building. "Do you know how to amplify the audio?" Ora asks.

"Yep." Tazib jumps up and grabs an ancient looking scanner. "Here, place your hand on this."

Ora presses her palm to the device and activates the video.

"People of the World Collective. I am at the Chrysalis today because I was summoned by the United People." Nela smiles at the camera, a weak, uncertain smile that is more of a grimace. "They claim there is something inside all citizens need to witness."

Nela turns to the wall of water that flows down the open spaces between the pillars of the bowl-like building, touching the scanner to open a gap.

It only takes the camera a second to adjust from the bright sunlight to the more muted tones of the glittering interior, but when it does, it reveals familiar faces milling about the large open space. Important faces.

The leaders of the World Collective.

"What is the meaning of this?" Merari storms towards Nela, fire in her eyes. "Did you send that cryptic message to ambush us? Your meddling has caused enough damage. We don't need the press here."

"It wasn't me." Nela moves to the stage, positioning the camera to capture a wide shot of all the leaders gathering around her.

"What do you mean, it wasn't you?" a small man asks. His round face and short stature are familiar from past broadcasts about improving WC efficiencies. "Why are we here?"

"I don't know." Nela opens a screen and projects a message for the others to see. "I was sent a message. From the United People."

"The United People," Merari scoffs. "Why would they send us cryptic messages? They haven't tried to hide themselves in the past."

"I know." Nela subtly waves her hand at her hip and a second camera feed appears, allowing the viewer to see both Nela's face and those of the leaders. There is no mistaking the alarm on all but Merari's. Merari just looks mad.

"Are you broadcasting this live?" she demands. "Turn them off. Now."

"I have a duty," Nela answers. "There's a reason you are all here. A reason I'm here. My vital role is to report and that is what I plan to do."

"Your actions have cost the Collective stability." Merari straightens, pulling at her blazer, and raising her chin. "Your reporting has led to disorder and unnecessary panic."

"Unnecessary?" Nela doesn't hide her astonishment. "The fact that thousands are dying early isn't reason to panic? Our vital roles are so short-staffed *children are dying*," Nela's voice quivers. "And what about the fact that your own offspring, Kyven, was kidnapped and murdered? You don't think that's worth reporting?"

Merari's face blanches as she presses her lips together in a harsh line. "You have a duty to the Collective, we all do. We are to serve where we are placed, doing our best to ensure that the order and peace of the World Collective remains for all ages. Your *reporting* has taken us back to the chaos and unrest of the days before the WC."

Nela's eyes flash. "You want to talk about keeping peace and order? Then why don't we talk about the patch? The one you have kept hidden from the citizens of the Collective, the one you keep denying exists. A patch that could protect us all."

"There is no—"

A startled scream cuts Merari short. She turns along with Nela and the cameras to a curvy woman in the back of the group.

"My... It's... How?" The woman reveals her wrist where the green light of an activated Thanatos shines under her skin. "You said we were safe." Her questioning eyes turn to Merari, confusion, hurt, and alarm flicking across her features.

"It must be your time," Merari says, though without her usual confidence.

"No!" The woman struggles to remain calm. "It's not. You said we were guaranteed 75 years!"

"Maybe that terrorist, Tazib, activated you," the short man cuts her off with a quick glance at Merari. "He did escape recently."

A loud exclamation has the group turning to another WC leader who also cradles a green-lit wrist. "How?" the man cries.

Now the whole group is swivelling around, eyes on their wrists as they shift nervously.

"I told you!" a woman screams at Merari. "We should have shared the patch—"

"We don't respond to threats from terrorists," Merari snaps.

"But if we'd released the patch when we first learned of the problem with Thanatos, none of this would be happening," a moustached man moans, staring at the little green light under his skin.

"You know why we didn't." Merari's eyes bore into the leaders around her. "Why we all agreed to keep the truth buried."

"Tell us." Nela has kept one camera on her and Merari while the second flits from person to person, recording each horrified reaction as more and more are activated for their Thanatos. "Why didn't you protect us?"

"We did protect you," Merari turns to Nela, a fierceness flushing her face. "We protected you from yourselves. If everyone had the patch, if everyone was guaranteed 75 years, it would be no different than disabling The Code. You know our history—you know we need The Code to govern every part of our lives." Merari's voice quivers with passion. "Without it, society crumbles, the planet dies, people turn on each other as each struggles—"

Another startled shriek pulls Merari's eyes from Nela and the camera. Her face pales. Every leader bares their wrists, each one displaying the green light announcing their doom. All activated but Merari and Nela.

On the screen, Merari transforms in front of our eyes. Gone is her larger-than-life stature. Now she is nothing more than an average woman, one who is afraid for her life.

"How?" She attempts to hold her head high, her shoulders rigidly straight, but she's unable to hide the tremor that shakes her hands. "They shouldn't all be activated at the same time. The Code would never allow it."

"The United People." Nela's voice is hardly more than a whisper. "They just sent a message." She looks up from her screen with wide eyes. "They say this is proof they've disabled the patch. They're claiming they activated each of you. Not an instant Thanatos, but what all citizens must face."

Merari raises her wrist and the second screen zooms in on her tan skin. "We thought we had time to fix it... I didn't think..."

"They say it is time for you to wrap up your affairs and say your goodbyes. In five days, the World Collective will end. It is time for a United People."

The broadcast ends on a single image.

The green light of Thanatos on Merari's wrist.

I rock back, blinking as Ora's screen closes.

"They've all been activated." Ora squeezes her eyes shut with a shudder. "Merari and every other top leader of the Collective. This happened four days ago. By end of the day tomorrow, all leadership within the World Collective will be gone."

"But won't someone be activated to fill their roles?" Loren asks softly. "Isn't that how it's supposed to work?"

"Yes." Ora massages her temples, stilling when her eyes fall on the blood on her sleeves. She drops her hands into her lap. "But things are too far gone. There's no one left with any experience. Anyone activated would be your age, not ready for the decisions and leadership that would be needed in a time of such great turmoil.

No," Ora sighs. "The World Collective will fall. In many ways, it has already."

Though the noise in the hall continues to buzz, those of us near Ora are still. Tali circles the raised spot on her wrist, her blue veins visible under her skin. Loren stares straight ahead, mumbling her disbelief. I look over to find Maisie watching us and my stomach hardens with jealously. She doesn't have to worry about suddenly dropping dead. She doesn't have to worry about anything happening to her dad or best friends.

"It's bad." Ora rubs her knees, her knuckles white. "We've been taught to follow The Code, to do our part for the Collective..." She shakes her head. "I'd thought... I thought people would keep serving, that they would see that's how we survived. But we started sliding into chaos the moment the news broke there was a problem with Thanatos, and now... When we lose all the leaders..." She stares unseeing across the hall. "Since Nela's broadcast was live there was no way to minimize the panic. Green-lots were raided, healing centres too. You walk down the street and people are either stealing from each other or strung out on The Light." Ora blinks, looking up at me. "The worst is in the dorms. Leaders have disappeared. I don't know if it's because of Thanatos or they've just stopped caring, but the children..." Her eyes fill with tears and she reaches for my hand.

"Arisu contacted me. She isn't safe." Ora's face crumples in pain. "I've always tried to do the right thing, to not build our bond too strong so she'd be equipped to serve her role when the time came. But Edju loved her so much. He was always planning adventures for us. I tried to keep my heart closed, but I couldn't.

When the World Collective sent me to Fordtown when you were in the coma, it was the hardest thing I've ever done, leaving her there, saying goodbye. When she called me, begging me to come and get her…" Ora hides her face as she struggles to stop the tears. I scoot closer, wrapping my arms around her legs and setting my head in her lap. When she collects herself, she brushes her fingers through my mess of curls.

"I couldn't bring myself to tell her about…" She waves her lit wrist. "But I can't leave her there, all alone… Not with what's happening. That's why I had to find you. I asked Aliah to help me because I knew we couldn't risk being followed. Wait." Ora's head swivels as she searches the large hall. "Where is Aliah?"

"She's in a secure location," Al answers.

"A secure location? Why?"

I bite my lip. "Because she works for the United People. We shouldn't trust her."

"Oh, Rygita," Ora caresses my chin. "Don't be so quick to judge. Aliah came because she wants to help."

It's hard not to roll my eyes.

"You need to speak to her, Rygita. At least listen to what she has to say because you're going to need her help," Ora adds with more emphasis. "I've been collecting data, ever since the report where the problem was made public." She opens a screen full of information. "It is clear Thanatos is very broken, but the speed at which things have changed—I don't know if it's because of what the United People did with the patch or if they've done more—but what I do know is that the danger is very real. Thanatos is speeding up much too fast. At its current rate, anyone over the age of 25 will be dead in the next ten days."

If the floor split open and I fell into an endless chasm I would feel safer than I do right now. Everyone over the age of 25? Ten days? So many lives cut short. And what about those left? How long until it's everyone over the age of 20? 15? How long until there's no one left at all?

"What about the leaders of the United People?" Jolan asks. "Aren't they at risk too?"

"They have the patch," I groan, pushing away from Ora as guilt and shame burn my face. "They've made sure to protect themselves." My anger flares. "But how can they let this happen? How can they be okay with this?! If Thanatos has sped up that much…" I struggle to take a breath, my lungs caught in a vice-like grip. "They need to be sharing the patch—not activating people's Thanatos'! At this rate, there won't be anyone left!"

"I agree," Ora says. "If I had more time… if I knew more about Thanatos… maybe there's more I could do."

"Before we left we had a plan," Tali says, perching on the edge of the couch. "DATA knew—well, Darr and Hyll—and they had a way to get the patch out to everyone, through one of Nela's broadcasts. It's why we agreed to free Tazib. We thought he had a copy."

"Do you?" Ora leans forward, a glimmer of hope in her weary voice.

Tazib shakes his head.

Ora flops back with a sigh. "Then this is the end."

A child's happy call echoes in the large cavern and Ora looks up in surprise, seeing the people of Sota. Understanding dawns on her face, but it is mixed with hurt. "Well, I guess it is not the end of humanity."

Momma Aimee reaches for Ora's hand. "My dear, don't mistake our separation from the WC as apathy. If there's some way we can help, we will do it." She looks to me. "If you could get your hands on a patch, would you still be able to spread it to the people?"

"We think so," I nod.

Momma Aimee stands and raises her voice, addressing the crowd around us. "I bring to The Table this urgent matter to discuss. People within the Collective are dying. Our guests have an idea of how to stop those deaths, but they lack resources and experience—things we have. We have resources we can share with them, experience that can guide them. It is my suggestion we equip our guests to save their people."

"Isn't that what we've been doing?" a voice calls from the crowd. "Isn't that why they're here?"

"Yes," Momma Aimee confirms. "But I think we should consider doing more. But I caution, doing so will involve risk."

The crowd around us shifts, voices slowly rising. Momma Aimee raises her hands and waits for the murmurs to settle.

"I understand your concerns. That is why I suggest we openly discuss this matter among ourselves. Let us gather at The Table and come to a consensus, but let us not waver. From what we have heard today, we don't have time for long debate. Look to your hearts, judge if I speak the truth."

"What happens now?" I ask, watching as the crowd breaks away, Mikom, Jolan, and Al disappearing into small groups scattered around the large hall, the noise of many voices bouncing off the walls and high ceiling.

"Now we will discuss," Momma Aimee says, observing the

people around her with tenderness. "Those with a spot at The Table will move about for the next hour or so, asking questions, sharing information, and weighing their hearts."

"And after that?"

"After that? You will know if you have the support of the Uncounted."

Ora pushes herself to her feet. "I should check on the new mother and baby." But as she turns to the medical tent, her face blanches and her body sways.

"Ora!" I jump to offer her the support of my arm.

"I'm fine," Ora says. "I simply stood up too fast."

"You need to lie down," Momma Aimee declares.

"Give me a minute and—"

"No arguments." Aimee waves Ora's protest away. "Loren, come take her other side."

Together, Loren and I brace Ora as we lead her into the tent where she collapses onto one of the empty cots.

"Thank you," she sighs, her eyes fluttering closed. "I'm suddenly so very tired."

Cold fear creeps up my spine. Ora's paleness, the sweat on her brow, the way her body appears to be drawing in on itself...

"Ora, when was your Thanatos activated?"

"Four days ago."

Loren and Momma Aimee meet my gaze over Ora's head. We know what that means.

Ora has one day left.

One day for us to find a solution.

"I should get out there." I nod to the voices outside the tent.

"The Uncounted need to understand why we have to do something. We need to get a patch from the United People. I know it won't fix the problem, but it will at least slow the deaths down."

"I'm afraid I can't let you have a place at The Table," Momma Aimee says.

"What?" Both Loren and I start.

Momma Aimee gently pulls the blanket to Ora's shoulders. "Only adults have a place at The Table; and even then, final decisions will be made by the selected few who have a permanent place at it."

"Let me guess, you have a place."

"I do," Momma Aimee states. "Along with Al, Priya, Jolan, and Mikom. Girls, I know you are worried—"

"These are our lives!" Loren blurts. "If you do nothing..." Her whole body shudders.

"Don't be afraid, child. The Table will choose the right path." Momma Aimee reaches for Loren's hand, but Loren pulls back with a jerk.

"Really?" Loren's tone is cutting. She waves to the hall outside. "Because you're safe here. This isn't really your problem."

"Loren—"

Loren's glare halts my tongue. "What? It's the truth!" Her nostrils flare and her cheeks flush. "They're unconnected. They aren't walking around with this death chip ticking away in them!" She thrusts out her arm, the skin rubbed raw at her wrist. "Look around, Ry. Look at this set up. They can hide here until everything calms down. They're safe from the World Collective, from the United People, from Thanatos. We're the ones who are going to die. Not them." Angry tears shimmer in Loren's eyes and she swipes at them with the palms of her hands.

"Child, I'd hoped you'd see we aren't like that. We want to help. It's why The Table brought you here."

"You didn't want me," Loren's voice quivers. "You wanted Ry. I was just extra baggage."

"You're not baggage—"

"You know what? Don't. Just don't." Loren swings away with a half-repressed sob, racing from the tent. I'm ready to start after her, but a low moan from Ora stills me.

"Ry?"

"Yes, Ora, I'm here." I drop to my knees besides the cot.

"I need to tell you…" Ora grimaces as she fights to hide another wave of pain.

"We need to help her," I plead to Momma Aimee. "Drugs, a medic, something!"

Ora shakes her head. "I've already been medicated, Rygita."

"You need more."

"What I need is to talk to you."

"That can wait. First, let me help you."

Ora opens her eyes and reaches for my hand. "Rygita, there's no helping me. Not now."

"Don't say that. We're going to fix this."

"There is no stopping Thanatos, Rygita. You know that."

"That's not true," I gasp, realization hitting me with a jolt. "We can stop this. Quick, Momma Aimee, bring back your healers. It is possible to stop Thanatos."

"Ry—"

"It is! I survived!" I grip Ora's hand in both of mine, needing to spread my hope to her weak form. "Ora, I survived Thanatos. Before, in Fordtown. Libni, the United People, they saved me! It is possible!"

"Oh, Rygita." Ora shakes her head. "It wasn't Thanatos—"

"It was!" My throat squeezes as I try to make her see. "The World Collective covered up the truth, but I survived Thanatos."

"You are young, Rygita." Ora raises her free hand to my cheek, her pupils dilating as she tries to focus on my face. "Whatever you survived, whatever assistance you had, I doubt it can be replicated."

"Ora—"

"It's okay, Rygita. I know it isn't right, it's not my time, but saving my life... I don't matter, Rygita. But Arisu..." Ora's voice cracks and she blinks rapidly as her eyes well with tears. "There was a fire in her building. She got out but couldn't find her dorm leaders. Rygita, she was so afraid. When she contacted me, she was hiding in a bush. I could hear the shouts around her." Ora pauses, her breathing rapid and shallow. "You have to go to her, Rygita. If Thanatos can't be stopped... Things are only going to get worse. I —" Ora swallows. "I don't want her to be alone. Please. She trusts you. She needs you. Rygita, take care of my little girl."

The ache in my heart is a living thing, fierce and ferocious, but it is equally matched by the drive to do something. All else fades away as I meet Ora's eyes, her cold hands clasped in mine. "I promise, Ora. I promise to take care of Arisu."

A tear slips free and rolls down the side of Ora's face. "Thank you," she breathes. "This is her last known location." She closes her eyes as she presses her palm against mine, but there is no familiar tingle to notify the passing of data.

"I don't think it worked." I squeeze Ora's hand, but her eyes remain closed, the rise and fall of her chest growing slower as a sheen of sweat collects on her brow.

"I think we should let her rest," Momma Aimee says softly. "Come."

She motions for me to leave the tent, but I don't move from Ora's side. "Why won't you let me have a place at The Table? At least let me talk to people."

"Child," Momma Aimee's raspy voice is soft and gentle. "Getting involved puts our community at risk. This is a decision that must be made by the Uncounted."

"Then give Tazib a place," I blurt, speaking the idea before I've even finished processing it. "He knows both worlds. I know he's young and he does really, really stupid things, but he'll be a voice for me, for the Collective." I haven't forgiven Tazib for what's he's done, not even close, but I need the Uncounted to help us.

Momma Aimee starts to object, but then she closes her mouth, her wrinkled brow puckering in a frown. "Alright. We will give Tazib a place," she promises. "Just for this. Now, let's give Ora space to rest."

I straighten Ora's covers, shaking my head. "If I can't have a voice in the discussion, I'll stay here." I watch the steady rise and fall of Ora's chest. "In case she wakes and needs something."

Momma Aimee nods, her eyes soft with compassion before she slips out to join the others.

It's strange, sitting in the dim light of the tent, the world at once both quiet and still and yet buzzing with voices and movement just beyond my sight. I feel the same way. Part of me is vibrating with urgency: to make a plan to recover a patch, to chase after Loren, to rescue Arisu. But the other part is still, unable to move from Ora's side.

I can't lose her. Not yet, and not to Thanatos.

"Please," I whisper, leaning my forehead on Ora's cot. "You promise hope and a future. Please help me know how to stop this." The tears slip free, wetting the blanket as I strain to hear the Composer's music. "I'll do whatever it takes, I promise. Just please, don't let me lose anyone else."

CHAPTER NINE

STAY WITH ORA FOR HOURS, KNEELING AT HER SIDE WHILE I HOLD HER hand. Eventually, I drift off, and I when I wake, the buzz of voices has stilled. My chest tingles. What did the Uncounted decide?

Careful not to make too much noise, I limp to my feet, my whole body stiff from sleeping in such an awkward position. Rolling out the kink in my neck, I exit the tent to find the lights of the large cavern dimmed. The space is empty of people, and the lack of chatter and movement amplify my anxiety to learn what has been decided. Drawn to the hushed tones and soft mewing of a baby, I move across the cavern to the couches around the command centre.

"Hush now, little one," Priya croons where she sits with Momma Aimee. "I'm working on it."

I pull up short, heat flooding my face. Priya has her robe pulled to the side, her breast exposed as she cradles the infant's head.

"Why isn't she latching?" Priya sounds exhausted, but there's something else in her voice. Joy. Wonder.

"Here, take your nipple like this," Momma Aimee mimes, directing Priya's hands. "That's it, now roll her lips on… There you go."

My eyes dart away, mortified for interrupting.

"Rygita, what are you doing up?"

I hesitate to look back to Momma Aimee, but when I do, I see Priya's breast is covered by the suckling baby.

"I need to know what was decided," I answer. "Will you help?"

Momma Aimee gives an understanding nod. "Come have a seat."

I pause, unsure where to sit in an effort to give Priya privacy, but she offers me a weary smile. "It's alright. I don't know how these things are done in the Collective, but here, nursing is nothing to be ashamed of. Come. Meet my little miracle." Her eyes are drawn like a magnet to the infant as I take a seat. "Isn't she perfect?"

"She is."

The baby's tiny hand curls around Priya's finger, her long lashes fluttering against her cheek as she drinks.

"I'm so thankful your friend was here. She saved our lives." Priya's voice trembles and she swallows. "Whatever happens, she will not be forgotten. I want you to be the first to know—" Her eyes shimmer. "I've named her Ora, to honour the one who served us even when her own time is so short."

"Thank you," I murmur past the lump in my throat.

"Here." Momma Aimee passes me a tin. "Have a cookie. Sugar is good for the soul."

Selecting a cookie, I take a nibble, my pounding head and aching shoulders curbing my appetite. "So?"

"Opinions were more divided than I liked," Momma Aimee says, dipping a cookie into her mug of tea. "I must admit, I'm disappointed more people didn't see the situation with compassion for their fellow man."

She sighs and my heart tightens. Does this mean they won't help?

"But we have a plan," Momma Aimee continues, cutting my racing thoughts short. "It's twofold. First, if you are still willing, we would like to do a MEMORY search. I understand your previous attempt was interrupted."

"It was, but I'm still willing. If there's any chance the key is hidden in my mind then I want to find it."

"I told you," Priya smiles. "Rygita is a very determined teen. Much like our Tazib."

I turn the cookie in my hands, uncomfortable with the comparison to Tazib. "Are you..." My tongue stutters. "Will you still be able to help?" Priya's presence was the only thing making me feel even a little okay with the idea of attempting MEMORY. If she can't be there... My body grows rigid.

"Give me a stool and I'll be fine," Priya reassures me. "You'll be the one doing the hard stuff."

"Okay," Momma Aimee nods. "We will notify the others and get the equipment ready. No point delaying because we will want the data before you leave."

"Leave?" I look up in surprise.

"Yes," Momma Aimee states. "The second part of our plan is to send a small team to Unity with the hope of securing a patch from a United People member. Too many are dying. If there is even the smallest chance we can find a way to upload the patch to the people of the WC then we must attempt it."

Hope jumps in my heart. "You're sending a team? Who's on it?"

A knowing smile plays at the corner of Momma Aimee's wrinkled lips. "You, obviously. Tazib insisted you wouldn't settle without being included. Warned us you'd likely do something rash if you weren't given the opportunity," she chuckles.

I blow out a long sigh of relief. One less fight. "Who else are you sending?"

"We are willing to give Tali and Loren a place if they wish to go, as this impacts them directly. And considering what is happening in the Collective, we understand the team needs to be manned with younger people. There aren't many adults left walking around Unity," she says with a sad sigh. "For that reason, we've agreed on Tazib, Eldon, and Maisie. Mikom will also be accompanying you because you will need at least one level head among you."

"Maisie?" I bite the inside of my cheek. Tazib and Eldon make sense, Tazib because of his expertise in all things tech, and Eldon because he's lived within the Collective and would know how to blend in. But how will Maisie blend in? Using sign language will be a dead giveaway she isn't a WC citizen.

If Momma Aimee hears the scepticism in my voice she doesn't acknowledge it. "Maisie is a keen observer. You will appreciate having her to watch your back. And that girl," Momma Aimee chuckles, a lovely musical laugh that makes the skin under her chin wiggle. "She can be most persuasive. Won her argument with her father hands down."

"Wonder where she gets that stubborn streak from?" Priya laughs.

"Yes, indeed."

"When are we leaving for Unity?" I ask, desperate to keep the conversation on track. "Because there is something I need to do first, for Ora."

It is impressive how high Momma Aimee's eyebrow arches. "Oh?"

"I have to find her daughter. I have to make sure she's safe." I've managed to decimate the cookie so I brush the crumbs into a pile. "I know we don't have a lot of time, but I have to do this."

"Where is her daughter?"

I swallow. "Ol'Syd."

Momma Aimee sucks in a sharp whistle between her teeth.

"That's a long way," Priya says.

"I know."

Momma Aimee frowns, her forehead puckering with lines. "I understand your desire to do this for your friend, but I think you need to consider the bigger picture. You don't have time to travel to the other side of the globe."

"Arisu is only 7." I slide forward, my foot tapping as my building anxiety demands release. "She's all alone. Separated from her dorm group. Lost and afraid. She needs to be here, with her mom, before…" No matter how often I swallow I'm unable to wet my dry throat. What if I can't get Arisu here in time?

"I understand," Momma Aimee says. "But, Rygita, people are dying everywhere. Across the globe, children are becoming orphans while we sit having tea." Priya pulls her sleeping baby closer. "I know you want to help your friend and this child, but it's more important that we stop Thanatos."

"But I can't just leave her there!" My imagination won't stop haunting me with little Arisu in a thousand situations, each more dangerous than the last.

"I'm sorry, but our resources are stretched thin as it is. We simply don't have the manpower or equipment for two missions. As it stands, you will leave for Unity as soon as possible, assuming all goes well with MEMORY." Her quick glance at me is enough to communicate what she does not say—that everything depends on me not reacting again.

"Your suggestion to invite Tazib to The Table was a wise one," Momma Aimee continues. "He spoke with the girl, Aliah, and has a plan. While you are gone, Priya will go over any remaining tissue samples and the data collected from MEMORY. Rygita." She finds my eyes, holding me in her steady gaze. "We understand that this mission, this attempt at finding the patch, is just that—a patch. We must keep searching for a way to end Thanatos completely." She pats my hand. "You will get to Arisu, but first you must travel to Unity."

"Tazib's going after Libni, isn't he?" My stomach flops in my belly. Of course that's Tazib's plan. He'll probably threaten to kill someone Libni cares about, forcing her to show herself. That is, if she cares about anyone. I can't believe I fell for her mumbo jumbo about being for the people.

"Unfortunately, we need the data she carries." Momma Aimee's cheeks sag, her age painfully obvious without her usual smile and twinkling eyes. "It wasn't a decision we came to lightly.

Abandoning Arisu fills me with dread, but they have a point. We need to stop Thanatos. "Thank you," I mutter, keeping my eyes down. "For getting involved when you don't have to."

"Oh, child," Momma Aimee says. "We are not so noble as you think we are." She sighs, a deep heavy sound. "We may live separate from you, but we still need you. In fact, we cannot survive without the connected world. Where do you think our equipment, medicines, and much of our food comes from?"

She waves to the hall and I realize the WC logo is everywhere: on tents, on equipment, the crates stacked against the wall, even the tin the cookies are in. Having seen it all my life, I'd become blind to its presence.

"The world is a big place," Momma Aimee says. "And while things have greatly improved, it is still a very harsh and dangerous place. Unless we find a way to stop Thanatos, I doubt humanity will survive."

Her statement, delivered in her deep raspy voice with no hint of sarcasm or exaggeration, makes my blood run cold.

"It's hard to believe it's gotten this bad." My voice trembles. "How could our leaders let this happen? Why didn't they stop it?"

"I'm sure they had many reasons," Momma Aimee says. "Disbelief that their perfect system could have any faults. Fear of change, of giving up the power they had. Power does strange things to people, Rygita. It's one of the reasons the Uncounted do not have one person in charge. We join at The Table to make our decisions because we know we are all connected."

The room blurs as I blink the tears away. I know I'm not alone, the Composer's music is a constant reminder of that, but it doesn't ease the stress. So much weighs on my heart: needing to find the crypto key, Ora's request to watch out for Arisu, Tali and Loren's struggles to move past their hurts, the brokenness of my relationships with Rube and Darr, the fear of all I will lose if we don't stop Thanatos.

"Rygita." Momma Aimee's voice breaks through my mental fog as Priya reaches for my quivering hand. "We know you carry the weight of all that is happening, but it is not yours alone. We are all part of this, Collective, United People, and Uncounted alike. And though it may not seem like it, you are surrounded by people who want to help." She nods in the direction Al led Aliah away. "Like the girl, Aliah."

"I wouldn't trust a word she says," I blurt, pulling away from Priya's touch. "She's a backstabbing, self-preserving—"

"—young woman who risked everything to come here to find you," Momma Aimee interrupts. "One who made sure what may be Ora's final wish, to speak to you, was achieved." I shift under Momma Aimee's gaze. "You can't do this on your own, Rygita. You need others. Aliah has information, details that will help you on your journey to recover a patch. I can have someone take you to her now."

"What about MEMORY?" I hurry to my feet. "I think we should do that right away. I can go find Mikom."

"Child." The simple word stops me in my tracks. "Speak to the girl. We will get everything ready while you do so."

She waves her hand and a man I had not noticed before steps forward.

"This way," he says, leading me across the hall and down a cement corridor. We stop at a simple wooden door guarded only by a woman half dozing in an armchair. "She's here to talk with the girl," the man says to the woman. When she nods her assent, he pushes open the door, waving me inside.

I'm stunned. That's it? That's all their security? No locks, no full body scan, no checking to see what I'm carrying. I'm not even escorted into the cell.

Cell isn't the right word for the space I enter. It's more like the room Aliah and I briefly shared in Unity, with a washroom, a sitting space with a worn table and mismatched chairs, and beyond that, a bedroom with a pair of beds, each decorated with warm, colourful quilts. A desk and chair sit between the beds, complete with a stack of worn paperback books. Other then the fact that there are no windows, there is no indication this is a prison.

"I was wondering when you would show up." Aliah is sprawled on top of the covers on one of the beds, staring at the nondescript ceiling. "Come to tell me what a traitor I am?"

I linger in the doorway. What am I doing here? I don't want to listen to whatever excuse Aliah has for what she did. I should just go. Let her rot in here while I do the hard work of trying to minimize the damage she's done with Libni.

But before I can turn to leave, the melody washes over me. Like always, it is both calming and reassuring, but there is something more. Though it is faint, there is another melody line, a thrill just under the main refrain, and it is telling me to stay. To listen.

So, I force my feet to move and I sit on the bed opposite Aliah. And then I wait. If I'm supposed to listen, then that's what I'll do. But don't expect me to do more. Aliah got herself in this mess and I'm not going to help her dig her way out.

Five minutes. That's how long it takes for the silence to become unbearable, but I refuse to break. Finally, Aliah jerks upright, swinging to face me.

"Would you stop staring at me," she snaps with a scowl. "Go

ahead, get it over with. Tell me what a terrible person I am. Scream at me for what I did. For not stopping Libni. For letting her kill Ky. I'm a monster—cold and uncaring. Go ahead. Tell me!"

It is only the presence of the music that stops me from blurting all the hate that is bubbling in my gut. I long to agree with her, to call her all the names and watch her deflate, but I bite my lip.

Aliah's eyes narrow as she leans towards me. "You must be so proud. So happy to see me locked up. It's where I belong, isn't it? Because of what I did, because I didn't listen to you. Ky's death is my fault. I picked the wrong side. I was so focused on vengeance I couldn't see the United People for what they really are."

"Vengeance?"

Aliah ducks her head. "I don't want to talk about that," she mumbles. She takes a steadying breath through her nose, gripping the edge of the bed with white knuckles. "Look Ry, I admit it. I messed up. I didn't think the United People would actually go through with it. They needed the world to know the truth of what was happening, of what the World Collective was hiding, and kidnapping Ky—making those demands—it was effective. But I didn't think they would kill him! Honest!"

I watch Aliah's bowed head, the way her shoulders curve in on herself. All her self-assurance vanished. When I say nothing, Aliah looks up, her brows pinched in a pucker.

"You're not going to gloat?"

Though I only shrug, I know my expression betrays me. She's right. I'm dying to gloat. But I also know it isn't going to fix anything.

"Ora said you had news?"

Aliah shoves her hair away from her face. "I told Tazib already —that was loads of fun."

"Tell me. What news do you have?"

Aliah shifts, scooting until her back is against the wall, feet stretched before her. "I was already thinking of leaving when Ora contacted me about finding you." She speaks to a point behind my shoulder, never making eye contact. "After they killed Ky, I knew I had to distance myself. The fact that they are so ingrained in every facet of the World Collective..." She runs her hands through her hair, pulling it together and over her shoulder. "I've been with the United People a long time. I'm not important in their organization," she huffs. "Nothing like you and the WC, but still, they trust me. They don't send me from the room when they talk, so I hear things."

"What are you saying, Aliah?"

Aliah bristles, jutting her chin and meeting my eyes with a pointed glare. "What I'm saying is I know what they are going to do, and if you want to have any chance of stopping them, of stopping Thanatos, you're going to need my help."

The challenge in Aliah's voice dissolves what little resolve I had to remain quiet and listen.

"You came all this way to help me?" I stand, heat rushing to my face. "You expect me to believe that?" My laugh is dry and cold. "Nice try, Aliah. But no. Not going to fall for it. I'm not letting you manipulate me or anyone else." I move to the door.

"It's bad, Ry," Aliah blurts. "I'm sure Ora's told you, about the leaders?"

"That they're all going to die? Yeah, I know. Is that why you're in a hurry to help? So you can get free in time to take your place at

Libni's side as she takes over the world?"

"Stop being a brat," Aliah snaps. "I'm not working for Libni anymore. Aren't you listening?"

"Yes, Aliah, I'm listening, and I know it's bad. Why do you think we're willing to walk into the city that wants our deaths? We have to do something to fix this mess!"

"You're going back?"

My hands ball at my sides, hating myself for revealing too much. "We have a plan," I growl. "A plan to stop the madness you helped create."

"A way to stop Thanatos?"

"A way to secure a patch."

"But…" Aliah sucks her cheeks in as she thinks. "To do that you'll need a copy, and the only copies…" Her features shift as understanding dawns. "That's why Tazib was asking so many questions about Libni…" She looks up. "You're going to try to get the patch from her."

I keep my face still, knowing I suck at masking my thoughts.

"I need to come with you," Aliah states, sliding off the bed.

"You will be staying here," I say pointedly.

"But I know Libni. I can get close to her without putting anyone else at risk." Aliah leans forward, her voice dropping. "You don't know what it's like. More is going on. The United People have thought of everything. *Everything*," she stresses. "If you're going back, you're going to need me."

"Why?" I bristle. "Why should I trust you? All along you've been acting behind my back. Tracking me, informing on me. I tried to tell you what was going to happen. I asked for your help for crying out loud!" My nails cut into my palms where my fists clench at my sides. "And what did you do? You locked me up! And now—" I step away, struggling to contain my anger. "Now you want me to trust you. To free you so you can travel with us into the very city that would lock me up without a second thought? Nope. No. Not going to happen."

CHAPTER TEN

FLEEING ALIAH'S CELL, I STORM DOWN THE TUNNEL. I TRIED, I really tried to do what the music suggested. I tried to listen, tried to wait and see what she had to say, but how? How can I ever trust her? She only looks out for herself, expecting her to be different now… Nope. It isn't going to happen, no matter what the music or Momma Aimee may say.

Reaching the large hall, I find it buzzing with activity. Under Jolan's supervision, people are dismantling the tents and stacking supplies neatly along the walls in what looks like organized chaos.

"There you are," Jolan says when she sees me. "There's no sign Ora's pod was followed so we're packing up and heading topside."

"Anything I can do to help?"

"Nope." Jolan grabs one of her kids before they're run over by a group of men moving a heavy cart of folded beds. "I would have you help with my brood, but they're waiting for you in the lab. The plan is to head to Unity as soon you finish, so you should go there now."

"What about you?" I ask. "Aren't you coming?"

"Put that crate with the ones over there," Jolan answers a woman's question before turning back to me. "No, I'm needed here. But don't worry. Mikom, Priya, and Maisie are there. Maisie's our MEMORY expert. Her powers of perception are so sharp she often catches details the others miss. It's easy to focus on what's being said in memories, but Maisie sees the whole picture: body language, the surroundings, the little inconsequential details. Plus, most of the modifications to the mechanisms are her own. So, see? You'll be in good hands without me."

The heat that carried me from Aliah's cell chills as I make my way down the long hall to the lab. No matter how I reason with myself that this is our best shot of stopping Thanatos, I'm unable to stop the tremors that shake through my hands and up my shoulders.

I find the abandoned healing centre gown in the bathroom and I hurry to change. If I'm doing this, I need to do it as quickly as possible before I chicken out. When I emerge, I find Priya, Mikom, and Maisie waiting by the modified couch and a cluster of computers while Momma Aimee rocks Priya's newborn in the small office. With determined steps, I cross the lab and lower myself onto the couch.

"Try not to worry," Priya says as she covers me with a warm blanket. "We're going to take care of you, promise."

I nod meekly, thankful for the blanket but still feeling naked and exposed.

Priya attaches cold sensors to my chest, wrists, and neck as she explains the changes they've made to the stolen WC equipment. Her movements are slow and stiff, a reminder that it's only been a couple of hours since her dramatic birth experience. Mikom and Maisie set up more monitors and equipment around me, silently signing to each other as they recheck the calibrations.

"It is our hope," Priya says, tucking a curl away from my eyes and giving my shoulder a reassuring squeeze, "that if we stay away from any memories of the accident, your vitals will remain stable. That's where our tracker program will help. It will guide you to the memories we think have the best chance of showing what we need. Ones with your parents and grandparents."

"What are grandparents?" I ask.

Priya blinks. "You know, your parents' parents."

"Oh."

I see the look of pity in Priya's face as she pulls a stool over to my head. "Alright," she sighs with relief as she settles. "We're ready if you are."

My eyes jump to the two metal panels on either side of the couch. I don't want to do this. I don't care how safe they say they've made it, they can't know how I'm going to handle it. No one reacts the way I do. I lick my lips, my mouth suddenly bone dry. I could still say no. I could jump up and run out of this lab. I could go find Tali and Loren and...

And what? Wait for their Thanatos' to activate? Watch from afar as the World Collective crumbles and the United People take over? Stay here and pretend nothing else matters but myself?

I draw a deep breath and close my eyes. I don't have to be afraid. I've survived MEMORY twice. Each time, the music met me when I needed it the most, and it is here now. I focus on the melody, letting it remind me that I'm not alone, that there is a plan, and that I can have hope.

"I'm ready."

My voice sounds hollow but determined. I set my hands on the metal plates, the tingle of the device almost reassuring in its familiarity after being away from Unity for so long. Immediately, I feel the drugs numbing my thoughts and my body grows heavy. I brace myself for the rush of falling through time and space, for the unbearable pain of reliving those moments of pure terror.

But it doesn't come.

Instead, I find myself in a strange, grey, empty expanse. Everything is formless, with nothing to define up or down; the space is warm and quiet, but not silent. The Composer's melody whispers around me, and beyond that I can hear Priya's calm voice.

"Look around you, Ry," Priya directs. "What do you see?"

I turn slowly in the grey mist, marvelling as thousands of feathers appear. They drift in the stillness, a variety of colours and sizes. I reach out and touch a purple and blue feather. As its softness brushes lightly over my fingers, I'm transported to a memory, the day Rube and Jep hid under my bed at the healing centre and scared my nurse so badly she asked to be transferred. When I pull my hand back the memory vanishes.

"Touch another," Priya instructs.

This time, I touch a small pink feather, and there's Loren in Year 8, laughing so hard at something she fell off her stool, which only made us laugh harder until the two of us both had stomach aches.

"Find a feather that shows your father."

I examine the feathers around me, beginning to understand the way the colours and variety are connected to people and places. Dad. Which feathers belong to him?

A step away, a large white feather twists in the grey. Though I am drawn to it, I hesitate to reach out my hand, some part of me knowing this memory is heavier than the others. When the tip touches my finger, I'm transported to when Merari had me question Dad at the holding facility. Time seems impossibly slow as I relive those moments, my last conversation with my father. My heart spasms as I look at him, at the way the pale grey suit he was wearing aged him, drawing attention to the silver in his beard. And, when I hear the anger that was in my voice when I turned to leave without telling him I loved him, I close my eyes. I would give anything to change these memories, to take back the things I said, to repair the divide between us. But I can't.

"Let it go." Priya's voice drifts into my consciousness, shattering the memory like smoke. "Find more feathers."

Time inside MEMORY is strange and fluid. I relive hours and days as Priya directs me through the storm of feathers. We touch everything, good memories and painful ones, big and little. Everything from meals in the dining hall, working in the green-lots, to tearful goodbyes and deep betrayals. Most of the memories focus on moments with my parents, some so far back that watching the memory is like living it for the first time.

One of those lost memories comes in the form of a lovely green feather. When I touch it, I'm transported to the Thanatos Hall in Ol'Syd where the smell of cedar and fresh flowers overwhelms me. A low sun floods the hall with warm light, the lit candles flickering at the end of each aisle. I'm sitting on a too-big bench, cheerfully swinging my feet.

My first Thanatos.

Wisps of moments flicker through my consciousness. The

sparkly emerald shoes that absolutely enthralled me and I'd been so disappointed I couldn't keep for everyday use. Laughing at dinner so hard my drink bubbled up my nose. A woman giving Mom a fancy box she clutched to her chest. Rube and I racing between the legs of the adults at the dance. I remember how little Year 4 me was so sure I'd stepped into a fairy tale. I was positive Thanatos was a magical thing where everyone wore their finest clothes and danced and sang and laughed and had the best day ever.

We were celebrating a woman's Thanatos. I don't know her name, but there was something familiar about her, something about her smile that reminded me of Mom. When the woman climbed into bed at the end of the night, I held Rube's hand and giggled when Mom kissed the woman on her forehead. It was so strange, to watch my Mom tuck a grownup into bed, but even more strange was the way the woman fell still. I didn't understand it at the time, but that was the first time I saw someone die. I recall the confusion I felt, the wrongness of seeing someone so full of life and stories suddenly become so motionless and empty.

But what shook me more was Mom's reaction. Mom's tears.

I remember how badly I wanted to climb into her lap, to put my arms around her neck and tell her everything would be okay: that we aren't meant to live forever and we can walk bravely into the future.

I pull my hand from the feather, shaking the memory away. It's hard to believe I once bought into the World Collective's propaganda about Thanatos. All too soon, that little me would learn the truth.

But watching that memory sparks an idea and I search the sea of feathers for more green, brushing them through my fingers until I find the one I'm looking for.

Mom's Thanatos.

Warm tears slide into my ears as I relive that day. I remember every detail, every decoration, every word and look. I see the hall set for the dinner, the tables decorated with green tablecloths and fine china, and Mom, so alive and so close. I relive the moment she saw me standing with Dad and Rube across the hall.

"There you are!" Mom's face was flushed with excitement as she rushed across the hall, her tall frame moving with grace between the round tables. "What do you think?" She struck a pose, waiting for our admiration.

"You look perfect," Dad said as he studied Mom's face with a softness I hadn't seen in years.

"Your hair is grey." I didn't mean to snap, but it was so shocking, so different from how I wanted to remember her.

Mom laughed as she touched her head. "Do you like it? It's all the rage right now as a Day of Thanatos style. I think it suits the event perfectly. Don't you?"

"I like it," Rube said. "Makes you look old."

"Rube," Mom laughed. "I'm not old."

"But isn't that the idea?" My voice betrayed my emotions. "That Thanatos and old go together?"

An uncomfortable silence fell upon us as Mom's smile dimmed.

"Rygita, don't be like that. This is supposed to be a happy day. A day to celebrate." She forced the laughter back into her voice. "A day to celebrate me!" She flung her arms wide and spun in a small circle.

"You look lovely and we look forward to celebrating you." Dad took her hand and gave it a kiss. "I'm honoured to have been a part of your story, Sabeen."

Mom blushed. "Thank you, Morrow. We certainly had an exciting one, didn't we?"

"That we did. And we were fortunate The Code saw fit to give us these two." Dad nodded to Rube and I.

"Yes, to carry the story forward."

"Let's move on," Priya prods gently, but I fight against her. These were my last moments with Mom. I'll never have another chance to sit with her, to watch her throw her head back in laugher, to have her cup my cheek. Not ready to move on, I pull the feather closer, time jumping forward to the dance that followed the dinner. I try not to compare Mom's Thanatos to Jep's. Mom's day was how it was supposed to be celebrated: elaborate and over the top, full with the ceremony, fancy dinner, and dancing. Jep's Thanatos was... wrong, so very wrong on so many levels.

In my memory, I'm in the Thanatos Hall, encouraging Loren to go dance with the other guests, knowing she was resisting because she didn't want to leave me on my own. When I finally convinced her I'd be okay, the voice I longed to hear the most spoke over the thumping music.

"Ry, you're not dancing."

I turned to find Mom sitting on one of the chairs set in the shadows.

"You're not dancing either."

Mom scanned the room, a blank expression dimming her usually bright features. I wonder now if she was counting down the minutes, knowing what was to come all too soon.

"It's been a long day," she answered.

Without thinking, I'd taken her hand and given it a squeeze. I'd expected her to pull away, she was always so conscious of drawing unwanted attention to open displays of emotion, but that night she had gripped my hand tightly.

"I didn't tell you earlier," she said, studying my face, "how lovely you look today. Sometimes I look at you and I'm just amazed." She touched my cheek and I leaned into her hand. "You are so strong. So brave. You fought through the worst thing that could ever happen to you and you came out the other side." She pulled her hand away to wipe at her tears. "And not only that, you remained so kind and loving." Mom shook her head with a bewildered smile. "What happened to you, the attack, it made me so mad and bitter, but you... You rose above that. You're amazing."

"Mom..." My tears blurred my vision.

Mom's smile grew wider though her own tears continued to drip down her cheeks. "That word: Mom. It's so antiquated. I can't imagine where you'd heard it." She squeezed my hand, her gaze drifting over the dancing crowd without seeing. "The first time you said it was the first time you woke up after the attack. I'd been sleeping in the chair by your bed. You opened your eyes, looked at me, and said 'Mom.' I'd never been happier in my life."

I choked back a sob.

"I knew I should stop it, you calling us Mom and Dad—the WC did away with such language years ago—but it never seemed like the time. And then we got used to it, I suppose. Look at us—" she laughed through fresh tears. "Crying like two emotional fools."

The laughter was a welcome aid to the pain that crushed my heart. Mom reached for her clutch, finding a cloth to wipe her eyes before passing it to me.

"I'm glad I caught you on your own," she said as I tried to compose myself. "I have something for you."

Mom pulled a long, thin box from her clutch, its velvet covering worn bare at the corners. The part of me that's aware this is a memory watches as I take the box, opening it and pulling out the long necklace that has become so important to me. Even here, in the grey mist of MEMORY, I long for its reassuring presence.

"It used to be a common thing—the Thanatos host passing on mementos to guests—but it's fallen out of fashion," Mom explained. "Still, I've wanted to give it to you ever since…" Her eyes dropped to the green light under the skin of her wrist. She forced a smile as she looked up, taking the necklace from me. "Here, let me."

Mom draped the long strand of beads on my shoulders, her face more serene than it had been all day. "It suits you."

I don't need MEMORY to recall every detail of this moment. I can still feel the music of the dance pounding in my chest, still hear the cheers of joy from those who weren't having their hearts torn to shreds. I threw my arms around Mom, my tears dampening her dress as she drew me close, her perfume enveloping me.

"I'm so glad you were part of my story," she whispered in my ear. "Now go, live your own."

01010111 01100101 00100000 01110001 01110101 01101111 00100000 01110100 01110000 01100100 01101101 00100000

01010101 01101110 01101100 01101111 01101111 01101011 01100101 01101110 01110100 01100101 01100100 00100000

Blinking, the mountain lab slowly comes into focus. Priya stands over me.

"There you are," she coos. "You did so well." She gently peels the sensors off my skin. "Don't sit up just yet," she instructs. "I'm going to get you some sugar. It will help with the lightheadedness."

I keep still on the couch as she leaves, only turning my head to look at the others in front of their computers. It seems impossible. I survived a MEMORY experience without a reaction. My head is spinning and my body trembles with the same exhaustion as after a long run, but otherwise I'm okay.

"Did we find what we need?" I ask.

"Not sure yet," Mikom answers. "But we have lots to look through. And if we don't have it yet, we can always try again later." He gives me a hopeful smile.

My eyes jump to Maisie who is watching me as usual, but there is something different in her expression. She taps Mikom on the shoulder and signs, waiting for him to translate.

"You want me to ask her?" Mikom asks.

Maisie nods, her eyes jumping to me.

"Maisie wants to know how you do it. How do you say goodbye to the people you care about without a fight?"

Despite Priya's warning, I pull myself to sitting, closing my eyes when the room tilts dangerously. "I'm here, aren't I? Doesn't that count as fighting?"

"It's just really hard for the Uncounted to grasp," Mikom continues to interpret for Maisie. "Thinking it's normal to end one's life like that, to not wait for death to come on its own."

My eyes burn and I squeeze them tighter to keep the tears at bay. Experiencing memories in MEMORY is so real, so life-like that it feels like it was only seconds ago Mom held me in her arms. I would do anything to have her here with me, to have one more day with her.

"We were taught that we needed to go when The Code told us it was time," I say, knowing it sounds lame, but needing to say something. "In school we spent a lot of time learning how bad things got before, about the global warming, the floods and famines, and all the displaced people because of climate change. We were told we needed shorter lives so we could all have one."

Mom believed she was doing what she was supposed to do. She was trusting The Code, doing her part for the whole. When I remember Mom's face as she stood on that stage, when I recall the way she looked at me, I know she believed she was doing it for me, for my future.

I open my eyes, finding Maisie's. "We were taught that by walking bravely into the future, into the unknown of death, we were doing the most selfless act we could. So don't you dare think less of my mom or Jep or any of the others." My voice quivers as a tear slips down my cheek. "But it doesn't mean it hurts any less for those of us left behind. Even if we've been taught not to show it, it's still there, the hole they left when they said goodbye."

Maisie's eyes aren't the only ones I feel on me as I pull the blanket tighter around my shoulders.

"You poor thing," Priya croons, setting a glass of juice and a pile of cookies on the metal panels. "You're so young and you've had to face so much. Thank you for sharing your memories with us. I'm sure that was very intimidating—letting us see those inner parts of you."

I close my eyes as I pull my knees up, resting my head on them. When Priya rubs my back it is all I can do to not break down into sobs.

"I'm sure she knows, Maisie, give her a minute," Mikom says from across the room. "Okay. Fine." I raise my head as Mikom,

Maisie, and Momma Aimee move to stand around me with solemn expressions. "You do know, right? What we really hope to do if we find the cryptography key? Our goal isn't to fix Thanatos. We're taking it down. It will be over, gone. No one else will die at a scheduled time."

I take a shuddery breath, searching for the music's calmness. "That's why I'm here."

CHAPTER ELEVEN

WE LEAVE FOR UNITY IN THE EARLY AFTERNOON. LOREN decides to stay behind, convinced she would only be a burden despite my assurances that wouldn't be the case. The six of us cram into two pods, with Mikom and Tazib flying manually. They land us well outside the city limits in one of the seas of solar panels surrounding the capital.

"This way." Mikom leads Tali and I to the shade of one of the panels as Maisie and Eldon wrestle a large tarp free of the sand, pulling it over the pods. I see the genius instantly. Before, the sun reflected off the glass and metal pods like a beacon, giving away our presence, but as the tarp slides over the round shapes, they are transformed into nothing more than another wave of sand.

"Let me double check your tech," Tazib says, waiting for me to raise my palm. I press it against his device and watch as he quickly enters some commands.

"Is it okay that it's active again?"

"It's not really active," Tazib explains. "You'll be able to use some features, but I've kept you and Tali offline. No need for anyone to realize we're here. But it will help to have real WC digital prints instead of our poor copies."

"Hey." Eldon jogs into the shade with Maisie. "It was good enough to pass me off as a citizen."

"But not the real thing." Tazib motions for Tali to scan. "I'm just double checking that your signatures are disguised."

I look across the shimmering sand towards the green haze of Unity. It's as impressive and larger than life as it was when I first saw it, but it seems different now, foreign and out of place, like a blight on the barren landscape. I hug my middle, trying to still my restless hands. Somewhere in that massive city, Darr is going about his life, probably at the DATA office or perhaps working in the green-lot. How is he handling everything that's happening? It's strange. When I think of Darr dealing with everything on his own, I both ache for him and boil with anger. If he hadn't turned me in, how different would things be?

Tali follows my gaze to the shimmering city. "I'm not looking forward to this hike."

"What?" Eldon looks between us and the distant city, a grin spreading across his freckled face. "You think we're walking? Guys," he calls to Mikom, who's fiddling with something at the base of a solar panel pillar. "They think we're walking."

Maisie laughs. She shakes her head at us and points to where Mikom works, signing.

"Oh," Tali gasps. "We're taking the trams."

"Got it." Mikom tugs a rusty hatch open, revealing an access shaft inside the pillar. "You got the helmets, Tazib?"

"Just about." Tazib tugs a strap, pulling a large bag from the sand. Unzipping it, he reveals a collection of scratched and dented helmets. "One for each of us," he says, tossing one to me.

I eye the cracked glass of the light before setting the helmet on my head. When everyone is outfitted, Tazib backs into the opening, holding the sides of the panel as he finds his footing. Slowly he lowers himself down into the shaft. Maisie follows after him, then Eldon.

"You next," Mikom instructs. "I'll come last and make sure everything is closed up here."

I move towards the opening and peer over the edge. The walls of the shaft are lit by Eldon's head lamp, but I can see nothing beyond that.

"How far to the bottom?"

"Best you don't know." Mikom twitches his wide nose with a mischievous grin. "And best you don't look down. Just take it one step at a time."

Cautiously, I back into the opening, lowering my real foot over the edge and reaching blindly for the rung below. Once I feel its solid presence, I move my prosthetic to join it, lowering myself into the narrow space. Then I repeat the process.

The little light from the opening is blocked as Tali inches onto the ladder, followed soon after by Mikom. When he closes the hatch, we are plunged into complete blackness but for the light from our helmets. There is a quiet gasp from Tali above me.

"You okay?"

"Not really," Tali whispers, her voice strained. "Not a big fan of the dark."

"Focus on the light," I encourage, watching my own small circle of light bob in front of me as I lower myself down another step. "And think about something else."

It is slow going, inching our way down the ladder with only the sounds of our feet on the rungs and our laboured breathing echoing back to us. I don't mind being up high, not when I'm in control of my movements, but I don't love the lack of clearance. My back brushes against the wall and I have to keep my elbows tucked to avoid bruising them in the tight space. Taking my own advice, I focus on the music as I try to imagine what we will find below. I've never given much thought to the trams before. It's a fully automated system that every city uses to move food and supplies from green-lots to complexes. For most citizens, our interaction with it is nothing more than putting our picked produce in the receiver and hitting a button, knowing it would zoom off to where it was needed. But how does it actually work, hidden deep underground? I guess I'm about to find out.

From below, new sounds echo up to me, the crunch of gravel under boots and a groan of someone stretching out tight muscles.

"You're almost there," Tazib calls.

It's a relief to set my feet on solid ground. I flex my stiff hands, my fingers cramped from gripping the rungs of the ladder too tight, and I look around at what I can see in the narrow beam of light. The tunnel is low, so low my helmet brushes the ceiling, and it is damp and cool. But instead of smelling earthy, there is a hot metallic odour, a mix of electrical and machine. To my left yawns a cavern of empty space, my lamp lighting only a few feet; to my right, I find Eldon, Tazib, and Maisie rummaging through stacked crates. When

Mikom drops to the ground they rejoin us, offering Tali and I what I at first think is a backpack, but on closer inspection I see it is too stiff and heavy to be a bag, plus it has a strange dangling piece on one shoulder.

"It's oxygen," Eldon explains. "The further we get from the access point, the worse the air quality will get."

"But don't use it too quickly," Mikom explains, double checking his own pack. "They're hard to come by and there isn't enough for the whole trip. Just use it if you start to feel lightheaded or queasy."

In the dim light, Tali's white face shines like a beacon as she struggles to secure the pack, her hands repeatedly reaching for the nozzle.

"Here, let me help." Eldon tightens the straps so it sits higher on her back, but as he moves, he accidentally blinds Tali with his light.

"I'm fine," she blurts, stepping back with a grimace.

Eldon ducks his head, his shoulders dropping. "Sorry," he mumbles.

Tazib holds a small device which he taps against his hand until it flickers to life. The light shimmers off the walls, revealing a hologram of the tunnels.

"The others know where we're going," Tazib explains. "But it never hurts to review. The trams are a maze and it's easy to get twisted around. Plus, things move fast, so try not to get decapitated," he laughs.

Mikom uses the hologram to show Tali and I our route into the city. We are currently on the furthest reaches of the tram line, an unfinished tunnel not yet connected to the rails that radiate out from the capital. Though the walk to the line isn't a long one, Mikom cautions us to not push ourselves too hard and to limit talking in order to save oxygen.

Together we move down the pitch black tunnel, helmets knocking against the lower beams. The further we walk, the noisier it becomes. What starts as a distant whine soon becomes an ear-shattering rattle of metal against metal with the squeal of brakes and the thunder of wheels on tracks.

When the tunnel branches, Mikom pauses. "It's going to get a lot louder," he shouts to Tali and I. "There's ear protection in the side pocket. But before you put it on you should know Tazib wasn't kidding. The trams move fast. If you can't get on in time, let it go. Stay where you are and we will come back for you. This is your first time. Don't try to navigate on your own. Got it?" He waits for us to agree before showing us where to find the ear plugs in our packs.

Wiggling the small spongy plugs into my ears is like sinking underwater. The noise from further down the tunnel becomes a bearable rumble I feel more than I hear, and the voices of the others are muffled and muted.

Making our way around the corner, I am hit with a gust of wind that lifts my curls from my sweaty forehead. Our lights swing over the space, revealing another joining tunnel, this one with a metal track secured firmly in the gravel centre. As we approach it, there is another lift of air and understanding hits me with a jolt. The noise, the rush of wind, both are caused by the trams flying down the rails at impossible speeds.

I sway on my feet, my vision blurring. We're going to attempt riding on that?

Mikom taps on my shoulder, pointing to the oxygen nozzle.

Taking a deep breath, my head clears, but my panic remains. No doubt seeing my alarm, Mikom signs to me, but I can do nothing more than watch his hands with confusion. If only I tried harder to learn, communicating through sign would be very handy right about now.

"There's a stop just down the line." Mikom leans close to my ear, shouting to be heard over the noise. "Just keep your back to the wall."

Maisie moves into the new tunnel, her back pressed firmly against the wall as she sidesteps out of view.

"You next!" Mikom waves.

"No way!" I shout. "I can't!"

"You have to!" Tazib yells, grabbing my hand. He pulls me into the tunnel, motioning for me to copy him as he lines himself up on the wall. Eldon comes after me, guiding Tali along the passage with Mikom following last.

It is absolutely terrifying. We inch along the wall, pressed as tight as we can to its solid presence as every minute another tram speeds past, blowing dust in our eyes and stealing the air from our lungs. It feels like an eternity before we reach a section where the tunnel is a little wider and it is safe to move freely. We seem to be below an access elevator. Every minute or so a tram screeches to a stop with an ear-shattering scream. Robotic arms then either lift a crate off the tram or load a new one before it streaks down the line. The whole thing happens with frightening speed, every moving part another painful way to lose a limb.

Since it is impossible to be heard, the others communicate in sign. Tazib continues to watch his handheld device, and when he nods to Mikom, the others move to stand as close to the track as they dare, motioning for Tali and I to join them. Again, Tazib takes my hand as Eldon takes Tali's.

It happens so fast I can hardly process. One second the space before us is vacant and the next there is an empty tram. Maisie scampers onto the flat surface, hurrying to stretch herself prone on the furthest edge while Tazib drags me up behind him. I don't have time to register who ends up beside me: Eldon, Tali, or Mikom, as Tazib shoves me to my belly, guiding my hands to the edge of the bed, and screaming at me to hold on.

And then we are moving. The tram lurches forward with such speed I'm lifted from the flat surface, my fingers aching at the force of my body being dragged back. Struggling to better my grip, I wedge my feet against the tram bed, raising up on my knees as I fight to pull myself forward. I've barely managed to move when a sharp kick knocks me flat. Turning my head towards Tazib, he shakes his head no, indicating with his eyes to look up.

Keeping myself flat on the tram, I crane my head up only to immediately jerk back and press my cheek to the rough surface. The tunnel has narrowed significantly, the ceiling now a couple feet above our prone bodies. Worse, every now and then, lower pieces jut out, flying over us at alarming speeds. If I sat up at the wrong time... I shudder, fighting the wave of bile that rises in the back of my throat.

The whole trip lasts only seconds, but they are some of the longest, most terrifying seconds of my life, and considering what I've survived, that's saying something. Curves are the worst. The pull of centrifugal force swings us to the side and it is all we can do to hang on. From the corner of my eye, I watch as Maisie struggles to not be pushed from her spot on the edge of the tram bed, the walls of the cave ripping at her clothing and making me very grateful for my spot in the centre.

But stopping isn't any better. After fighting the pull of force trying to rip us free, when the tram stops, we all tumble forward, summersaulting or skidding across the gravel.

"MOVE!"

Mikom's volume is impressive considering the noise has only grown louder. Impressive and effective in reminding me the tram won't linger long before taking off again. I leap to my feet and rush to press my body to the wall as the others do the same.

Once the tram is gone, we slide along the wall to another wider, safer section. Mikom motions for us to use our oxygen and I'm grateful for the relief it provides to my tight lungs and pounding head. Meanwhile, Tazib pokes through a mess of wires, clipping his device to one and tapping the screen. When a panel drops from above, revealing another long narrow ladder shaft, I don't need to understand sign to know this is the way out. Wordlessly, we each grab the lower rungs of the ladder and pull ourselves up and away from the madness.

01010111 01100101 00100000 01100101 01101101 01100101 01110010 01100111 01100101 00100000 01110100 01101000 01110010 01101111 01110101 01100111 01101000 00100000 01100001 00100000 01110100 01110010 01100001 01110000 00100000 01100100 01101111

We emerge through a trap door in the floor of a supply closet. The space is small for the six of us, but we hardly notice as one by one we wearily climb off the ladder and flop onto the floor. Mikom emerges last and he closes the heavy door with a thud. He pulls out his ear plugs and I do the same. For a moment, we remain silent but for our heavy breathing, the quiet so welcome after the roar of the tunnels.

"I'd call that a success," Tazib says, shrugging off his pack and tucking it behind an inactive cleaning bot. "We all lived and we have all our pieces. Pretty good for first timers."

"First timer?" I croak with disbelief. "You've done that more than once?" My hands tremble as I try to shake the dust out of my curls, my nose wrinkling at the strong metallic smell.

"We're all pros," Eldon grins, his face smeared with grease. "But I did roll off at a curve my first time."

"Seriously?!" Tali squeaks. "What did you do?"

"Well, I'd lost my helmet so I had to inch along in the pitch black to the next access point."

Mikom takes my equipment, placing it with the other supplies. "It took us nearly a day to find him. But you did the right thing," he says to Eldon. "You stayed in one spot and waited."

"I didn't know what else to do," Eldon shrugs. "I didn't know how to access a shaft ladder yet and I wasn't about to go exploring the tram tunnels."

"I can see why." Tali shivers.

"We should keep moving." Tazib stands, dusting his pants before pulling his device from his pocket. "I'm not registering any heat signatures so we should be set." He moves to open the closet door, but Mikom blocks him.

"Hold on. Don't rely on technology alone. Look and listen, make sure it is safe."

The light in the closet is dim, but I'm pretty sure Tazib rolls his eyes. Still, he does as he's asked and places his ear to the door, waiting a moment before pulling it open.

We step out into a wide hallway lined with oversized images of perfect-looking people in perfect-looking outfits. I recognize these images, I've seen them hundreds of times before whenever I've had the opportunity to select new outfits.

Tali sucks in a breath. "Oh."

"Tali?" I turn to find her staring at one the images, her large blue eyes swimming with tears.

"It's Ky."

Dominating the wall is a larger-than-life picture of Ky. It was taken a couple of years ago, he can't be more than 10, but the sparkle in his eyes, his mischievous grin, and signature long bangs are the same.

"That's why he looked familiar." Eldon looks from the picture to Tali. "I've walked by these dozens of times but never really looked. This is the kid the United People kidnapped, right? The one…"

Maisie shakes her head and Eldon falls silent.

I reach for Tali's hand, giving it a squeeze as she rests her head on my shoulder. She presses her trembling lips together, a single tear slipping down her cheek.

"Don't worry, Tali," Tazib says. "We'll make them pay for what they did to Ky—to everyone. Them and the World Collective."

Tali nods, taking a steadying breath and pulling her shoulders back.

Mikom leads the way through the empty building, passing by the large windows without concern, and taking the elevator to the top floor. There we find an office full of desks and built-in scanners. Unlike the other spaces we passed, this one has a lived-in feel to it with empty water bottles and the remains of half-eaten sandwiches. Mikom, Eldon, Maisie, and Tazib each head to a desk where they place their hands on the scanners, flickering screens coming to life before them.

"How did you do that?" My head swings between Maisie and Mikom. "You don't have tech."

Mikom points to Tazib. "That young man is a bit of a tech genius if you haven't realized. He wrote a bypass that allows us access through our palm prints alone."

"Won't that give away you're here?" Tali glances at the closed door, her body ready for flight.

Tazib laughs. "You were looking for us and you never noticed. We weren't even a blip on your radar."

My frown is matched by Tali's. "You're saying this is where you were, all that time?"

"Not all the time, we move around, but yeah, basically we were right under your noses. The DATA headquarters are just a couple of blocks that way." Tazib points out the window.

I wander over to the wall of windows overlooking an outdoor courtyard. The low sun casts long shadows over the manicured lawn and gardens; as I watch, the path lights blink on, blanketing the area in a warm glow. It's pretty and perfect, as all things are in Unity, but something is off.

"Don't you worry about someone seeing the lights on?"

Eldon sniffs a sandwich before wisely deciding to set it aside. "Nothing's happened so far," he shrugs. "It's one of the things I find so strange about the WC. Nobody really knows anybody. I'm sure people have seen the lights, but they don't know who actually works here so they just assume everything's fine."

Eldon has a point. I wouldn't think twice about seeing a light on in a building. Crime is so rare within the Collective that I would assume whoever was there was supposed to be. It's only more recent events that have made me so suspicious and jumpy.

"What is this place?" I ask, wandering around to look at more catalogue pictures. "You've never been caught by the people who serve here?"

"They wouldn't," Tali says softly. "This is one of the WC design headquarters, isn't it?" When Tazib nods, Tali explains. "There haven't been any new clothing designs in years. I'm guessing those who used to work here were reassigned ages ago, before we even knew anything was wrong with The Code."

"New fashion isn't really essential," Tazib points out.

"So you have the whole place to yourselves."

"A convenient set up."

A loud thud sends my heart rocketing into my throat as I spin to the door.

"Maisie," Eldon laughs, signing as he speaks. "That was mean. You know they're on edge."

Maisie grins at her desk. She points to her screen, signing quickly.

"Good work, Maisie." Tazib crosses the room to peer over her shoulder. "She's found Libni."

"Really?" That was fast. Chances are Maisie would make a better DATA candidate than me, not that that's a hard thing. On her screen I see streams of data with one section highlighted, but I can't make any sense of it. "Where is she?"

"The good news is she's in the city."

"Sounds like there's bad news," Mikom says.

"She's in the air."

"Please don't tell me we got here just as she's leaving."

Maisie shakes her head. "No," Tazib says. "Just moving within the city." Tazib taps his chin. "This could be a good thing…"

Maisie's fingers fly across the keys.

"Exactly," Tazib grins. "If we can get control of her pod—"

"We can bring her to us!" Eldon shouts, jumping from his chair.

"Hold on," Mikom raises his hands. "Think this through. Where would we send her? We can't bring her here. She'd have us apprehended before we even made it to the roof."

"We send her outside the city, far from her resources."

"You're still not thinking." Mikom speaks with calm patience. "By the time we made it back to our pods she'd be long gone. She's connected, remember?"

Eldon drops back into his chair, but Tazib only looks more determined. "I meet her in the air."

"Are you not listening?" Mikom sighs. "Our pods—"

"Are too far away. Yes, I'm listening." Tazib paces behind Maisie's desk, his face growing more and more animated. "I'll use a WC pod. There's a community station two buildings down. I get a pod, fuse with Libni's, and get what we need."

"What then?"

Mikom voices the question that has been bugging me since we left Sota. How does Tazib plan to pull this off? Does he think Libni will simply hand him a copy of the patch? That's unlikely. It's possible he could obtain it through physical contact, but Libni would have to give mental permission. Again, unlikely. And, supposing he gets the patch, what happens after that? Making contact with Libni will alert the United People to what we are doing; and chances are, they'll retaliate.

"I have ways," Tazib shrugs. "Look, don't worry. This will work. I get a pod, intercept Libni, download the patch, and then, I don't know, push her out of the pod, activate her Thanatos, something. It doesn't matter how I get rid of her, the goal is to get the patch."

"Tazib." Mikom stands slowly, his face darkening. "We are here to save lives."

"Exactly." Tazib straightens, his gaze unflinching. "Isn't it better that one dies so many live? Isn't that what's been taught?"

"The death of one is a sacrifice, a sacrifice that must be given willingly," Mikom stresses.

"Well, I disagree. People are selfish, especially those who've lived in a protective bubble all their life. No one within the WC is going to give their life for their fellow man because they don't even know them."

"And you aren't selfish?" Mikom rests a heavy hand on Tazib's shoulder. "Look at yourself, Tazib. Look at your actions. Over and over you act on your own, without thought to the rippling consequences those actions have on others. When will you learn you are stronger and better when you work with others? There are other ways to get the patch, ways that use all of our skills and don't involve murdering this woman."

"But there isn't time!" Tazib snaps, shrugging away from Mikom. "Look! Mikom, look at the data! Each second we waste arguing, more people die from Thanatos. I don't care what you say,

I'm going. I'll get the patch from Libni and then make sure there's no way she can hurt anyone else." Tazib swings to me, his eyes blazing. "Isn't that what you want, Ry?"

"No... I mean, yes." The suddenness of his question has me stammering. "I mean... Why is this something either of you should get to decide?" I look away from Tazib, disliking the way his eyes sparkle. "Thanatos doesn't impact you. It's part of my world," I touch my chest. "It impacts my friends, my family."

"So, what would you suggest?" Mikom eyes me warily.

"I don't want to hurt Libni, but she did betray us. I trusted her. I told her about the patch and she turned around and took that information to the United People, and what did they do? They disabled it." My voice quivers as heat rushes to my face.

"I will not condone killing this woman—no matter how badly she hurt you."

"No, I don't want to kill her. *I* would never do something like that," I hiss in Tazib's direction. "But we do need the patch, and fast. I say we kidnap Libni and take her back to Sota with us."

Maisie snorts as she signs to Eldon.

"Maisie has a point," Eldon says. "Al isn't going to love having a leader of the United People around."

"So," I shrug. "You disable her tech. She's just a person. Disconnect her from the system and what threat does she pose? If we do this right, no one will know what happened to her. She gets in a pod and vanishes. We can do that, we can erase all digital traces and poof." I mime the motion. "Libni disappears."

"Sounds good to me." Tazib bounces on his toes. "I mean, if trouble arises, we still have options."

"It's too rushed," Mikom states. "She could be landing any second."

Maisie shakes her head, signing.

Tazib squeezes her shoulders. "That's my girl," he grins. "I've taught you well." At Tali's questioning look, he explains. "She's slowed Libni's pod. Not enough to be noticeable, but enough to give me more time."

Tazib moves to the door, but Mikom blocks his path. "I still don't agree with this. There is too much that can go wrong. How are we going to steal enough pods for the six of us?"

"The six of us?" Tazib echoes. "No, there's no way the six of us can pull this off without getting caught."

"Tazib—"

"Look, if you're worried I'll go rogue, I'll take Ry with me." Tazib looks back at me, rocking on his heels. "The rest of you can monitor from afar. That's what's safest, isn't it?" The sarcasm is so thick you could choke on it. He ducks under Mikom's arm. "Come on, Ry. We should hurry."

CHAPTER TWELVE

"RYGITA, WE NEED TO THINK THIS THROUGH." MIKOM steps towards me, but I don't wait to hear what else he has to say. I dash down the hall after Tazib.

Mikom isn't wrong; this is all happening really fast, but Tazib's right too. Every minute we waste perfecting plans costs another person their life. Besides, this will work. Maisie will look out for us from afar, Tazib's technical skills can handle any challenges, and I know Libni. She should listen to me.

Right?

Tazib leads me out of the design headquarters and down Unity's green paths at a steady jog. Rounding the corner, we arrive at an open-air pod station where a few people mingle and I shoot Tazib a worried glance. Thanks to Nela's many broadcasts, all it will take is one person recognizing us to find ourselves locked up as terrorists again.

"Don't pay them any mind and they won't pay you any," he

says, moving through the public space like we have every right to be here.

"That doesn't usually work for me," I mutter.

"Sure it can," he answers. "Just act like you're in a hurry to be somewhere important, which we are. Works for me and I have hands like this." He holds up his deformed hands with a grin. "The trick is to not have a care in the world, like everyone else within the Collective."

Tazib heads to a scanner, using his handheld device to call a pod, while I look around the station. None of the people here look like they don't have a care in the world. In fact, the longer I watch, the more I sense an anxious tension. The young man nearest to us sits unmoving on a bench, starting blindly into the empty space before him while a pair of teen girls lean their heads together as they share a screen, their brows puckered with worry. A pod pulls into the station and a young man jumps from it, sprinting away into the darkening city with a pale, sweaty face.

"Citizens of the World Collective." The large screens around the station flicker to life, the sudden audio making me jump. Nela's familiar face beckons and I find myself drawn towards the nearest screen.

"This is Nela, broadcasting live from outside Unity's largest healing centre. It is with great sadness I bring to you the news that today, at 6:49, our leader, Merari, stepped bravely into the future."

The girls gasp behind me.

"Our greatest minds were unable to undo the early Thanatos activation caused by the terrorist group, the United People." There are dark shadows under Nela's eyes and a tightness around her mouth. She swallows, like each word is painful.

"I have done my best to uphold the high standard of excellence that is demanded of all journalists. My goal has always been to speak the truth, to verify the facts, and to inform you, the people." Her eyes glisten as she forces a smile. "I've loved my role, even now when I'm daily delivering news none of us wish to hear.

"People of the Collective. I admit I don't know what comes next. What happens now that we are leaderless? The United People have claimed they work for a future for all, but we have yet to see how that applies to us, the citizens. I don't know if The Code will select a new leader or who that will be. I don't know if Thanatos will slow, or stop, if there is a way for us to recover from the staggering loss of so many." She shakes her head. "There is much I don't know, but what I do know is that the time has come for me to say goodbye."

I am standing directly in front of the screen and Nela seems so close I have to fight the urge to lift my hand to reach for her as she raises her wrist into the camera's frame, revealing the green glow of the Thanatos light under her skin.

"It is my turn to face what none of us can escape. I may not be able to stop Thanatos, but I can and will walk bravely into what comes next. I am choosing to spend my remaining days on my own terms, visiting those I care about, revelling in the sun on my face, in the simple joy of a hot-from-the-oven roll. I *refuse* to submit to panic or despair." Her voice quivers with conviction. "I choose joy and I encourage you to do the same. This is Nela, signing off for the final time. Goodbye all."

The screen blinks and disappears, but I remain fixed in place. In the distance, there is a smash of shattering glass, a disembodied shout, and the pounding of feet racing from the station.

"It's time for us to go." Tazib grabs my arm, pulling me from my trance. "Choose joy," he snorts. "Like people are going to do that. They're going to choose chaos, they always do. But hey, it will give us an advantage. Come on."

Tazib leads me to an empty pod, pulling me in behind him. The doors slide closed and the pod drifts out of the station, rising slowly into the sky as I stare unseeing at the city that was supposed to be my home.

The World Collective is leaderless. Even if we do find a way to stop Thanatos, what will happen now? How will life go on?

I lift my eyes to the sky, stilling myself to hear the strains of notes that remind me there is a plan. I don't have to be afraid. Find Libni. Get the patch. Stop Thanatos. The rest will work itself out. Later. When we have time to breathe.

Tazib settles himself on one of the seats, his attention absorbed in his handheld device.

"Anything I should be doing?" I ask.

"Not really."

I blow out a frustrated huff. This whole trip I've done nothing of value. "Please, give me something to do," I press.

"There isn't anything for you to do," Tazib answers. "Maisie's controlling Libni's pod and will make sure we line up nicely without changing her course. Don't want her to suspect anything until it's too late."

"What about when we connect with Libni's pod? What should I do then?"

"I don't know," Tazib shrugs. "I only brought you along to make Mikom happy, the whole 'don't work alone' thing, you know? I don't really need you. Handling Libni won't be a problem," Tazib says with confidence, lifting his device. "I have certain *tools* at my disposal." Seeing me start, Tazib adds, "Don't worry, I'll only threaten her. I won't hurt her... if she cooperates."

Cringing, I turn to the unfamiliar skyline of Unity. It's strange, this was to be my permanent city, the place I would know better than any other; but so far, I've hardly spent any time here. I wonder, when everything goes back to normal, will it start to feel like home? When I'm not worried about the people I care about losing their lives, will I build relationships that last until I'm old and grey, like Mom and Dad should have been able to do?

"That was a big sigh." Tazib sets his device in his lap, watching my anxious swaying. "This is going to work. Stop stressing."

"Stop stressing? We're about to kidnap the leader of the DATA team, my boss essentially, with the hope, and I must emphasize hope because I highly doubt she's just going to hand it over, that we can get the data we need to distribute a patch to stop the population from prematurely dying. Yeah." A strangled laugh bursts from my chest. "Not stressing should be easy."

"Do that thing," Tazib waves dismissively. "You know, that calms you down. Sing or hum or whatever it is."

The click of my teeth clamping together is audible in the quiet pod. The perfect refrains of the Composer's music is exactly what I need to hear right now, but it feels so wrong to have Tazib suggest it. Thankfully, a beep from his device saves me from having to explain my sullen silence.

"Oh, good. We're coming up on her now." Tazib waves to a glowing orb of light on the skyline. "Quick, duck down. Your head of hair is way too recognizable."

I slide off the seat and crouch on the floor as Tazib watches our pod close the gap to Libni's. As the pods align, he raises his hand in a friendly wave, but not before I see a flicker of worry cross his face.

"What's wrong?"

"She isn't alone." Tazib answers through a forced smile.

"What?!" I hiss. "You didn't think to check that before?"

The pods beep, signalling the two are fused together.

"Change of plans," Tazib says, both to me and into his device. "Ry, you handle Libni. Don't let her send a message."

Before Tazib can step across the small space to activate the door, before I even scamper to standing, the doors between the two pods open and a figure charges into Tazib with such force the pods sway violently.

My heart lodges in my throat.

It's Darr.

Darr is here, in the pod, throttling Tazib.

This can't be happening.

How is this happening?

Darr kneels on Tazib's legs, pinning him to the floor as his fists pummel Tazib's head and face. Tazib tries to protect himself but he's so small compared to Darr, he doesn't stand a chance.

"Ry!" Tazib splutters through a bleeding lip, struggling to wiggle from Darr's grasp. "Get Libni!"

I stumble to my feet, my movement distracting Darr just enough for Tazib to jerk his knee upward. Darr groans, rolling to the side and freeing Tazib.

"Move!" Tazib shouts. "Get Libni!"

I sprint into the adjoining pod. If Libni's sent a message, everything will be lost. Our plan hinged on catching her by surprise, whisking her away before she could alert anyone.

But as soon as I step into the pod, I know I'm too late. Libni stands with a communication screen open before her, as collected and calm as always even though she has to press her hand to her ear to hear over the commotion from the other pod.

"Yes," she says cooly to whomever she is speaking to, her eyes meeting mine. "I have the location of both Tazib and Rygita."

Spots dance before my eyes as I struggle to control my runaway breathing. There has to be something I can use to stop Libni, something to disrupt her call. But the simple travel pod is empty. There is only me and Libni.

"Hang up." My shaking voice lacks authority and Libni doesn't even blink, her piercing stare as intimidating as ever. I hold up my palms as I step closer. "We don't want to hurt you. All we want is a copy of the patch. That's it. Give me a copy and we'll let you go."

"You and Tazib are going nowhere," Libni says, her eyes narrowing as she looks over my shoulder. "Except perhaps a holding cell."

From the way the pods continue to sway, and the combination of grunts and heavy thuds, it's clear the struggle between Tazib and Darr continues. It takes all my willpower to resist the urge to turn to see what is happening. Darr is here. My mind keeps stalling on that fact. If we can't get what we want... What will Tazib do to Darr?

"You think I'm going down without a fight?" My whole body quivers, every sense heightened in fight-or-flight response. "You think I'm going to sit on the sidelines and watch the world die?" My voice cracks as I step closer until only Libni's shimmering screen separates us. Fear gives way to anger and desperation and I straighten my spine to match Libni's stare with my own. She's always been so intimidating, so larger than life, but now, face to face, eye to eye, I realize she's just a person.

A person who lies, betrays, and kills to get what she wants.

Libni takes a step back, like she can read my thoughts. "What are you going to do? Are you going to wrestle me to the ground and take the patch by force?"

"If I have to."

I don't think. I grab her wrist, yanking it towards my other hand. Libni pulls away, but I don't let go. Instead, I lock my fingers tighter and twist so she is pushed against the glass, my back to her stomach.

"Give it to me," I yell over the noise from the other pod.

Libni struggles against me, but she can't pull free. I'm actually stronger than her. But her erratic movements make it impossible to press my palm against hers. All my energy is spent on keeping her in one place.

"Still thinking like a child," Libni growls from behind me. "Never planning, always jumping from reaction to reaction."

I slam my weight against her, pressing her into the side of the pod. "At least I'm actually interested in helping people," I seethe. "You were the leader of DATA, a team that was supposed to protect people, but you went and took the only thing that could save us and gave it to the United People! To destroy!"

"The World Collective must fall!"

Hearing Libni raise her voice, abandoning her stoic nature, is both alarming and telling.

"And then what? The United People take over?" I twist her wrist, ignoring her cry of pain. "There'll be nothing left. Thanatos will kill everyone."

"Not everyone. The essential will survive, those we select. We'll start over. Write a new history. It's been done before."

Rage bubbles over, a dormant volcano that has been building for years. Live our stories, trust The Code, these things are necessary to survive. Years of lies. Years of rewriting the story, rewriting the truth. It needs to end. It must end.

I twist with surprising speed, grabbing both of Libni's hands and slamming them against the glass, my face inches from hers. "You don't get to decide who lives and who dies. No one should. That's why we're going to end Thanatos. No one should have that power. Ever!"

"Ry?"

All it takes is one word. One word, my name on Darr's lips, all his confusion, pain, and longing infused in that one gasp to totally disarm me.

Libni twists a hand free, swinging her elbow into my nose. I release her other hand as I bring both of mine to my face, my eyes watering and nose throbbing as blood drips between my fingers, falling in large fat drops to the pod floor. Libni shoves me back, straightening her shirt.

"Tazib is contained?"

"He's unconscious."

Through my watering eyes I'm able to make out Tazib's slumped form against Darr's legs. His face is a bloody mess, his head hanging lifeless as Darr drags him by the arm into the pod.

"Secure Rygita." Libni doesn't look at me or Darr as she moves to the pod's panel. "They've overridden the controls. We should have landed by now."

Darr steps towards me, his dark eyes a storm of emotions. "What are you doing?"

There is so much in that question. Why am I here with Tazib? How far am I willing to go? What line have I crossed if I've chosen Tazib over Darr? I see the hurt on his face, For Darr, the world is black and white, right or wrong, good or evil. My being here, now, with Tazib, means I've chosen wrong. It won't matter that it was out of necessity, or that I wanted to make sure Tazib didn't hurt Libni. All Darr will see is that I chose Tazib over him. But it isn't that easy. None of us are all good or all bad.

All these thoughts fly through my head as I pinch the bridge of my nose, but I don't get to voice any of them as, without warning, I'm thrown against the wall of the pod. Everything is a cacophony of sound: breaking glass, crunching metal, frantic shouts. Instantly, I'm taken back to that other time: the pod crash that changed my life. My screams drown out the shouts from Darr and Libni as I drop into a ball, hands over my head as I cower, waiting for the stomach-lurching drop.

But it doesn't come. Instead, a hand shakes my shoulder.

"Ry, Ry. It's okay." I'm shocked to look into Tali's wide blue eyes. "You're okay. But we have to hurry."

Wind whistles through the pod's broken glass, whipping our hair into our faces as Tali pulls me to my feet. Somehow, we're still in the air. The damaged pod's lights flicker and I scamper after Tali into the adjoining pod which appears to be less damaged. Tazib lies limp on the floor, unconscious, but I hardly notice him. Instead, my eyes are drawn to Darr. Blood runs down his cheek from a gash on his forehead and he stands with his weight on one leg, his shoulder tilted. Eldon is waving a strange metal device at him, screaming at him to raise his hands as he directs Darr into yet another pod that is joined on the other side. When the door closes, I can still hear Eldon's panicked shouts.

The lights blink off as the joined pods sway violently, sending me stumbling into the wall. "Tali!" It feels like I've been punched in the chest; I can't draw a full breath. "What do we do?"

Tali runs back into the damaged pod and climbs up to the broken window, waving her arms. My muddled brain has trouble processing the sight of yet another pod flying only a foot away, one with a large, splintering crack wicking its way across the glass. In this fourth pod, Mikom is tying Libni's feet together as she sits in one of the seats cradling her arm, her shoulder strangely misshapen. When he finishes, he takes the controls from Maisie who then, without hesitation and to my utter amazement, leaps from the open door of the pod into the broken window where Tali catches her arm and pulls her inside. Together they race back to me and the unconscious Tazib. Maisie quickly takes over the manual controls, closing the door between the pods. The second she disengages us from the damaged pod, it plummets to the earth with a deafening crash, exploding into flames and leaving a smouldering crater where there was once a perfect Unity garden.

"You're bleeding."

The front of my shirt is covered in blood and it runs hot and sticky down the back of throat. "Libni elbowed me." I pinch my nose, tilting my head back as I try to slow the flow. Out the window, I see the other pods zoom away in opposite directions as ours shoots higher into the sky. "How? What happened?"

Tali's face is white and she's as breathless as I am. "Tazib had his comms open. We could hear everything. Mikom moved so fast I was almost left behind. It was crazy. He just smashed the pod into yours. I thought for sure we were all going down."

Maisie signs to Tali and Tali nods.

"Maisie wants to know if Libni called for help."

I drop my head. I had one thing to do and I failed. "She did."

"It's okay. We're splitting up anyway, just to be safe."

My head swings to the city already growing smaller as we speed away.

"Will they be able to track us? These are WC pods."

Tali signs the question to Maisie and then translates her answer. "She says they've got a code that disables tracking, but it doesn't do any good if they have a visual."

"Meaning if they see us and follow us…"

"We'll have to out-maneuver them."

With a sinking heart, I watch what has to be at least twenty pods fanning out from the glimmering skyline. They break into three groups, each heading in a different direction, one of those being straight for us.

Maisie's face is a mask of determination. She hits a button and the pod speeds forward, throwing me off balance. I watch the glowing orbs close the gap between us with alarming speed. How are we going to lose them? We're a big ball of light flying over an endless expanse of nothing.

The pod suddenly drops, throwing me in the air with a startled scream, only to stop just as suddenly metres above the sand. Maisie's fingers fly over the keys, and when she hits a stroke, we're plunged into darkness. Then the real flight begins.

If you had told me a month ago it was possible to fly pods manually, I would have laughed. If you had told me it was possible for them to weave and loop, to change directions without hesitation, to evade and defy gravity, I would have thought you were insane. But that's what Maisie does. The ride is something from a nightmare, alternately sending me sliding across the floor, lifting me to my feet, or throwing me down. I don't know how Maisie manages to remain at the controls. Rube would probably enjoy the madness, but all I can think about is that ball of fire in the courtyard, about how little is between us and death.

Maisie directs our pod into a great chasm in the earth. We sail between solid rock walls at alarming speed, twisting around corners, and passing under natural bridges. Flying though this area should be impossible, but Maisie is pulling it off. The pods behind us aren't so lucky. Of the five chasing us, three don't even attempt to follow. The remaining two don't last long. First one and then the other crash into the earth. We don't see their pods fall to the ground, we are already around the next bend, but that doesn't stop me from imagining the terror of their occupants and I cringe at their painful deaths. When we planned to get the patch, I didn't want this. Those poor security forces where just doing their roles, serving as they were called to do. And now their deaths are on our heads.

We linger in the chasm until Maisie is confident the other pods are gone before we rise into the sky and head north. When she is sure we are safe, she opens up a line of communication with the others pods. Tali explains that she kept it silent to increase our chances of escaping, but it has been hours since we fled Unity and all three of us are more than ready to connect with Eldon or Mikom.

Tazib stirs with a groan. "What happened?" He rubs his jaw which is already turning a deep shade of purple. Both of his eyes are swollen and he squints as he looks around. "Maisie? Tali? Where's Libni?"

"She's with Mikom," I explain. "They came to rescue us."

"We had it under control." Tazib struggles to stand before swaying violently and sliding to his bottom with a moan.

"Ah, you were unconscious," I point out. "I think we both owe Mikom an apology. He totally called it. We didn't think things through."

"Hello? Hello?" A garbled voice crackles through the intercom. "You guys there?" Eldon's panicked voice cracks loudly through the pod speakers.

Maisie motions me to the panel.

"Hey Eldon, it's me, Ry. I'm with Tali, Maisie, and Tazib." I answer.

The sigh is audible despite the distortion. "You got away? No followers?"

"It took some impressive flying from Maisie, but yes. You? Are you guys alright?" The image of Darr's bloody face clouds my mind.

There's a pause before Eldon answers. "We got away."

"That's good."

"But..." The intercom crackles.

"Could you repeat that?" We all flinch as the system screeches with feedback. "Eldon?"

"Not really okay," Eldon's voice is high and squeaky.

"What happened? Did you crash? Eldon are you okay? Is Darr okay?"

"He was trying to stop me..." Eldon sounds breathless. "I had to do something. I couldn't keep control of the pod and fight him at the same time... I didn't have a choice..."

"What happened, Eldon?"

"I... He's... I shot him, Ry. I shot Darr."

CHAPTER THIRTEEN

"**Y**OU SHOT HIM? WHAT DOES THAT EVEN MEAN?**"
Tazib is translating for Maisie and the way her face drains of colour raises my alarm.

"Eldon, is he okay? Is Darr alright?"

"I…" Static interrupts Eldon's answer. "— still alive."

"Send Maisie your coordinates," Tazib instructs. "We'll come to you."

I slide to the floor of the pod, my shaking legs refusing to hold me any longer as Maisie redirects us to the west.

"What does he mean when he says he shot him?" I ask Tazib, who leans against the shelves on the other side of the pod.

"It's old tech, rather primitive, but what the Uncounted could get their hands on."

"What does it do, Tazib?"

Tazib's face is a bloody mess and I can't be sure if he winces because of the pain or because he doesn't want to answer. "Let's just say, the Uncounted's weapons aren't as neat and tidy as what they have in the Collective."

"Do you have guns?" Tali asks, her voice hardly more than a whisper. "Like the bullet kind?"

Tazib nods.

"Tali?"

"It fires a small piece of metal at high speeds into the target."

"Metal?!" My chest constricts. "Couldn't that kill someone?"

Nobody answers.

Maisie keeps the communication line open, and as we close the gap, the distortion of Eldon's transmissions lessens.

"He isn't moving." It sounds like Eldon's been crying. "I'm so sorry. I didn't want to, but he wouldn't stop."

"Eldon, calm down." Tazib seems untroubled by this turn of events. He licks his cracked lip, wincing at the taste of blood. "You did what you had to do."

"I've been calling and calling." Eldon's voice cracks painfully. "I was beginning to think I was the only one who made it. Have you heard from Mikom?"

Tazib clears his throat. "Not yet. But I wouldn't worry. He's probably out of range. And you know Mikom, he'll wait until it is safe."

"Yeah, sure."

The comm falls silent and I stare out the window at the sky that stretches impossibly huge above us. With so much chaos, there is something reassuring in the familiar stars and quarter moon.

"What's that?" Tali points to something glowing in the distance, a faint light that flickers like a beacon.

Tazib struggles to his feet to look in the direction of the flare. "It's probably nothing, a forest fire from a lightening strike or something."

"A lightening strike on a clear night?" I frown.

Maisie huffs, signing rapidly.

"Why waste time?" Tazib says, dropping again to the floor of the pod. "Besides, we should take a cue from your dad and Mikom and play it safe."

Maisie shakes her head, her eyebrows wiggling as she scrunches her face. Her signs are large and dynamic and her expressions super animated as she proceeds to argue with Tazib. It's a silent argument but for the occasional grunt or the sound of their hands slapping from the forcefulness of their signing.

"Fine," Tazib sighs. "Have it your way."

Maisie swings the pod towards the distant glow, flying us over a heavily forested land of large hills and deep valleys. As we draw near, we see there isn't one light, but many. Scattered across the area, small fires splutter and smoke, their light jumping as the blaze spreads.

"What started them?" Tali asks.

I peer into the trees of the nearest fire, my stomach sinking as I recognize the twisted remains of a pod. "Mikom flew north, didn't he?"

The anxious look on Maisie's face is answer enough.

"There's another one." Tali points to a broken tree, the shattered glass of a second pod glinting in the little moonlight.

"They're probably the remains of the pods sent to chase us. Bet they couldn't handle Mikom's skilled flying," Tazib says.

Maisie drops the pod lower, slowing us as we move from fire to fire, drawing close enough to scan the wreckage, but out of the reach of the growing flames. I don't know what we're looking for or how we'll be able to distinguish Mikom's pod from the others, but I understand the need to look. If there is any chance there are survivors, no matter who they are, we can't leave them to die alone in the wilderness. And if one of the pods is Mikom's...

Our pod lifts over a small ridge, revealing a wide swath of broken trees ending at a mighty pine. Here the moon glints off the wreckage of a pod. Little of it remains. The glass sphere has shattered into a thousand shards, and there is a gaping wound in the metal floor where the two seats were once bolted.

Landing next to these disturbing remains, Maisie is out the door before the pod has even steadied. She runs, not to the broken pod, but into the woods beyond.

Tazib shuffles to the door, his hands on his ribs. "You should follow her," he nods in the direction Maisie disappeared. "I don't think I'll be much good maneuvering that underbrush. There should be an emergency kit in the seats. I'll contact Eldon and let him know we're delayed."

I retrieve the first aid kit from the hidden compartment under the seat cushion, also collecting the flashlight and flares before cautiously climbing out of the pod. I step carefully, the ground littered with broken branches, pieces of glass, and twisted metal. I sweep the flashlight in wide arcs for any sign of survivors.

"Listen," Tali whispers, as she picks her way to me through the wreckage. "Do you hear that?" A repetitive, rhythmic beat sounds from deeper in the woods. "I think it's Maisie, letting us know where she is."

Following the sound, Tali and I move deeper into the woods. Breaking through the thick undergrowth, we find Maisie beating a stick against a tree. A dark form is at her feet, and when our flashlight illuminates it, my stomach heaves.

It's Mikom.

Or rather, what is left of Mikom.

I jerk the flashlight away as Tali claps her hand over her mouth with a startled cry.

Maisie whacks the stick against the tree again and I scowl at her. I don't know why she rushed us here when there's nothing we can do. But Maisie points with her stick to something beyond Mikom. I raise my flashlight a little higher.

Libni.

Propped against the trunk of a large tree, her chest rises and falls with laboured breaths. I pick my way around Mikom, careful not to look at his remains, but I stumble when I see Libni's hands are wrapped around a large piece of metal that protrudes from her stomach.

"Order and reason," I swear. I kneel beside her, dropping the flashlight as I fumble to open the first aid kit. It pops open, scattering the contents onto the ground.

"He... used... his... body... to shield me..." Libni gasps, her glassy eyes locked on Mikom's still form.

"Don't try to talk." I grab the roll of bandages, but freeze when I turn back to her wound. Am I supposed to pull it out? Wrap around it? All my first aid training vanishes. The only step I remember is the first: call for help. But who do I call? The World Collective would be able to handle this no problem, but it's in shambles. I suppose the

United People would have control of the medical staff, but I don't know how to contact them; and if I did, we'd have to leave Libni here alone to avoid being captured.

"Help me get her to the pod." I loop my arm under Libni's as I attempt to lift her to her feet, but she's a dead weight. She moans as I jostle her.

"We can't move her." Tali is so pale she nearly glows in the moonlight.

"We can't just leave her here to die."

Libni coughs, blood bubbling from her lips.

Maisie grabs Tali's arm, signing frantically.

"She's right," Tali says. "Libni's not going to make it. You have to get the patch before it's too late."

It seems like such a cold thing, collecting data instead of trying to save her life, but I don't know what else we can do. Libni is going to die. And if she dies before I can get the patch then all of this was in vain.

Grabbing Libni's hand, I press my palm to hers. "Libni, you have to give me the patch. Let this be your last act, a selfless one to stop the deaths."

My palm rests against Libni's cold and clammy hand. Nothing will happen until she consents to a transfer. All she has to do is think it, to want to give me the information, and it will happen. It is possible for me to retrieve it manually but it will take too much time since I'd have to open the programs running on her personal system and dig until I find the patch to copy it over. But this? If she consents, it can be done in the blink of an eye.

Libni's pulse beats weakly beneath my fingers as I wait for the brief tingle, the alert of a transfer.

But nothing happens.

"We... had... a plan..." Libni gasps. "For... the... good... of all."

"Please, Libni. Sharing the patch is for the good of all."

Libni blinks, her eyes slowly focusing on me. "I didn't mean for this to happen."

"It's okay," I murmur. "We all make mistakes. But this is a way to fix it. Come on, Libni, make the transfer."

Her face twists in pain and a tear slips free from the corner of her eye to roll down her cheek. It is the most human, most fragile, I've ever seen Libni. "I'm afraid," she breathes.

Tali crouches beside us, and though she's visibly trembling, she takes Libni's other hand. "We're here," she says with impossible kindness. "You aren't alone."

Not alone. The words heighten the Composer's music where it plays in the back of my mind. I take a deep breath and push it out slow, trying to find that calm stillness. I hum only a note, one low tone, vibrating with frustration and desperation. What am I missing? How can I get Libni to give me what we need?

Libni's hand slips from mine, falling limp in her lap. I pick it up and place it on mine again. "Please," I whisper. "You don't have much time."

"How did you survive?" Her voice is nothing more than a puff of air. "Even with all our care, you shouldn't have survived Thanatos."

I nearly groan with exasperation. Why does she keep delaying? The desire to shake her to her senses, to demand she give the patch, nearly overpowers me, but I push it down.

"I think it was the Composer," I answer, hoping speaking the truth will prompt her to do the right thing. "The one who created everything. The Composer's music pulled me back."

"Oh."

It is such a sad sound, a release of air, a moan of emptiness. A final note.

Libni's head slips to the side, her eyes no longer focused on me or anything else in the woods.

"She's gone," Tali says softly, carefully setting Libni's hand in her lap.

In the silence, the woods hum with invisible life: the song of the crickets, a distant hoot of an owl, the creak of the trees. My frustrated cry cuts them all short.

"Argg!" I shout, jumping to my feet and kicking the undergrowth. "Why wouldn't she give me the patch?!"

"She was in a lot of pain." Tali raises her hand to Libni's face, hesitating a moment before closing her eyes. "It might have been impossible for her to make that conscious choice."

"It's the simplest thing! You can make a transfer in your sleep, for crying out loud!"

"Ry."

I spin away only to be confronted with Mikom's broken body. Every part of me trembles as I watch Maisie poking around in the brush, struggling to pull two long branches through the growth. Dropping them next to Mikom, she pulls off her sweater, using it to tie the branches together in a lopsided X.

"What are you doing?"

It's too dark for Maisie to see my lips so she doesn't answer. She steps over the twisted remains of Mikom and with a determined, stoic grunt, grabs him under the arms and heaves him onto the X frame.

"Tali, what is she doing?"

Maisie moves to the other end of the X, wedging her shoulders under the frame, and awkwardly tugging it back the way we came.

"She's taking him home."

My skin crawls and my stomach rolls. I don't want to travel with that bloody mess in the middle of the too-small pod. It was already crowded with the four of us; a dead body is not a welcome addition.

But then I'm flooded with guilt. Maisie grew up with Mikom. He's her friend. A heaviness pulls at my limbs. Mikom's a husband. A father. The hole he's going to leave in Sota…

I rush to catch up with Maisie, grabbing part of the X frame. Tali is quick to join on the other side. Together, we struggle to carry Mikom though the scarred woods back to the pod.

"That's not good."

That's all Tazib says as we lift Mikom into the pod. I try to read his face, to see if he feels any sorrow, but his usual mask of indifference is firmly in place.

"Libni?" Tazib nods to the woods.

"She's dead." My eyes drop to my hands. When did they get covered in blood? Is it Libni's or Mikom's? I wipe them on my pants. "She died before I could get the patch."

"Should we…" Tali stands outside the pod, her eyes dancing everywhere but to the body on the floor. "Should we bring her too?"

I look back to the dark forest. The image of Libni's body slumped against the tree is imprinted in my brain. I shudder. "It does seem wrong to just leave her here."

"What are you going to do with her?" Tazib asks. "Take her back to the city? Bury her in Sota? I wouldn't bother."

"Is there a chance we could still get the patch off her system?" I ask.

Tazib shakes his head. "Data is stored using your natural electrical impulses. With those gone…" he shrugs. "There might be faint traces, but it wouldn't be enough for what we need."

"Oh."

"We should go," Tazib says. "Eldon's still freaking out, but I've managed to convince him to head straight for Sota."

Tali climbs into the pod and stands facing the window, careful to put as much space as possible between her and the body. Maisie returns to the controls, her fingers leaving bloody prints as she raises the pod into the sky.

I sink to the floor and cradle my head in my hands. When we left Sota, we were so sure that in a couple of hours we'd have the patch and be figuring out a way to send it to everyone. And now? Now we will return with no patch, a dead loved citizen of Sota, and another captive. Heck, we aren't even coming back in the pods we left in.

01010111 01100101 00100000 01100001 01110010 01100101 00100000 01110100 01101000 01100101 00100000

01010101 01101110 01100011 01100111 01101101 01100110 01110100 01100101 01101101 01100100 00101110

A blanket of shadow rests over the mountain community when we return, the morning sun not yet high enough to break the gloom. A small crowd waits at the edge of the clearing where Eldon's pod sits empty. I search the faces for Darr, desperate to know if he's okay, but I don't see him. I do see Eldon, practically vibrating as he shifts from foot to foot, and with him, Momma Aimee, Al, and Jolan.

Jolan and her children. Mikom's children. She holds the youngest in her arms, her cheek pressed against the child's dark hair, as the others hug her legs, their bodies tucked against her as if she will be able protect them from the coming storm.

As the pod touches down, I see there are others gathering at the edge of the landing zone. There are faces I haven't seen before, but there is something familiar about them. Understanding hits me with a pang: they all share Mikom's wide nose, dark hair, and gentle eyes. It's his family, and they know. Eldon has delivered the devastating news and Mikom's family has gathered. What I am seeing is something that would never happen in the WC. Multiple generations —parents, aunts and uncles, cousins, siblings—all standing together, clasping hands and supporting one another as the ground shifts beneath their feet.

When the doors open, Jolan breaks apart from her children, setting the youngest on the ground. With determined steps, she approaches the pod, but Maisie intercepts her, leaping from the pod and wrapping her arms around Jolan's shoulders, turning her away. Jolan struggles against her, lunging for the door, but Tali and I wordlessly move as one to stand in the way, blocking Mikom's broken body from view. Jolan's eyes lift to mine and I shake my head ever so slightly. She doesn't need to see him, not like this.

Jolan's face pales, her mouth dropping open as she sags to the ground, pulling Maisie down with her. A piercing wail rips from her lungs, echoing over the lake and mountains with soul-shattering power. In an instant, the pair are encircled by her children and

Mikom's family. Together, they kneel around Jolan's crumpled form, their own voices joining the cry of sorrow.

I reach for Tali's hand, glancing to see her face streaked with tears. We watch from a distance, unsure how to respond.

In the World Collective, death is a celebration. With The Code we had assurance we would die at the right time, and that assurance wasn't just for us, but for those around us. Why grieve if it was the right thing happening at the time it was supposed to?

But none of that took into account the heart, the way it can be so connected to another, that regardless of timing or correctness, it is rendered severed and broken by goodbye. Maybe that's why no matter how neat and tidy Mom's death was, it still hurt. It still left me with an empty hole. Jep, little Mart. All these people carried pieces of me, and with them gone...

A moan slips from my lips as all I have lost overwhelms me. The pain in my chest isn't just symbolic but real and powerful. Jolan continues to wail, and the people of the Uncounted stop what they are doing and gather around the broken woman. More and more people gather. Even Priya appears on the upper paths, working her way down with careful steps, her newborn tied to her chest and with her, Loren. When Loren's eyes meet mine over the crowd, my chest constricts and I know, I know without her saying, that Ora is gone. Thanatos killed her.

The voices of the people of the Uncounted rise together in the powerful music of grief.

And I want to be a part of it. I *need* to be a part of it.

I take a stumbling step towards the huddle. Momma Aimee raises her tearstained face and, seeing me hesitate, reaches out and grabs my hand. With remarkable strength, she pulls me to my knees, wrapping her arm around my shoulders.

"Let it out, child," she says in my ear. "All that pain and sorrow you are carrying. Set it free."

I close my eyes and raise my face to the rising of the sun, opening my mouth to release a wail that's been building for years. A pitchy, screaming, sobbing mess of a wail, full of all the emotions I've tried to contain for so long. For Mom, Jep, Ora, and Little Mart, but for me too. For being activated too soon, for learning the world isn't what I thought it was, for the fact that there are people willing to maim and kill to get what they want. I wail for all that is wrong in this cold, harsh world.

But as I release all the pain, anger, and longing, I recognize another sound carried on the cries of the Uncounted. The perfect melody is here, hidden in the sorrow, woven through the wails. It rises and falls with us, tying our voices together into something else, something more, and as I listen, the layers of music increasing, building in their variety and complexity, I am reminded.

There is plan.

A plan for good.

And I am not alone.

I am not alone. The Composer's music has told me this since the beginning, and I thought I knew what it meant. But today, here, huddled in this circle of living grief, I understand the words in a new way. I am not alone. I do not grieve alone. I do not rage against all the wrongs alone, and I am not alone in wanting—*needing*—things to change. But even more, I do not have to act alone. It isn't up to me to fix everything. Even if the cryptography key is hidden in my mind or body, it still doesn't fall to me alone to end Thanatos. Over and over I've tried. I've tried so very hard to fix things. And over and over I've failed. But maybe that's because I've tried to do it on my own. Isn't that what Mikom cautioned Tazib against?

Gradually, the wails of grief grow softer. Sobbing gives way to sniffles, low voices murmur words of love, and the people slowly shuffle to their feet. I am utterly and completely drained, but a part of me feels lighter, freer. Though my eyes are puffy, my nose drips over my lips, and I'm sure my skin is a blotchy mess, there is relief. All the mess, all the rage and grief and fear, has been given a form and edges, and for once, I feel like I'm able to contain them in a way that's manageable instead of stuffing them aside, hoping they'll fix themselves.

The crowd breaks apart, people drifting back to their homes. Seeing Momma Aimee struggling to stand, her legs stiff from the time on the cold ground, I offer her my arm. She squeezes my hands, her eyes understanding so much without asking a question.

"You best get cleaned up, you look a mess. Then straight to bed. Come back to my place this afternoon," she instructs. "We have much to discuss."

"What about Darr?" I ask, helping Momma Aimee to her door. "Is he okay?"

"Darr? Oh, you must mean the lad that was with Eldon." Momma Aimee pauses, seeing the worry on my face. "I will not lie, he was wounded, but Priya tended to him. I have no doubt he will make a full a recovery."

"Can I see him?" My heart races at the thought of facing Darr, but it's something I need to do.

"Child," Momma Aimee cups my cheek. "It can wait. He needs rest and so do you. Just look at yourself."

My eyes drop to my bloodstained shirt. Some is my own, but not all. I'm covered in dust and sweat and my limbs have started to shake as my body crashes.

"Come back this afternoon and I'll make sure you're able to see him," Momma Aimee promises.

The long climb to Al's is a feat of endurance. I will myself to take one step at a time, and then one more after that. My mind is as numb as my body, my thoughts just as sluggish. There is almost too much to think about, too many worries and images I'd rather forget, that it's a relief as my tired brain dismisses them one by one.

Only one conviction remains. I don't have to solve this on my own. I am not alone.

CHAPTER FOURTEEN

T IS LATE AFTERNOON WHEN MY RUMBLING STOMACH WAKES ME. I jump in the shower, washing the grime and evidence of failure from my skin before hurrying to dress and jog down the mountain. I have some time before I'm expected at Momma Aimee's for dinner and there are two things I need to do: see Darr, and figure out a way to get Ora's daughter, Arisu.

Reaching the grassy clearing of the landing zone, I find Eldon leaning against a pod, playing with a blade of withered grass. Seeing me, he thumps the side and Maisie emerges with grease-streaked arms.

"Have you guys seen Loren?" I ask.

Eldon shakes his head no but signs the question to Maisie. "Maisie saw Loren and Tali down by the lake."

"Great. Thanks."

I hurry down the steps that lead to the wooden pier that juts out over the clear blue lake. Despite the insanity of the last day, I haven't stopped thinking about Ora's request to protect Arisu. She's all alone on the other side of the planet, afraid and with no one to help her. Since we failed to get the patch, everything now rests on finding the crypto key, which means I need to stay here until we do. But who says I have to be the one to rescue Arisu?

Loren and Tali sit at the end of the pier, their legs dangling over the water as they hold long, thin sticks.

"What are you doing?" I ask as I near them.

"Fishing," Tali explains, patting the spot between her and Loren. "They don't farm fish here. Instead, they use these," she lifts the apparatus in her hands. "See the line? It has a hook on the end. You put a worm on the hook and the fish are supposed to bite it and get caught. Then you reel them in."

"Seriously?" I scoff. "That sounds disgusting. What do you do when you catch something?"

"I don't know," Loren laughs. "Even though Momma Aimee sends me out here once a day, I haven't caught anything. I think the fish have caught on and are steering clear," she stage whispers.

I laugh. "Then why do you stay?"

Loren shrugs. "I don't know. I wonder if Momma Aimee needs a break and wants me out of the house. Or..." Her face grows more solemn as her eyes drop to the water. "Perhaps she is giving me time. Time to think about everything that's happened."

"Were you with Ora at the end?" I ask quietly.

Loren keeps her eyes down. "I was," she says softly. "It was so different from a Thanatos celebration to see her die like that."

"I'm sorry I wasn't there. That you had to watch her on your own."

"No," Loren shakes her head. "Don't be sorry. I wasn't alone. Priya was with me and Momma Aimee too. And…" She swallows. "I wanted to be there. The idea of her being surrounded by strangers when she… You were off saving the world, it was the least I could do."

"Great job I did," I huff. "We failed, Loren. Epically."

"At least you tried." Loren looks between Tali and I. "Seriously, trying is better than doing nothing. Trust me. I know."

I eye Loren. The idea struck me the moment I woke. If I couldn't travel to Ol'Syd, who better to send than my best friend?

"Why are you staring at me like that?" Loren asks. "Do I have something on my face?" Hurriedly, she runs a hand over her cheeks.

"No, your face is fine." I smile as I grow more convinced my idea is the answer. "I actually have a favour to ask. A really, really big favour you have to say yes to."

"Okay…" Loren sets her pole aside, her eyes narrowing. "Spill."

"I need you to go to Ol'Syd."

Her eyes widen.

"I need you to find Arisu," I rush. "With Ora gone… She needs to know and she needs someone with her. There was a fire and Arisu got separated from her dorm. Ora asked me to get her, to keep her safe. I'd go, but I'm needed here. We have to find a way to stop Thanatos and my connection to the cryptography key is the only thing we have left. But you, you can go. You can help. We can't leave Arisu there all alone."

Loren stills, a frown shadowing her face. "I get it. I mean Arisu needs someone with her, especially now, but…" She looks away. "But Arisu is a kid."

"Exactly. She needs our help. She's scared and alone. Ora tried to transfer me her last known location, but it didn't work, I'm guessing since my tech was off. But I bet Arisu will be near her complex or the school."

"But Arisu is a kid," Loren repeats.

"Yeah, a kid we know, in the neighbourhood we grew up in. You know the area. You'll be able to find her and bring her back here."

"No, Ry," Loren snaps, her eyes blazing. "Don't you get it? You can't trust me with this. I *killed* Mart."

"How many times do I have to tell you it wasn't your fault?"

"And how many times do I have to tell you it *was*!" Loren shouts with a strangled cry.

"Oh, Loren." I pull my friend into my arms, muffling her sobs against my shoulder. "What happened with little Mart was terrible, something that's going to leave a mark on you for the rest of your life. But it isn't who you are." I close my eyes as I rub her back, listening for the familiar refrains of the Composer's melody. "The things that happen to us don't define us. We were made to be loved, and you are loved, Loren, you are loved so much."

Loren continues to cry, wetting my shirt. Over her bowed back, I meet Tali's eyes.

"Do you mean that?" Tali asks, picking at the sleeve of her sweater. "Do you think we were all made to be loved?"

"I do."

"Then why do we hurt so much?" A large tear rolls down her cheek.

"Come here," I instruct, making space for her at my side.

I hold my friends, hating that their hearts have been so wounded.

This isn't the life we were promised. The Code was to give us perfect lives: all our needs met, fulfilling work, a story laid before us with all the time we needed. But that's not what happened, and now we have to learn how to deal with this, how to process and move on.

"When I feel overwhelmed, I listen for the music," I whisper to my friends. "It helps me with everything. If you want, I could sing now."

Tali's head bounces on my shoulder, so I close my eyes. At first, it's hard to hear the melody, my exhaustion and the thousand thoughts competing for space and crowding my mind. So I visualize closing a door on the noise and opening the door in the wall, the one that opens to the perfect woods. There, the melody floats through the trees, a multitude of voices and instruments playing in harmony. I know the music won't erase the pain that weighs down Loren's and Tali's hearts, but I do know it is able to offer peace. Because it's in the music I hear how loved I am—a perfect love that doesn't change with circumstances—and I'm learning it's better when shared with others.

Slowly, the melodic strains wash over me, filling me with calmness, and when the words come, I open my mouth and sing.

When the storms rage,
when the floods come,
I will hold fast to you.
When the wind howls
and the sun scorches,
I will hide in your arms.
You hold me fast. You protect me.
All is yours and I won't be afraid.
No, I won't be afraid anymore.

As the last note wavers into silence, I become aware of how loudly I was singing. I'd started softly, but it was impossible not to let my voice climb, to follow the melody where it led me. The final note echoes back to me over the lake, solid and clear.

"You have a really beautiful voice," Tali says softly, pulling back. "And I don't know, there's something almost magical about listening to you." She blushes, turning away. "It doesn't make sense, a song helping, but it does."

Loren uses her sweater to wipe her face clean of tears. "I agree with Tali," she says. "That did help, a little. But I don't get who you are singing about."

"It's hard to explain because I don't totally understand myself. It's just, when I hear the music, I know someone made it. And when I listen, I hear stories in the melody. My story. It makes me realize I was made too, you know? Like someone had to create the music and that someone created me too. And composers, well, they work to get the piece of music just right. They think it out, they have a plan for how it will sound and…" I shrug, fiddling with the handle of the reel instead of meeting their eyes. "The longer I listen to the melody, the more I know—I mean really know, deep inside at my core—" I press my hands to my chest. "I know I'm a piece of music too, and the Composer, well, they're going to take care of me. You guys too."

The water laps gently against the dock supports, the late-day sun warming our faces as we sit in silence.

"I'll do it," Loren says with surprising resolution. "I'll find Arisu. I'll keep her safe."

"Really?" I spin to my friend.

Loren nods, her cheeks puffed in determination.

"Oh, Loren, you're amazing," I gush, pulling her back into a hug. "You too." I look over Loren's head to Tali. "I'm sorry for what happened with Ky. I thought I had to be the one, that everything was resting on me, but I was wrong. We all have something to offer, a part to play in all of this. I'm going to work on remembering that."

Tali's red-rimmed eyes drop to her wrist, her dark hair falling across her face.

"So, what do we need to do?" Loren asks. "How do we get me to Ol'Syd?"

"Eldon and Maisie were with the pods in the clearing," I answer, getting to my feet and pulling Loren up beside me. "We ask them."

We make our way up the steep flight of stairs to find Maisie still working on the two pods we used to flee Unity.

"Are these pods okay to fly?" I ask, eyeing the abandoned parts scattered around Eldon.

Maisie nods, her fist bobbing up and down, one of the few signs I understand.

"Can Loren use one to get to Ol'Syd?"

"Why?" Maisie questions through Eldon.

"I'm going to help a kid," Loren answers. "Ora's kid."

"I heard she passed," Eldon says softly. "Didn't know she had a kid."

"Well, she did. And now her kid's all alone. I'm going to get her."

Maisie looks at Loren with respect, signing slowly so she can understand.

"Thanks," Loren's expression is grim.

Eldon activates the door of the pod, stepping inside with Loren.

"This is a good pod for you to take," he says. "Maisie hasn't completely converted it yet so you won't have to fly it manually."

"Manually?" Loren's eyebrows arch. "No way. This thing better fly itself."

"No worries." Eldon grins. "Maisie will get it ready for you. Where about in Ol'Syd do you want to go?"

Loren and I agree that the best place to start looking for Arisu will be around her dorm and school so we get Maisie to program the pod to drop her at the closest station.

"How will we get back?" Loren asks. "There's no way to make sure I get the same pod and I don't know our location."

"And it's going to stay that way," Eldon says, looking around the clearing with a nervous glance. "Al will kill us if we give you that information. Why don't you just stay there in Ol'Syd?"

"What?" Loren snaps. "Stay? Have you forgotten what's happening? The world's imploding! It isn't safe, not to mention I'm a wanted criminal. I helped Tazib escape, the world's worst terrorist!"

"But he's not a terrorist." Eldon's cheeks flush. "That's just what the WC wanted you to think."

"Does it matter?" Loren snarls, taking a step towards Eldon, her fists clenched and her face almost as red as his. "It still isn't safe."

"But it keeps this safe." Eldon takes a step back, waving to the mountain community.

"So I'm just supposed to start a new life, in a fallen society, with a kid, all by myself?!"

"Hold on, Loren." I reach for my friend, holding her shoulders and willing her to calm down. "It isn't a bad idea—" When Loren huffs, I hurry to continue. "You find Arisu and lay low until we find a way to stop Thanatos. Then, when things settle, we find a way to get you both back, either to here or Unity."

"Um... are you forgetting the fact that I broke you out of a secure holding facility?!" Loren shakes with fury. "You know what kind of consequences that carries? Because I do!"

"But Loren, the WC has no way of knowing you were involved. And besides, you aren't heading back to Unity. You're going to Ol'Syd. No one's going to be looking for you there."

Tali hugs herself against the cold mountain wind. "From the sounds of it, things are so bad, I doubt anyone's looking. The World Collective has fallen. I bet you could scan like normal and nothing would happen."

"Speaking of scanning..." I turn back to Eldon and Maisie. "Loren will need to be reconnected."

"No, no way!" Eldon's voice squeaks. "Reconnecting Loren, here, in a hidden community... Al says we have to be at least 200 kilometres away before we connect."

"But I can't do anything if I'm disconnected." Loren straightens to her full height. "How will I find Arisu?"

Maisie rolls her eyes. *You WCers are so dependent on your tech. You use your eyes and your brain*, she signs.

I stretch a calming hand towards the heat radiating off Loren. "She will need to be connected if she doesn't want to draw attention to herself. You can't even open doors without tech within the Collective."

Eldon groans. "Fine, you're right. You can't live within the Collective without being connected," he signs to Maisie. "It's why

Tazib had to give me implants."

"So?" Loren crosses her arms over her chest, her hands still balled into fists. "Will you reconnect me or not?"

Eldon sighs but pulls a familiar device from his coat pocket, running it over Loren's wrist. "If Al kills me, this is on your head," he mutters. "There, you're all set."

And the pod is good to go, Maisie signs, closing a panel with a bang.

Loren straightens, her tiny chin jutting forward as her brow furrows.

"You got this." I pull my oldest friend into my arms. "You can find Arisu and keep her safe because you're amazing."

"I know it," she laughs awkwardly, pulling away. "Ry, just promise you'll stop Thanatos. I don't want to drop dead on the other side of the world. Okay?"

"Promise."

01010111 01100101 00100000 01100001 01110010 01100101 00100000 01110100 01101000 01100101 00100000

01010101 01101110 01100011 01101111 01110101 01101110 01110100 01100101 01100100 00101110

Maisie returns to working on the remaining pod while Tali and I watch Loren's pod grow smaller until it disappears over the far mountains.

"Al is going to kill us," Eldon mutters, returning to his spot on the ground where he plucks another blade of grass.

"I'm sure it will be fine," I say. "Especially when he understands it's to save an innocent kid."

"Wait, Al doesn't know, like at all?" Eldon looks up from his mangled piece of grass, his eyes wide. "I assumed you had permission to take a pod. Oh man, oh man," he mutters, shaking his head. "I don't like secrets."

"It's not a secret," I reassure. "I'll tell them at dinner."

Other than my empty stomach, dinner is not a welcome thought. Momma Aimee and the others will be looking for a recounting of what happened in Unity and I do not look forward to reliving that failure.

"Hey, do you know where I can find Darr?" I ask, changing the subject. "I'd like to see him before we eat. Make sure he's really okay, you know?"

Eldon groans, covering his face with shaking hands. "I'm sorry, alright. I didn't know what to do."

"It's fine, Eldon. Momma Aimee told me he's going to recover. I just need to see him."

"Priya said he's in the lab," Tali says. "It's where they have the best equipment so it kinda doubles as a healing centre when they need it."

"Thanks, Tali."

I waste no time sprinting to the mountain base. It's hard to tell if my heart pounds because of the run or because I'm about to see Darr. Darr, the guy I absolutely fell for and the same guy who betrayed me and got me arrested.

Heaving the heavy door open, I dash into the large lab where I am met with a low, guttural groan. Racing around the jumbled assortment of equipment, I pull up short.

Tazib has Darr connected to MEMORY.

CHAPTER FIFTEEN

DARR DOES NOT LOOK OKAY. THE BLOODY REMAINS OF HIS TORN shirt exposes a swath of white bandages covering his lower abdomen. Sensors are attached to his chest, fingers, and forehead, but I don't need to look at the monitors to know he's in trouble—his ashen skin and rapid breathing show that plainly. Darr's head rolls to the side, another moan slipping from his lips.

"Darr," I gasp.

Tazib spins from his screen with a start, squinting at me through swollen eyes. "Ry. What are you doing here? Shouldn't you be with everyone else?"

I step closer to Darr, noting the sweat on his upper lip, the sporadic twitching of his closed eyes, the bruised cheek and split lip.

"What are you doing?!"

Tazib turns back to his screen. "Just checking his memories, seeing if there's anything useful."

"Did Momma Aimee ask you to do this?" I bristle. "And where is Priya? She should be here, watching the monitors, making sure he's okay!"

"Momma Aimee," Tazib scoffs. "No, she didn't send me. She'd rather sit at The Table. We all join at The Table, we all share the burdens together,'" he mimics. He hits a key and Darr cries out, thrashing violently against the straps that bind his hands to the metal panels.

"Stop," I gasp, horrified. "This can't be normal." I wave at the monitor showing Darr's vitals.

"What do you know about normal?" Tazib mutters, continuing to tap keys. "Look, I know it looks bad, but I'm doing the hard things. The others won't use MEMORY on him. They'll want to question him in a civilized manner." He rolls his eyes. "A waste of time. This way we get the whole story—no lies, no twisting the truth—and we get to see it all in a matter of minutes. Honestly, there are times I wished Uncounted citizens had tech so we could use this on them. It's much more efficient."

Darr's breathing has grown erratic and his chest heaves. Around us, alarms beep, warning of the strain on Darr's heart.

"Tazib stop. You're hurting him."

"I may be pushing things a bit fast," Tazib shrugs. "But he's strong. He can handle it."

"Look at him! He's NOT okay!"

Tazib barely glances at the screen that shows Darr's racing heart and dropping blood pressure. "Darr was with Libni. He probably has inside knowledge of what's happening with the United People. We might find something that can help people."

Darr thrashes as more monitors begin to beep.

"Turn it off," I growl.

Tazib shakes his head. "You know, I don't think I will. There's some good stuff inside Mr Dimple's head. A lot about you. You'd see his true thoughts a lot clearer if you come stand by me."

"Turn it off!"

"Mikom's dead because of him!" Tazib yells, his swollen face contorting. "If it wasn't for him it would have worked and we'd have the patch!"

"This isn't his fault! Stop it, Tazib!"

Tazib doesn't move from his screens.

Desperate to do something, I struggle to unbind Darr's hands from the panels.

"I wouldn't do that," Tazib mumbles.

Pulling the restraints aside, I slide Darr's limp hands off the plates. Instantly Darr stills, his body suddenly calm, but the monitors continue to alarm.

"What's wrong?" I reach for Darr's hand, feeling his racing pulse under my fingers. "Why isn't he waking up?"

Tazib sighs. "You can't just snap someone out of MEMORY. There's a sequence to bring them back to the present."

"Why didn't you say that?!" Panic floods me and I reach for Darr's face. Though his eyes are closed, I see the rapid movement behind the lids. His skin is slick with sweat. "What do we do?"

"I don't know," Tazib shrugs. He begins turning off the screens. "Lost all that great data I was retrieving. What a waste of time."

"Wait!" I grab at his arm. "Help him!"

"I already said I don't know how." Tazib pulls his arm free, brushing his sleeve back into place. "My expertise lies in the technical side. You need someone like Priya." He moves to the exit.

"Where are you going?!"

"I expect Momma Aimee is waiting for us. She'll want an update on what happened in Unity." Tazib pulls open the lab door and raises a hand in a wave. "Good luck," he says, then disappears.

A frustrated scream bursts from my chest as I swing back to Darr. Though he's stopped thrashing, the muscles in his neck bulge, his hands clench and unclench at his sides, and his chest continues to heave like he can't catch a full breath. Thanks to my years spent in healing centres, I know Darr is in serious trouble. The amount of stress on his heart... He needs help, and fast.

I search the room for some way to notify the others. Darr needs Priya. If I were back in the WC I would use my personal system to alert the others in seconds.

Darr moans softly and I cradle his face as I lean in, aware of his shallow breath on my cheek. "Hold on, Darr. Keep fighting. I'm working on it."

My eyes drop to my wrist and the useless tech embedded under my skin.

Wait. Is it useless, or simply disconnected?

The alarms fade into the background as my mind races. Tazib has repeatedly used WC tech, both when we were attempting to rescue Ky and in our mission to Unity. How did he explain it? Something about using the local signals instead of the network? So maybe, maybe there is a way I can use my dormant tech to get help by contacting Tali.

I pull away from Darr and hurry to open a screen, spreading my hands wide so it hovers in front of me. When Eldon said he turned everything off, I didn't bother looking to see what I could and couldn't do, but now I see many systems remain untouched, like my personal music and other features that connect occasionally to the WC interface but are capable of running separately. Unfortunately, sending a message to another person is not one of those features. But that doesn't mean I can't get into the background of the programs. Even with my little time working with DATA, I've amassed more skills than the average citizen. I'm sure there's a way to send an SOS to Tali.

It's a struggle to remember the needed commands, my attention distracted by the frantic thought that this isn't enough. Maybe I should run to Momma Aimee's or try to find Priya. Maybe I should restart the MEMORY system and try to pull Darr out that way. But neither idea sits right. I won't leave Darr alone, and all of my MEMORY experiences have been on the wrong side to be of any use. So I continue to work furiously, cursing when my shaky hands fumble the commands.

But it works. Tali's confused face shimmers into focus before me. The relief that floods through me is short lived when I look back at Darr's monitors.

"Ry? What? How did you contact me?"

"I need help," I rush. "I'm in the lab. It's Darr. Tazib was using MEMORY on him and now something's wrong. Hurry!"

Tali's eyes widen as she looks up. "You used MEMORY on Darr?"

Voices rise in anger and there's no mistaking Al's swearing.

"We're coming," Tali promises, the camera bouncing as she runs. "Just hold on."

01010111 01100101 00100000 01100001 01110010 01100101 00100000 01110100 01101000 01100101 00100000

01010101 01101110 01100011 01101111 01101101 01101110 01110100 01110100 01100101 01100101 01101100 00101110

Maisie is the first to arrive. She bursts into the room and heads straight for the computers Tazib turned off only moments ago. Tali and Eldon arrive next, hurrying to restart the MEMORY system following Maisie's signed instructions.

"What should I do?" Their drawn faces and hurried actions only tighten the heaviness in my chest.

"Get his hands on the plates," Eldon says. "And try not to worry. Al went to get Priya. She'll know what to do."

Jolan arrives next and she moves to the computer Mikom used when I was hooked up to MEMORY. Tali joins me, holding my hand as the other three move around us in a fluid dance, double checking the sensors on Darr's chest, reviewing the computer's data, and confirming his racing pulse with their own hands.

"Tell me what happened," Priya demands when she arrives, breathless, and with her new baby strapped to her chest with a long piece of purple cloth.

"I found Tazib using MEMORY on him," I explain. "Darr was groaning and thrashing. I told Tazib to stop but he wouldn't so I took Darr's hands off the plates." My chest tingles. "I didn't know. I didn't know it would hurt him. I thought it would make it stop."

Priya gives my shoulder a squeeze. "It's not your fault," she says. "Tazib is responsible for this. Not you." She bustles over to Maisie's screen, her hand on her infant. "What do you see?"

Maisie signs and Priya nods. "Okay. We need to walk him back to the present. Do you know how to do that?"

Maisie shakes her head. Priya looks to Eldon and he too shakes a no.

Priya blows out a long breath, her eyes jumping to Jolan, and I know. We need Mikom. He was the expert. Without his expertise... Spots dance in front of my eyes. This can't be happening. We might lose Darr and there's nothing I can do about it. If only I knew more about MEMORY. If only Mikom hadn't crashed. If only...

My trembling body slumps onto a stool as my vision blackens, my breathing raspy. Not again. I can't do this again.

Do you see?

You are not alone

The melody is faint, hardly audible over the screaming monitors and my pounding heart, but it is enough to pull me from my panic. Do I see? That I'm not alone? I look up, blinking as my eyes struggle to focus. The others move around Darr's still form, doing everything they can to save him, their faces drawn but determined. They may lack the experience needed, but they are not giving up. So why should I? And who says I have to be the one to save Darr?

"Aliah," I gasp, jumping to my feet. "Aliah was there, when I crashed in MEMORY the first time."

Jolan glances at me with a sad shake of her head. "Isn't that the girl you said we shouldn't trust? The one you insisted we lock up?"

"Yes." My cheeks burn. A part of me still doesn't trust Aliah, but right now she's our best chance of saving Darr. "Aliah's smart, really smart. She'll know how to help. I'm positive."

"Run and get her," Priya nods to the door. "We'll try to get him stabilized."

I sprint from the room, racing down the long tunnel to the holding cell. An older man is lounging in the armchair outside the wooden door, a mug of cold tea on the floor. He looks up from his book and rises to his feet before I even reach him.

"Based on that face I say something's wrong and you need me to open the door."

"Yes," I pant. "I need to take Aliah with me."

He doesn't hesitate to fish a key from his pocket. I'm stunned at his willingness: no calling to confirm with a leader, no requesting of data, he just simply takes me at my word.

The second the door is unlocked, I shove it open so hard it bangs into the wall. Aliah jumps to her feet, her hands wrapped in a long necklace of black and white beads.

"Ry." She looks from the beads to me, her eyes wide. "I meant to tell—"

"Is that my mom's necklace?"

She unwinds the long strand, thrusting it at me. "I took it from your room after... I was going to give it back," she blurts.

I grab the necklace, balling it in my fist. "You have to come, now. Darr's in trouble."

I don't wait to see her reaction. I'm already turning back to the lab. My anger at finding her with my necklace is nothing compared to my worry for Darr, and from the sound of Aliah's shoeless feet slapping on the cement floor as she chases after me, I can tell she understands this is serious.

Reaching the lab, my gut sinks when I see a defibrillator has been pushed next to Darr's still form. Tali trembles in a corner.

Aliah pauses only for a moment, taking in the scene with

remarkable calmness, before joining Jolan at her computer. "He was interrupted?"

Jolan hesitates, glancing at me with scepticism.

"Tell her," I insist. "She won't hurt Darr."

"Yes, he was interrupted," Jolan answers Aliah's question. "He's stuck reliving one of his worst memories. We keep trying to pull him out, but it isn't working."

"May I?" Aliah motions to the computer and Jolan gives up her seat, watching as Aliah opens a new screen and begins reviewing the information.

I'm torn between wanting to return to Darr's side and finding a screen of my own. There must be some way I can help.

The Composer's music.

It hits me like a fist. Each time I've been lost in MEMORY, it was the flawless music of the forest that brought me back. Why didn't I think of it sooner? I hurry to Darr's side, reaching for his palm, pressing mine tight against it. I close my eyes to the chaos of the alarming monitors and shouts of commands, quieting my racing mind as I listen for the melody. Not the faint notes that play in the back of my mind, but the whole thing in all its perfect completion.

It isn't easy. I can hear the strains whispering at the edge of my consciousness, but when I try to pull them forward, to join my voice with them, I am sidelined by the memory of Mikom's broken body, Libni's face twisted in pain, Tazib's disregard for others, my worry for Loren and Arisu.

"Rygita, you need to move."

I open my eyes to find Priya across from me, her face pale. "Let go of his hand," she says, holding two paddles at the ready. "We need to shock him."

I stumble back in a stupor, watching as Priya touches the paddles to Darr's smooth skin. His chest leaps from the bed, his back arched unnaturally, before dropping back, limp and unmoving.

The world slows around me. This can't be happening. Darr will be alright. He has to be alright. We need more time. It can't end like this.

As Priya shocks Darr again, I continue to back away from the couch, away from the circle of computers, the push of bodies scrambling to save Darr's life. I back away until I hit the wall and then I slump to the ground, pulling my knees to my chest. I bury my face in my hands, desperate to stop seeing Darr's lifeless body crash again and again on the bed, the flat line on the monitors unchanging.

CHAPTER SIXTEEN

"**H**E'S BACK!" PRIYA CHEERS WITH RELIEF. "AND HIS VITALS are returning to normal. Now, let's see if we can bring him out."

I raise my tear-stained face, my heart leaping along with the steady blip on Darr's monitors.

"You're sure he's stable?" Aliah asks.

"As stable as he's going to be while still under MEMORY," Priya answers. She shakes her head. "He should never have been placed under so soon after the trauma of being shot."

"He was shot?" Aliah's glare is withering. "Why would anyone shoot him?"

Eldon twists his hands, cracking his knuckles. "It was me. He was so much bigger and I didn't know how to restrain him," he rushes. "Tazib told me to use this if I was ever in an extreme emergency." He pulls a strange metal device from where it was tucked into the back of his pants. "I didn't know… I didn't want to hurt him… I just panicked."

Aliah frowns at the data on her screen, her lips a thin line of determination and her nose scrunched in concentration. "No wonder he crashed. His body was already too stressed."

"We need to get him out." Priya continues to monitor Darr's vitals. "Can you do it?"

Aliah blows a long breath. "I think so. But if I'm honest, I don't know for sure."

"Jolan, what do you think?" Priya asks.

Jolan stands behind Aliah, watching her work. "It looks good to me," she says. "But it's beyond my knowledge. I say it's Aliah's call."

"Wait, what?" I jump to my feet, hurrying back to Darr's side. "Why is it her call?"

Jolan sighs and rubs the bridge of her nose. "It's her call because she's the one with the knowledge. It's her call because she is a fellow WC citizen, one who worked with him."

"But—"

"If we make the call and something goes wrong it will be on our heads. Leaving the decision to Aliah places the responsibility for his life in the right hands."

"What about me?"

Priya takes my shoulders, her tired eyes finding mine. "Do you want that responsibility?" she asks. "When you don't know how MEMORY works and aren't able to check what Aliah's doing?"

"I…"

I look past Priya to where Aliah is double-checking her work. In my balled fist, the beads of Mom's necklace cut into my palm. I don't like Aliah, I never have, but am I going to continue holding a grudge when it could cost Darr his life? Aliah is capable and she would never hurt Darr intentionally. The whole time we've been working on DATA, Darr and Aliah have always gotten along. If I'm honest, Darr and Aliah's friendship has been way more consistent than my relationship with him. She has every reason to want to save him. Because the thing is, Darr is a really good friend. To me, to Tali, to Hyll, and Rube. And Aliah.

"It's your call, Aliah," I say softly.

Aliah meets my eyes and I hate the fact she can see how much this costs me—no doubt she'll find some way to gloat in the future—but it's worth it if she can save Darr.

"Okay," Aliah says, turning to her screen. "Here it goes." She takes a deep breath and hits enter.

The room falls silent but for the beep of the monitors. I untangle Mom's necklace and drape the long strand over my head, running my fingers over the familiar beads as I lock my eyes on Darr, watching the twitching of his lids and the shallow rise and fall of his chest.

"It's working!" Aliah exclaims. "He's coming back."

The others continue to monitor the progress from their screens and devices, but I watch only Darr. I note the colour returning to his cheeks, the way his rigid body slowly relaxes, and the evening of his breathing. I'm the first to see when his eyes flutter open.

"Where..." Darr's voice cracks and he licks his lips, his forehead puckering as he looks around in confusion. "Where am I?"

Priya is the closest to the makeshift couch and she places a hand on his shoulder. "Try to stay calm," she croons. "You've been hurt, but you're safe now."

"Don't touch me!" Darr jerks away from her, rolling off the couch. He groans, his hand finding the wound on his side. "What? What have you done to me?" He grabs at the sensors, pulling them from his skin as his voice grows louder. "What were you doing to me?"

"Please," Priya steps in front of Darr, her hands raised. "You are safe—"

"Let me go!" Darr yells, shoving Priya aside. She falls hard, her hands wrapped protectively around the infant strapped to her chest.

Like the flip of a switch releasing a jolt of electricity down a wire, the reactions roll through the lab, growing in intensity. Jolan rushes to help Priya as Darr lurches towards the door, his eyes wild with fear. His unsteady steps send him crashing into the defibrillator cart and he swears as he tries to right himself.

"Stop," Eldon yells over the wail of the baby, his voice pitching painfully as he fumbles for the weapon tucked into his pants. Seeing the gun, Aliah cries out a warning, grabbing at Eldon's arm and sending the device skittering across the floor.

Do something! my brain screams while my body remains frozen, watching as Eldon drops to his belly to scramble after the gun and Darr continues to knock over equipment as he storms for the exit. I manage a startled cry when Maisie sprints forward, tackling Darr around the middle and sending them both crashing to the ground. Darr is quick to twist, pinning Maisie beneath him as he grabs her wrists, bending them backwards. When she cries out in pain, he gives a frustrated yell before shoving her aside, staggering back to his feet, and charging again for the door.

"Watch out!" Aliah cries, jumping between Darr's exposed back and Eldon who waves the gun with shaking hands and a face flushed red. Tali screams.

I don't hear the shot, but I see its impact. Aliah's shoulder slams backwards and her face drains of colour. She slumps to the floor with a piercing cry of pain. Darr turns, and seeing the blood seeping between Aliah's fingers, his panic transforms to rage.

"You!" he shouts, barrelling towards Eldon.

"No, stop!" Finally my body responds to my commands and I leap between the pair, aware of the weapon still clutched in Eldon's trembling hands. "Darr. It's alright." I raise my hands, hoping my familiar face and soft voice will break through his fog of terror. "It's me, Ry. It's going to be okay."

"Ry?" All his fight vanishes. His eyes cloud with confusion as he looks between me and Aliah. "Ry, what have you done?" Darr's face falls slack, his eyes roll back into his head, and he sags to the ground, out cold.

"I have half a mind to throw you in the lake—with large boulders strapped to your ankles!"

Tazib sits on the couch before Al, his chin held high though he winces with each thunderous word Al spits.

"Calm down, Al," Momma Aimee says from her spot by the fire. She rubs her eyes, her wrinkled hand quivering. "We're not going to drown the boy."

After Darr collapsed in the lab, Priya hurried to give him a mild sedative to avoid a second disastrous waking. Checking he was stable, she moved him to the holding cell where Tali volunteered to stay with him until he wakes, confident the sight of a friend will calm Darr enough for her to explain where he is and what has happened.

I marvel at Tali's conviction. I wish I could be so sure of Darr's reaction. If I was, maybe I would have gone with her. But the truth is, the moment Darr's eyes found mine, I was suddenly aware of how things must appear to him. We *attacked* him. There is no other way to define what happened in the pods above Unity. Worse, what's going to happen when Darr learns Libni's dead? I knew Libni was working for the United People, but Darr didn't—his memories were changed. He believed Libni was one of the few people who had any power to stop the madness that's thrown the world into turmoil. When he hears that Libni is gone it will only cement his thinking that I've chosen wrong.

"Tazib needs to learn a lesson!" Al's signing only accentuates his rage. "We've been too lenient with him! He thinks he's above everyone, acting without thought to the consequences: to himself, to others, to this community!"

I watch Tazib's verbal beating from the table with Eldon and Maisie, where loaves of bread and pans of roasted vegetables sit forgotten. Aliah is with us. Priya says she was lucky, the bullet only grazed her upper arm, and after carefully tending to her wound, Priya insisted Aliah came with us to Momma Aimee's. It seems fair. She did save Darr's life. Twice.

"I've helped this community." Tazib straightens his spine, but he still looks small in Al's shadow. "You were starving and dying of preventable causes before me. Sure, maybe I push things a bit far, but I make things happen!"

"You-You—" Al looks like he's ready to strangle Tazib.

"Your disregard to the well-being of others is concerning," Momma Aimee says. "And I fear we've allowed you to run unchecked for too long. What you have done—"

"It needed to be done."

"—shows you are nothing more than an impulsive, dangerous teen with no common sense and no human decency."

"One who has gotten more done in four years than your community has in a hundred!"

"You nearly killed the boy."

"But he's not one of us," Tazib shouts. "So what if he dies? He's on the other side."

Anger bubbles in my gut, hot and bitter. There have been moments since arriving in Sota when it was almost possible to believe Tazib was like any other teen. Hurt and angry and prone to making bad decisions, but at the heart, just trying to do the right thing. But now…

I shoot up from my chair and cross the small space so swiftly there's no time for anyone to react, least of all Tazib. I slap him, the sound louder than the impact, so startling it shocks the room into silence.

Tazib sits stunned, a red print rising on his cheek while I stand before him, my hands balled at my sides.

"Darr is the kindest, most thoughtful person on the planet." My voice quivers. "All he's ever wanted is to do the right thing, to serve in the role he's assigned, and to help others. It's not his fault if he's on the wrong side. A year ago, no one in the World Collective would have thought things were broken. And now that we do see, we can't change overnight. You... You nearly killed him. Who are we doing this for?" I fling my arms, motioning to the bigness of what I'm trying to say. "Isn't it for people like Darr? Those still in the WC who don't know, who are going to die if we don't stop Thanatos?" I meet Tazib's eyes, my voice dropping. "I'm trying to believe everyone is worth saving—even you, Tazib—but I won't let you hurt any more of my friends. You either change, apologize to Darr, or we do this without you. Because I see you, Tazib, you want everyone to think you're so smart, that you're the only one who can save the day. But you're wrong. We can do this without you. You aren't needed."

Those words—*you aren't needed*—seem to strike the strongest blow. Tazib rocks back, sucking in the tiniest of breaths, blinking through swollen eyes.

"Well," Momma Aimee heaves herself to her feet. "I think that settles it. Tazib, you are dismissed. Head back home. I'm sure Al has some chores to keep you busy."

"You bet I do," Al grumbles. "Firewood to be chopped and stacked, a kitchen that needs a deep-cleaning, and laundry, you can do everyone's, for the next week—no, month."

"Come, the rest of you, we need to eat and talk." Momma Aimee takes her spot at the table, settling with a tired sigh.

Tazib remains frozen on the couch before he shakes himself and stands. "You can't just kick me out," he says. "You need me. To stop Thanatos."

Momma Aimee doesn't look his way as she takes a large knife and begins slicing the loaves.

"What, you're just going to ignore me?" Tazib's voice rises, but it lacks its usual confidence. Instead he sounds whiney. "You *need* me," he repeats.

Al gives Momma Aimee a look, but with a subtle nod of her head, he remains quiet. Tazib blusters a bit longer before storming from the house, slamming the door so hard a frame falls from the wall.

"You think it wise?" Al asks. "Letting him wander around unsupervised?"

"Eldon, run and let the others know Tazib is being reprimanded." Seeing my confusion, Momma Aimee explains. "He won't be allowed back in the lab or any other important areas." She waves us over to the table. "We are all worn. Let's eat as we talk. Jolan, if you want to join your family..."

"No," Jolan shakes her head, her eyes shining despite the exhaustion written on every feature. "I need to know what is happening. I need to know what Mikom died for."

Momma Aimee nods and begins passing the still-warm bread around the table.

"I can't believe I slapped him," I mutter as I take a seat. "I've wanted to, so many times, but..." I shake my head.

"It was about time someone put him in his place," Al mutters.

When everyone is served, Momma Aimee leans back in her chair. "Normally, we eat and then open The Table for discussion, but under the circumstances, I think we should keep things moving." She butters her bread as she talks. "Eldon wasn't the best communicator when he returned, but from the state of things, I understand your trip to Unity was a failure."

Hearing it put so bluntly is painful. I slouch in my seat, shame heating my face as I nod. "That's right. Tazib and I tried to intercept Libni's pod, but we didn't know she wasn't alone. Darr..." I stutter to a stop, a tremble shaking through me. "Mikom saved us," I swallow. "We got split up when we were chased. His pod crashed. He tried to protect Libni when they went down, but... it wasn't enough. I wasn't able to get the patch from her before she died."

Aliah sucks in a breath as Al curses.

"All that risk for nothing."

"Al," Momma Aimee warns, glancing at Jolan who stares into the empty space before her, her food untouched. "Not now." She balances her bread on the edge of her bowl. "What's done is done. In light of these events, I believe we should abandon the idea of attempting to find a patch."

Maisie signs and Momma Aimee shakes her head. "When you were away, Priya, Jolan, and I went through all the data we collected from Rygita." She looks at me and the sympathy in her eyes erases what remains of my hunger. "First, I have to thank you for letting us look so closely at your memories. I promise those of us who saw them will hold them in confidence." She takes a steadying breath. "Unfortunately, we didn't find anything."

I stare at my steaming bowl, blinking as I try to process. "Nothing?" My voice is hardly more than a whisper. "But Tazib was so sure."

"I'm sorry," Momma Aimee says. "You did have secrets buried in your memories, the truth about the accident, and your father's involvement in covering it up, but there was nothing that could help stop Thanatos."

My chest squeezes as I raise my head, feeling, more than seeing, all eyes on me. Momma Aimee's chair squeaks as she shifts her weight, her raspy voice halting as she speaks. "We discussed it at length, what was driving Tazib's belief that you held the answers. What happened to him as a child, it left more than physical scars. The boy was cut off from all he knew, a living ghost. When he arrived, well, we did our best, but he never truly belonged. A part of him will always be a citizen of the WC. I suspect you became his link, his way back to his old self. That drove his obsession, his conviction that you were the answer. It became his reason to make contact with you, to bring you here."

I drop my eyes back to the table, worried my thoughts play out on my face. How long have I suspected the same thing? Sure, Dad admitted I have genetic ancestors who were involved in the creation of The Code, but did I ever truly believe I carried the key? Didn't I know all along it was wishful thinking? Irrational hope in the impossible miracle that maybe, just maybe, I could fix it all and save those I love.

"So, what now?" I ask. "How do we stop Thanatos?"

The table stills around me, a subtle shift in the energy of the room.

"Now you live out the days you have been given."

Momma Aimee's words are certain and final. It is like that moment when you turn off a screen, one second there is light and data, and the next—nothing. Everything fades but the rise and fall of my chest.

"Thanatos is unstoppable," Momma Aimee continues. "Those who carry its programming must be resigned to its fate. It is a dark and terrible evil, but one we cannot fight."

"I'm afraid I agree," Priya says, looking at the old woman instead of me. "I motion we allow these youth to return to their communities if they wish. We should not force them to spend their last days here."

"What about the risk of them revealing our location?" Al asks.

"I doubt they have the resources or time to do us much damage," Priya answers.

"Then it is decided?"

There is a murmur of agreement.

That's it? They give up? There's nothing else to try? A familiar fire burns in my chest. How can they expect me to quietly live out the days I have been given? How can they ask me to sit back and watch all those I love die years before their time?

"No." My hands shake as I set them on either side of my bowl, pushing myself to my feet. "No. I can't do that. We can't do that. There has to be another way. Something else we can try." My mind scrambles for a solution. "We find someone else with a patch, we hack the database and find a copy, there has to be something we haven't tried!"

"The Uncounted will help you get back to Unity," Momma Aimee says. "What you do after that is up to you."

"But you won't continue to help us?" I slump against the table. "You drop us off and wash your hands of the whole thing?"

"Child, we have tried to help, but the cost was too great. There is nothing more we have to offer."

I fall back into my chair, my mouth agape. "What about all that stuff you said before? About helping your fellow man?"

"The Table has decided."

"The Table?!" Heat rushes to my face. "This isn't some decision about chores or where someone lives! We're talking about the life of every citizen of the World Collective! It isn't something some table with a handful of 'special' people get to decide. This is when you need to consider all voices: mine, Tali's, heck, even Aliah's. We should have a say!"

"No," Momma Aimee states, her voice ringing with calm authority. "Not in the involvement of the Uncounted. You are not one of us, and you don't know us. The Uncounted have survived this long because we have been careful. We do not take unnecessary risks. I'm sorry." Momma Aimee reaches across the table for my hand, but I pull away from her touch. "If there was something we could do we would, but this is beyond us. We will bury our dead and mourn the lost. This is our way."

CHAPTER SEVENTEEN

THE CONVERSATION CONTINUES AROUND THE TABLE AS the adults plan how to transport Tali, Darr, Aliah, and I back to Unity, but I don't hear much of it. I can't believe they've given up. There has to be something else we can try.

When the meal finally ends, Aliah is sent with us to Al's. She hangs back as we trudge up the mountain, watching Eldon and Maisie's signed conversation with a quirked brow. Reaching the small house, Maisie leads us to her room before disappearing to find more pillows and blankets.

"So, Libni's dead."

It's the first Aliah has spoken since everything happened in the lab. I drop onto the window bench.

"Yeah."

"I'm not surprised." Aliah's back is turned as she picks up a random part from Maisie's desk. "I told you there was no way you could get close to her without me. I knew it was going to fail." She sets the part back, running her finger over the wrenches and tools. "But it sucks we're all going to die."

"I'm not giving up." Despite my complete lack of ideas, my voice rings with conviction. "I'll never give up. I can't."

"No, you never do, do you?"

Aliah wipes the dust from her hands as Maisie returns, dumping an armload of bedding onto the floor. Aliah works to make a comfortable nest while Maisie perches on the edge of her bed, studying both Aliah and I with an unsettling intensity.

"Do you have something you'd like to say?" Aliah snaps, sinking into the pile of pillows. "'Cause spit it out. I'm exhausted."

"She's deaf, Aliah."

Aliah continues to glare at Maisie. "So? I doubt that's going to stop her from giving us a piece of her mind."

Maisie smiles and gives Aliah a nod of approval. She grabs an ancient-looking device off her headboard, giving it a few firm shakes before it flickers to life. The room is quiet as she taps the screen before lifting it towards us.

Turn on your translators.

"Our what?" I frown.

"How would our translators help us understand you?" Aliah challenges. "You don't talk."

Just do it.

"What is she talking about?" I ask Aliah.

"In our tech we should have a translation option." Aliah presses the connection points on her arm before bringing her fingers together to make a screen. "See, here." She shows me the buried file. "It's an old program, used when the World Collective was first formed and we hadn't adopted one language. I still don't see how it's going to help." She switches the program to *enable* and turns back to Maisie. "Happy now?"

Maisie signs and Aliah's eyes widen with shock. "No way."

"What happened?"

"Here, see for yourself."

Aliah shows me how to access the program. I slide the button to ENABLE, turning eagerly to Maisie. As Maisie signs, a robotic-sounding voice speaks in my ear.

So what now?

"I can hear you!" I exclaim. "How is this possible?"

Your visual implants track my movements, translating them to audio for you.

"Why didn't you tell me this before?! All this time we could've been talking, getting to know one another."

Tali got to know me without it, Maisie's eyes flash.

My mouth snaps shut as my frustration fizzles. She has a point.

"Okay, now that the drama's over," Aliah says, facing Maisie. "What did you want?"

I want to know what now? How are we going to stop Thanatos?

"We?" Aliah questions. "Why do you care? Thanatos won't kill you, you're safe."

The Uncounted won't last on our own. Not for long. Besides, it's wrong—to have your life determined by a computer code. I'm not going to sit back and do nothing while the world dies.

"You sound like Ry," Aliah mutters.

"Thanks, Maisie." I make a point of using one of the few signs I've learned. "It means a lot. But we have no patch, no crypto key, and no more ideas." I sigh. "Thanatos seems unstoppable."

But it's a code, Maisie signs. *There has to be a way.*

"A code designed to kill us." I shake my head, fighting the helplessness that threatens to suffocate me.

"A code…" Aliah repeats, her gaze distant.

Maisie leans forward, her eyes locked on Aliah. *What are you thinking?*

"We can't stop Thanatos on individuals." Aliah fingers her scar. "Any tampering with the implant results in death. The patch would've protected us, but it was an individual thing too, something each citizen would have to install. But the servers…" She looks up, a fierceness transforming her face. "The Code tracks everything, every detail of our lives. All that data is sent to the servers. It's there that The Code makes its decisions: about our roles, where we live, when we die. It then sends that to our implants. If we stop the servers—"

"You know where they are?" I interrupt. "Because I thought that information was classified. Darr tried to find them when we first realized the problem was with Thanatos."

Aliah leans back on her hands. "I've told you, I've been with the United People a long time."

"So?"

"So, the United People are everywhere. All levels of leadership, all kinds of roles, all different levels of classification. It's part of what made them super effective. Obviously they would know where the servers are located."

"Okay," I concede "But why would they tell you."

"Like I said before," Aliah scowls. "I was with the United

People a long time and I worked hard, especially at winning Libni's trust. Nobody thought anything of it when I was in the room. I heard and saw a lot."

Maisie signs, *How would you stop the servers?*

"I'm not sure," Aliah admits. "Not yet anyway. But there's more than one way to kill a server," she adds with a smirk.

"Do we know what will happen if we do that?" I ask. "What will happen to us if the servers are suddenly destroyed?"

"I don't know, and I doubt I'll be able to find any information because the WC probably assumed it would never happen. It's possible we'll all drop dead." Aliah's expression is grim but determined. "Or nothing will happen at all and we'll get to live until we die naturally."

"You're suggesting blowing up the Thanatos servers without knowing the consequences?!"

Aliah flicks her hair over her shoulder, her signature *I know everything* move. "Look, we'll know more if we can physically see and interact with the servers running The Code but, yeah, we can't know anything for certain until we're there. We're going to die if we do nothing, so why not risk it? It's a whole lot better than sitting around waiting for this to turn green." She extends her arm, wrist up, exposing the white skin and blue veins.

For a moment we sit in silence, our eyes on the small scar. Behind me, the cold seeps in through the glass and I pull a cover around my shoulders, wishing it was that easy to shake the chill that grips me.

I'm in. Maisie signs. *Eldon too. We already agreed, we'll do whatever you need.*

"Your dad isn't going to let you come," I point out to Maisie. "And I doubt 'The Table' will agree either."

I don't plan on telling them. Maisie grins. *I also don't think we should wait.*

"What do you have in mind?"

When the adults send you back to Unity tomorrow, Eldon and I will steal a pod and join up with you. We could go straight for the servers after that.

"It won't be that simple, but I'm willing to give it a shot." Aliah yawns, wiggling down into the covers. "Hey, what was that stuff at dinner about looking in your memories and genetic make-up?" she asks me.

"Tazib lied," I huff. "Again. He claimed he'd find the crypto key either in my genes or hidden in my memories. But it was all for nothing."

It wasn't unfounded, Maisie signs. *There were real clues someone in your past had connections to creating The Code.*

"Really?" Aliah looks mildly curious, but it quickly disappears. "I'm sure poking around in Ry's head was... interesting," she finishes with a smirk.

There was some good stuff in there.

"I'd love to see it."

I'll get you a copy. Maybe you'll see something we missed.

"Hey!" I snap. "Don't share anything with her."

"Whatever," Aliah rolls her eyes. "Like I want to rewatch all the times you've made a fool of yourself."

"I'm going to change," I grumble, grabbing my pjs and heading for the bathroom.

I linger in the hall, my emotions churning at the soft murmur of Aliah's voice. Her idea to go to the servers is a solid one. We're bound to be able to do more if we can physically interact with the Thanatos server, and though shutting it down is risky, it *is* better than doing nothing. I just wish it hadn't been Aliah's idea. Trusting her with Darr's life and trusting her with Thanatos are two different things. She did work for the United People after all. Maybe there's some way to drop her off in Unity and go on to the servers without her.

Laughter from Tazib and Eldon's room startles me and I dash into the bathroom when their door opens. Listening to the two teens chatter as they move away to the kitchen only deepens my confusion.

I don't know how to wrap my head around Tazib.

Here in Sota, among the Uncounted, Tazib is like any other teen. At times, he's almost likeable. But then he shows his true colours.

He nearly killed Darr.

Sure, you could say he faced the consequences tonight with his verbal berating from The Table, but he didn't seem at all remorseful. And hearing him banter and laugh with Eldon now, without a second thought to whether Darr's okay... How is it possible for him to be so warm and cold at the same time?

When I return to the bedroom, Maisie has turned off the lights. I pick my way to my bed, careful not to step on Aliah, and slip under my covers with tired relief. The small house is quiet but for the occasional laugh down the hall.

"I know you don't trust me." Aliah speaks softly in the darkness. "You have every reason not to."

I stare at the ceiling, watching the long-fingered shadows sway.

"Look, I should have given you your necklace right away. I had every intention of giving it back."

My hand finds the strand where it pools around my neck. Hot anger burns in my chest. If I hadn't caught her with it she probably would have kept it for herself.

Aliah blows out a long breath. "You're terrible at hiding what you're thinking, you know that right? I can tell you're trying to figure out a way to go to the servers without me."

When I stay silent she continues, her voice even quieter.

"I never wanted to hurt anyone. What the United People did to Ky…" She draws a ragged breath. "I know you don't believe me, but I don't work for them anymore. All I want to do is stop Thanatos before more people die."

I turn away with a huff.

"You aren't the only one who lost people. Does the name Malien mean anything to you? No, of course it doesn't. The Collective made sure they never used names in any of the broadcasts. They couldn't make them too human, couldn't tell you too much about the lives of their scapegoats, or else you wouldn't be satisfied with their deaths."

My breath fogs the cold glass of the window as I stare into the dark, refusing to understand what she's suggesting.

"Malien was the kindest person you could ever meet. The best dorm leader ever. And she would never, *ever* do anything to hurt another person, let alone kids." Aliah's voice quivers. "Her only 'crime' was getting involved with the United People. And for that, the WC sentenced her to death." Her laugh is cold. "But they couldn't even admit that. They couldn't report there was a group of people who wanted something different from the World Collective.

No, they had to create false charges, blaming her to cover up their own accident."

I squeeze my eyes shut, but it doesn't stop me from seeing the faces of the terrorists the WC sentenced to death. I've wondered about them since learning it was an accident and not an attack. Wondered who they were and how they ended up blamed for something that wasn't their fault. Did the WC murder them for the sake of their narrative?

Aliah sniffles, her words choked by suppressed tears. "I know now the United People are no better than the Collective, but at the time, when they came to me after Malien's death, I got involved. I was just a little kid, but I could see the WC needed to change, and I thought the United People were the ones to make it happen."

Why is she telling me this? Does she expect me to roll over and forgive her? To suddenly trust her every word? I press my head into my pillow, trying to block Aliah's soft voice.

"I got it all wrong. That's why I have to be a part of ending this. I have to do it for Malien, for Ky, for myself."

The silence stretches, long and heavy. Hot acid burns at the back of my throat as I stay absolutely still. Internally, my mind and my heart are in turmoil. I understand choosing wrong. How many times have I made the same mistake?

But this is Aliah. Aliah who always needs to have the best score, to pick the winning team. She's probably only here because things were getting too out of hand and she wants to save her own skin. I won't give her the satisfaction of acknowledgment and she doesn't deserve my pity.

I'm done giving second chances.

01101011 01101101 01100000 01100001 01110010 01100101 01100000 01110100 01101000 01100101 01100000
01101010 01101110 01100001 01101101 01100001 01100001 01100101 01101110 01110100 01101101 01100100 01100100

I dream of the ancient city.

The stone structures rise around me, their simple adornments giving them an elegant old-world beauty. The cobbled street is uneven under my feet, often catching me, but not deterring me as I wander, always working my way up the hillside. I'm aware of the city's citizens watching, their eyes following me like I'm a parade of one, their work interrupted and conversations forgotten. It's unnerving, but the moment I crest the hill and step into the city's garden centre, I forget my discomfort. The space is so alive, so vibrant, and though it can't be more different from the woods, it has the same presence.

Ignoring the onlookers, I rush into the space, spinning on the grass as a clear note bursts from my lungs. There is no doubt music formed this space at the heart of the city. And there is no doubt this place was made for the music.

It spills from me, pure and joy-filled, and as I sing, the Composer's symphony joins me. Layers upon layers of sound. Bass that rumbles in my chest. Strings that bring tears to my eyes. Melodies that rise and fall, sending shivers of pleasure down my spine.

It's perfection. It's hope, joy. Love.

But all too soon, my feet tire and my lungs demand I slow before I draw another breath.

That's when the stern voice snaps me back to the present. "What are you doing?"

My skirt twists against my legs as my feet fall still, shame overwhelming me. Faces watch from all sides with bewildered expressions. My hands tremble and my mind blinks blank. What explanation can I give?

A small hand slips into mine and I glance down to find ageless eyes in a child's form. "Do you see them watching?" The Composer smiles.

I answer with a strangled laugh. "Ah, yeah, I see them." I attempt to step into the shadow of a tree, but the child holds me in place, allowing no obstacles to block me from my unwanted audience.

"No, Rygita," the child Composer says. "You don't see them. Look again."

Heat fills my face as I draw my eyes up from the ground to the faces that surround me. All ages are present: children, teens, adults, and the very old, and they study me intently. But as I look from face to face, I realize not all carry judgement. Many watch with confusion, some curiosity, and others have soft smiles, their feet twitching like they're waiting to be invited.

"Do you see them?" the child repeats. "Do you know who they are?"

My confidence grows as I continue to search the faces around me, the Composer's hand in my own.

"Do you know whose they are?"

The question is sung and it dances around the garden, stirring the leaves and tussling my hair.

"They're yours." I spin slowly as I look at the people again. "You made each of them. Just like you made this place, like you made me. Like you create the music."

The child laughs, a trill of notes that amplify the melody that builds all around us. "Yes!" they call, pulling me forward. "Do you see why I made them? Why you're here together?"

From our vantage point on the hill I can see how the city spreads out below us, all the streets leading to this spot in the centre, this garden that demands the Composer's song.

"They were made to sing," I say, understanding snapping the world into focus. "We're made to sing together, to join in your symphony."

A fresh breeze blows through the square, raising the hairs on my arms as the Composer's music washes over me. Laughter fills my chest as I throw back my head.

What have I been so afraid of?

The music has always told me I am loved. Nothing will change that. Not the opinion of others. Not whether I am alone in a jungle or surrounded in a city.

The music tells me there is a plan.

A plan that isn't just for me, but all of humanity. All those gathered around me are loved by the Composer too. They have a part to play, a melody line all their own.

I look down where the tiny hand is wrapped in mine, then to the eyes that shine with unfathomable wisdom. I know what I'm supposed to do.

"There is something you need to do first." The Composer nods to my pockets with solemn eyes. I'm suddenly aware of how heavy they hang at my sides; and reaching inside, I pull out a handful of smooth stones that are impossibly heavy for their small size. "You need to let them go," the Composer says. "Don't carry them any longer."

"I don't even remember picking them up." I roll the stones in my hand, recognizing the rocks that tripped me on the journey. Why did I choose to carry them?

"It is easy to pick up that which is not ours to carry," the child explains. "Especially when one's been hurt. But they're not yours. They're mine." The child opens their empty hands. "You may need to check your pockets again," they say with a smile. "When you find your feet heavy and your lungs too tired to sing. Leave the hurts and anger with me. I don't find them heavy at all."

I drop the stones one by one into the tiny hands, and as I do, I begin to laugh. For as I drop the stones, they shrink until they are nothing but grains of sand in the hands of the Composer.

"Now, what are you waiting for?" The child grins, dragging me to a woman who watches with glistening eyes. "You know what you're supposed to do." Taking the woman's hand, the child places it in mine.

My heart races and a flash of fear crowds my thoughts but I quickly push it aside, focusing on the lightness in my chest and the music that dances around us.

I sing to the woman before me.

Do you know?
Do you know who you are?
That you were made
To love, to be loved

Do you hear?
Do you hear the music?

That dances around us
A living thing, Reminding us

As I sing, the melody grows in complexity and I realize I no longer sing alone. The woman throws her head back, joining her voice with mine in beautiful harmony. She reaches out and grabs the person next to her and soon they too join the song.

There is one who weaves the notes together
One who composes the refrains
And we are all invited to join the song
Each voice an instrument

More and more people join until the garden thunders with hundreds of voices. Emotions crash over me. I know this, I caught a glimpse of it as the people of Sota mourned Mikom. But this, this is overwhelming in its beauty. The way all the different voices blend together creating something so complex out of nothing but the air in our lungs, this is indescribable. Happy tears stream down my cheeks.

And one voice sings over us—a voice that carries all knowledge and all power—uniting us into one masterful symphony. A symphony of hope and life.

Do you see?
You are not alone
I've woven you together
Into my perfect melody.

A loud boom startles me awake, shattering the dream and the wisps of song from my mind. I roll over to find Maisie illuminated by a flashing red light as she shoves things into a bag, nudging Aliah with her foot.

"What's happening?"

A thunderous crash rattles the window and Aliah sits up with a shriek. The door slams open, Al's large frame looming in the doorway.

"Quick, to the tunnel. We're under attack."

He grabs Maisie's arm and pushes her from the room. Aliah and I scamper after them. Eldon and Tazib join us as we rush through the house.

"Stay close," Al calls, throwing open the door and hurrying out into the dark. "It's not far, but we can't use lights."

I stumble after the others, wincing when I trip over roots as we hurry down a pitch black trail behind the house. Another crash echoes over the lake and I turn to see the glow of a pod as it falls from the sky, spinning madly before slamming into the mountainside.

"Here." Al stops suddenly, the line of us bumping into each other as he flings open a hatch. "Quick, inside. The light will turn on when I close it."

We tumble into the dark space, reaching with our hands to find the rough wall as Al closes the hatch behind us. Immediately, the tunnel is flooded with light, making us squint as Al pushes past us in the tight space.

"Quickly, we need to get to the Ark." Al's large frame barely fits in the rock-hued tunnel, forcing him to stoop as he hurries down the passage. "I knew this was going to happen," he mutters. "I just knew it. No advance warning. None. They used something to block their signal so we didn't see them until they were on top of us," he grumbles.

"Do we know who it is?" I ask.

"Does it matter?" Al barks. "World Collective or United People —they aren't ours, that's for sure."

A muffled boom shakes the walls of the tunnel, showering us with dust.

"What is that?" Aliah asks as two more low rumbles follow in quick succession.

"Tazib's self defence system," Eldon answers, shooting Aliah a grin. "It can take out any pod within a kilometre radius of Sota."

"You shoot them down? Without knowing who they are or why they came?"

Eldon's grin falters. "Well..."

"This place is hidden for a reason." The swelling on Tazib's face has gone down, but the bruising has turned a deep purple. "The World Collective has known about the Uncounted since the beginning and they've never stopped hunting them. Having protection against attack is a necessity."

Our tunnel reaches a T where it joins a larger passageway bustling with families moving in an orderly line deeper into the mountain. They step aside for Al, allowing us to hurry down the long corridor to the Ark where Al rushes to join the other Table members at the command centre.

"How many?" he asks Jolan who is manning Mikom's old computer.

"At least a dozen." Jolan's eyes are rimmed red, dark shadows aging her face. Her youngest child is wrapped around her neck like an extra appendage. "The SDS shot down three so the others are keeping their distance."

Al swears, his voice echoing in the large space, turning many anxious faces in our direction. "Tazib, do your thing." He waves to a computer. "Find out who they are, how they found us, and what they want."

"I thought you didn't *need* me anymore."

Al spins to Tazib, fire in his blue eyes. "You little—"

"Al, now is not the time to lose your temper," Momma Aimee emerges from the crowd. Her cheeks are pink and her breath short as she sets a calming hand on Al's arm. "And you—" She turns to Tazib. "You need to decide where your loyalties lie. Are you with our community or not?"

I shouldn't be surprised Tazib hesitates. The whole hall seems to hold its breath as we watch the unreadable features of his bruised face. But then Tazib is moving, sliding into the empty chair, the stubs of his fingers flying over the keys.

"Okay," Tazib says, the flickering screen casting a strange glow over his features. "The who is United People. The how isn't clear. But the why…This is interesting." On the screen, Tazib enlarges the blueprints of a pod. "The why is that they're here to annihilate us."

CHAPTER EIGHTEEN

A CHORUS OF VOICES ERUPT, MY OWN INCLUDED. MOMMA AIMEE restores order by getting Eldon to produce a piercing whistle.

"I understand we all have questions." Her throaty voice carries over the crowd. "But the most pressing matter right now is to protect our people. Tazib, you use the word annihilate. Why? Are we not safe here?" She motions to the mountain walls surrounding us. "There are no guns that can penetrate our fortress."

Tazib shakes his head. "They don't need guns. Look." He sends the image of the pod to the larger screen, pointing to a strange protrusion hanging beneath. "They're here to release a virus. Blowing up the pods has probably already exposed us and now, being in here all together, we're only going to speed up the spread of whatever they've released."

Al isn't the only one who swears at this news.

"Are you certain?"

Tazib nods, opening another screen with footage of the attack. He plays the recording of the approaching pods and I watch in astonishment as a bright flare temporarily blanches the screen before the first pod spins out of control, smashing into the side of the mountain in a ball of fire. "Here," Tazib says, reversing the video and pausing it just before the flare. "Look right here." He enhances the image and points to a strange shape hanging below the pod. "The WC built these years ago. They were originally for firefighting but have been modified many times since. One set of plans, the ones here, were developed with the idea of using pods to spread vaccines, but they could just as easily be used to infect."

Priya instinctively cradles her baby closer. "What makes you think that's how they are being used now?"

"Because the United People had a plan like this. A plan to gain absolute control." Aliah stands off to the side of the main group, her arms crossed across her middle, her back straight. "Thanks to embedded tech, they have a way to control the citizens of the World Collective. The threat of an instant Thanatos is a pretty effective mode of persuasion. But that doesn't impact you." She nods to the gathered people. "They wanted a way to control the Uncounted or any other groups that have remained separate. So, they decided to use viruses, ones they have vaccines for."

"YOU!" Al spins to Aliah, a red vein throbbing on his forehead. "You brought them here!"

"No," Aliah shakes her head, backing away from Al. "I didn't. I promise. I did everything I could to make sure we weren't followed."

"It wasn't her," Tazib says from his computer. "Her stuff was good. It's hard to say how they found us, but it doesn't really matter. They're here now."

"But why?" I turn to Aliah, desperate to understand. "Why are they doing this? All of this? Ky, not sharing the patch, letting so many die from an early Thanatos? And why come after the Uncounted? They aren't hurting anyone. How does this fit with their claims about a future for all?"

"Because they want control!" Aliah's shout startles us all, herself included. She grinds her teeth, her face red and eyes shining. "You can give a future to all if you control who is a part of that future." A stillness falls on the crowd around us. Aliah trembles. "They want to control everything, but Thanatos especially. What better way to control people than with death? They can't stand the idea of you, the Uncounted, because they have no power over you. That's why they want to infect you. They can use the vaccine as a bribe, a way to make contact, then they'll upload each of you with the chip, bringing you under their control. Those that resist and fight, they'll eliminate."

"But Thanatos is killing too many. At this rate, no one's going to be left."

"You've got to remember they didn't know what was going on," Aliah says, regaining her composure. "No one knew why Thanatos was speeding up, only that it could move up their timeline, help them achieve their goals. They certainly wanted to get their hands on a patch—you helped with that." Aliah nods in my direction. "With the patch they could protect those they counted worthy, another tool in their arsenal of control. But I don't think anyone understood how fast the problem with Thanatos was spreading, how quickly it would decimate the population."

"I don't mean to be insensitive," Al says in his typical booming voice. "But can we focus on the issue? What do we do right now?"

"Do you know what they released?" Priya asks Aliah. "How we might protect ourselves?"

Aliah blinks and looks around. "It's measles, one of the ancient strains. The best thing you can do is isolate any who get sick."

"We should leave immediately," Al barks. "Abandon this location."

"No," Aliah rushes. "You shouldn't travel, at least not to a new location with a new group of people. You'll spread it further, faster. Exactly what the United People hope you'll do."

"So, what do you suggest?" Al asks. "Wait here to die from sickness, or for the United People to barge in to finish us off?"

Aliah doesn't answer. She bows her head, her voice soft. "I'm sorry. So very sorry."

A child whimpers in her father's arms and quiet tears drip down Priya's chin onto her daughter's head. I look around at the pale and drawn faces. It would be so easy to give up, to find a quiet corner and wait for the inevitable, but Momma Aimee straightens, her grey head held high and her eyes bright.

"This is not your fault, child," Momma Aimee says. "And we don't give up that easily. Okay." She claps her hands. "Table, gather, let us decide what is to be done."

The command seems to shift Priya, Jolan, and Al out of their apathy.

"I motion we take the threat of measles seriously," Priya says. "But not panic."

"What do you suggest?" Momma Aimee prompts.

"We start by setting up a quarantine area, I suggest using the holding cells in the tunnels. Anyone who was near the pods that crashed should separate from the main group. We will take names and monitor for symptoms." The sleeping baby in her arms shifts and Priya cradles its tiny head. "Our children face the most risk. All who are able should wear masks to help prevent spreading it to our little ones. We'll need a team to sew masks." She looks around the gathered crowd and a number of people raise their hands, volunteering to sew and offering clothing to use as material.

"Al, do we need to do anything to fortify ourselves more?" Momma Aimee asks.

Al strokes his beard as he thinks. "Not really. But we should keep an eye on all external monitors. Watch in case the United People change tactics. We can equip nearly every man and woman with a weapon."

"I'd rather it not come to that."

"Me too," Al agrees, his blue eyes piercing Eldon. "We've seen not everyone can handle the responsibility of a weapon with a level head."

Eldon blushes a deep crimson.

"Jolan, how long can we wait the United People out?"

"Not as long as I'd like," Jolan answers. "Shorter if people start getting sick."

"How long?"

"Two weeks tops."

"Two weeks is a long time." Momma Aimee nods thoughtfully. "While we may be isolated, we are still connected to the greater world. We must not forget that the United People are dealing with a virus as well, one that threatens to decimate their population. Two weeks might be more time than they have to spare. Alright, let's get to work."

Priya, Al, and Jolan disappear into the crowd, collecting people for the various tasks as Momma Aimee turns to Aliah and I. "I'm sorry, girls. But we will not be able to return you to Unity as planned. I'm afraid you will have to wait this out along with the rest of us."

"What?" Aliah gasps as Momma Aimee moves to join the others, the large hall once again filled with sound as the people get to work. "She can't keep us here! They might be fine if they wait it out, but us, with Thanatos, we're going to die if we do nothing!"

She moves to charge after Momma Aimee, but I grab her arm.

"Don't bother, Aliah. They've made up their minds, and really, we can't expect more from them. Our being here has already cost them so much." I wave to the screen showing the glow of the remaining pods hovering on the other side of the lake.

"But we can't just sit here and do nothing!" Aliah paces between the computers.

I look around the hall at the people of the Uncounted. When I arrived, all I could see were the differences. They were so foreign to me, with their lack of tech, the way they spoke to each other, the multiple generations living side by side, their openness to share their emotions and burdens, and their willingness to forgive and give second chances. I watched them with fascination, but kept my distance. I didn't even try that hard to get to know Maisie. Because why should I? This was only a temporary stay, a blip until I could find a way to fix everything and return life to normal.

But what if I had it all wrong? What if I wasn't seeing what was right in front of me?

The Composer's music swells around me, reminding me of the truth: every person was made for a purpose and each has their own unique notes to play. And it hits me. The answer doesn't lie with fancy tech, but with people. People equipped to play their part. All around me, the Uncounted work together, using their various skills to handle the problem at hand. Many parts joining in unity to create a solution. Like the music, each one is unique, each needed and wanted, and working together they're able to create a symphony.

Hope expands in my chest, lifting the suffocating weight and filling my lungs with sweet oxygen.

Aliah stills, her eyes narrowing. "Let me guess. You have some impulsive, half-thought-out, irrational plan, don't you?"

"Of course she does." Tazib spins his chair towards me, his light-filled eyes sparkling. "That's Ry. She never gives up. The WC's little fighter."

Tazib. How do I reconcile Tazib? How do I see Tazib beyond the hurt he has caused? It is one thing to trust Aliah. Hearing her story last night helped. It opened a window into her past and what may have motivated her poor choices. And who am I to judge mistakenly trusting the wrong people? I too fell for Libni's lies. Plus, Rube seems to see something in Aliah that I don't, so perhaps I should give her another shot. But Tazib?

"What are you thinking?" Eldon asks. "Because Maisie and I are in."

Maisie nods with a grin.

"Here isn't the best place to discuss any marvellous plans."

Tazib indicates the people within ear shot. "Why don't we take this somewhere more private?"

"The holding cell," Aliah states. "Because Darr deserves to be part of this."

"Tali too."

"Great, let's go!" Tazib jumps to his feet, but Aliah steps in his way.

"Not a chance. You stay here. Or better yet," she turns to me, "we lock him in the cell and forget he ever existed."

"You're going to need me," Tazib drawls. "Whatever plan you're concocting is going to involve tech, and I'm the best."

"As if." Aliah flicks her hair over her shoulder, hopping off the platform and heading to the tunnel that leads to the holding cell, but I hesitate.

Tazib *is* skilled and he claims he wants to help, to end Thanatos. But he has killed and lied. Jep is dead because of him. He tried to kill Rube and he nearly killed Darr.

So what do I do? I can't forget what he's done and I'm not ready to forgive. But we have to stop Thanatos. No one will be left if we don't. I don't like it, but something tells me Tazib has a part to play in ending this. An image forms in my mind of heavy stones passing from my hands to a child's.

"I think Tazib should come with us."

Aliah stops, spinning on her heel. "No. We can't trust him."

"But you expect me to trust you?" Aliah flinches but doesn't back down. I turn to Eldon and Maisie. "You guys have known him longer. What do you think?"

"I trust him," Eldon blurts, his cheeks flushing. "I mean, I know he's made mistakes, but so have I. I mean look, I shot someone! Two people!"

"But you feel bad about it," I point out.

"So?" Eldon's hands fidget at his sides. "I still thought it was the right thing to do in the moment. Tazib's done bad things, but he thought they were the only choice. Right, Tazib?"

"Absolutely." Tazib grabs Eldon, pulling him in for a side hug.

"Maisie?"

Maisie waits for Eldon to step away before she positions herself in front of Tazib. Without a clear view of their hands, I have no translation of their silent conversation, but I watch Tazib's posture change, his shoulders growing rigid and his face serious. Whatever she has to say to him holds a lot of power.

Finished, Maisie turns to me. *You have my guarantee he will stay in line.*

In Maisie's eyes I see the weight of that promise. Tazib is her family. I know what it is like to have family do something you question, the conflict of emotions, your love at war with what they've done. I also see the need to give them another chance, let them prove to you they are who you believe them to be. Isn't that what I wish I could have with Dad? Isn't that what I hope will happen between Rube and I?

"Alright," I nod. "Let's make a plan."

There is no guard at the door to the holding cell. The chair sits empty, the novel resting open across the arm to keep the page.

"Where's the guard?" Aliah asks.

Tazib shrugs. "The Uncounted aren't accustomed to having prisoners. They probably went to the Ark when the alarm sounded."

"How will we get in?"

Tazib points to the door handle. "The key is in the lock."

It hardly seems possible, but there it is, the key sitting unattended in the door's lock. Tazib reaches to push the door open, but I intercept him.

"I think you should sit this out."

"How can I help plan if I'm out here?"

"Tazib." I level my gaze on him, trying not to be distracted by the discolouring of his bruises. "Darr is not going to want to see you. Convincing him to trust me is going to be enough of an issue. You wait here."

When we enter, Tali leaps to her feet from her spot at the small table. "What's happening? We heard the alarms, but the guard said I should stay with Darr since he's still unsteady on his feet."

"We're under attack," Aliah states, moving past me into the small bedroom where Darr rests in bed, his usually rich dark skin grey, his eyes dull, and his face drawn.

"Aliah?" Darr struggles to sit, wincing as the movement strains his side. "How? Did they kidnap you too?" His eyes jump to her bandaged arm. "You're hurt!"

"No and it's just a scratch." Aliah sits on the bed opposite Darr. "Ry? You want the honours or should I try to explain this madness?"

I step into the small space, forcing my eyes up from the floor to meet Darr's. They are like two dark pools, swirling with so much unsaid. There is both good and bad in his look. I'm sorry. I missed you. But also, why? How? And what now?

I take a deep breath. Half of me wishes we were alone, that this could be a quiet moment between the two of us, a chance to say all those unsaid things.

The other half is grateful that isn't the case.

"Darr, I don't know what Tali has told you, and I'm sure your thoughts are muddled so I won't smother you with details. Most of it doesn't matter at this point. All you need to know is everything is really messed up, no side is the right side, and we are going to stop Thanatos."

"Stop Thanatos..." Darr rubs a hand down his worn face and something in my heart does a strange flip. If things weren't so messed up between us I would be tempted to sit on the bed, taking his hand into mine, leaning forward until our foreheads touch. "Ry, I don't think it can be stopped, not anymore. It's killing too fast."

"That's why it's time for a new plan. One where we all band together." I look to where Maisie and Eldon stand with Tali in the other room. Darr follows my gaze.

"You!" Darr throws the blanket aside as he swings his legs to the floor. "You're the guy who shot me!" He pushes off the bed and takes a step towards Eldon.

"I'm sorry!" Eldon stutters as he throws his hands up, side-stepping so Maisie is between him and Darr. "I didn't think... I didn't want to hurt you... I'm never going to carry a weapon again!"

Darr moans and sways on his feet and I hurry to grab his arm, bearing his weight on my shoulder as I guide him back to the bed.

As he slumps down he takes my hand, his eyes finding mine. "Why are you here? Why are you with *them*?"

I marvel at the warmth of Darr's hand on mine, the way our fingers entwine. "It isn't us and them," I say. "World Collective, United People, Uncounted, we're all just people. We like to stick everything in boxes, the good guys versus the bad guys, but it's never that simple."

"How would we even stop Thanatos?" Darr pulls his hand from mine to run it through his rumpled hair.

"I know where the servers are," Aliah says.

"The Code servers?" Darr glances up in surprise.

"Yeah, they're hidden in the Atlantic," Aliah continues. "If we can interact with them, we might have a chance of ending Thanatos, but first we have to get there, and to do that we'll need special pods."

"Wait." Tali's face scrunches in confusion. "Didn't you say we're under attack? Is it even safe to leave the mountain?"

We'll have to be careful, Maisie signs. *But if we aren't seen, we should be okay. There's another way out, a tunnel that leads out the back of the mountain. We have extra pods hidden there.*

"Ah, guys?" Tazib sticks his head around the door. "I think we need to get moving. Darr's not-so-great guard was just here. I sent him off to get himself a coffee, but we don't have a lot of time. Oh, hey." He salutes Darr. "Look at you, awake and everything. Ready to save the world and be Ry's hero?"

"Tazib."

With frightening speed, Darr transforms from weak and shaken to pure rage. He launches himself across the small rooms, shoving Tazib back through the door and out into the hall. Tazib tries to protect his already mangled face, but Darr's blows are relentless. In his struggle to escape, Tazib trips over the armchair, landing on his back. Darr is on his chest in an instant.

"Darr! Stop!"

I'm not the only one shouting. Both Eldon and Maisie jump for Darr, trying to grab his arms. Darr's elbow catches Eldon, splitting his lip, but Maisie locks on to his neck, wrestling him away from Tazib.

"Stop Darr!" I yell, hurrying to pull a gasping Tazib to his feet. "You're going to kill him!"

"He deserves it!' Darr thunders. "He deserves to die! It's all his fault!"

"But it's not" I shout back. "Thanatos speeding up has nothing to do with him. It was there before, from the very beginning!"

"He nearly killed me!" Darr tries to wiggle free of Maisie's grip, but she holds firm.

"I know!" I scream. "I know and I will never forget what he's done!" My throat aches and my eyes burn as I reach out a hand to Darr, trying to calm myself as much as him. "You're right. He's done terrible things, things he needs to be held accountable for. But Darr, now is not the time."

"How can you defend him?" Darr's nose wrinkles with disgust when he sees I'm still holding Tazib steady. "How can you touch him?"

"I'm not the bad guy—"

"Don't," I cut Tazib off. "Don't minimize what you've done. And Darr, I'm not defending him."

"I'm just so mad." Darr's chest heaves but as he looks down at his bloody knuckles the fight drains from him. Maisie releases her hold and he sinks to his knees. "It isn't fair, everything that's happened. Someone needs to pay."

"I understand. I'm mad too. We all are."

I note Darr's drooping shoulders, the clouding of his eyes, and the clenching of his jaw. He isn't just angry, he's hurting. Seeing it so plainly makes me wish there was a way to change the past, a simple way to erase the pain. Perhaps that's why the World Collective liked using MEMORY so much. Burying the hard things is easier than dealing with them. But maybe it's better to look at them. To face and identify these traumas so we finally learn to let them go. Haven't I seen how carrying the anger only weighs and encumbers? Letting go, passing it on to one who is able to carry them, is the only way to move forward.

I crouch in front of Darr. "I'm not asking you to trust Tazib and I'm not asking you to forget what's happened, but if we want to stop Thanatos we're going to have to work with him, and to do that you're going to need to set aside your anger. It doesn't mean he's off the hook, it's just now is not the time to pass judgement. Later, when we have time and we can look at all the pieces, all the people and systems responsible for what's happened, then we can seek justice. But not now and not with our fists."

Darr cups his face with his hands. "I know. I know violence isn't the answer. It's just..." He sighs. "I don't know what's the right thing to do anymore. I feel so lost."

My heart aches and I lean closer. "Stopping Thanatos. That's our goal. For all of us. Can you do that?"

The echo of a door closing reminds us we don't have a lot of time.

"We need to go," Aliah says. "Darr, it's like Ry said, there are no more sides. It's just us. If we want to stop more people from dying we're going to have to work with Tazib. Though," she shrugs with her typical smirk. "If you want to stay here, that's your choice."

"No," Darr sighs, shaking his head. "No, I want to stop Thanatos."

"Good." Aliah grabs Darr's arm, pulling it over her shoulder and helping him to his feet. "Then let's go. Ry, give me a hand."

I slip my arm around Darr's waist, steadying him between me and Aliah.

"Took long enough," Tazib says, wiping the blood from his lip.

"Do us a favour and keep him far away from us," Aliah snaps to Eldon and Maisie, who willingly comply, hurrying Tazib down the long hall.

The air is stale and warm, making me sweat where Darr's arm rests heavy on my shoulders as we follow the others deeper into the mountain. I listen for the melody, clinging to its hope that this rag-tag group of teens, half of whom hate each other, have what it takes to save the world.

CHAPTER NINETEEN

GOLDEN HUES PAINT THE UPPER SLOPES OF THE MOUNTAINS IN shades of light when we emerge from the secret tunnel. Aliah and I set Darr down to rest under a towering pine while Maisie leads the others to the hidden pods. When they are free of their covering of fir branches, Aliah joins Maisie in making sure they are fit to fly, but I hang back, remaining at Darr's side. The morning air is heavy with the smell of earth and pine, and it is chilly in the shadow of the mountain. I wrap my arms around my middle, the sweat cooling on my skin as my breath escapes in puffy clouds. Though my instinct is to blurt the thousand thoughts swirling in my head, I force myself to remain still. To wait. To listen for the melody in this amazing landscape.

"I thought I was doing the right thing," Darr says quietly. "Turning you in to Libni. I knew it would hurt you, but freeing Tazib... I was trying to save you from yourself. You know the WC can't tolerate terrorists. Lumping yourself with him equalled death."

I lower myself to the ground, sitting beside Darr but not facing him. "And then I went and did it anyway."

Darr laughs dryly. "I should have known locking you up wouldn't be enough to stop you."

We are silent a moment as we watch Aliah and Maisie argue about something.

"Libni's dead."

"I know. Tali told me."

"She was with the United People, Darr."

"Tali told me that too."

"Do you believe it now?"

Darr answers with a heavy sigh. "I don't know. What's happened, what the United People have done... It's hard to believe Libni would help them."

"I did too." I pick up a pinecone, pulling at its closed seeds. "Helped the United People that is. I thought they could fix things. I bet Libni believed that too." I look over at Darr, finding his eyes already on my face. "It's easy," I say. "To choose wrong. To have good intentions but be misguided. We've all done it." I hold his gaze, hoping he understands what I'm trying to say.

"Is that why you're giving him another chance?" At "him" Darr tosses his head in Tazib's direction, the word filled with disgust.

"Him, and others." I watch the group. We are such a mix of people: World Collective, United People, and Uncounted all represented in our midst. "I know I've made mistakes. I'm no different than Tazib, or Aliah, or you. We're all broken people trying to survive in a broken world."

Darr leans back against the tree, his hand covering his side as he moves. "Do you think there's any point?" he asks. "In trying to stop Thanatos? Maybe we should just let it come."

"No." I scoot so I'm facing him. "Don't think like that."

"Why not?" Darr looks over my head at the tree-covered mountains. "You said it. We're just a bunch of broken people in a broken world. Even if we do manage to stop Thanatos, what then? Things aren't really going to change. If anything, they're only going to get worse." His eyes drop to mine. "The World Collective is leaderless and the population count so low The Code is ineffective. Every system is at risk of collapsing if it hasn't already. I don't see how we can come back from this, Ry."

"But we can!" I press the pinecone between my hands, fighting the urge to grab his. "I'm not saying it will happen all at once, but things can get better, Darr." I rock up on my knees, my chest squeezing. "Just look." I wave at our group. "Look at what can happen when we work together. We don't need The Code or the Collective. We just need to start seeing people as they are, not one-dimensional tools, but complex, growing people. People who change, who dream, who create and love and feel. Darr, all our lives we've been taught to trust The Code, but we were living on autopilot. We did what we were told, when we were told to do it, but what if there's more? More to who we are? What if we all have more to offer?"

"Wow." The tiniest of smiles pulls at Darr's lips. "You feel really passionate about this."

"Guess so," I laugh.

Darr looks past me, his face falling slack once again. "How do you do it? How do you keep going despite everything? Doesn't it crush you?"

"I feel it, Darr, all the time." I run a finger along the bumps of the pinecone. "But I can walk through it because I know I'm not alone. And you aren't either. The music shows me we all have a part to play. None of us are an accident or a number in a code. We're here for a reason. And everything is going to work out because the Composer is in control, weaving all the notes into something beautiful. A plan for good."

"Please don't." Darr stiffens, his eyes pleading. "Just don't. I can't... I don't want to hear about the music stuff. Not now, Ry. I'm too sore and too exhausted."

I force a nonchalant smile. "Yeah, I get that."

"Everything's ready," Tali calls from the pods. "Do you need a hand, Ry, getting Darr up?"

Darr is already pushing himself upright, using the tree for support, and I hurry to assist him. "We got it," I call back.

It's strange, this conversation didn't go at all the way I'd imagined. There was no kissing and making up. Things aren't fixed between us. But instead of being crushed, I'm okay. I see now I don't have to rush or push. If something's going to happen between Darr and I, it will. And whatever happens isn't a reflection of who I am. My worth is found in the melody, in the song the Composer invites me to sing. And though I'm disappointed Darr once again brushed aside the music, that's okay too. Over and over, the Composer has reminded me that the choice is and always will be mine to make. I don't choose for others, and them choosing differently doesn't mean the music ceases to exist. It will always be present, even if I'm the only one who hears it.

"Alright," Aliah says as Darr and I reach the group. "We have three pods ready. Two to a pod with one carrying three. To avoid detection, we need to fly the pods manually until we're sure we aren't being followed. Because I don't trust you—" Aliah glares at Tazib. "—I'll man one, Eldon another, and Maisie the third."

"Will we link up once we are safely away?" I ask.

Aliah nods. "Yeah. We still need to finalize our plan."

Maisie signs, *Let's get going. Dad's going to realize I'm gone any minute.*

"Hold on." Aliah squares off with the three from Sota. "I'm not going anywhere until you reconnect me, all of us from the Collective."

"But it isn't safe." The tips of Eldon's ears turn pink. "We need to wait until we are away from the community so we don't reveal our location."

"Ah, it's a bit late for that," Aliah snaps. "Come on." She thrusts out her arm. "If anything happens and we can't meet up, I need to be able to connect to the system."

"She's right," Tazib says, stepping forward and waiting for Eldon to hand him the special device. "Quick, I'll reconnect each of you before we go."

We each step forward, exposing our wrists for Tazib's device. When he scans Darr's arm, Tazib's face darkens.

"That explains how the United People found us. You were still connected."

"I'm sorry!" Eldon squeaks. "Everything was crazy! Oh man, oh man, if Al finds out…"

"Bit late for stressing about it now." Tazib shrugs.

Now back online, Eldon, Maisie, and Aliah each climb into a

waiting pod while the rest of us glance at each other. Who should go where? In the end, Tazib boards the pod with Eldon, Tali climbs in with Maisie, and I help Darr into Aliah's pod, lowering him onto the chair where he leans back and closes his eyes, his hand covering his side where fresh blood seeps through the bandage.

"You okay?" Aliah asks Darr.

Darr nods, his lips pressed together. "It's not as bad as it looks."

Aliah meets my eyes over his head. He shouldn't be here, he should be resting and healing, but neither of us will say it because he deserves to be here as much as the rest of us.

"All set?" Tali asks over the pod speakers. "Maisie says we have to fly low and quick."

"Copy." Aliah stands at the manual controls, pushing her sleeves up over her elbows.

"How do you know how to fly a pod?" I ask.

"There's lots you don't know about me," Aliah scoffs, touching her hand to the panel. The pod sways as it lifts off the ground and Aliah shoots me a glance over her shoulder, a mischievous twinkle in her eye. "You might want to hang on."

I've hardly dropped into the second seat before the pod streaks forward, barely high enough to clear the trees. I grip the armrests as branches scrape along the bottom, the pod swaying from side to side as Aliah weaves around the taller trees, racing after the other pods as they fly down the valley away from Sota's mountain.

"Keep watch for the United People. If you can keep your eyes open." Aliah lacks her usual sarcasm, all her attention focused on keeping our pod from smashing into one of the many solid surfaces.

"All good so far," I answer. Looking behind is easier than facing forward since I can't see the many obstacles that could send us to our fiery deaths. That is, until I see the glint of sun on glass. "Shoot. Spoke too soon."

"We have company," Aliah transmits to Eldon and Maisie. "Split up. And you guys," she says to Darr and I. "Hang on."

Aliah struggles to maintain her footing as she manoeuvres the pod into a hard turn, sending Darr and I slamming into our armrests. "Ry, can you find a topographical map?" she asks when we straighten out.

"A what?" It's hard to hear over the screech of branches slapping the pod and the whine of the engine as it's pushed to its limits.

"You know," Aliah shouts. "One of those maps that show hills and valleys."

"They're gaining on us," Darr grunts. Sweat dots his forehead and he grits his teeth as he struggles against the swaying force as we swing around a large tree.

"Ry! Hurry!"

I bring my fingers together, searching through maps as I fight to not be thrown from my seat. I don't want to be doing this again: weaving dangerously close to the ground, trying to outrun, trying not to crash, worrying about the other pods. It didn't go so well the first time.

"Found one," I say, enlarging a map of the area. "Should we go higher?" I ask. "Avoid the trees to go faster? That's how they're gaining on us."

"But we won't lose them that way." Aliah's arms shake as she fights to keep control of the pod. "Look for a narrow gap, or an abandoned structure, something we can hide in."

I study the map. "It looks like there used to be a tunnel through that mountain." I point to the imposing mass. "But it's old, really old."

"Then let's hope to The Code it hasn't collapsed," Aliah says, swinging the pod towards a ribbon of decaying road. Here the trees are smaller and we have more space to push the pod faster as we fly towards a dark gap in the wall of rock.

"Aliah…"

Entering the tunnel, we are plunged into darkness, the lights of the pod only illuminating the area around us.

"I can't see!" The alarm in Aliah's voice amplifies my terror. She's forced to fly blind, the pod light not carrying far enough into the distance to illuminate our path, especially at the speed in which we race down the corridor.

"You're doing great," Darr encourages. "But we haven't lost them." He points to where a glowing ball follows behind us.

Aliah struggles to control the pod in the small space. Occasionally, we knick the wall, sending bright sparks jumping where the metal and glass scrape against stone. The map shows the tunnel isn't that long, only eight kilometres, but in the dark, time feels unmeasurable. My heart leaps when we finally see a prick of light ahead. Aliah pushes the pod to go faster, the force resting heavy against my chest.

"Hold on!" Aliah instructs as the pod breaks from the tunnel, the light temporarily blinding us. She slams down on the controls, shooting the pod upward like a rocket. We barrel into the sky, stomachs left below. "Please work," Aliah mumbles as she watches the shrinking tunnel opening. "Please work, please work…"

The pursuing pod streaks from the tunnel at high speed, crashing into the trees that have grown in the empty space.

"Yes!" Aliah shrieks, watching as the pod tumbles into dense woods.

"That was some serious flying," Darr says with admiration. "If we survive this, you'll have to teach me."

"Deal." Aliah grins.

01010111 01100101 00100000 01100001 01110010 01100101 00100000 01110100 01101000 01100101 00100000

01010101 01101110 01100011 01101111 01110101 01101110 01110100 01110100 01101000 01101001 01100100 00101110

When we are certain we're no longer being followed, we connect with the others, meeting up to fuse the pods, and cramming together in one to discuss next steps.

"We're going to need supplies," Tazib says from where he sits with his back against the lower shelves. "Access to the mainframe, weapons, the works."

"No weapons." Aliah drills Tazib with a pointed stare from where she perches on the shelf, as far from Tazib as possible in the small space. "You people can't be trusted with weapons."

"I'm so sorry." Eldon drops his head, his hands quivering where he flexes them at his side.

"The servers will be guarded," Tazib assures. "And they will not hesitate to take us out. If not weapons, then we need tech so we can connect to the system. Take out any opposition by activating an instant Thanatos."

"No!" Tali gasps. "We can't go around killing people, especially not with Thanatos! That's what we're trying to stop."

"Besides," Darr's dark eyes are shadowed by his frown. "We'd be killing innocent people. Just because they're guards doesn't mean they deserve to die. They'd only be doing what the Collective told them to, serving in their vital role without questioning."

"So what do you suggest?" Tazib's bruised face contorts. "We walk in and ask nicely? Say 'pretty please' and they'll let us do what we want, no questions? As if. Look, I know it isn't tasteful, but sometimes you have to do the hard things. We would have been able to save that kid, Ky, if you'd let me do my thing."

Tali cries out and I jump to my feet.

"Hold on now." I stretch my hands between the group, noting how those from the Uncounted sit on one side of the pod and those from the WC on the other. "We need to work together if we're going to pull this off."

"Exactly," Tazib nods. "You need my skills."

"You little—"

"We do," I cut Aliah off. "But we aren't going to use your 'skills' to kill innocent WC citizens."

"Then we're going to fail."

"No, we aren't." I look around the crowded pod. "We failed to rescue Ky because I thought I could do it myself. I didn't consider the abilities of those with me." I offer Tali an apologetic smile, then face Tazib. "And we failed to get the patch from Libni because we rushed into it without considering all the risks. But we can do this if we work together."

There are a few noncommittal grunts, but Maisie watches me with a smile. *I've been thinking,* she signs. *From the sound of things, the World Collective is gone. So, who's to say there'll be any guards? If I thought I could die at any time I wouldn't stick around to watch a bunch of servers.*

"Good point, Maisie." I sign a silent thank-you.

"Even if there are no guards, there will still be security," Darr says. "We're trying to get into a place we aren't even supposed to know exists."

"Where is this place?" I ask Aliah. "You said something about the Atlantic."

"The middle of the Atlantic," she says grimly. "And I mean middle. It's on the Mid-Atlantic Ridge, about 3000 metres below the surface."

"3000 metres *below* the surface?" Tali echoes.

"Sounds fun," Tazib deadpans.

"That's why we need the special pods, ones that can submerge," Aliah explains. "But I don't know where they are, only that they're on the east coast. I need access to the WC system to pinpoint their location."

"How do you know all this?" Darr asks.

Aliah shrugs. "I was with the United People a long time. I think, because I was so young when I joined, they weren't so careful about what they discussed around me, and well, if you watch and listen long enough, you pick up things."

"Sounds a bit like me," Tazib says, drawing a sharp look from Aliah. "Most of my tech knowledge is because this guy at the healing centre thought it would be a good distraction for me as I recovered from the burns. If only he knew how far I'd take it." He grins.

"So, to paraphrase," I say, bringing the conversation back on topic. "We need tech to connect to the system without getting caught, find this hidden facility, grab some submersible pods, and go turn off the Thanatos server."

Darr blows out a long breath, running his hands over his head and ruffling his hair. "This is crazy. All of it. What if harming the server kills us? Tampering with our embedded tech does, so it's logical to reason that they would have built similar protective measures into the servers."

"We don't know that for sure," Aliah says. "There's a lot we don't know. But being there, being able to interact with the servers in person, we should be able to learn more."

"And Thanatos is going to kill us if we do nothing," Tali whispers. "So why not risk it?"

A sombreness falls over the pod, only to be broken by a noisy rumble from Eldon's stomach. Eldon winces, but Tazib chuckles, leaning over to sign to Maisie what she missed.

Guess we also need food. She laughs.

A hot blush creeps across Eldon's freckles. "What?" he squeaks. "It's been a long time since we ate."

"So, where do we go?" I ask. "Where is it safe for us to get tech and food without drawing unnecessary attention to ourselves?"

"Fordtown is on the way to the coast," Aliah states.

"Rube?" My chest squeezes. How long has it been since I've spoken with my brother? I duck my head, misery washing over me. "I'm not sure he'll help."

"He will," Aliah says with confidence. "And before you start whining and getting all emotional, he does want to see you. So save us the drama and keep your feelings to yourself."

"I wouldn't want to inconvenience you," I mutter.

"Tazib, I hate to say it, but I'll need your help." Aliah hops off the shelf, crossing her arms. "We need to connect to Rube without the WC or United People seeing. I could figure it out myself, but you might as well just tell me how and save us the time."

"Of course." Tazib stands, dusting his bottom as he moves to Aliah's side. "Happy to share my skills with one who can appreciate the genius."

Aliah rolls her eyes but watches closely as Tazib shows her how to connect without being detected. She then steps into the adjoining pod to make the call.

I watch through the glass as Aliah brings her fingers together, waiting for Rube to answer. Though I can't see her screen, I can tell when Rube connects from the glow that spreads across her face. For someone whose default is snark, it's such a contrast to see the emotions flick across her features. Happiness, uncertainty, fear, longing. At one point she even blushes. It appears the Aliah Rube knows is very different from the one I've been forced to tolerate.

"It's all set," Aliah announces, stepping back into the crowded pod. "I gave Rube a list of what we need and he's going to meet us outside the city."

"Great." Tazib pulls Eldon to his feet. "I suggest we get some sleep in the meantime. It's a long flight to Fordtown."

He and Eldon move to an empty pod and Maisie and Tali move to another. Darr drops with a grateful sigh into the cushioned pod seat as Aliah turns to go.

"Wait, Aliah," I stop her. "We should change your bandages. You've bled through."

Aliah looks down at the small stain on her sleeve. "I can do it myself."

I raise my brows. "Really? With one hand?" I grab the small first aid kit from the lower shelf. "Come on, let me. I have some experience with this medical stuff you know."

Aliah sits with a huff, pulling her sweater over her head and staring forward as I kneel between the two seats. I'm careful as I unwrap her arm; thankfully, the wound wasn't deep. Five of Priya's neat stitches track across her smooth skin, the edges raw where she's pulled them when flying the pod manually.

"You're going to have a cool scar after this," I say as I apply the antibacterial cream.

"Great," Aliah mumbles. "I'll be marked."

"You might be able to get it removed." Scars are a thing of the past thanks to all our medical advancements. Even if it takes a couple of days for Aliah to get it treated at a healing centre she has a good chance of complete removal.

"I doubt there are many healing centres still running." Aliah stares stoically at the ceiling as I rewrap her arm. "Anyone with experience is gone. Those left will have more important things to do than erase a scar."

"Then it will be your battle badge. A mark of honour."

"Whatever," Aliah mutters, grabbing her sweater and leaving the pod.

"Can I get some of that care?" Darr asks with a tired smile.

"Of course."

Darr struggles to pull his shirt up, revealing a blood-soaked bandage.

"Sorry if this hurts."

Darr sucks in through his teeth as I pry the dressing from his skin. I try to keep my face neutral as I take in the torn stitches. Darr's wound is much worse than Aliah's. He really needs more care than simple first aid can provide.

"I need to apologize," Darr says, wincing as I clean the wound. "For being so abrupt before, about the music."

"It's okay, Darr. Really."

"No, it wasn't." Darr closes his eyes, his face paling even though I work as gently as I can. "I didn't need to be so cold. I struggle with it, this idea of special music. I like things I can see and touch and hear for myself, you know?"

"I understand."

"But even though it makes zero sense, what I *can* see is how it's helped you." Darr releases a breath as I press a fresh bandage to his skin. "I've been trying to imagine what comes next, if we're able to stop Thanatos, and all I can think about is all the ways we can fail. All the things that can go wrong. The population has already been decimated. How does a society function when there is no one left? How will we grow food? Keep the lights on?"

"We'll adapt." I give his arm a squeeze. "We'll learn to do multiple roles, to help one another. We'll start small and figure it out as we go, one thing at a time."

"See?" Darr opens his dark eyes to look at me. "You're doing it again. Seeing good, seeing hope, when everyone else would give up."

"Oh, I have my moments when I want to give up," I assure him, securing the fresh dressing and pulling his bloody shirt back into place.

"Yeah, but you don't." Darr turns his head to look me in the eye, our faces level as I kneel beside him. "And I have to think it has to do with this music you hear. Look, it isn't for me, and I still don't think it's something you should go around announcing to people, but I can see it helps you. And the way you see the world, that you believe we can have a future, a good one, well, that's special, Ry, and something we need just as much as we need a way to stop Thanatos."

"Thanks, Darr."

We are quiet as we study each other's faces and I feel something shift. An understanding and a letting go.

For years I've had a serious crush on Darr. So many of my daydreams centred around him smiling at me, the possibility of seeing his dimple, of one day feeling his arm around my shoulder. Loren and I spent so much time sneakily trailing after Rube and Jep whenever they were hanging out with Darr, hoping for another glimpse of the cutest boy in Ol'Syd. When I was activated, when I saw him in the pod travelling with me to Unity, it was all my dreams come true, and the friendship that blossomed into a relationship was more than I could have ever hoped for.

But so much has happened since then.

Now my thoughts are occupied with how to stop Thanatos. My time is spent struggling with forgiveness and next steps if we manage to pull this off. And the biggest change is that I'm learning to see the world differently, to see myself differently. Though I will always treasure my friendship with Darr, I don't *need* him the way I did when I was activated.

Darr must sense the change too. He reaches out and cups my cheek, his expression filling my eyes with tears, before he pulls away. He leans back into the chair with an exhausted sigh.

"If you don't mind, I think I'll try to get some sleep." Already, his eyes are sinking closed. "I don't want to hold us back when it comes time to do all the things."

"Yeah, for sure." I return the supplies to the kit before getting to my feet. "I think I'll go check on the others, see if anyone else needs first aid."

For a second I pause, watching the steady rise and fall of Darr's chest, my heart still doing that happy little flutter it has always done when he's near, and then I turn and slip out.

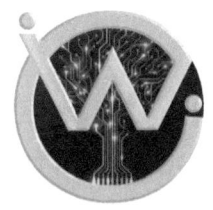

CHAPTER TWENTY

E FOLLOW THE CURVE OF THE RIVER AS WE APPROACH
Fordtown, landing on an island within view of the
distant skyscrapers. Leaving Darr to sleep, we step out
into a small clearing of heavily forested woods. A
variety of trees with mature canopies hide our presence from any
pods that might fly this way, though the skies are eerily empty. Faint
traces of gravel paths lead to a curved living building. Formed by
the bending and twisting of three willows, it must have been
stunning when it was created, but now its branches grow unbidden,
blocking the windows and obscuring the door. We duck inside the
dim interior.

"What is this place?" Eldon asks, walking between one of the
many tables bolted to the cement floor. Its entire surface has been
claimed by creeping vines.

"This is one of the first New Growth Groves," Tali says, arching
her head to marvel at how the branches are intertwined to form a

solid ceiling. "I've read about this island," she explains. "It used to be popular for the people of Fordtown to celebrate their Day of Thanatos here. Then their trees were planted outside."

Kind of morbid, isn't it? Maisie signs. *Celebrating your death in the middle of a graveyard?*

"What's a graveyard?" Aliah asks. She waves Tali's ready explanation away. "Never mind, I don't care. What matters is no one comes here anymore—no more room. That's why Rube picked it as a meeting place."

Finding it impossible to stay still, I wander back outside, peering into the lush growth for a sign of my brother. I'm eager to see him. I miss his crooked grin, his recklessness, his easy-going nature. I even miss him messing up my hair. But despite how desperate I am to see him, my gut rolls with nerves. I feel like I've been smushed and pulled in a hundred directions and I can't help but wonder... if I've been so changed by everything, what about Rube? How has he changed? What if the collapse of the WC has made him harder, colder? What if it isn't my goofy, open, loving brother, but someone new who emerges from the woods? Someone calculating and cold.

Wrapping my arms around my middle, I close my eyes, enjoying the fresh air on my face and the distant sound of water lapping on a beach of stones. I can understand how this place was chosen as a New Growth Grove. It's peaceful. I let the voices of the others fade into the background as the sun warms my cheeks, listening for the melody.

"Fancy finding you here."

My eyes fly open. "Rube!" I don't hesitate to throw my arms around his neck. It isn't until I pull away that my brain catches up to remind me of my nerves. I drop my arms to my sides. "I've missed you."

"I've missed you too, Little Sis." Rube grabs me and rubs his fist against my head. "Missed this most."

"Rube!" I screech, trying to hide my massive grin. Freeing myself, I struggle to temper my joy, knowing we don't have time to waste. "Rube, I'm sorry about Dad. I—"

"He messed up, Ry. Not you," Rube cuts me off. "I see that now. It sucks, massively, but considering everything, we were lucky. We got lots of time with him. More than most get with their genetic sources. I'm going to focus on that, remember the good, forget the bad."

"I'm forgiven?"

"For the stuff with Dad, definitely. For letting Aliah know it was you leaving flowers... not so sure about that." He flashes his lopsided smile.

"Ha, ha," I deadpan, punching Rube in the shoulder. I turn with him to watch the others emerge from the Thanatos building. Rube's always been a terrible flirt, terrible in that he flip-flopped between crushes like they were the flavour of the week. The fact he and Aliah have stayed in contact says a lot. "Looks like you two are still a thing."

"I have no idea how, but yeah. I like her, Ry. A lot." Rube gives my shoulder a pat before rushing to meet Aliah, swinging her around in one of his signature hugs. Aliah is caught off guard, but her surprise quickly gives way to flushed cheeks and a smile that crinkles the corners of her eyes.

Setting Aliah down, Rube takes a step back, his face darkening as Tazib steps forward.

"Did you bring the things we need?" Tazib asks.

"The only thing you need is my fist in your face," Rube rumbles. "But from the looks of it, someone beat me to it."

I move to put a calming hand on Rube's elbow, but Aliah's already there. "Darr put him in his place," she says. "Though I don't think anyone here would object if you wanted a turn."

"Nah." Rube shakes his head though his fists remain clenched at his sides. "He isn't worth bruising my knuckles."

"We should keep moving," Tali adds, glancing around. "It isn't safe to stay in one place long, not so close to the city."

"I wouldn't worry too much," Rube says, leading us down a path. "No one even looked my way when I collected what you asked for, or even when I stole the canoe. Nobody cared. Not that there are many people around to notice. There are no elders to report to, and all the WC safety and order drones were taken offline when the United People stepped in."

"What's it like?" Tali asks. "In the cities? Now that our leaders are gone."

Rube sighs, his face going slack. "It's messy. Most people have stopped serving and spend their time doing fun things or using The Light. But not everyone." He squares his shoulders. "Some of us are trying to keep things together. I have a small team putting in extra hours at my green-lot. It's a struggle, but we are keeping people fed. Not great food, but fed. And there are others who have gathered dorms together—gotten the older years, the Year 8, 9, and 10s—to help with the younger groups. It seems to be working. It reminds me of us," Rube says, nodding to me. "It's like the kids are learning how to be siblings. They're looking out for each other, building connections. The littles love following the older kids around and copying them. The dorm leaders who are left say it's been a huge help. Here we are."

Rube stops at a canoe pulled onto the beach, its back end resting low in the water with its burden of old tech and bags of fruit and vegetables.

"I hope I got what you needed," Rube says to Aliah. "I tried to find older-model stuff, like you asked. Your tip about looking for abandoned towers was super helpful. I had no idea so many were sitting empty."

"Thanatos has been at work for a while," Aliah says dryly as she inspects a dated screen. "What do you think, Tazib, will this work?"

"We've worked with less, haven't we, Maisie?" Tazib grunts as he struggles to lift an old console over the edge of the boat. "Eldon, give me a hand. Let's get this stuff back to the pods."

Tazib, Eldon, and Maisie grab armloads of tech and head back into the cover of the trees. Tali and I collect the food.

"Come on," Tali nods. "Let's give them a minute to themselves."

I glance to where Rube leans towards Aliah, speaking in soft tones for her ears only. I want to object, to claim every second I can, but I follow Tali back to the Thanatos building where Eldon hurries to take the bags from us, eager to dig in. With his mouth full of green beans, he doles out food to the rest of us, making sure some is set aside for Darr. I take a bunch of carrots, snapping off their green tops as I watch Maisie and Tazib connect the old tech to the interface of the pods. When Rube and Aliah return, Aliah joins them, double checking their work. I hand Rube a carrot where he leans against the pod, his eyes rarely leaving Aliah.

"Come with us."

"What?" Rube barely glances at me. "Why would I come with you? I can't help."

"Sure you can."

Rube snorts. "How? By identifying underwater plants? I don't think so."

"You're strong and fast. And the more of us there are, the better the chance we can overpower any resistance we meet."

"Ry." Rube turns to me, his voice dropping into that familiar big brother tone, tender and understanding. "We'll see each other again."

Unexpected tears fill my eyes and I blink to keep them at bay. "We can't know that for sure."

"No," Rube says slowly. "But I believe it." He throws an arm over my shoulder and for a moment, my heart stutters at how much he reminds me of Dad. "We will see each other again. I'm sure because…" He hesitates, taking a slow breath before continuing. "Because the music tells me."

"You hear it?" My heart leaps.

"I do. Not all the time," Rube rushes. "Usually only when I'm dreaming, but sometimes, when I'm in the green-lot, down a row of plants where I can't see anyone else and all I can hear is the whir of the fans… sometimes I hear it then too."

"Rube—"

"It's the reason I have to stay here," Rube continues. "The music knows me. It's helped me see I'm good at what I do. I can provide food for a lot of people, and right now we need it. And I'm meeting people who want to help, it's like a whole new community is forming. It still sucks, and we disagree all the time, but at the heart we want to help. We want to keep people safe and fed. We'll figure out the rest later."

"Wow." I bump my shoulder into Rube's side. "Who would have thought Rube-the-goof could become Rube-the-responsible?"

Rube laughs. "If you had told me back in Ol'Syd I'd be passing on the chance to sink to the bottom of the ocean to stay behind to grow food, I would have laughed in your face. Jep too." His voice grows softer. "Jep would choose to help others, wouldn't he?"

"He would've."

"I don't know if I'll ever stop missing him." Rube swallows, dropping his head. "Sometimes I feel bad that I miss him more than Mom and Dad."

"He was your brother," I say, lacing my hand with his. "Not by genes but by choice."

"He was."

We are quiet as we watch the others. Eldon has settled not far from Tali and he massacres a pile of leaves as he sporadically chats with her, the tips of his ears turning pink at each attempt.

"Loren contacted me."

"Really? Is she okay? Did she find Arisu?" I rush.

"From the sounds of things, it wasn't easy, but she did find Arisu and a bunch of other kids. Things are going down in Ol'Syd a lot differently than here. People are fighting, like with actual weapons. It's really dangerous."

I chomp on my lip as my stomach knots. I shouldn't have sent Loren, especially not alone.

"Loren says she hooked up with someone from her old complex.

They're hiding the kids in the school. She contacted me because she didn't want to risk your safety."

"How did she look?" I ask.

"She looked exhausted," Rube answers. "But determined. You know Loren, she'll be okay. I feel sorry for anyone who walks into that school thinking they're going to hurt those kids."

For a split second I debate telling Rube what happened with little Mart and Loren's guilt, but I decide against it. It isn't my story to tell.

"Hey, can you do me a favour?" Rube says, rubbing the back of his neck and fluffing his shaggy hair. "Watch out for Aliah for me?"

"You guys have gotten really close."

"We have." Rube is silent a minute. "She doesn't open up to others easily. And with good reason. I won't betray her by telling you anything but... don't let her take unnecessary risks."

It's my turn to snort. "You're asking the wrong person. I'm always rushing into things without thinking."

"Not as bad as me," Rube chuckles. "But no. Aliah is still healing, and I just think... She wants to fix this so badly. She'll justify almost anything, even sacrificing herself. She's never thought about a future, never imagined what her life could look like, and I just..." He blows a long breath, his eyes jumping to Aliah. "I worry about her."

"I'll do my best," I promise, watching Tazib and Maisie light up with satisfaction as they finish connecting the tech. Looks like it's time to leave.

"Hey." Rube senses my mood change and he pulls me into a hug. "It's going to be okay, Ry. Listen to the music."

I tighten my arms around Rube's middle, lingering a moment longer before climbing back in the pod where Darr continues to sleep. I watch as Aliah approaches Rube, her head bowed. He takes her chin, tilting her face up as he talks, brushing a tear from her cheek. When they press their palms together, I turn away, allowing them this short moment of privacy, knowing that despite what Rube says, there's no guarantee this isn't their last.

Aliah avoids eye contact when she joins me, activating the pod and raising it from the ground. I move to stand beside her, looking down to where Rube waves enthusiastically as the leaves swirl over his feet, politely ignoring the silent track of tears that slip down Aliah's cheeks. As his form is swallowed by the canopy of trees, I cling to his last advice and listen for the symphony.

Using the stolen tech, it doesn't take long for Tazib and Aliah to pinpoint the location of the secret pod station. We use the travel time to dig through WC records for information on the security at both the pod station and the underwater servers, wanting to be as prepared as possible. Unfortunately, details for both locations are limited. Darr surmises it's likely for a reason; after all, secret information can't be stolen if it isn't recorded, but it leaves a sour taste in my mouth as we approach the island where the special pods are hidden.

"It's a lot smaller than I was expecting," Eldon says as the pods slow for descent.

"And closer to land than I thought it would be," Tali adds.

The tiny island is nestled in a bay surrounded by sloped hills covered in the remains of a crumbling ancient city. The island itself is nondescript. No trees grow on its gentle hill and the brown grass is bent flat from the fierce Atlantic wind that rocks the pods.

"Time to split up," Aliah announces from the doorway of the adjoining pod. "Everyone know what to do?"

We nod. From the little information we could glean, we know the pods are being kept underground. The first objective is to find a way in.

"I wasn't expecting it to be so empty," Tali says as she scans the mound below us. "You'd think finding an opening would be easy, since there's nothing here, but I can't see anything that looks like it might lead underground."

I have to agree. The only structures on the island are ancient, like before-the-fall ancient. A few straight lines of stone mark where an octagonal fortification once stood. There is nothing to indicate the World Collective has ever been here.

We split into our groups before the pods separate, each landing in a different spot on the island; Aliah with Darr, Eldon with Maisie, and me with Tali and Tazib.

Stepping from the pod, I'm immediately chilled to the bone by the bitter wind. Tali pulls her sleeves over her fingers as she scans the area.

"Looks like there's an old dock or something over there. That might be a good place to start."

Tali leads the way as we move to the water's edge. The waves lap at the rocks, spraying our already cold faces.

"This place gives me the creeps." I shiver.

"Me too," Tali agrees.

"Come on." Tazib's smile is more of a wince. "Use your imagination. This could be a lovely place. Build a little house, plant a garden."

"Who would want to live here?" Tali shakes her head. "It's so isolated and lonely."

"Exactly," Tazib motions. "No one to tell you what to do. No one to judge your decisions. It's practically paradise."

I roll my eyes as I pick my way to the remains of an old foundation, checking the ground for any sign of a hidden hatch.

"Any luck?" Eldon's voice transmits to my tragus implant.

"Nope," I answer. "Darr and Aliah?"

"Nothing yet," Darr answers. "Wait. Aliah's found something."

I look up the mound to where Darr and Aliah's pod sits near one of the remaining walls. I can't see them from this angle, but I hear Aliah's cry of alarm.

"Darr?" I transmit. "What's happened?"

"She just disappeared," Darr answers, his voice bouncing as he runs. "She was just—"

He too is cut off by a sharp cry.

"Darr? Darr!"

There's no answer.

I race up the hill, my long strides quickly distancing me from Tali and Tazib. Cresting the hill, I find more windswept grass and a couple scraggly bushes tucked against the remains of the walls. I spin in a circle, scanning the area. From here I have an unobstructed view of the whole island. Maisie and Eldon are climbing over large rocks on the south side while Tali and Tazib scramble after me. There is no sign of Darr or Aliah. But what's more puzzling is there's no sign of what could have happened to them. They've simply disappeared.

"What happened?" Tali gasps as she reaches me. "Where did they go?"

"I don't know." I hurry to Darr and Aliah's pod, trying to retrace their steps. "Fan out," I tell Tali and Tazib. "But be careful."

Tali moves away, her hands outstretched and head swinging from side to side like she expects to run into an invisible wall. Considering the WC and the secrets they've managed to keep, it is a possibility, but from the way the wind relentlessly tears at us, it's unlikely there are any invisible structures nearby.

"This is strange," Tazib says, disregarding my instruction to fan out and instead staying by the pod with his little device. "I can't get a read on either of them."

"What does that mean?" If I wasn't so cold I would be shaking from anxiety. I don't like this.

"It means we're in the right place." Tazib tilts his screen towards me. "Look, even Eldon and Maisie's signals are weak."

I move along the low wall, running my hands over the stones worn smooth from years of being battered by the elements. Perhaps there's a button or switch to open access to the tunnels we know must be here.

"Ry!"

I spin towards Tali's short scream, but I don't see her anywhere on the barren hill.

"Tali!" I yell, straining to hear over the whistling wind. I spin to Tazib. " Did you see anything? Where did she go?"

"She was over there." Tazib points to an innocent looking patch of grass. "Then she wasn't."

"Come on." I grab Tazib's arm, tugging him along with me.

"I don't think so." Tazib tries to pull away, but I hold firm. "Whatever's happening doesn't sound inviting. I think I prefer finding a more controlled method of entering the pod station, one that doesn't involve dropping into the ground. For all we know, it could be a safety measure. An elevator shaft that lowers people with the correct digital signature to the submersible pods while dropping those without it to their deaths."

"Tazib!" I screech, freezing in my tracks. "Why didn't you say anything sooner?"

"It was only a suspicion until Tali disappeared."

"What do we do?" I squeeze Tazib's arm. "We need to go after them. They could be hurt!"

"Eldon," Tazib speaks into his device. "We've found something. You guys should join us. Bring the pod."

Impatient, I watch as Maisie and Eldon hurry back to their pod, flying it to the top of the hill to rest next to Darr's and Aliah's.

"Where are the others?" Eldon asks as he hops free.

"I think they've found the entrance," Tazib explains.

"That's great!"

"Not if it dropped them down the shaft."

Eldon's face pales.

Tazib signs to Maisie and together they climb into the pod.

"What are you doing?" I shout over the wind. "We can't leave. We need to help them!"

"We need to find someone with clearance to the station," Tazib says.

You should help, Maisie signs, beckoning for me to join them in the pod.

I eye the strange assortment of servers and screens jerry-rigged to the pod. Chances are, if I touch anything I'll start a fire. "I'll stay out here, see if there's anything I can find."

No, Maisie signs. *You know the WC,* she explains. *Who might have clearance to the submersibles?*

"I don't know!" I snap. I don't understand how they can be so calm. The others could be seriously injured or dead, and other than Eldon turning a little pale, they don't seem to care.

Would Merari have access? she presses. *Or your dad?*

"I don't think so," I huff. "Why would they ever want or need to visit servers? Besides, they're dead. How could their credentials help?"

"Considering the state of everything, I doubt anyone has removed their clearance," Tazib answers. "But you're right. We're looking at this wrong. Maisie, search for those in the WC with the most experience managing a data centre. That's who we need."

While they hack away at their computers, I pace outside the pod. At least my anger heats me.

"Okay," Tazib calls. "Give me your arm, I think we got this." Tazib scans my arm as the others hop out of the pod. "I've changed your digital signature to that of a data centre technician. Let's hope it works."

Where did you last see Tali? Maisie asks.

"Over here." Tazib leads the way to a spot that looks exactly like every other, but as we get closer, I notice a subtle crunch under my feet betraying something more lies hidden below the long, thick grass.

"Now what?"

A faint rumble vibrates from below. I throw out my arms as the area begins to sink, lowering us into a cement shaft. The moment we step off the patch of grass into a damp brick-lined tunnel, it rises, blocking the sliver of daylight and quieting the howling wind with a resounding thud.

CHAPTER TWENTY-ONE

"**T**ALI! DARR! ALIAH!"

My voice echoes back to me. The tunnel is empty. I don't know whether to be grateful or alarmed. Grateful we haven't found their broken bodies. Alarmed because if they aren't here, where are they?

"Hello?!" I call again. The drip of water and our too loud breathing is the only answer. "Anything on your fancy little device?" I snap at Tazib.

"Nope, nothing. It doesn't even show us anymore." Tazib shows me the screen, all our previously flashing dots now gone. "Guess we're going in blind."

Together we creep down the brick-lined passage. It is a claustrophobic space. There is little headroom despite the few lights being hung at waist height, and it is so narrow we are forced to walk single file. When we reach a branch in the tunnel, Tazib signs for us to go right. I'm thankful the translator feature allows me to understand the silent signals since speaking aloud feels wrong in this oppressive space. We continue in the same manner, each turn and passageway looking identical to the last. Its labyrinthine nature reminds me of the holding centre in Unity, but nothing else about the underground tunnels is like anything found in the World Collective. It feels old, really old. The floor has a worn track down the centre and the brick walls are discoloured from years of water damage.

Tazib stops suddenly, signalling to stay quiet and listen. I lean forward, my teeth clamped on my lower lip, hearing only ringing stillness.

But there.

A low murmur.

Voices.

We inch around the corner and down the next tunnel, the voices growing steadily louder until we can distinguish one from the other. One voice is confident. The other pleading. One voice is a deep, low baritone and the other…

I gasp.

The second voice sends me tumbling back in time. Images of laugher, sun, trees. The feeling of strong arms keeping me safe, a kiss on the forehead. A voice reassuring me to trust.

Dad.

I push my way past Tazib and Maisie in the narrow tunnel, twisting my arm away as Tazib tries to grab me.

And there he is.

Dad.

The world slows. A thousand thoughts race through my mind, memories and promises, disappointments and lies. I thought I'd never see him again. That surely, with all the Thanatos deaths, he was already gone. But here he is, alive and well. And while I'm still hurt by the secrets he kept, I still love him—and I know he loves me.

"Dad."

I crash into Dad's arms and he pulls me close, his chin rubbing into my hair as I bury my face in his collar, his familiar smell filling my eyes with hot, stinging tears.

"My little survivor."

"I'm sorry," I rush, the words tumbling from me. "For not saying I love you. I was mad, I'm still mad, but I get it. We all make mistakes, we all hurt people, especially when we are hurting. You love me. That's why you did it."

"Rygita," Dad sighs into my hair. "My darling girl. Don't forgive me—what I did was unforgivable—but yes, I love you. Every day I've loved you. You and Rube and your mother, Sabeen. I had the whole world. The best life any man could hope for."

"Ry?" Tazib's voice pulls me back to the present and returns the world to normal speed. "This isn't really the time for a touching reunion."

"I tend to agree."

I turn to the deep voice, knowing I will find Kohath, the leader of the United People.

Dad gently tugs me back until I am tucked safely behind his shoulder. "Let her go." Dad's tone is no longer pleading. "Don't do this. They're children."

"I'm afraid I can't do that, Morrow."

"Wait." My brain is only now catching up to fact the that Dad is here, here in a secret pod station on the remote coast. My head swings between the two men. "Do you know each other?"

"We met a long time ago," Dad says. "Back when Kohath worked in the healing centre in Ol'Syd."

"I don't understand. Why are you *here*?"

"That's a question for him." Dad's voice rings with scorn. "Why am I here?" He glares at Kohath.

"I rescued you from the plastic mines because I saw your value." Kohath smiles at Dad before turning to Tazib. "Just as I saw your value all those years ago, and how I see Rygita's now."

"My value, huh?" Tazib steps further into the small space where multiple tunnels join. His eyes catch mine, flicking to the corner where Eldon and Maisie remain out of sight and then away, a silent signal to keep their presence hidden. "What do you know of my value?"

"It's good to see you again, Tazib," Kohath's rich voice rumbles.

His genuineness makes Tazib pause. His eyes narrow as he studies Kohath, his brow wrinkled in confusion.

"Come on now, you can't have forgotten me. I'll give you a hint." Kohath lowers his voice even further so it thunders like a gentle giant. "Come on, Tazib, don't you remember Mr. Toad?"

Recognition flashes on Tazib's face, his eyes widening as he rocks back on his heels. "You."

"Yes, me," Kohath smiles. "I really am glad to see you, Tazib. To see how you have grown into an intelligent, capable young man. They didn't want to save you at first, but I knew you were a fighter. That you could be useful."

"You're…" My mind scrambles to make sense of what is

happening as I look between Tazib and Kohath. "You're a medical officer? It was you who saved Tazib's life after the accident? But... how? You're with the United People."

"I wasn't always. When the accident happened, I was the lead at the healing centre. I actually triaged both of your care when you arrived." His eyes grow dark. "When the World Collective began their cover-up, when they decided we shouldn't heal you completely, that we should leave you marked, well that was my turning point."

"Marked?" My question is nothing more than a puff of air.

"Yes," Kohath nods. "They wanted a permanent reminder of the event. It was genius, really. By spinning the accident as a terrorist attack, they were able establish a zero-tolerance stance towards any groups that opposed the WC while garnering support at the same time. Who could look at a little scarred child and not feel rage?"

"But they didn't show me," Tazib's voice cracks. "You're telling me you could have fixed this?" He thrusts out his scarred hands. "Why? Why let them do that to me when they were erasing me anyway?"

"I'm sorry, Tazib," Kohath says. "When I realized what they were doing, that's when I knew I could no longer serve the Collective so blindly. I sought out the group being blamed, knowing if the Collective believed them to be so dangerous, there must be something to them."

"You left me." Tazib's voice is so small, so child-like. "You were the only one who treated me like a human, the only one who took time to make me laugh or ask about my nightmares. And then one day, you were gone."

"I made the mistake of objecting and they transferred me."

"You abandoned me!" Tazib's voice cracks.

"I saved you," Kohath answers calmly. "Twice. First, by keeping you alive, and then by getting you out."

"I got myself out." Tazib scowls, crossing his arms over his chest.

Kohath tilts his head. "You were a child, yes—one with impressive hacking abilities—but come on, Tazib, we both know the events of that day went too smoothly, too perfectly to be completely your own doing."

Tazib huffs, but his eyes betray his doubts. "Don't listen to him, Ry. He's no different from the leaders of the Collective. He's twisting everything around to suit his fancy. We can't trust a word he says. Next, he'll be claiming he wants nothing to do with The Code."

Kohath laughs, a disarming smile on his face as he shakes his head. "No, Tazib. We need The Code. Look at the control it provides. The United People have never wanted to abolish it, not completely. Change it, yes. Rewrite sections that have allowed citizens to become lazy, self-entitled, and mindless, but never abolish it."

"Of course not," Tazib mumbles, rolling his eyes dramatically. "I should've known. You love The Code because you love Thanatos. You like being in control of it, don't you?" he asks Kohath. "It's helpful to your objectives if you can kill people off with a few strokes of the keys, isn't it?"

Kohath isn't fazed by Tazib's dramatics; rather, he seems glad to have an audience. "It's the United People's goal to start a new age. Yes, recent events have been upsetting, but we will rebuild, as we have in the past. Only this time, it will be different. We will live alongside The Code, with elected leaders who have the power to modify The Code when needed."

"And I'm sure it will just be a lucky coincidence if you're elected."

"No coincidence—simple planning, as any good leader would do."

"What does that have to do with us?" I ask.

"I would think it was obvious." Kohath smiles, that easy smile like Merari was so good at. "The people love you, Rygita, they have from the beginning. I may have thought it cruel to choose one child over the other, but the WC did get it right. Who could resist the gap-toothed grin of the girl with the curls? You chose to work for the United People once and I'm here to remind you why it's the right choice. Think of the world you could help build. A world where we recognize The Code is only a tool, not the giver of life and death, but a program to help us as we govern ourselves."

My fingers reach for my necklace. Why do his words make my skin crawl? Haven't I wondered the same things, about what the world could look like if we weren't so dependent on The Code?

"You're doing a lot of talking," Tazib drawls. "Without really explaining anything. Like why is Ry's dad here? 'Cause that seems pretty random."

"Nothing random about it at all." Kohath faces me, his expression serious. "Your misguided attempt to rescue Merari's offspring, Kyven, told me exactly what I needed to ensure your cooperation. And as you know, our embedded technology is very useful in tracking movement and conversation." He smiles. "It was so easy. All I had to do was monitor those you cared about. We followed Darr's signal to the Uncounted; and once you escaped the mountain, I knew it was only a matter of time before you made contact with your brother, Rube, letting us know where to intercept you."

"And here you are," Tazib deadpans.

"Yes," Kohath says. "Here I am."

"But why is Dad here?" I don't like the worry I see in Dad's eyes, the anxious gathering of his brows.

"I should think it was obvious. He's here to ensure you make the right decision, Rygita." A new fear whispers in the back of my mind, turning my hands clammy. "What I didn't count on was the added bonus of having so many of your friends walk themselves in as backups."

Kohath taps his wrist and from the opposite tunnel come the sounds of shuffling feet. Darr, Aliah, and Tali are escorted into the small space by armed guards, their feet restrained by linked metal cuffs. All three are covered in dark grime, skid marks on their knees and elbows, scratches on their hands and faces. Aliah and Tali look sore but otherwise unharmed. The same can't be said for Darr. His wound oozes dark red blood that stains his shirt and he sways on his feet, his shoulders hunched as he clutches his side.

"This is what's going to happen," Kohath says, taking a device from one of the guards. "First, you will tell me how to fix The Code. I know you have the answer. It's the only logical reason for you to break Tazib out of the WC's holding cell or for you to be here, at the submersible pod station. Two," he continues over the pounding of my heart. "You will film a broadcast explaining to the world how the United People have saved them."

"And if I don't?"

"You will." Kohath's confidence raises my alarm even more. He motions with the small device. "Because if you don't, I will activate an instant Thanatos on your paternal source. And if that doesn't convince you, then I will take your friends from you, one by one, until you have no one left."

The edges of my vision darken as a loud ringing in my ears muffles Kohath's words.

"I see you understand. So, Rygita, are you ready to cooperate? After all, the choice is yours."

The choice is yours.

Those words break the fog. Blinking, my eyes refocus as a melody whispers in my mind. I may be deep underground in a brick room too small for all the bodies crammed into it, but I am not trapped. Over and over the music has shown me that I'm never alone, and in this moment, with the lives of those I love on the line, I cling to that promise. The choice is mine and I choose not to live in fear.

"No," I say aloud.

"No?" Kohath is genuinely surprised. "Are you sure you don't want to reconsider?" He waves the device and a screen shimmers into focus. With a quick swipe, Dad's image is displayed, the place on his wrist where our tech is embedded, highlighted.

"We don't have a fix," Darr groans. "Tell him, Tazib. It's impossible. We can't stop Thanatos from speeding up."

"He's right," Tazib says, taking a small step backwards. "I was sure the answer lay with Rygita, everything pointed in that direction, but we found nothing. There is no fixing Thanatos."

"Then why are you here?"

"To kill it, obviously," Tazib grins.

Kohath blanches. "But that could kill everyone."

"Maybe." Tazib shrugs. "With no way to fix Thanatos, you're all going to die anyway. Some sooner than later."

"What is that supposed to mea—"

"Now, Eldon!"

Tazib spins to the tunnel opening, catching the small device Eldon tosses him. He swings back to Kohath, a screen of his own shimmering into focus, this one with Kohath's image. Understanding dawns on Kohath's face and he grunts as Tazib strikes enter, one hand grabbing at his chest, his eyes bulging as he sinks to his knees.

But his other hand remains on his own device.

"Ry."

Dad's voice twists with pain as he falls towards me. I struggle to catch him, but I'm unable to support his weight. We sink to the ground.

"Dad!"

Dad's face is ashen and his eyes roll back in his head as he clutches at his chest.

And then he is still.

It happens so fast. Commotion erupts. One of the guards rushes to perform CPR on Kohath while the other shouts in alarm, brandishing his weapon at Tazib who yells at him to lay down his arms or face the same fate. But it all happens in the peripheral: a blurred, muted action swirling around me while I, in the centre, am unmoving. All I see is Dad. It seems impossible, that this man who used to appear so much larger and wiser than anyone else, is so suddenly gone. He made mistakes, so many terrible mistakes, but his motive was always his love for his kids, for me. I stroke Dad's cheek, my fingers tracing where his beard meets his skin, before sliding my hand to his forehead, slowly drawing my hand down to hide his now empty brown eyes. Salty tears wet my lips as I rock forward to kiss his still warm cheek.

I am an orphan.

The World Collective would say it doesn't matter. We live collectively, meeting each other's needs so we don't need parents in the ways of our ancestors. But I've seen how things can be different. I've *lived* differently. My parents mattered because they were mine. And now they are both gone.

A yawning chasm of emptiness threatens to swallow me, a black hole of sorrow ready to rip my heart into tiny pieces.

But something holds me back.

Something holds me together.

Gentle refrains wash over me. Music filled with sorrow and loss, but also laced with hope. Though the grief threatens to consume me, a bigger presence envelops me, reminding me I am not alone. Notes climb and twist and promise this is not the end. Death is not the end.

CHAPTER TWENTY-TWO

"**R**Y, WE HAVE TO MOVE."

Tali tugs me to my feet and I stumble after her down the narrow passageway. I'm not sure what happened, how Aliah, Tali, and Darr got free from their restraints or what happened to the guards, but from the faces of the others, I know things are bad. Aliah is swearing, Tali looks absolutely terrified, and Eldon is flipping out, his hands flying madly as he signs with Maisie. Only Tazib appears calm as he briskly leads us away.

Warm fingers wrap around my hand with a gentle squeeze and I glance over at Darr through my haze of tears. He doesn't say anything, he only nods at me with compassionate eyes. He knows how close Rube and I were to our paternal source. He understands how deeply this loss strikes.

"I thought we'd agreed there would be no more killing!" Aliah snaps.

"You had a better idea?" Tazib skids to a stop in front of a polished metal door. He waves his device over the built-in scanner, motioning Maisie forward to check out the lines of code. "He was going to kill you—all of us."

"We don't know that for sure." Tali's voice wavers and her forehead creases in wrinkles. "He could have been bluffing."

Tazib snorts. "Sure. That's why Ry's Dad is dead."

My breath hitches as all eyes swing to me.

"It's okay." I cling to Darr's hand. "Tazib's right. Kohath would have done anything to get what he wanted."

"But the guards?" Eldon flops back against the tunnel wall. "You killed them, Tazib. They were just following orders. Didn't you see them? They weren't much older than us."

"They chose the wrong side and it cost them." Tazib doesn't look away from his screen.

"Maybe we should have tried talking to them?" Tali glances at Eldon who's begun to tremble. "Maybe if they knew what we're trying to do, maybe they would have helped us?"

"It's a bit late for that." Aliah edges her way between Tazib and Maisie, pulling the device from Tazib's hand. "You need someone with clearance," she declares.

Ry, Maisie waves me over. *Use your palm. The stolen digital print should work.*

I slip from Darr's side and touch my hand to the metal scanner. The doors open with a rusty squeak and together we step into an underground cavern that is large and open after the claustrophobic narrowness of the tunnels. Lit with floor lights that cast ominous shadows on uneven walls, the space is dominated by a large pool of black water where two pods sit ready. Unlike the standard glass sphere, these pods are completely encased with heavy metal, their shape more egg-like than circular, with a rudder, fins, and propeller cluttering the usually sleek surface.

Aliah and Tazib hurry to the pods, activating the scanners and working to bypass the security.

"Two." Tali steps towards the strange submersibles. "There are only two."

Two pods and seven people. Three people is pushing it in a normal pod and the submersibles are much smaller. Two seats barely fit in the confined space and extra gadgets litter the walls and floors, leaving no room to squeeze in a third. Only four of us will be able to travel to the servers.

"Good." Eldon lowers his shaking limbs to the ground, his long skinny legs stuck out straight before him. "I don't want to come. Not anymore. I can't. I can't do it again. I can't be a part of this if there's a chance we'll hurt more people. I'm done."

Tazib glances up from his screen, his light-filled eyes shadowed by his brows. But he doesn't argue with Eldon. "Don't stay here," he cautions. "Get topside, back to the pods. Get away."

"I'll go with him," Darr says. At my cry of protest he pulls his hand away from his side, showing the fresh blood that seeps through his bandages. "I'm no good to you, not like this. I'll only get in the way."

"But Darr, you're good at what you do."

"So is Aliah. And Tazib. And she's pretty impressive too, considering she's tech-free," Darr nods at Maisie. "No, this is the right call."

"I'll stay with you," I declare.

"No," Darr shakes his head, reaching again for my hand. "You started this, Ry. You're the one who got us this far. You need to see it to the end."

"But what can I offer? I'm no good with tech. The others will be fine without me."

"I'll stay too." Tali shifts from foot to foot, tugging on the hem of her shirt. "I don't want to go without you."

"Tali…"

"It works," she rushes. "Then the others will fit."

Aliah looks up from her panel. "I don't think so," she scowls. "I'm not going on a suicide mission on my own with him and a bunch of Uncounted." She juts her chin in Tazib's direction. "Not a chance."

"You don't need to stay, Tali. There's room for you."

I'm staying, Maisie signs. *Eldon isn't fit to fly and Darr can't go back to the Collective, not yet anyway. I'll take them both somewhere safe. That means Ry, Tali, Aliah, and Tazib can go on.*

"Are you sure?" Tazib abandons his device to take a step towards Maisie. Of course, the first time he's worried is when both of his friends volunteer to leave him with a group of WCers.

I'm sure, Maisie answers. *This is their world, their lives. Killing The Code impacts them the most.*

"With that argument, I shouldn't go either."

It is your world too. Maisie touches Tazib's arm where his damaged tech lies dormant under his scarred skin. *This is a part of your story, more than mine. You have a right to be there. See this to the end.*

Maisie pulls Eldon to his feet, pushing him towards the swaying Darr. It's surreal to see Darr drape his arm over Eldon's thin shoulder, thanking him for his help, when only a day ago he was ready to pummel him.

Maisie steps towards Tazib, turning her body so we can't see what she signs; but, from the emotions flickering on Tazib's face, I can guess. There's a chance those of us who go on may not come back. I turn to Darr.

"Don't." Darr shakes his head. "No goodbyes." Darr's dark eyes are soft as they study me. "Every moment with you is an adventure, isn't it?" He smiles, his dimple setting my heart racing. "You've always accused your brother of being over the top, but you're a hundred times worse." He chuckles, wincing at the movement. "I'll see you later."

I force a smile, blinking away fresh tears. "Of course. Later."

"Take care of Tazib for me, will you?" Eldon asks, readjusting Darr's weight on his shoulder.

I try not to grimace as I nod, my gut squeezing uncomfortably.

Eldon helps Darr hobble to the cavern door as Maisie pulls Aliah close, signing something I cannot see, before hurrying to grab Darr's other arm. Together, the three exit the underwater pod station.

"I am not travelling with him," Aliah declares, opening the pod she'd been working on with a flourish. "Tali, come with me."

Tali offers me a bemused expression before climbing into the pod after Aliah. Tazib and I watch as their pod seals and lowers into the water, the lights disappearing from view beneath the inky blackness.

"After you." Tazib waves to the opening of the second pod.

I grip the edge of the pod to steady myself as I lean into the cramped space, dark but for the few blinking lights and a large screen.

"Stop!" An unfamiliar voice echoes in the stone cavern. "Back away from the pod with your hands raised or I'll shoot," they command.

I raise my hands in submission, turning to face a young guard who stands in the doorway. My heart gallops at the sight of her weapon aimed at my chest, one that looks frighteningly similar to what Eldon used.

"Aren't you the brave one." Tazib's hands remain at his sides, his fingers twitching where his device lies in his pocket. "You might want to reconsider your stance. Your leader is dead."

"He wasn't my leader," the guard snaps as she inches towards us. "I follow the movement, not a person."

"My, my, what forward thinking for a WC citizen." I shiver at the shift in Tazib's tone. This Tazib sounds like the Tazib I first met, back when he would whisper in my ear: cold, calculating, and manipulative. "You and I think alike, desiring a new world. Why don't you put down your weapon and we can discuss this, civilized-like."

The guard hesitates, her weapon lowering just a fraction, before she straightens, determination written across her features. "I know who you are, what you've done."

"And what about her?" Tazib asks, tossing his head in my direction. "Do you recognize her?"

"Of course I do," the guard snaps.

"So you know the United People want her on your side. How do you think threatening her with a gun is going to go over?"

The guard glances at me, uncertainty creeping into her eyes. Again her weapon lowers, and this time Tazib capitalizes on the hesitation. With one hand, he shoves me into the pod, while with the other, he whips out his device, quickly opening a screen.

Understanding hits the guard and she gives a cry, again levelling the gun on Tazib. But before she can fire, Eldon barrels across the room, plowing into the guard's middle. The shot ricochets off the pod.

"Go!" Eldon grunts as he wrestles with guard. "Tazib, get out of here!"

"Give me a second," Tazib answers, typing quickly into his little device. "I can get rid of her."

"No!" Eldon screams. "No more killing!" He grunts as the guard's knee connects with his head with a sickening hollow thunk. Eldon slumps unconscious.

"Almost got it," Tazib mutters, his eyes locked on his screen and not the guard who untangles herself from Eldon.

"Tazib, watch out!"

Tazib looks up from his screen, his eyes widening as the guard squeezes the trigger. He's out of time. Even if he could activate an instant Thanatos there's no stopping the speeding bullet. His mouth gapes in surprise.

But it isn't Tazib's body that slumps to the ground.

It happens so quickly my brain doesn't even have time to process her presence. One second, her form was in the doorway, and the next, she had thrown herself in front of Tazib, knocking him to the ground while she took the bullet meant for him.

"No!" Tazib's startled cry rips from him. "Maisie! Maisie, no!"

He scoots forward on his knees, his device forgotten as he rolls her to her back. "Maisie, why would you do that? Why?" He cups her face and her eyes roll as they try to focus on his lips.

"Don't move!" the guard screams, her eyes wide with terror and something else, something twisted and full of pain. She waves the gun at Tazib but cannot keep her eyes from dropping to the red stain that grows across Maisie's chest. "Don't move!" she screams again, her voice breaking. "I mean it!"

Tazib doesn't look up. He continues to lean over Maisie as his scarred fingers caress her cheek. "Why Maisie? You know Al will kill me if I come home without you. Why would you sacrifice yourself for me?"

Maisie raises her hands, her movements slow and laboured.

"Stop!" the guard screams, growing even more unhinged as Maisie struggles to sign. "I said don't move!" She steps towards Tazib, the gun aimed at his forehead.

"Tazib." Eldon struggles to rise, a large welt already forming on the side of his temple. "Tazib, watch out," he croaks as he crumples to his knees, clutching his head with a groan.

"Don't move," Tazib urges Maisie, pressing his hands firmly over her wound, the blood seeping between his fingers.

Brother, Maisie signs. *Choose wisely.* Then her hands fall to her sides, her unseeing eyes still locked on Tazib.

"No," Tazib moans, pulling her limp body to his chest, rocking back and forth. "No, please, no."

"Put your hands up!" screams the guard.

"Tazib! Move!"

Darr's deep voice breaks Tazib's trance. He jerks as the weapon fires, the cement splintering where the bullet strikes. Darr barrels into the guard and together the two crash to the ground, the gun skittering across the stone floor.

Tazib glances between the fallen weapon and the wrestling pair. "You killed her." His voice is low and quiet. He takes a shaky step towards the gun. "You killed her!"

"Tazib, no," Eldon moans, again struggling to stand. "No more killing. Please. For Maisie."

Tazib stills, his shoulders sagging. I grab his arm, dragging him to the pod and shoving him inside as Darr continues to wrestle with the guard. I hesitate, glancing between the weapon and Tazib's fallen device.

"Go," Darr grunts. "Now, Ry. Get out of here."

My blood feels like it's on fire, pounding through my veins, screaming at me to stay and fight. But there's no time. Stopping Thanatos is the goal. I have to trust the others will be okay.

I scoop up Tazib's device and dive into the pod, activating the door. The heavy metal closes with a strange sucking sound, cutting us off from the struggle outside. Through the small sliver of window set into the roof, I watch the light fade as we sink into the depths.

Darkness and silence envelop us as the pod speeds away from the station. Self-guided to the data centre, there's nothing for either of us to do but wait.

I peer at Tazib in the dim light where he sits beside me in the cramped space. He's curled in a tight ball, his knees pulled to his chest, his face tucked away. But he is unable to stop the tremor that shakes his shoulders or the muffled snuffle of his tears.

"I'm so sorry, Tazib." I rest my hand over his and though he flinches, he doesn't pull away. "I know Maisie meant a lot to you."

"Why?" Tazib's voice cracks as he struggles to swallow back a sob. "Why would she do that? I almost had it."

"Because she loved you."

It feels strange to say that word to Tazib, loved, but I know it's the truth. Despite my feelings, despite my inability to forget the ways he has hurt me, I know Maisie loved him. For her, Tazib was family, and I know how confusing and impossible our feelings for family can be. I loved Dad. Despite everything he had done, the ways he too had hurt me, I loved him. My eyes burn as the tears rise and I reach for my necklace, rolling the familiar beads between my fingers.

Beside me, Tazib takes a deep shuddering breath, raising his head and straightening his shoulders. "I don't deserve Maisie's love. Not yet." Gone is his quivering tone. He speaks with a steady, low-pitched determination that sets my heart thrumming. "Her death won't be for nothing. I will stop Thanatos. I'll fix this. I'll fix everything."

CHAPTER TWENTY-THREE

T IS SILENT IN THE UNDERWATER POD. THERE IS NOTHING TO SEE ON the screen but empty space broken only occasionally by an underwater landform, and with Tazib remaining quiet after his declaration, I'm unable to fight my exhaustion any longer.

When I wake with a terrible crick in my neck, I'm momentarily confused by the shapes on the screen before me. I blink the sleep from my eyes, anticipation flooding me with adrenaline at the sight of straight lines and right angles. A man-made structure.

"Looks like we're here."

I follow Tazib's gaze, peering out the tiny window as I roll out my stiff shoulders. Underwater lights illuminate a cement structure and the two large doors that slide open as we approach. As the pod rises, light floods our small space, highlighting the colourful bruises on Tazib's face and the bags under his eyes.

"You ready?" he asks.

"As ready as I'll ever be."

Tazib activates the pod door and we step out in a space nearly identical to the one we left, though the air is much cooler and the walls smoother. Tali and Aliah's pod surfaces beside ours, filling the space with the sound of cascading water as it pours off the pod. When their door opens, we are met with two solemn faces.

"What's wrong?"

Aliah holds up her wrist, showing the green light glowing under her skin. "Happened on the way here." She shrugs like it's nothing, but the tremble in her voice betrays her. I glance at Tali who has her hand clamped over her own wrist, like applying enough pressure will stop it from happening to her.

"Guess that means we need to hurry."

Aliah nods, her expression grim, but also grateful I say no more.

"Do you think there will be guards?" Tali asks as we move to the door leading into the main structure. "Or alarms?"

"I doubt there's any guards," Aliah's says. "Ours are the only pods here. There might be alarms, but who's left to monitor them?"

"And if there are, by the time anyone reaches us, we'll have done what we came to do." Tazib waves his device over the palm scanner but the door remains closed. "Ry, you should scan. The fake identity should get us in."

I press my palm to the cold metal, the familiar tingle twitching my fingers the same moment the door glides open. Together, we step into a sterile hall. All is quiet but for a distant hum and our wet shoes squeaking on the white floor. Doors line each side, neatly labelled with things like bathroom, storage, switch room, and generator, but we are drawn to the door at the end, the one marked servers.

"Wow," Tazib breathes as he leads us inside.

Wow is right. We step into a room lined on two sides with lockers and benches, much like a green-lot. White suits hang from hooks with white slippers neatly aligned below. But what catches our attention is the wall directly opposite. Lined with glass windows, it overlooks a large, long room, brightly lit from both the floor and the ceiling, with rows upon rows of towers filled with blinking servers. This is it. This is the heart of The Code.

"This looks like a clean room," Aliah says as she picks up a suit. "We should put these on to prevent carrying any dirt into the servers."

"I don't see why," Tazib shrugs. "We've come to kill The Code. We don't need to get all dressed up for the occasion. Come on." He moves to the glass door that leads into the server room. "Let's find the off switch." Once again his device produces no results. "Guess you get the honours, Ry."

I press my palm against the cool metal, but nothing happens. "Why isn't it working?"

Aliah elbows her way to the scanner, running her fingers over the smooth surface. "There's something off about this device, something different."

"Oh," Tali gasps. "I know what it is. I've read about these. It's old. Instead of using your digital print, it actually scans your fingerprints. It isn't working because your fingerprints don't match the identity you're using."

"What do we do now?" I shake the door handle, peering at the servers just beyond our reach. "We need in there."

"Let's smash it," Tazib says, knocking the glass. "I'm sure we can find something heavy enough to break through this."

I shoot Tazib a scowl. "And risk leaving the rest of The Code unprotected? No way. There's got to be another way."

"Don't see why you want to protect it," Tazib shrugs.

"I've seen a few different data centres." Aliah rubs the green light under her skin. "They all tend to have a couple of things in common."

"Sounds like you have an idea."

"It'd be good to find some blueprints of this place, but yeah, I think there's another way."

Aliah motions for us to follow her down the hall to the room labelled "Air Filtration." Stepping inside, we are forced to shout to be heard over the deafening whir of huge fans.

"I thought so," she shouts. "Look, this is how they keep everything cool." On the wall is a large diagram of the underwater structure. "This system is drawing the warm air out of the server room and sending it through those pipes where the sea water cools it." She points to large conduits. "Then it goes through that," —she indicates the large refrigeration machines— "to cool the air further, before pumping it back through those ducts. If we access the ducts, someone should be able to crawl through to the server room and then open the door from the inside. See?" She points to where the ducts run the length of the server room.

"Is that safe?" I eye the ventilation shafts. Though they look large enough for someone to wriggle through, the noise level suggests the air inside would be pretty forceful. "How would someone breathe in there?"

"I didn't say it would be comfortable."

"Sounds like a plan." Tazib looks between us. "So, who gets the honours?"

"Me." Tali bites her bottom lip, but her chin is held high, her large blue eyes determined. "I'm the smallest."

"Tali—"

"I can do this, Ry, I know I can. Is there anything else I should know?" she asks Aliah.

"Not really. From the drawing, it looks like a straight shot." Aliah runs her finger along the diagram. "They vent through the floor in a number of spots before turning to run up the wall and along the ceiling. If you come out any of the first ones, you'll be right in front of the door."

"How will she get the vents open?" I ask. "I doubt they'll just pop open with a push. She'll be trapped."

"Didn't we pass a tool room?" Tali tugs at her shirt while she hops from foot to foot. "I bet we can find something in there."

"Good thinking," Aliah nods. "Go, look for wire-cutters, something strong. And see if you can find a wrench or something that can help us open this." Aliah stomps on a large access panel on the floor.

"Got it," Tali nods.

"I'll come with you."

I follow Tali back down the hall to the tool room. Like everything else in the building, it is neat and organized so it doesn't take us long to find a wrench and bolt cutters. The bolt cutters have long handles that will be awkward to crawl with, but they look like they could cut through anything.

"Tali, are you sure about this?" I ask. "It doesn't have to be you."

Tali shoots me a glance. "Don't."

"Don't what?"

"Don't baby me. I can do this. I *want* to do this."

There are so many arguments I could use to counter her, to suggest Aliah go herself since this is her idea, or to do it myself. But I bite my tongue as I look at the way Tali squares her shoulders, the jutting of her chin. Ever since our first meeting on the steps of the Poulia, I've seen her as a little sister, someone to look out for and protect. But protecting doesn't mean limiting—I know that better than most. If I want to watch out for Tali like a big sister, then I need to be her support system and encourager. Not that it makes it any easier to watch her do the scary things.

Back in the Air Filtration room, we take turns wrestling with the wrench to loosen the bolts holding the access panel in place. When we pull the heavy metal covering aside, Tali cautiously pokes her head into the opening, her hair immediately streaming away from her with startling force.

"It's so strong," she yells as she pulls herself free. "I won't have to crawl at all. It's going to pull me through."

Aliah frowns. "It might pull you too far. There's no vent where it goes up the wall. You'll have to grab on to one of the floor ones before you get that far or else you'll be stuck."

Tali's face pales, but she nods resolutely. "I can do it."

"Hold on." I grab Tazib's arm. "You're the tech genius. There has to be a way to control the air flow so it doesn't blast Tali to pieces."

"She'll be fine," Tazib says, shrugging free and moving to the door. "Come on, let's get back to the server room to meet her on the other side. We've got a code to kill."

"No." I block Tazib's path, looking between him and Tali and Aliah. "We aren't going to rush this. We need to think it through. How about we split up? I'm pretty sure we passed a network room. Tazib, you go there and find the controls for the fans."

"Look at you," Tazib says. "Taking charge."

"Aliah, you go to the server room. You'll be able to watch Tali's progress through the windows. I'm going to stay here, in case she needs any help from this end."

"Sounds good," Aliah nods. She taps her ear. "We can use our implants to communicate."

Aliah and Tazib slip down the hall as Tali and I stand by the whistling opening. Tali shifts from foot to foot.

"It's okay to be nervous."

She glances at me. "Thanks for not trying to talk me out of this. I want Thanatos stopped. If this is the way I can help, then I have to do it, no matter how terrified I am." She crouches by the opening, her knuckles white where she grips the bolt cutters.

"Okay," Tazib says in our ears. "Turning off the fans in three, two, one."

Tali doesn't wait for the air to slow before taking a deep breath and sliding forward on her bottom. Dropping into the duct, she half crawls, half slides away, the bolt cutters clanging on the metal shaft as she moves.

"I see the first vent," she calls.

Across from me, a light blinks on the panel of the refrigeration controls, keeping time with the long seconds while I anxiously listen to Tali's grunts as she struggles to manoeuvre in the small space with the long handles.

And then the system restarts.

There is no warning. The silence is shattered with the screech of the fans resuming their spinning, once again pumping the air through the ducts with frightening force.

"Tali!" I scream, but it's pointless. There's no way she can hear me or me her. "Aliah?" I cup my hand over my ear. "Can you see anything?"

"She was cutting the grate, but now she's stopped."

"It's because the air is circulating again. Tazib!" I shout. "Do something!"

"I'm trying, I'm trying," Tazib drawls, clearly lacking the same level of urgency.

"Try faster," I bark.

"Wait, I see her fingers," Aliah says.

Relief floods me, but it's short-lived when Aliah swears.

"What's wrong? What's happening?"

"It looks like Tali's barely hanging on. I mean, I see both her hands, and she isn't cutting the grate."

I glance down at the vent opening, feeling the pull of the air. If Tali is holding on with both hands, it means she's lost the bolt cutters. They've likely been blown down the vent, and if she lets go to find them, there's no way she'll be able to crawl back to the grate.

"Tazib, do something!" I cry, swinging around the room, desperate for some way to help.

"I'm working on it."

Spying the abandoned wrench, I grab it from the floor, its weight heavy in my hand. I rush for the refrigeration controls. Half my brain knows there's probably a more logical way to handle this—I should flip switches instead of smashing them—but the other half thinks only of Tali, trapped in that screaming tunnel, the force of the air so strong it's being pulled from her lungs, her skinny arms shaking as she desperately tries to hold on.

With a battle cry, I swing the wrench again and again. Sparks fly and the metal buckles before the ear-shattering wind quiets. Dropping the wrench, I run back to the vent opening, sliding onto my knees with a painful grunt.

"Tali!" I cry as I duck my head into the darkness. Whatever damage I caused has stopped the powerful fans, but air still moves through the vents. It has a strange smell, almost sweet-like, and when I peer into the darkness, it leaves a dampness on my cheeks. I jerk my head out of the opening when my eyes begin to burn. "Tali," I cough, wiping at my face with the hem of my shirt as my lungs tingle. "Are you okay?"

There is no answer, but I do hear movement, the clang of metal on metal.

"Aliah? What can you see?"

"She has the cutters. She's working on the grate. She should be out soon," Aliah answers. "Good work, Tazib."

"Wasn't me," Tazib chirps. "But I'm on my way."

"Me too." I jog down the hall, joining Tazib and Aliah in the clean room where we watch through the glass as Tali finishes cutting the grate. I give a whoop when her head emerges, throwing my fist in the air. "Good job, Tali!" I call.

But Tali doesn't react. Tears are streaming down her face and she wipes them away with her shirt before stretching out her hand. With cautious steps, she fumbles to the window where she runs her hands over its smooth surface.

"What is she doing?" Tazib asks. "Why doesn't she open the door?"

"I don't know." The hair lifts at the back of my neck as a cold chill creeps down my spine. I knock on the glass. "Tali, open the door."

Again, Tali doesn't react. It's like she neither sees or hears me.

"Knock again," Aliah instructs. "Knock where her hand is."

I hit the glass with my palm, watching as Tali's tear-filled eyes widen.

"She feels it," I gasp, knocking again.

Together, we pound on the glass, moving towards the door as Tali follows the vibrations with her fingers. When she pushes the door open, Tazib is quick to grab it, wedging a white suit under the frame to stop it from closing.

"You did it!" I cheer, grabbing Tali for a hug.

"Ry?" Tali clings to my arms, her voice shrill with pain. "Ry, my eyes! I can't see!"

CHAPTER TWENTY-FOUR

"**R**Y," **TALI WHIMPERS. "MY EYES, THEY'RE BURNING."** I cup Tali's face, my gut sinking. Her deep blue irises are hidden by a cloudy substance, the whites marred by blood-red threads as tears leak down her cheeks.

"We need to rinse her eyes. Fast. I think there was a chemical in the air."

"I'll find water." Aliah runs from the room.

"It hurts."

"I know, hold on." I cradle Tali in my arms.

"Here." Breathless, Aliah hurries to my side, a bottle of water in hand. "Tilt her head back."

I tip Tali's head and Aliah pours the water into her eyes. At first, Tali jerks, confused and surprised, but once she understands, she takes the bottle from Aliah, pouring it into her eyes herself before taking a drink, coughing and spluttering when it hits her lungs.

"Thank you," she gasps. "They don't hurt as much now." She

takes a shuddery breath as she continues to blink. "I'm sorry I took so long. I dropped the cutters."

"It doesn't matter. You got us in."

"What did you say?" Tali shakes her head. "Never mind. It's a bit hard to hear right now. But don't worry." She wipes her face dry with the edge of her shirt "I'm sure I'll be fine in a minute or two. It's just…" She bites her lip. "I might need a little help."

"For sure."

I extend my hand, waiting for her to grab it, but Tali doesn't respond. I meet Aliah's eyes over my outstretched hand, knowing the concern on her face mirrors my own.

Tali can't see.

"Here." I grab Tali's arm, pulling her to her feet. "You ready?"

"Ready." Tali nods. "Let's go do what we came to do."

"She's tougher than she looks," Aliah whispers as she leads the way into one of the many rows of servers.

"She sure is." I loop Tali's arm in mine, keeping my gaze away from her eyes. "I can't believe Tazib didn't wait for us. How will we know which one is Thanatos?"

"We'll know."

We wander up and down the corridors, our footsteps barely audible over the hum of the servers.

"There." Aliah points to a cabinet encased in a metal frame with a glass door and large locking mechanism on the side. "That's it."

We hurry down the row.

"I can't believe this is it."

"Well, we won't know for sure until we get in," Aliah says, peering at the lock.

"I bet Tazib's device can unlock this."

"Why wait?" Aliah steps back against the opposite row of servers, her hair swinging along her back as she bounces on her toes. Then she shouts, delivering a swift kick that shatters the glass front of the cabinet. "What?" she shrugs at my stunned expression. "It isn't like we're worried about leaving a mess."

My laugh echoes in the sterile room. There is such sweet relief in the fact that we're here. Soon this will all be over.

"So?" Tali asks. "Is this it? Can we turn Thanatos off?"

"Give me a sec." Aliah places her hand on a scanner within the cabinet before opening a screen. "This is it. This is the server running Thanatos." She opens a new screen and quickly types out a string of commands.

"What are you looking for?"

"Everything we saw from a distance said we couldn't change the Thanatos coding."

"Yeah, that we needed a crypto key, which we don't have."

"Yeah, but I just thought maybe there's no key because they did away with it. Maybe we can modify the code when we're here in person."

"And?" I prompt.

"And... we need the key." Aliah turns so I can see her screen.

"We can't turn it off?" Tali echoes.

"Changing the code and turning a server off are two very different things," Tazib calls as he strolls towards us from the back of the room. He cocks an eyebrow at the broken glass. "Looks like you beat me to it. What have you got?" He peers at Aliah's screen and then at the wiring of the server. "This'll be easy," he grins, elbowing Aliah out of the way and pulling his device from his pocket.

"Now that we're here, do we have a better idea what will happen to the rest of The Code if we turn off the Thanatos server?" I ask, looking down the row of humming cabinets.

Aliah huffs. "From what I could see before *he* got in the way, it shouldn't do anything. It looks like the Thanatos program accesses the rest of The Code for data but runs separately from it. Everything else should keep functioning as normal."

"Why don't we kill it all?" Tazib asks, running a hand over the shelving of the next tower. "Aren't you tired of having a computer decide your life?"

"I am," I admit, drawing raised brows from both Tazib and Aliah. "But I don't think the world can handle that much change, not yet. We start here, with ending Thanatos. Then we'll have time to consider doing more later, when people aren't dying."

Aliah nods. "I have to agree. I mean I'm sick of having other people decide what's right or wrong for everybody else. If the four of us decided to kill The Code now, we'd be doing the same thing: deciding for everyone else and not giving people a chance to figure out what they want."

"Exactly. We need to take small steps to changing things. There's enough chaos as there is."

"You guys are so melodramatic," Tazib drawls with a grin.

"Aren't you the one always saying chaos wins?"

"Sure." There is a strange sparkle to the light flecks in Tazib's brown eyes. "And ending Thanatos will be no different. So, are we doing this? Can I shut Thanatos down?"

"Do it."

"Finally." Tazib connects his portable device to the server as Aliah watches over his shoulder. When the screen fills with green commands I take my cue and lead Tali clear of the broken glass, finding a spot for the pair of us to sit with our backs to the towers.

"We're turning it off," I say, leaning in to her ear. "Tazib's doing it now. No more Thanatos."

Tali's face brightens. "Good."

"How are you feeling?"

"My ears aren't ringing as much," Tali says. "But my eyes hurt a lot. Everything's fuzzy. I can't make much out, except where the lights are."

"I'm sure they'll clear with a little more time."

"I hope so," Tali's voice drops to a whisper. "Not being able to see... I feel so lost, like I'm disconnected..."

"Here." I pull Mom's necklace over my head, placing the long strand in Tali's hand. "Take this."

"Is this your necklace?" Tali asks.

"It helps ground me," I answer. "When I feel like I'm spinning out of control, I run my fingers over the beads, and I don't know... it calms me. They stay the same no matter what's happening."

"Tazib, stop!"

Aliah's cry turns my attention back down the row. She snatches the device from Tazib, her face pale.

"Didn't you see what it said? We need the key!"

"No, we don't." Tazib reaches for the device. "There's always a work-around."

"This is Thanatos!" Aliah snaps, frantically tapping the screen.

"It's tied to our lives!"

Tali gives me a gentle push. "You better go."

"What's wrong?" I ask, hurrying to intervene.

"Whoever created this was a psycho." Aliah's voice trembles. "Any interaction with the Thanatos server without the crypto key risks activating a Thanatos on every citizen. Look!"

Aliah pushes the device into my hands. On the screen, red letters spell out a warning while blank spaces blink, waiting for the special key we don't have.

"I'm sure it's nothing," Tazib says. "A scare tactic that won't do anything."

"And what if it isn't?"

"Trust me, Ry. I can stop Thanatos." Tazib reaches for the device. "We have to try something. We covered this: if we do nothing, everyone dies. So let me. I can get around this. I know I can."

"Seriously?!" Aliah's voice cracks as she pushes Tazib against the servers, jabbing her finger into his chest. "You really believe you can waltz in here and hack The Code? You're a kid. Just like the rest of us!"

"Um, guys?" Tali calls from her spot on the floor. "Do you smell that?"

"I got us here, didn't I?" Tazib shoves Aliah back.

"No, you didn't!" Aliah shouts. "I'm the one who knew where the servers were."

"Yeah, well, you wouldn't have made it here without me taking out Kohath!"

An acrid smell hits my nose the same instant a loud alarm cuts off Aliah's reply. Instantly, the colour drains from Tazib's face.

"Fire. There's a fire somewhere. We have to go." Already he is inching away.

"But Thanatos," I protest.

Tazib shakes his head, the panic in his eyes palpable. "There's no time. Once the fire suppression system kicks in..." He doesn't finish, but takes off for the exit.

"Ry?!"

I grab Tali's arm, pulling her to her feet and ushering her down the row. Barely audible over the din of the alarm is the sound of turning gears and the metal click of shafts closing.

"What's that?" Tali yells.

Aliah grabs Tali's other hand, helping me rush her to the exit. "The system is isolating the server room. Once it's sealed, it will release a gas to neutralize the oxygen, snuffing out any fires."

Fires aren't the only thing that need oxygen. No wonder Tazib rushed for the exit.

Our feet skid on the floor as we race out of the row and turn towards the door where Tazib is bracing it open with his body.

"Hurry!" he shouts. "We have to get out of here."

I dash through the gap, pulling Tali into the clean room with me, but Aliah hesitates in the doorway, still holding Tali's hand.

"Come on," Tazib grunts, straining against the mechanism forcing the door closed. "We have to get back to the pods."

"I know how to stop it." Aliah pulls her hand away from Tali's, Mom's necklace slipping between her fingers. "I know how to get into Thanatos."

Aliah turns and dashes back into the column of towers as Tazib stumbles. I lurch forward, wedging my prosthetic in the gap before the door can close.

"Ry, we have to go. If there's a fire…" He pulls at my arm. "Don't you see? We're trapped in a burning can at the bottom of the ocean. We *have* to get out of here."

"But Aliah."

"She's dead either way. Once the room seals, she'll have only a minute or two before all the oxygen is gone."

"Then don't let it seal."

I twist from Tazib's grasp, wiggling through the door, and racing after Aliah. When I slide to a stop at the Thanatos server, Aliah looks up from Tazib's abandoned device, her surprise evident only for a second.

"I figured it out," she gasps. "Tazib was right. The answer lay in your past. It was this." She thrusts my necklace into my hands. "Hold it out so I can see all of it."

"Aliah, we can't stay. We need to get out."

"Not yet." Aliah runs her hands over the beads. "Don't you see? The pattern, it's binary. You've been carrying the key the whole time! Now let me think." She taps her finger along the strand, counting quickly, her brow wrinkled in concentration.

I stare at the necklace in my hands, its random pattern of light and dark metallic beads broken into sections with white pearls. This was the answer all along? This final gift from Mom?

"Arg, I can't think straight," Aliah pinches the bridge of her nose, squeezing her eyes shut. "Help me. Open a screen and write down the letters I tell you."

"Okay." I drape the long necklace between my two arms so I can use my hands to open up a screen and type the letters as Aliah identifies them. My head is pounding and I pant in an effort to draw more air into my starved lungs.

"Aliah, we have to go," I repeat, my words slurring.

Tears stream down Aliah's face, but she shakes her head. "I have to do this. We can't let anyone else die."

"We're going to die if we stay."

Aliah glances up, her eyes slightly unfocused but surprisingly soft. "At least it will mean something," she says. "Our deaths wouldn't be for nothing. Ry, don't you get it? Everything has led to this. This is what I am meant to do. And if doing this, if this is the way to set right all the wrongs that have happened, if this is how I can make meaning from all the deaths, then it's okay. But if I fail..." She swallows back a sob. "If I fail... then everything... everyone I lost was for nothing." She sways on her feet, crashing heavily into my side.

I try to focus on Aliah, this person who has been my torment. She's so desperate, driven to the point of being frantic. I made a promise to Rube to protect her, but right now I realize *I* want to protect her. While she's never liked me and we've never gotten along, I see that she too was made for a purpose. And if this is it, if this is how we save the world, then I'm honoured to be with her for the end.

I sag to the floor, propping Aliah against my shoulder. "Aliah, stay with me. You got this, keep going." I hold the necklace in front of us. "We're so close."

Aliah's head rolls, but her fingers return to the beads. As her breathing grows more laboured, I keep encouraging her, decoding each section until we've reach the end. With clumsy fingers, Aliah types out the completed cryptography key.

"Together?" she asks, her finger hovering over enter.

"Together."

As one, we strike the key and watch as the red lettering disappears to be replaced with a standard coding command page.

"Aliah, you did it," I gasp. "We're in."

"Now to end this." Aliah taps the screen, quickly entering the commands to disable Thanatos. "Here it goes."

There are no more passwords, no warnings or alarms. Only a simple text box asking if we are sure we want to disable Thanatos. Aliah doesn't hesitate to hit accept.

"That's it?" I ask, looking up at the looming Thanatos server. It is so strange that this hunk of metal and wires determined the deaths of thousands.

"That's it." Aliah holds up her wrist and it takes a moment for my oxygen-starved brain to understand.

Her Thanatos light is gone.

"Aliah, you did it. You saved everyone," I whisper.

We should be jumping and dancing, celebrating our success with shouts. We've done it. We've stopped Thanatos. No one else will die an early death.

But my head is pounding too violently and my body is too weak. In my arms, Aliah grows heavy, her eyes sinking closed. I know we should try to find a way out of the server room, that we desperately need oxygen, but I can't move. I can hardly focus more than a couple feet in front of me. My only coherent thought is how heartbroken Rube will be.

"Aliah." I slip my hand into hers, Mom's necklace linking our hands together. "I'm sorry it took me so long." My words are garbled, my tongue refusing to comply. "I'm glad we made a connection."

CHAPTER TWENTY-FIVE

THE PERFECT MUSIC DANCES AROUND ME, ITS MELODY intertwining with the hum of the servers, the screech of the alarms, and the sound of breaking glass. Darkness creeps at the edge of my consciousness, but I'm not afraid. We stopped Thanatos. Rube, Tali, Darr, Loren—they'll be safe. If this is the end, it will be okay.

"Hold on, Ry."

Hands stroke my cheek, pushing back my hair and securing something to my face. My lungs sing with the sweet relief of oxygen.

"Don't leave me. Keep fighting. I can't lose you too."

My muddled brain struggles to place the voice, confused by its urgency and pleading. When my eyes flutter open, it takes another minute for the haze to clear.

"Tazib?"

Relief floods Tazib's face and his eyes shimmer with tears as he squeezes my hand. "That's it, there's the curly haired survivor, fighting the odds once again. Come on." He pulls me to my feet, his arm wrapped tightly around my middle to hold me steady. "We have to get out of here."

"Aliah."

The rooms tilts as I struggle to focus on the forms on the floor. Tali is draped over Aliah, fumbling with a canister and another mask.

"Tali's got Aliah," Tazib says, steering me down the row of servers.

"No."

I pull away, my head pounding as I drop to my knees next to Tali. Tears continue to leak from her eyes, her wide blue eyes that stare forward, unseeing. She uses her fingers to find Aliah's mouth, struggling to place the mask.

"Let me." I touch Tali's hands and she starts.

"Ry?"

"I'm here," I say louder, taking the mask from her and securing it over Aliah's mouth and nose.

"Ry. It's not getting better." Tali's hands search the empty space between us and I lean forward, letting her find my arm which she grips tightly. "My eyes aren't clearing."

"This isn't the time to catalogue our injuries," Tazib says, once again pulling me to my feet. "We have to go. Now."

"Not without Aliah."

"Fine," Tazib huffs, releasing me and grabbing Aliah's arms. "You lead Tali."

Tazib drags Aliah's limp form down the row as I follow, leaning on Tali for support. As we near the server room door, glass crunches under our feet.

"We had to break the window," Tali explains. "It was the fastest way to get to you."

"I didn't think it was breakable," Tazib grunts, shoving the empty door frame open to pull Aliah through. "But we didn't have a lot of options. Couldn't go back through the ducts." He drops Aliah, wiping sweat from his forehead. "What did you do in there, Ry? The room's engulfed in flames."

"I did what I needed to do to save Tali." With each deep breath, my head clears a little more. I drop to my knees by Aliah, feeling for her weak pulse. "She needs a healing centre."

"If we don't get out of here, a healing centre won't save any of us."

Tazib grabs Aliah's arm, pulling it over his shoulder, and I hurry to lift her other side.

"Tali, hang on to me." I grab Tali's hand, handing her the edge of my shirt.

With Tali trailing, Tazib and I stagger out of the clean room and into the hall where we are assaulted by a billowing cloud of smoke and a wave of heat. Long fingers of flames leap from the Air Filtration room, blocking the way to the pods.

"It's spread." Tazib coughs, pulling his shirt up to cover his mouth, his eyes wide with terror. "We're trapped."

"There's an escape hatch." Tali tugs me in the opposite direction. "I saw it before."

Sure enough, at the far end of the hall, red lettering points to an emergency exit.

"Thank The Code for your amazing memory, Tali."

Bowing under Aliah's dead weight, we hurry away from the flames to the round hatch. I struggle to keep Aliah upright when Tazib drops her arm to grab the wheel set in the centre.

"It won't move," he grunts. "I can't get it open."

Setting Aliah on the floor, I grab the opposite side of the hatch wheel, straining with Tazib as we try to budge the mechanism. The smoke is growing thicker. Thanks to my oxygen mask, I'm protected, but Tali and Tazib struggle to breathe, coughing as the fumes hit their lungs.

"Come on!" I shout, throwing my weight onto the wheel. With a rusty screech, it begins to turn. "Hurry."

Tazib continues to spin the now loosened wheel as Tali helps me lift Aliah. As soon as the hatch is open, we scramble through, pulling the door closed behind us. Inside, we find walls lined with strange-looking hoods and a metal grate for a floor. There is no exit.

"No, no, no." Tazib grabs his head, his whole body trembling. "It's a dead end! We're trapped!"

"We're underwater," Tali says. "It's got to accommodate an underwater escape. Is there anything above us?"

In the centre of the low ceiling is another hatch wheel. From the look on Tazib's face, he understands what we have to do.

"You've got to be kidding," he mutters. "We have to swim out?"

I remove one of the strange hoods off the wall. It appears to be a combination life jacket and oxygen device with a hard top and long flaps to cover the chest and back. Pulling off my mask, I struggle to lift the heavy hood over my head, wrestling to pull the thick rubber sleeve over my curls to seal around my neck. Tazib grapples into a hood of his own as I help Tali and then Aliah.

"We have to flood the hatch," Tali says, her voice transmitting between the hoods. "Then we open the second door. These hoods should lift us slowly to the surface so we won't have to do anything but stay calm."

"Sure, great, whatever." Tazib paces in the small space. "Whatever we've got to do to get out of here."

"How do we flood the room?" I ask Tali.

"There should be a valve."

Searching the walls, I find a valve labelled Flood and Drain. I twist the handle to Flood and shiver as cold water rises from the grated floor. I pull Aliah's arm over my shoulder, her limp form already easier to manage with the quickly rising water.

"Let's get out of here."

As we are lifted off our feet, Tazib grabs the hatch wheel above. He waits until the chamber is completely flooded before twisting it open and swimming through. I steer Aliah through the small circle, letting go once she is free of the structure, and allowing her hood to lift her to the surface.

"Ry? I'm scared."

"I'm here," I reassure Tali, grabbing her hand. "I won't let go. Promise."

Together we wiggle through the hatch, floating up after the blinking lights on Aliah's and Tazib's hoods. I can't imagine what Tali is experiencing. Even with sight, the water is cold and dark and oh so silent. I try to quiet my imagination, reminding myself that many of the dangerous sea creatures have gone extinct.

"Can you hum?" Tali asks. "Or sing?"

"Of course."

Through all of the chaos of the last hours, the Composer's music has not ceased. It ran in the back of my mind, a soundtrack not of alarm but promise. Even now, as we slowly rise from the depths of the ocean, it continues to reassure me.

Though darkness drowns me
I will not fear
For the music calls to me

And though the fires rage
I will not fear
For the music reminds me

I am more than a code
More than a body
In the cogs of the world
I am an instrument
A voice with a song
To join in the symphony
Knowing tomorrow will come
Tomorrow will come
And I have nothing to fear.

I continue to sing as the black gives way to deep blues and then lighter teals. When we break the surface, our eyes are dazzled by the shimmering waves, the sun high in the sky. Water stretches in every direction and we bob on the waves as I let the last note fade to quiet.

Aliah groans then jolts, arms flailing with a startled scream.

"Aliah!" I grab the back of her hood, turning her so she is able to see us through her visor. "Aliah, it's okay. We're out."

"Okay?!" she exclaims. "How is everything okay? We're in the middle of the ocean!"

"She has a point," Tazib says, his earlier panic now replaced with dry sarcasm.

"No, really," I stress. "We're going to be fine. Look." I tap the flap of the hood that rests on each of our chests where a light pulses with a steady rhythm. "Don't you see? They're transponders. I bet emergency pods are already on their way, automatically launched the moment we put these on."

Aliah calms, her breathing ragged. "Oh, my head," she moans.

"Killer headache?" I guess. "Just keep taking deep breaths. The oxygen will help."

I demonstrate by taking a couple steadying breaths myself as I rise and fall in the gentle swells.

"I guess the fire will do the job for us," Tazib says, kicking to stop a wave from pushing him away. "Guess we'll know soon enough if that warning about the crypto key was a bluff or not."

"No, we don't have to worry." Relief floods through my body as a tired smile grows on my lips. "Aliah figured it out. She ended Thanatos."

Tazib sucks in a sharp breath. "No."

"Yeah. It was Mom's necklace." My heart sinks momentarily as I realize the strand of beads, my last link to Mom, is long gone, dropped in the server room. "You were right. The answer was in my past, a memento passed down through the generations on their Day of Thanatos. The key was the pattern of the beads, a binary code. Aliah figured it out."

"I knew I wasn't wrong." His voice is so soft I barely hear it.

"How did you know?" I ask Aliah. "I had the crypto key all along and I had no idea."

"Maisie gave me the data from your experience in MEMORY," Aliah says. "Tali and I watched it on the journey to the server station. I think I only caught it because I'd been carrying your necklace around ever since I turned you in." She looks away across the waves. "I was going to give your necklace to Rube, so he'd have something of yours, but then you broke out with Tazib and I hung on to it. But I was never going to keep it, really. I brought it with me to the Uncounted to give to you. I just hadn't done it yet. Anyway, when I saw it again in the server room, it just clicked. It was in your memories not once, but twice, so it had to be the answer."

"I'm glad you figured it out."

"Me too." Aliah leans back, floating on the surface of the water. "I can't believe it's over."

"We need to make them pay."

The three of us turn to Tazib.

"The United People need to pay for what they did. Without Thanatos, it will be harder, but not impossible. Aliah, you must know of a database, a list somewhere naming every person who's ever aligned themselves with the United People. We find the list and then track them down, one by one until there's no one left."

"What are you talking about?" Aliah's scorn is obvious despite the foggy visors. "I'm not going to hand you a list so you can go off and get some twisted version of revenge."

"This whole thing was about stopping unnecessary deaths," Tali says.

"But they need to pay for what they did. For releasing the virus among the Uncounted. For Maisie. For everything."

"Seriously?" Aliah sighs dramatically. "You want to talk about settling scores? How are you going to pay, Tazib? What's your punishment for the lives you took?"

"*This* was supposed to be my redemption!" Tazib slaps the water. "*I* was supposed to be the one to end Thanatos. I was supposed to figure out the crypto key. By ending Thanatos, I was going to show the World Collective they needed me just as much as they needed Ry. She would have given the world hope, but I would be the one to give the world life!" Tazib slumps, only his hood keeping his head above the waves. "But I did nothing. I didn't figure out the key. I didn't stop Thanatos. And when things got dangerous, I ran." His voice drops to a whisper. "The World Collective was right. My life is worthless."

"Tazib—"

My words are cut off by a loud whirring, the water spraying upwards to block the sun with a mist of droplets as a pod lowers itself to skim the surface. The doors slide open and we quickly swim over, dragging our tired limbs into the pod where we lie on the floor, soaked and exhausted.

As the pod lifts into the sky, we struggle to break the seals of the hoods, freeing ourselves of their heavy weight. Aliah moves to the panel, activating the highest heat setting while the rest of us settle ourselves on the floor.

"We should send a message to the others," Aliah says. "Let them know we're okay."

"And let them know we did it, we stopped Thanatos," Tali adds.

Aliah glances at her wrist. "I bet they already know."

"Nela." I bring my hands together to activate a screen. "This is the news the world nears to hear. She can make a broadcast."

"There she goes, doing her thing. The bringer of good news and hope yet again." Tazib clamps his jaw so hard his teeth snap together with a loud clack.

"Tazib—"

"Where is this pod taking us?" Tazib interrupts. "We should redirect it. Drop me off somewhere remote. Make me disappear. Again."

"Tazib, you were a part of this."

"Really?" His voice wavers. "And how are you going to describe my involvement? Are you going to tell them how I killed Kohath and his guards? I'm sure the citizens of the Collective will love that. I'll be their hero," he sneers. "Or better yet, you can use me the way I've always been used. Cast me as the bad guy, the unhinged teen. Tell the story in black and white, the good versus the bad."

"It's not that simple."

"Sure it is," he snaps. "I *killed* people, Ry. Worse, it was easy. I mean, all I had to do was think about how the World Collective treated me and I could justify anything. And besides, what was me activating a few Thanatos' when The Code was killing hundreds? But now, with Maisie gone..." Tazib swallows as his eyes well. "What do I do now? I was supposed to fix everything. This was my way to return to the Collective. But now, I can't even return to Sota. Al and Eldon..." He moans, cupping his face in his hands. "Maisie is dead because of me."

"Oh boo hoo," Aliah snaps, swinging from the panel. "You think you're the only one hurting? We've all lost someone!"

"Aliah..." I caution.

"If we all gave up as soon as we got sad, we never would have stopped Thanatos!"

"Stopping Thanatos doesn't fix anything!" Tazib shouts. "We can never undo what's been done!" He heaves a shuddering breath. "Don't you see? No matter how much you wish and hope, plan and scheme, there's never a way to turn back time. Chaos wins. Always." He grows quiet, studying the scarred skin of his hands. "You'd think I'd have accepted that by now, that the world isn't fair. It certainly showed me when it first scarred me and then forgot me. And killing Maisie..." He shakes his head. "No. We haven't fixed anything. The world is just as broken as it was when we started."

Tazib's anguish is like a spotlight shining on all the broken pieces I've yet to reconcile. He's right. No matter what we do, we can't change the past, we can't bring back those we've lost. Sorrow clutches at my heart, squeezing my chest with an intensity that physically hurts. Mom, Jep, Dad, little Mart, too many are gone. A glance at Aliah's white face and locked jaw is enough to remind me of her beloved dorm leader, and I don't need to look at Tali to know she will never forget Kyven. We've all lost someone we've cared about, the whole world has by this point. Thanatos may be gone, it will never kill another person, but that doesn't mean we're all magically okay. Stopping a computer program has done nothing to fix all the things that are broken. All the people that are broken.

I lean my head back against the wall of the pod, looking out the glass sphere at the expanse of sky. I'm so small in the grand scheme of things. A tiny speck with no true power. But that's only part of the picture. Though it's unseen, the Composer's song dances around our pod, a living thing weaving everything together. I sense it in the big and the small. From the sun in the sky, to the drops of water condensing on the glass, to the quiet breathing of my companions.

I let my gaze drop back to Tazib. Our lives have been so different and yet so similar. Both of us were marked as children by an event outside of our control. We've struggled to be seen for who we really are in a world that wants to label us in neat boxes. We've been hurt by those we should have been able to trust. We've lost those we loved. And while understanding Tazib doesn't forgive his choices, it does provide insight. I can understand his hopelessness; but unlike him, I know I'm not alone. My voice is one instrument in a symphony of unmeasurable size. And that gives me hope.

I shuffle across the pod, settling next to Tazib. "You're right. We can't change the past. There's no way to undo what's been done, by the World Collective, the United People, or even ourselves. But we can move forward."

Conviction grows in my chest. The Composer's song promises a tomorrow, a better tomorrow.

"Don't look at this as an ending, but a beginning. Yes, terrible things have happened. So many are dead, and coming back from this will be hard, really hard. But it *is* possible. We can have hope. We can have a future. Don't you see? We can do things differently. We can learn from the past. We rebuild, but in a way that *sees* people. We aren't cogs in some great system. We are each unique, each important. What happened to you, to all of us..." I look up at the others. "It gives us insight into how to move forward." I smile at

Tali. "We can learn to not minimize based on age." I nod at Aliah. "That we never really know a person until they let us in." I look back at Tazib. "And that even the most callous person still has a heart that can be broken. We all deserve second chances. We are all capable of change."

"But Maisie's gone," Tazib chokes. "Eldon and Al will never forgive me."

"You don't know that."

"Yes, I do!" Tazib gasps. "Because I will never forgive me!"

I take Tazib's hand and he looks up in surprise, his eyes glassy with tears. "You're right," I say quietly. "Forgiving yourself will be the hardest thing you ever do because you can't bring Maisie back. There is no button you can push to fix everything." I take a deep breath. "But you can let her death change you. Become a person Maisie would be proud of. Take ownership of what you've done and work to make the world a better place."

For a long time, the pod is silent. Tazib doesn't lift his eyes from our hands as tears drip from his chin. Across the pod, Tali leans back, her eyes closed as she faces the sun, her cheeks also wet with tears.

Aliah keeps her back to us. "You really think that's possible? That the world can get better?"

"I do." Around us the Composer's music feeds the hope growing in my chest. "I believe it because we're going to be part of it. It isn't one of us fixing the world. It's all of us." I fling my arms as I struggle to explain. "All of us playing our parts. Together we can make something beautiful."

"It's a lot to ask," Aliah huffs. "Getting people to work together."

"But we can do it." Tali's voice is so soft I barely hear her over the whir of the pod. "I mean, look at us. Collective, Uncounted, United People." She smiles. "We came together to do something and we don't even like each other that much."

It must be exhaustion. Or maybe the relief of knowing Thanatos is gone. The music definitely plays a part, the way it rises, a thousand instruments dancing in harmony. But for whatever reason, Tali's comment makes me snort with a barely suppressed laugh. Aliah catches my eye. She smirks, but it doesn't have its usual edge. "You do realize our four names are going to be recorded in history for this. Together. Forever."

"No," I groan dramatically, my grin growing wider. "Now I'll never be free of you."

Tazib looks between us, his brow furrowed. "I thought being tied to me was your worst fear."

"Naw," I say. "You're nothing compared to sharing a room with Aliah."

That does it. Aliah snorts as Tali's giggles grow louder. Tazib shakes his head as I lean back against the wall of the pod, a smile on my face, hope in my heart, and the melody in my ear.

I understand now. All along, the song has been rising to a crescendo. For so long, I mistook it for the climax, the high before the end, but now I see this isn't the ending.

It's only the beginning.

CHAPTER TWENTY-SIX

GRAVEL CRUNCHES UNDER MY FEET AS I JOG DOWN THE TWISTING path. The sun lingers on the horizon, casting long fingers of light between the towering buildings as my body finds a comfortable rhythm, the thud of my feet and the pounding of my heart in time with the music that dances around me.

Six months have passed since Aliah disabled Thanatos. Every morning, I rise early to beat the heat of Unity, the routine of running a reassuring constant in a world recovering from the fall of the World Collective. It's strange, how a place can look untouched, and yet every aspect of it has changed. The same buildings tower around me, but their windows remain dark behind the plant life that grows up their sides. Large sections of the city sit empty, their paths quiet but for the birds and bubbling streams. I run past abandoned green-lots that grow foul with their crops slowly rotting and their steamy windows morphing to green with mold. Everywhere I look, I feel the absence of those we have lost.

Yes, we were successful in stopping Thanatos—no citizen will be forced to celebrate their day of death at the whim of a code—but the world has been marred by the loss of so many. Every citizen over the age of 30 is gone, and the numbers of those in their 20s is terrifyingly low. Too many tiny trees line the paths, their frail stems bending in the hot southern winds, their leaves growing brown with too few left to care for them.

When our pod landed in a World Collective city on the Atlantic coast six months ago we were able to watch Nela's broadcast live. The reactions of the young citizens who had gathered in the city square surprised me. Many were joyful, especially those who had, like Aliah, been waiting for their death day. But most remained afraid and uncertain. While no more would die, how were we going to live? We had no leaders, no healers, few people left with any experience to keep society running.

And there were many who didn't know how to handle their grief. Stopping Thanatos didn't end death within the Collective. Without support, many couldn't process their losses, their desperation driving them to find a drastic escape. Others turned to anger, demanding retribution for the state of the world. But who remained to blame? Every leader of the World Collective was gone, and the United People dissolved into obscurity after the death of Libni and Kohath. Even if we managed to hunt down any remaining members, how could we ensure we would judge them correctly? Not all who were a part of the United People agreed with their actions. Just look at me. Or Aliah.

I glance at where Aliah jogs beside me, impressed at her ability to keep pace with my long strides. If you had told me a year ago that

Aliah would become my morning run partner I would've questioned your sanity. We certainly aren't best friends, but something happened between us back in the server room. We still push each other's buttons and there's a lot of eye rolling, but despite the abundance of empty rooms, neither of us have moved from our shared space. Neither of us will admit it, but we need each other.

Aliah turns down a familiar trail and I follow her lead. We won't stop, but each day we wind by the trees marking those we have lost. Libni, Dad, Hyll, Ora, little Mart, Kyven. The WC may be gone, but we continue to plant trees to remember those we have lost, now marking them with ribbons and pictures, flowers and rocks that sparkle. It's one of the small changes our young society is leaving on our surroundings as we learn how to grieve.

Jogging alongside one of Unity's rivers, we twist around the glittering Chrysalis. Screens flicker on each of the columns as Nela's broadcast explaining the upcoming election runs on repeat. She's chosen to use a close-up shot, one that shows the way her eyes crinkle when she smiles, a deliberate reminder she's one of the few remaining with experience. Elections are happening around the globe as each city chooses its leaders to represent it as we build a new form of leadership.

Our pace slows as we return to the Psari. As usual, Aliah lingers in the lobby to call Rube while I head upstairs for a shower. The idea of Rube and Aliah as a couple has grown on me. They balance each other, her instilling a level-headedness in my brother, and him bringing light and laughter into her life. I wish Aliah could convince Rube to move to Unity. Without The Code directing our every step, we now live with a freedom we never knew we were missing. Much of The Code was destroyed by the fire in the underwater server location; but surprisingly, parts of it survived. We use what remains as a tool to guide and inform but not dictate. It lets us know where we need people in order to keep the lights on and food in our bellies, but we're given the choice of what role we want and where we want to live. Even so, Rube insists on remaining in Fordtown where he's built his own community. Maybe one day, he tells me, when things are more settled, he'll move to Unity. After all, he reminds me, we have time.

Today's an important day, so after my shower, I spend extra time on my hair, ensuring each curl is perfect. My physical appearance is one of those things that's remained the same despite how much I've changed. I'm still tall and curvy, still recognized by my curls and prosthetic, but I couldn't feel more different from the young teen I was a year ago. I thought I understood death, and right and wrong, but I see now I still have so much to learn.

I'm still learning.

My growling stomach reminds me of the time and I hurry to the dining hall—though it hardly resembles what it used to be. The clean, uniform rows of tables have been pushed into groupings, and the once sterile walls are now a kaleidoscope of colour, decorated with names and pictures of those we have lost, intertwined with our youthful dreams for the future. Even the windows haven't escaped our creativity and the sunlight casts rainbows over the tables. A group of pre-teens pass out paint to a mixed dorm of children, leading them to a free section of wall and supervising as they add their own unique touch.

"Ry! Ry!" Small voices call my name. "Come see my painting."

"They look lovely," I praise the smiling faces. "Arisu, you're getting better every day."

Arisu looks up, her brush poised over her painting as she glances at the hovering image of her parents she's using as a reference. "You're being nice." She eyes her work with a furrowed brow. "Ora's eyes are two different sizes."

Art was never a priority in the Collective, but it's clear Arisu has a natural talent. Every morning she adds another layer as she hones her skill.

"You'll get it. Just remember, there's no rush, you can take all the time you want."

"We get to skip school," a child sings as they paint their palm to press against the wall. "Because we're coming to see you!"

"We still have to go to school afterwards," one of the pre-teens corrects.

"Need a break?" I ask Arisu, who continues to frown at her painting. "You could come wth me to help with breakfast."

After she drops her brush into a cup, we bid goodbye to the group and head into the kitchen. It's a large, industrial space, built to churn out nutritious food for a large population, but it too has been touched by our young hands. Colour has been added to each stainless surface and music echoes a steady, lively beat as we enter.

"There you are," Loren calls over the music. "We've finished the bread, but we still need more fruit and veggies chopped, and I think the porridge needs your touch, Arisu. Come on, hurry up, breakfast starts in ten minutes!"

As I wash and slice strawberries, I watch Loren and Arisu. They have their own harrowing story to tell of what happened in Ol'Syd and the struggle to get back. Now, they are like sisters, sharing a room, bickering and laughing, teasing and encouraging. Arisu tastes Loren's porridge and makes a face, pretending to gag. Loren huffs, but she tosses two spices to Arisu, getting her to add them to the pot. It's funny, The Code reassigned Loren to the kitchen, and now that we're free from it, she could leave. But she's found a new home in this space, her aptitude for science lending itself to food as she tests and experiments with our limited ingredients. Plus, her powerhouse nature is just what we need to keep track of supplies, menus, and the roving groups of helpers.

"Are you nervous?" Loren asks as we carry out the large trays of food to set in the middle of the tables.

"A little," I admit, settling myself on the bench between a pair of toddlers. I scoop porridge into their bowls before topping it with fruit. "But I went over everything with Tali and Aliah last night. I'll say what I have to say and then it's out of my hands."

"I don't know how you stay so calm." Loren shakes her head, pouring and passing out cups of water to the table. "The fact that there are people still fighting this blows my mind. Didn't they see how bad things got? Why would they want to go back to what we had?"

"Change is hard," I shrug, getting my own breakfast. "Sticking to the familiar isn't as scary as restarting."

"You're too nice," Loren huffs. "I just want to slap some sense into them. 'Bring back The Code,'" she quotes. "Crazy fanatics."

"And that's why it's Ry going up there and not you," Arisu teases as she takes her own spot at the table. "She's good at seeing things from every side."

"Thanks." I grab a bowl from the edge of the table before the toddler manages to dump it. "I'm working on it. Sometimes it's still hard to move past the hurt."

"The Tazib stuff happens today too, doesn't it?"

"Yeah." I don't need to say more. Countless nights have been spent reflecting on everything that's happened and how Tazib factors in. It isn't just me who struggles to reconcile the kid from his actions. Today's assembly is his chance to present his side. I know what he will be sharing. I've helped him dig through WC records, finding evidence of the truth about the attack that was actually an accident, his recovery and erasure. I've even travelled back to Sota to use their MEMORY machine under Priya's guidance, looking for the little boy who was once my friend. None of it changes what's happened—being hurt doesn't justify hurting others—but it's important to understand the why. What Tazib does next? Well, that's up to him.

Our conversation drifts to other topics, constantly interrupted by the little ones at our table. The dining hall is a buzz of noise, each table-grouping responsible for caring for the younger children seated with them. Dorms still exist, but instead of dorm leaders and a bunch of children all the same age, we use the large spaces to create families with groupings of children of different ages. The older kids watch out for the younger ones, helping them dress, moving them between spaces. At meals, everyone helps, whether you've been paired with a kid or not. It hasn't fixed everything, there are still kids who go missing, older and younger, and not everyone is happy with the added responsibilities. There are no days off in this new world and no magic to instantly mature the young population. But it's better than what would have happened if Thanatos hadn't been stopped.

After clearing the table and making sure everyone is with their buddy, Loren and I wait for Tali and Aliah to finish with their table. It's hard not to notice Tali's eyes with a pang of sadness, but I try to focus on her bravery, watching as she uses her cane to manoeuvre between the tables. She has her bad days, days where she wets my shoulder with tears and rages at what she's lost, but she's learning to navigate her new normal with such courage and determination. She's been instrumental in educating people about democracy and the election process, finding ways to research the distant past without her sight so she can explain the benefits and caution against repeating the mistakes of our ancestors.

"Morning, Tali," I say as she approaches.

"Morning, Ry," she chirps. "Priya called me, told me to wish you luck."

Tali's been back to Sota many times since that late fall day. First when we rushed to deliver medical supplies for their sick. Then again once Aliah found a vaccine for the measles the United People had released. Priya was determined there was something she could do for Tali's eyes; but eventually, she had to admit defeat, pulled in too many directions with too many to care for. Despite our best efforts, the small mountain community lost many children to the virus. They too are struggling to come to terms with their losses.

"Are you still thinking of moving there?" I ask, walking beside her as we exit the Psari.

"I am," Tali says. "But not until everything is settled here. Priya could use the help with baby Ora and I like it there. The quiet, the smells, the fact everything is tiny and rarely changes..." She shrugs.

"I don't know, it just seems like where I'm supposed to be."

"Well, you know I'll support you no matter where you end up," I promise. "Though I'm guessing Eldon has a preference," I add with a smile.

Tali blushes but doesn't deny it. Eldon's been in touch with her constantly. Together, the two have learned how to grieve for Ky and Maisie.

"I could never imagine living in such a primitive location," Aliah says with a shake of her head. "Especially since they keep insisting on remaining uninvolved with what happens within the Collective."

"Can you blame them?" Loren asks, swinging her arms as we walk down the sandy path towards the Chrysalis. "Many of them have lived separately for generations. No matter how much has changed here, they're not going to want to jump into our society."

"But we aren't connected anymore," Aliah argues. "And we're doing all this stuff to change, to be better."

I, too, am a little disappointed at how distant the Uncounted have remained. We could use their guidance and wisdom, especially since we're so young. But other than welcoming us with food when we visit, Momma Aimee and The Table have chosen to have no influence on what happens within the Collective. Other than the occasional word of advice, we are on our own.

Reaching the dome of the Chrysalis, we are met by Nela and her cameras.

"Rygita, good, you're early. Could I go over a couple of things with you before the assembly starts?"

The others wave goodbye, passing through a gap in the water to head into the dim interior. Nela opens a screen with the assembly's itinerary, projecting it so we can go over the schedule.

"I'll have cameras at multiple locations," Nela reviews. "I'll do my best to keep the feed interesting, but since I'm also moderating, it may be a little rough."

"I wouldn't worry about it," I reassure her. "Our goal isn't to produce a show but to communicate the facts. Just keep the cameras on who is speaking. We don't have to show everyone's reaction. Let the viewers decide for themselves. Okay?"

"Good idea. I'm working to keep my own opinions out of my broadcasts, but I know my face sometimes betrays me. What if there's unrest?"

"Having the smaller children here will help. The buddies will want to keep them safe, so that should minimize reactions. But we also want to let everyone voice their feelings, so yeah, it might get heated. There is a plan for how to evacuate the space quickly if the need arises. Darr should have sent it to you this morning."

Nela checks her messages, finding the memo from Darr. "Oh, I must have missed it. I'll read it over now in case we need it. See you inside." She disappears behind the curtain of water.

Knowing I have a couple minutes before I'm needed, I move to a shaded bench, breathing in the smell of roses that wafts on the breeze from the nearby garden. I touch my fingers together, creating a frame and waiting for the call to connect.

"Ry! All set to change the world? Again?" Rube's crooked grin bounces as he jogs down a row in his green-lot.

"Rube, you're going to be late. You should be in Fordtown's centre square by now."

"I know, I know," Rube pants. "But one of the water lines broke last night and I had to fix it before it flooded the whole section." He pushes his bushy hair out his eyes, leaving a streak of dirt on his forehead. "So, why are you calling? You want me to compliment you on your hair or something? 'Cause it looks good, practically perfect. You need me to come and mess it up a little? Make you look more natural?"

"Nah," I laugh. "I just wanted to see my big brother."

"Translation: you have time to kill and you're nervous."

"Exactly."

Rube slows, taking the time to focus on me instead of where he's walking. "Hey, don't sweat it. This is what you're supposed to do. Listen to the music and follow where it leads."

"But what if no one listens? What if things only get worse?"

"You can't control what everyone decides," Rube says. "People have to take responsibility for their own actions. If we want to come back from this, they'll have to see the truth of what you're saying. We need to see each other as we are, we need to use our individual strengths to work together." He laughs. "It's a bit like it was before, with The Code, but it's also *so* different. Harder. Figuring out our own strengths and what we want to accomplish is a lot more work than letting a computer to do it for us."

"You have that right," I sigh. "But it's also freeing. I like that we can change now. We can be good at more than one thing, help in more than one area."

"Exactly," Rube grins, resuming his quick trot down the green-lot's long centre aisle. "Hey, before you go. Have you talked to Darr?"

I look down. "Other than messaging to arrange everything for today, not really." I haven't seen Darr in months. Once his wounds healed, he decided to join Rube in Fordtown. We talk regularly but only about the things we need to, never more.

"He's ready, Ry," Rube says softly. "He needed time to process everything. He wasn't just betrayed by you but by everything he believed in. But he's starting to heal. I think now would be a good time to reach out. He still cares about you."

Heat floods my cheeks and my stomach flutters. I'm not sure I want the same things I did when Darr waved at me that day in the pods. I'm glad he was part of my life when I first arrived in Unity— he was my connection to home, a security when I was overwhelmed with change—but it was a season. A good season, but one that's ended.

"Sorry." Rube's bark of a laugh calls my attention back to the screen. "This was totally not the time to tell you that. Please forgive your clueless big brother for being totally insensitive!"

"I'll try," I huff, grinning so he knows he's already forgiven.

Rube signs off and I watch his image fade. The chatter of voices and the happy shrieks of children are muffled by the falling water of the Chrysalis. It's almost time.

"They told me I'd find you out here."

Tazib joins me on the bench, his guard keeping his distance but remaining watchful. Like me, Tazib is dressed in his best, in dark blue pants and a green shirt that makes the gold in his eyes pop.

"I'm just taking a moment, making sure I stay focused on the right things."

"I thought maybe it was nerves, or regret."

"No regret," I say, watching a lone pod cross the city skyline.

"You deserve to tell your story."

"It might not change anything." Tazib stretches his legs in front of him, leaning back on the bench. "I'm still going to need my shadow." He nods to the silent guard, a young twenty-something who Aliah vouched could remain impartial. His role has been two-fold: to assure the public that Tazib is being watched, and to keep Tazib safe from those who blame him for the Thanatos deaths.

"You could always leave," I say. "Go back to Sota and the Uncounted. You'd be safe there."

Tazib grunts. "I can't go back. Al would never allow it."

Tazib stares straight ahead, his brow puckering as he frowns. He won't admit it, but Al isn't the reason Tazib won't return to Sota. I see it in his body language, the way he will grow distant, his eyes shining as his mind carries him away. He can't go back because every place and every face will remind him of Maisie.

"Besides," Tazib says. "I want to be here. I'm a World Collective citizen after all. I want to be a part of what comes next."

"Speaking of which, we should head inside." I stand, brushing the dust from my pants.

"They're going to elect you," Tazib says as we move to the column where there's a break in the water.

"We don't know that."

"Sure we do." Tazib pauses, turning to face me. "You're exactly what we need."

"It's crazy." I take a deep breath, trying to calm the fluttering in my gut. "I used to want the world to forget me, to treat me like a normal kid, and here I am, asking them to elect me." I laugh. "I wanted to be a dorm leader, not a world leader."

"And because of that, you're perfect for it," Tazib smiles.

"I kinda thought you wanted the job."

"I did," Tazib admits. "But I'm beginning to see I'm not ready for it. Not yet anyway. First, I need to atone for the mistakes I've made. I want to make Maisie proud, and to do that I need to learn who I am before I ask the world to know me. I've got a long way to go."

"And you think I have it figured out?"

"No, but you have time." Tazib tilts his head. "Hey, I've been wondering, the crypto key, was it anything significant? I mean, for them to go to all that trouble of hiding it in a necklace, I'm guessing it was more than a string of numbers and letters. So, what was it?"

"Make every day count."

"Huh." Tazib is silent as he gazes at the waiting crowd. "Figures they would be interested in counting. But it does give you something to think about."

He waits a beat more before he passes into the dome, walking to the stage and taking his place by the far podium. The crowd falls silent as Nela moves to begin the assembly. It's time for me to take my place.

I take a deep breath, listening for the music which is as familiar as my own heartbeat. *Make every day count.* I've thought a lot about this phrase these past months. It's good advice. Timeless really. The Code was created to ensure everyone had days to count. As wrong as it may have been to assign our deaths to a computer program, its ultimate goal was to give life, and I'm sure its creators wanted to make sure they didn't lose sight of that gift. I certainly don't plan to. Whatever time I have, I want to use it in a way that's going to help people. And though I may not know exactly what the future will look like, there are a few things I know for certain.

I am loved.

There is plan for a future. A good future.

And though I have a lot to learn, though I'm young and will make mistakes, it's okay.

After all, I'm only 15. I have my whole life ahead of me.

ACKNOWLEDGEMENTS

It's hard to believe The World Collective started as a NaNoWriMo project way back in 2018. It feels both like yesterday and decades ago. From the beginning, I believed in Ry's story. I was certain there were young readers looking to get into the dystopian genre but also seeking stories where the darkness would give way to the light of hope.

But my belief alone would not have had the power to carry me to here, where I am publishing the final book in the series. That took a lot of time and work, not to mention a world of encouragement and support. Seriously, without the support of so many, this dream would have never made it to print. And so, once again, I search for the words to express my appreciation for all those who have played a part in making The World Collective series possible.

To Alanna and Chicken House Press, thank you for taking a chance on me. For believing in this story so much you committed to publishing all three novels before they were even finished. Thank you for doing all the "stuff" I have no idea how to handle, like page layouts, margins, ISBN numbers, and so much more. And of course, thank you again for another amazing cover. These books are going to look stunning sitting together on bookshelves.

To Becky, Hannah, Kaitlyn, and Heather, thank you for the honest feedback and critical eyes. Everyone needs good typo finders and I'm grateful I have you.

To my family, ALL my family. I won the lottery when it comes to great families. The fact that you are all so different and yet all champion my writing… I can't express how wonderful that is. I can go to a book event without fear of no one showing up. You will be there. You listen when I ramble, encourage me when I want to give up, and remind me to be proud of this amazing thing I have accomplished. Thank you.

To author hopefuls and the author community. If you are thinking of writing a novel of your own—find your people! The writing community is one of the most accepting, encouraging, and lovely communities I have ever been a part of. There are so many names I could list, but I'm afraid I will miss someone. So, to all the fellow authors, writers, and book publishing people I have met over the last five years, thank you. You have supported me in so many ways, whether through helpful criticisms or unbridled enthusiasm, tips about selling books, ways to promote, contests, conferences, or simply hitting like on every post. We are not in competition. We are fellow creatives on a journey to fill the world with more stories and I couldn't ask for better travel mates.

To the book community, without you there would be no story. Some may say YA dystopian has had its time, but I knew that wasn't the case. I wrote this series to bridge the gap I could see between young readers interested in the genre and the books currently on the market and I knew that fans of a genre are always hungry for more—for a library isn't made up of one book but many. Thank you to every reader for taking a chance on me. May Ry's story remind you that you are never alone and that you too have something to offer the world.

ABOUT THE AUTHOR

Susan Cullen is the author of *The World Collective*, a Rakuten Kobo Emerging Writer finalist, and winner of a Word Award. A lover of all four of Canada's seasons, Susan lives in Chatham-Kent where she is raising two story-loving teens with her husband. She spends her time cheering on her fellow NaNoWriMo writers, criticizing Marvel movies, walking her pup, playing boardgames, and dreaming new stories to tell.

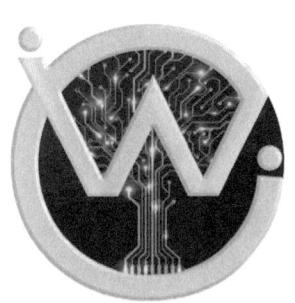

www.ingramcontent.com/pod-product-compliance
Lightning Source LLC
Chambersburg PA
CBHW021434240626
47153CB00001B/145